FAKE IT TILL WE MAKE IT

NOOR SASHA

Copyright © 2024 by Noor Sasha

All rights reserved.

No part of this book may be reproduced or transmitted in any form or by any means, electronic or mechanical, including photocopying, recording, or by any information storage and retrieval system without the written permission of the author, except for the use of brief quotations in a book review.

This book is a work of fiction. Names, characters, places, and incidents either are products of the author's imagination or are used fictitiously. Any resemblance to actual persons, living or dead, events, or locales is entirely coincidental.

Cover Illustration: @cozka_art

Contents

Playlist		VI
Content Warnings		VII
Dedication		VIII
1.	Cheese Cappelletti	1
2.	Troublemaker	8
3.	Sky	15
4.	F.C.K.	22
5.	Mustafa's Calling!	30
6.	Jia's BBQ House	38
7.	Tae-hyung and Hye-jin	47
8.	Sun Tower Hotel	53
9.	Nyx	63
10.	Abe's Deal	71
11.	A Sexy Viking	83
12.	Mannequin	91
13.	Potato, Potahto	98
14.	Rodney The Rooster	105

15.	Principal Frederick	114
16.	Family Trauma	122
17.	The Origins of Arain	130
18.	Mr. Chewy	138
19.	Cookie	146
20.	Grocery Shopping	152
21.	Thank You, Chef	159
22.	What Do You Love About Alyn?	170
23.	Phoenix	176
24.	Our First Date	181
25.	The Show	189
26.	Nyla Ghilzai	194
27.	People Pleaser	201
28.	Rhode Island	208
29.	Independence Day	216
30.	A Garden For Her	224
31.	Caffè di Matilda	229
32.	Pride and Prejudice	238
33.	Caramel	247
34.	Happy Birthday	255
35.	Flirt With Yourself	271
36.	Ketchup Packet	278
37.	Talk	288
38.	Nylana and Shahzad	299
39.	See You In A Minute	308
40.	EPILOGUE	316
Acknowledgements		327

About the Author

playlist

Man's World	MARINA
Pray For Me	The Weeknd, Kendrick Lamar
Mrs. Potato Head	Melanie Martinez
You're On Your Own Kid	Taylor Swift
What Was I Made For	Billie Eilish
Doubt	Mary J. Blige
On My Own	Jaden, Kid Cudi
The Only Exception	Paramore
Mirrorball	Taylor Swift
Hey Jude	The Beatles
Family Line	Conan Gray
Call It What You Want	Taylor Swift
Jealousy, Jealousy	Olivia Rodrigo
Ya'aburnee	Halsey
Pretty Hurts	Beyonce
Idontwannabeyouanymore	Billie Eilish
You're Losing Me	Taylor Swift
People You Know	Selena Gomez
Talking To The Moon	Bruno Mars
Seven (Explicit Vers.)	Jungkook, Latto
Green Eyes	Coldplay
Nonsense	Sabrina Carpenter
Sure Thing	Miguel
Long Story Short	Taylor Swift

Content Warnings

Dear reader,

Fake It Till We Make It contains mentions of eating disorders (binge-eating), body dysmorphia, mentions of severe harmful diets, slut-shaming, fat-shaming & body shaming, disordered food & weight thoughts discussed, mention of emesis, parental abuse & neglect, mild sexual scenes (closed-door), and anxiety & panic attacks. The portrayal of the main character's struggles with BED is drawn from my encounters with the disorder. It is essential to recognize that individuals cope with eating disorders in diverse ways, and the narrative may resonate differently for each reader. Please take caution if you find such content triggering, and prioritize your well-being while engaging with this material.

Reader discretion is advised.

To me.
You're almost there.

1

Cheese Cappelletti

Nyla

"Your fiancé left you at the altar almost a year ago, Nyla. This is getting out of hand. I expect you to return to New York as soon as you get my voicemail, no questions asked. I'll set you up with the agency's trainer—"

"Nope."

Ending Baba's voicemail, I pull myself out of the tub and strip out of my tracksuit, flicking on the bathroom light. The full-length mirror shows me my reflection: a protruding gut that could pass for a four-month pregnancy, thighs, and arms that have bulked up and jiggle a bit as I do a little jig, and my breasts have grown from C-cups to 38-DD. Even my baby fat has magically cursed my face again. I mean, shit. How is the latter even possible?

I want to skin myself. Yeah, that's exactly how I'm feeling. Maybe a Great White Shark or a malnourished jungle cat would be interested in me.

"'I expect you to return to New York, Nyla. I'll set you up with the agency's trainer, Nyla.' Meh, meh, meh," I mock Baba's hundredth voicemail and pull back on my clothes.

Dragging my feet inside my bedroom, I drop face-first onto the mattress.

If I had only prioritized myself for once, I wouldn't have ended up face-deep in a pig's breakfast. Eight months of self-isolation, and I still can't muster up the guts to get back on track.

Not that I was exuberantly in love with *the* Glenn Jackson. Maybe a teeny-tiny crush? Yeah. Very tiny.

NOOR SASHA

My ex-fiancé is a groundbreaking Hollywood director who got his glamourous breakthrough from his godfather, James Cameron. He chose to cut the cost of hiring a male lead, co-starring with me in his debut directorial *The Wilted*, a movie about a deranged couple living in a trailer wagon, bartering Kafkaesque psychedelics that allow them to travel through the quantum realm. A publicity stunt was needed if we wanted to make box-office sales.

Modeling was a stepping stone into acting, anyway.

Alas, our agencies managed to pull the wool over the public's eyes, going as far as tying the knot. Glenn would flaunt me like a shiny ring on his finger and smoothly transition me into the current trending genre in Hollywood: A24-esque movies. Plus, the only man Baba would ever want me to be seen with is an A-lister, so naturally, it was a golden feather in his cap.

However, my expertise lay—*laid*—on a narrow, polished catwalk. Amy Adams can't close a Prada show, and I certainly can't act as Giselle from *Enchanted*. We're better off conforming ourselves to our respective roles. Unless your agencies want you to branch into national politics or feed people without homes. Ah, don't forget the twenty cameras documenting every bite and swallow to prove you're one with the common people.

I'd be damned to the depths of hell if I was forced to return.

Half an hour in, and my Uber Eats order is *finally* here.

They usually get it to me faster, but hey, I'm not gonna gripe when I've got a container of cheese cappelletti ready to be devoured.

I wrap myself in my robe and shield my eyes with my sunglasses.

Peeking at my doorbell cam, I spot my Uber Driver waiting on the porch, his beat-up leather belt in full view. *Jesus Christ, he's a skyscraper.*

I tap the button, and with a high-pitched voice and a killer French accent I've honed with my accent coach, Clara, I chirp, "Drop it at the door, s'il vous plaît et merci!"

He locks his sharp eyes with the camera.

I stagger on my heels and accidentally hit the shoe closet behind me.

Oh my god.

"I know you're watching me, Troublemaker."

Oh. My. God.

My knees weaken from the reminder of that nickname. The reminders of one night that was so good I couldn't sleep with any other man for a whole year. The bane of all my depraved fantasies, the leading actor in my wildest dreams, the douchebag who left me high and dry in a hotel room the very next day—he's here.

Shahzad Arain is *at* my doorstep.

How did he find me?

Did Azeer tell him?

Did Alina tell him?

No, she wouldn't dare. She was sworn to secrecy.

And there's no way he used his extreme body-guarding skills to track me. Just a week after our one-night stand, he resigned and hid somewhere in the hinterlands of America.

But now he's here.

On the other side of the door.

With my cheese cappelletti and his signature frustrated expression.

No way am I allowing him to see me like this. The Nyla he remembers strutted down runways in flashy clothes, not lounging around in tracksuits. That Nyla had sleek, brown, Garnier-advertisement locks. Not this riotous mane dyed the color of the pink bubblegum that I chew every night, hoping it'll sculpt back my jaw.

He remembers worshiping a body that inspired women to sign up for annual gym memberships. A body that was admired universally, on billboards, jumbotrons, and in magazines. If there's one thing, just one thing I really liked about myself, it was my physique. But at the same time, it's the one thing I despised because it wasn't truly mine.

"Nyla," Shahzad's deep, raspy voice snaps me out of my pity party. "You know I'm not one to sugarcoat my words or beat around the bush, so I'll come clean about why I'm here. Press the button to talk to me."

I tap the silver button with my trembling index finger and lick my parched lips. "It's nice to see you, Shahzad."

He nods. "It's nice to hear you're alive, Nyla."

I smile a little. "Barely."

He lowers his eyes to the floor. "How long do you plan on living here?"

"Until I die," I joke but fail to entertain him.

He shoots me a quick glance with those obsidian eyes, then looks away over his shoulder. I can't see what's back there, thanks to his big Captain America build. He's always taken space in my vision, both in a literal and metaphorical sense. "I've got a bit of a tricky situation."

"Oh, no. Do you need money?"

"What—?"

"Because if you do, I'll tell you now, my father and I had a joint account, which I have no control over, by the way, *and* Alina's been transferring me funds for food—"

"Nyla, I don't need money," he grits out, planting his palms on both sides of the ring camera. "How could you even come to such a conclusion?"

I let out a breath. "If Baba has sent you to drag me out of hiding, then know that your attempts are futile. I'm not going back to him *or* Hollywood."

He's staring at me, penetrating my thoughts through the screen like he's right here in front of me. Chest to chest, breath to breath. "I . . . *I* need you, Nyla."

And I need a For Dummies textbook on "How Not To Lose Your Brain Cells When The Man You've Been Dumbly, Desperately, Despairingly Crushing On Confesses That He Needs You."

"Well, I need you to live with me for a couple of months," he clarifies, but I'm still not breathing in the least. "My best friend Mustafa's little sister, Maira, is about to start her internship at some fancy marketing firm. I just picked her up from the airport. She's in the car right now as we speak."

My first thought is: *Is she pretty?*

But instead, I remain silent.

"Mustafa and I practically grew up together. He was worried about sending her from Toronto to New York to live by herself, but I offered temporary rooming. She's like my little sister, too. Like Dua and Zineerah. You remember my sisters, right?"

"I do. How are they?"

"They're great. Yeah, no, they're doing pretty great. For the most part." He gives a little nod. "Maira's like them. She's a good kid. Intelligent and hardworking. But the only issue is Mustafa refused to let her live on her own or with roommates. He doesn't easily trust people. Not with Maira. He wouldn't ever trust her with anyone except for me." He licks his lips. "And that's because he thinks I live with my girlfriend."

My heart dips to my stomach. "I'm your *girlfriend*?"

"Technically, no, you're not," he murmurs, getting nearer to the camera. "I just need you to act like one and live with me until the end of July. The two siblings will sort out a separate apartment and trustworthy roommates for her afterward."

It's currently the first week of May, which means I'll have to spend the entirety of this month, June and July, in close proximity, sharing meals at the same dining table, drinking from the same cups, and utilizing the same shower with Shahzad Arain.

Suddenly, I'm shuddering from the mixture of excitement and trepidation.

"Do you have a middle name, by the way?" he questions.

"I— Yeah, I do. It's Inayat. Why?"

"For the sake of our façade, your name is Alyn Inayat."

Alyn? My name . . . reversed?

"Wait, hold on. Can we please just boomerang back to what you said? You want me to *pretend* to be your girlfriend?"

"You're an actress. I'm sure you'll have no issue—"

"Shahzad, I haven't been in the public's eyes for eight freakin' months. How did Mustafa possibly believe you? How did *Maira* believe you?"

"Because he doesn't indulge in social media, let alone gossip, and Maira would rather every celebrity and their private jets in this world disappeared to save carbon emission consumption or some shit like that—I don't know. She's a political, environmental junkie." He half-rolls his coffee-brown eyes, and the butterflies in my stomach dust off their wings and take flight.

I sink my teeth into my bottom lip. "Uh, okay, just— Give me a minute." *Wait, you're actually thinking about this?* The voice in my head tries to reason with me. *You're not just doing this because you're attracted to the man?*

Absolutely not. No, that's just—it's laughable. Shahzad may be a towering six-foot-three sculpture, resembling Hercules with his beefy bicep and pronounced veins, not to mention his intentionally tousled Prince Caspian-esque hair, but that doesn't mean my attraction toward him would extend to *fake*-dating the man.

Yeah, right.

I've read tons of Alina's novels, and every fake-dating scenario ends with the couple dropping the fake.

Yet, you want this.

Except that's impossible because I'm a burnt-out celebrity, and he's my father's ex-bodyguard. Plus, we hooked up once, and living in close proximity would be disastrous to my imbalanced hormones.

Oh, shut up, Nyla!

"Just till July," Shahzad says. "That's all I ask."

"Why would you want *me* to act as your girlfriend?"

He tears his fingers through his hair. "Because I know you in more ways than one."

I shove the memories of our hook-up into the recesses of my mind.

"Look, just put on your best act, and in return, I'll make sure *nobody* aside from Maira and I know you're in New York. You know I can keep you safe, right?"

Well, yeah. He *was* my father's former bodyguard at First Class Faces before unexpectedly quitting the job. Even Baba couldn't shed light on the reasons behind Shahzad's sudden departure. After he abandoned me at said hotel, I didn't bother going over it with a fine-tooth comb.

Oh my god.

How can I possibly forget him abandoning his duty of protecting me after a long night of breaking the goddamn hotel bed? And let me assure you, I am *not* exaggerating about the bed-breaking. The following morning with the housekeeping lady was nothing short of pure humiliation.

And now he's expecting *me* to help *him* out?

"Go home, Shahzad," I snip out. "And leave my cheese cappelletti at the door."

"Nyla—"

"I don't want to see you again. Is that clear?" *But you do.* No, I don't. *But you really do.* "J-Just tell Maira we broke up or something. I'm sure she'll keep it a secret from her brother."

"Mustafa video calls her *every* night, Nyla," he pushes out the words through his gleaming, pearly whites.

"That's not my problem," I fire back.

Shahzad coughs out a scoff, his hands dropping and disappearing into the pockets of his sleek leather jacket. Damn, he looks *ultra fine* in that black leather. "Okay," he concedes, opening his eyes and staring directly into the camera with a grim gaze. "I'll find someone else and give her your name. Like you said, Maira will keep it a secret, and Mustafa won't know."

Anger swells within me, driving me to swing the door wide open. I stride out, forcefully shoving against his chest. He stumbles down the porch steps. "Give her *my* name? *My* name? Do you know who you're talking to, Shahzad Arain?"

"Yes, my girlfriend, *Alyn*." His gaze spears into me, his eyes widened, while he shakes his head slowly. "*Please*."

"My name is Nyla," I hiss for his ears, my voice dropping to a clandestine whisper. Just. For. Him. "Do you know who you're making demands from? I've had my whole— My whole *life* has been stripped from me. My dignity, pride, privacy— But my name is the only thing I still have power over— Y-You douche nugget!"

The second I choke up, the harsh reality of my mistake hits me like a ton of bricks.

FAKE IT TILL WE MAKE IT

I'm outside.

In front of Shahzad.

Here I stand in my pink tracksuit adorned with Kit-Kat stains and shorts that barely qualify as such. My hair, greasy and unkempt, hastily clinging to the side of my face. It feels like ages since I last bothered to shave, leaving my legs looking downright Amazonian. And my feet are bare, toenails unclipped, and unpedicured.

Shahzad *only* stares at my face.

Nowhere else.

Only. My. Face.

If he wasn't distraught, he'd be drinking my body like he did before shit hit the fan. Even in the midst of our hook-up, he couldn't control his compliments about my beauty. My sculpted, small breasts cupped in his palms like pomegranates. *So gorgeous.* My taught stomach carved with soft abs that he marveled at. *So fucking sexy.* Gracefully toned legs that he effortlessly positioned on his shoulders. *So perfect.*

The Nyla he was attracted to wasn't . . . whatever I am now.

And Maira.

Maira, poor thing, leans out of the passenger seat window, her eyes blank yet filled with curiosity. She offers a static wave, and I find myself inexplicably craving for her approval.

I stagger back.

Step.

By.

Step.

I scramble to grab my bag of cheese cappelletti from my welcome mat, holding it close as I retreat back into my house and forcefully slam the door behind me.

Leaning against the frame, I catch my breath.

In and out.

In and out.

In and out.

I retrieve my umbrella hanging in my shoe closet. Without a second thought, I stab the pointy finial into the doorbell's screen until Shahzad's retreating figure disbands into a mosaic of smashed, vibrant pixels.

2

Troublemaker

Shahzad

"Maybe I can talk to her."

Maira gives me a cold glare.

"It's fine," I mutter, pressing the pedal down and turning my rented car's key in the ignition. Piece of overpriced junk, but it somehow covered the three-and-a-half-hour trip to Rhode Island. "We just had a bit of a fight last week."

"That made her move all the way to some beach cottage in Rhode Island?"

"Okay, it was a *big* fight."

"About?"

"Grown-up shit."

Maira's got those intense dark eyes that seem to see right through you. Considering her and Mustafa's whole anti-social media upbringing, there's no way she could've known about Nyla. That is until their father passed away, and Maira got a bit of breathing room to chase a marketing degree in New York. Mustafa still lays down their father's old-school rules on her every now and then. Honestly, I was fed up with Dua constantly bugging me to persuade Mustafa to greenlight her best friend's summer internship.

So, I did what any sane person would do—I lied.

Told them I had a girl from our own culture to put Mustafa's mind at ease about his precious little sister bunking with me for her first year. Spent hours scrounging through

Google for low-quality pics of Nyla and made them look as fuzzy as hell like I was the one behind the camera.

Mustafa was a piece of cake to swindle, and Maira? She couldn't give a damn. As long as she's on track for her dreams, she's all smiles.

Once she's settled in and made some friends on campus, I'll help her find roommates who aren't a 29-year-old dishwasher with a Siberian Husky obsessed with ham and, fingers crossed, his pink-haired girlfriend. *Fake* girlfriend.

"Breakups happen all the time," Maira comments as I veer us back onto the road.

I grip the steering wheel. "We didn't *break up*."

"No, of course, you didn't. I'm just pretending you two did, and it was all your fault. There's something oddly satisfying about seeing a man beg and plead with his girlfriend to return home."

"I didn't even do any of that nonsense."

"Therein lies the issue." Maira grins pleasantly, straightening her posture and slipping her earphones back in.

What the fuck was I thinking involving Nyla Ghilzai in this scheme of mine?

I've never had much patience for celebrities, especially after my time with that arrogant Abdul 'Abe' Ghilzai and having to endure his daughter's endless complaining and privileged behavior. She's a true-blue Nepo-kid, waltzing her way into Hollywood thanks to some shady deal her old man orchestrated with a neophyte director.

And what did she get in return? Left in the lurch with a tarnished image, having to pick up the pieces on her own.

"Where are we staying?" Maira asks. "We can't drive back another four hours. Should we just crash at a motel or something?"

"Look one up."

I clutch the steering wheel even harder just thinking about how Nyla acted. Here I am, giving her an out, making sure she stays hidden, and she goes off on me like a firecracker. Even after all I've done for her stupid fucking father over the last five years. I mean, sure, I wasn't officially her bodyguard, but she was always shining in my field of view somehow. I was looking out for her from the shadows until I stuck myself right in her spotlight and screwed up my whole damn career.

"There's a Motel-6 close by. About thirty kilometers away. It's by the beach, too."

"Great." I switch gears and start driving to the location.

While Maira unpacks her toiletries, I head into the bathroom and give Jia a ring—she's my boss over at Jia's Korean BBQ joint and also happens to be my landlady. Sweetest lady you'll ever meet—treats me like her own since her son passed away a while back. Besides, I'm fucking great at scrubbing the dishes.

"Shahzad?"

"Hello, Jia. Sorry to bother you so late. I was calling to ask if I could take the day off tomorrow. A family emergency came up, and I have to take care of it." Technically, I'm not lying. As her guardian, Maira *is* family; her living situation is my emergency. "If not, I can work a late-night shift. I'm just not sure when I'll be back home."

Jia sighs. "No, don't worry. You can come when your emergency is okay. I'll ask Tae-hyung to cover for you."

"That's perfect. Thank you for understanding, Jia. I owe you one."

"You can *owe me* by cooking. Your kimchi-bokkeum-bap recipe is da-bomb-dot-com."

My brows furrow. "The what?"

"Tae-hyung taught me that phrase. It means very good. Your version of the recipe is *very, very good*." Her words bring a smile to my face, a gesture I refuse to shake hands with. Happiness is a privilege I sacrificed a while ago. "You *are* okay, yes?"

"I'm okay. Thank you for asking. And tell your grandson to stop teaching you weird phrases. They'll get you in trouble with the wrong crowd."

"Okay, okay. Don't lecture me, adeul. Make sure to eat and get a good night's rest."

"You, too, Jia. Goodnight."

By the time I've showered and dressed in my sweats and tee, Maira is fiddling with the television remote, attempting to get it to work.

"Give it here."

"Damn, Shahzad. Relax." She passes it to me, grumbling about my lack of manners. "I'm gonna go shower."

Once the bathroom door is locked, I grab some fresh batteries from the drawer to replace the expired ones, switching on the tele—

Nyla's crying face pops up on the screen.

Ah, Christ.

I clear my throat, making sure the shower is still running, then crank up the volume and plop down on the bed. Nyla starts spouting off her gloomy lines in this killer British accent. She's decorated in one of those old-fashioned milkmaid get-ups with a cloak, and the sky above her is all gloomy and churning with a storm—personifying the climatic shit that's about to go down.

Even if Nyla weaseled her way into Hollywood with Abe's trickery, I can't deny she's an incredible actress. Those large jade eyes and that soft yet powerful voice? They're like a damn trance, pulling me right in.

"*I love you, Jameson Whitehorn!*" Nyla cries through the pouring rain, massing her dress in her hands and breathing heavily, anticipating his fast turn on his heel.

"Whitehorn," I mumble, scoffing. "Stupid fucking name."

The soldier circles his neck around, undoubtedly battling his emotions. "*What was that?*"

"*I love you, James! I am unbelievably in love with you!*"

"*Again?*"

"*Good Lord, James Whitehorn. I said I love you!*"

He ditches his artillery and ruggedly strides up to her, yanking her close by the waist and pressing his lips firmly against her admission.

I roll my eyes at the escalating intensity of their kiss as they seem hell-bent on consuming each other. Memories of my own passionate encounter with Nyla a year ago flash like bullet shots to my brain. Frenzied kisses, the sound of buttons popping off my dress shirt, the sharp clack of her heels against the cold marble floor, smoky jade eyes holding me in place, hot breaths against my neck—

"Nope."

I turn off the television.

Around midnight, with Maira fast asleep and the room cloaked in darkness, I reach for my phone and type Nyla's name into the search bar, clicking on the News tab.

The articles mainly speculate about her abrupt departure from the entertainment scene or meticulously outline the roster of men she's been linked to. Some lists count fifteen, others tally eight, and People Magazine even stretches it to twenty men in just five years.

Short-lived affairs, courtesy of her alleged control issues. Publicity stunts masterminded by her father. There are even pieces that drop names like my older cousin Azeer and his wife Alina, highlighting their familial connections to Nyla. Fortunately, nothing negative has been penned about them since Azeer's smartass quickly dealt with any questionable articles concerning his girls.

I switch to the Images tab, filtering through a plethora of editorial photo shoots, runway shots, movie posters, and candids of her navigating New York or Paris with her fraternity of celebrity friends. Most of them abandoned her like a used tissue. She may be a brat, but she's a brat with a heart of gold. She's overly concerned with what others think, and that's her Achilles' heel. She'd go to great lengths to keep everyone pleased with her.

And look where that's gotten you, Troublemaker.

I pause at a photo from the day we ended up sleeping together. She looks like a completely different person in it, all sweetness and light, compared to her current gloomy and chaotic state. But man, seeing her again after eight months of secretly listening in on Alina's phone calls with Nyla whenever our group got together made me nervous.

My thumb barely grazes over the image of her in a black mini-dress with her voluminous brown hair tied up high on her head. Her smile is so big and full of life like nothing, and no one can hold her back from getting what she wants. She even somehow managed to have me that very night.

I won't make the same mistake as last year.

I power down my phone and tuck it under my pillow, hoping to catch some sleep without her face invading my dreams.

The sound of low chattering gradually wakes me up from my sleep.

I toss and turn, patting the area on my bedside table for my phone. "Hmm?" Lifting my head, I find only the ghost of it and the charging wire lying limp on the floor. "Maira?"

Her indistinct laughter comes from behind the bathroom door.

"Fuck." I fall back on the pillows, giving my face a good rub before sliding my legs off the bed. My hair's a mess of dark, frizzled chaos, which I quickly comb through as I scan the room for my phone. "Where the hell is it?"

Just then, Maira exits the bathroom with my phone in her hand. She gives me a chirpy smile and wiggles the device. "Congratulations, Shahz bhai. You're a taken man again."

My veins run ice-cold.

I stride up and grab the phone from her grasp, quickly scanning my call history to locate Nyla's number, courtesy of my niece Zoha. Thank fuck I saved her contact as 'Troublemaker.'

"You talked for *three* hours? How'd you know my password?"

She shrugs. "Saw you entering it in the car. Four, three, two, one? Seriously? You worked in security, Shahz bhai. You're practically asking to have your identity stolen."

FAKE IT TILL WE MAKE IT

"Maira, you *do* realize this is an invasion of privacy?"

She spins on her heels, hands planted firmly on her hips. Maira's practically a carbon copy of her older brother. A small button nose, those large, warm brown eyes, and lips that barely ever seem to smile. "I'm sorry I touched your phone without your permission. But I'm not sorry that I called Alyn and explained my situation again. She understands how difficult it is for the two of us to live together. *Alone*. With a little rationality, I managed to convince her." She shrugs languidly and resumes packing.

"What'd you say to her?" I ask, grabbing a towel for a quick shower before we return to pick up my "girlfriend."

"Oh, you know, just that you were crying your feelings into a liquor bottle about wanting her back in your big, strong arms, then bruised your knuckles punching a wall because you missed her so much."

"*What*?"

"Here, you might want to wrap some of this around your knuckles for the next couple of days." Maira tosses me a roll of gauze, which, for reasons only known to her, was stashed away in her backpack. "She folded pretty quickly at the bare minimum. Kinda pathetic when you really think about it." She zips up her bag and slings it over her shoulders. "I'll be outside if you need anything *except* relationship advice." With a deadpan expression, she grabs her wallet and heads off for a vending machine breakfast.

"Little shit," I grumble, quickly deleting my Safari history.

As we pull up outside Nyla's hideout, Maira hops out of the passenger seat and strolls up the driveway and porch steps with an air of nonchalance, ringing the bell.

The door creaks open like Dracula's casket, letting a sliver of light into the darkness that she's confined herself in for eight months.

I turn off the car and step out, clenching my keys tightly in my fist.

"—can get ice cream afterward," I hear Maira say when I approach her. She looks at me with a stern look. "Help her with her bags, please."

Nyla eases the door open, hesitating at the threshold. The first thing that catches my eye is her vivid flamingo pink hair. *Definitely not a wig*. She's gone and cut her bangs, too, framing those enchanting green eyes of hers. If I wasn't so familiar with her, I wouldn't be able to recognize her at all.

Thankfully, she's dressed more conventionally this time—a soft pink sweatshirt and sweatpants, a sight I never thought I'd see. She unfurls her heart-shaped sunglasses and slips them on, keeping her head down as she steps out, standing behind Maira like a drenched pup.

I get a playful nudge in the ribs from Maira. She shoots me a warning glance, her eyes fixed on the luggage gathered in the alcove.

The next fifteen minutes are dedicated to securing Nyla's trio of oversized pink suitcases and a carry-on. She clutches her petite designer backpack to her chest, settling into the passenger seat. Maira takes the back, a mischievous grin playing on her lips in the rear-view mirror.

"Seatbelt," I tell Nyla. She complies swiftly, offering a small apology. She slouches deeper into her seat, hiding her face in the curve of her neck, out of my view.

"He won't get under your skin again, Alyn," Maira assures, swiveling to face her. "I'll make sure he's on his knees, begging for forgiveness on the rough ground until he's bleeding through his jeans. Right, Shahz?"

"Right," I grind out, firing up the engine and giving the stick shift a bit more force than necessary. Nyla sinks even lower into her seat. "I'm sorry for upsetting you, Aly. I shouldn't have done that."

She nods. "It's okay. I'm sorry for running away."

"Don't be. Relationships are a two-way street, and I messed up," I admit. I don't often pat myself on the back, but *holy shit*, I'm nailing this.

"Got it."

I keep my gaze locked on her as I ease the car into motion. She clings to her backpack, taking a deep breath. "Hand?"

Nyla glances up at me from her goofy sunglasses and down to my open palm. She slowly runs the tips of her soft fingertips over my palm, provoking goosebumps across my skin, and weaves her fingers through mine.

We stare at each other for a long, tension-filled minute before I turn the steering wheel and accelerate away from the vacation house.

Maira pokes my shoulder with a hint of excitement as she whispers, "Told you I could talk to her."

3

Sky

Nyla

It's not until we're at a gas station halfway to Shahzad's rundown apartment in Koreatown that I realize how much I regret agreeing to his bizarre plan.

While Shahzad pumps gas into the Nissan, Maira and I browse the empty convenience store, picking out snacks for the trip back.

"Milk or white?" She holds up the two chocolate brands, raising her perfectly threaded brows. "Choose wisely."

"White."

"Both it is." She tosses the chocolate bars into the basket and glides down the aisle towards the chips and gummies.

Maira, petite and composed, is a picture of aloof stoicism. Brown and beige seem to be her go-to colors, especially in the form of trousers and sweatshirts, as she made a point of mentioning. Her gaze, a rich cocoa shade, appears as if it holds the universe's most guarded secrets. The front strands of her short, dark hair are dyed a bold blonde, a move she made to ruffle her brother Mustafa's feathers when he discovered her plans to apply to a digital marketing internship abroad and leave Toronto for good. "*You only live once,*" she declared in the car. "*And I want to spend the rest of my life in New York.*"

"Are you looking forward to orientation next week?" I ask, snagging a pack of mint gum.

"I guess," she replies, giving a nonchalant shrug. "I've never been good at making friends or conversing with strangers, to be honest."

I let out a laugh. "Well, coming from someone who's also working on her social skills, I'd say you're doing pretty great so far."

"Yeah?"

"Oh, yeah."

"Well, I get why being in a relationship with Shahz bhai diluted your social skills," Maira remarks, raising her fist for a friendly bump. "Consider this the start of our anti-social friendship."

I hold onto the basket a little tighter in my left hand, my heart swelling with her gesture. *Your first friend out of hiding.* "To our friendship," I say, returning the fist bump.

Maira was a big factor in me going along with this plan. Well, mostly. That and the fact that Shahzad ended up drunk out of his head, bawling his eyes out about how much he misses me, then took his frustration out on a wall. And when I saw the gauze wrapped around his knuckles in the car, my cataclysmic crush on the man last year revived in a heartbeat. After all, a person's genuine feelings are revealed while they're under the influence. Which means, Shahzad didn't miss his Alyn, he missed *Nyla*. He missed what we shared last year, and he's been missing me ever since.

Right? Or am I just delusional?

"Why the fuck is there gelatin in each one of these gummy-bear packets?" Maira grumbles, and just before I can let out a chuckle at her outrage, I catch a glimpse of my face in the magazine section. "I mean, seriously. Not to be *that* Canadian or whatever, but do Americans forget there are Muslims living in this country, or do Fox and Friends only recognize us? I wouldn't want *gelatin* in my system because, first of all, that's. . ." Her rant trails off into something I can't focus on fully.

I take a step forward.

Once.

Twice.

Five and some more.

As I stand in front of the rows of magazines, my heart sinks.

Tucked behind the latest gossip tabloids and fashion magazines, I see my face. Each one prints a different story, but they all reduce me to one harsh word: slut. Faces of men I barely know are splashed across the covers, accompanied by insolent headlines screaming, "Dirty, Dumped, and Destroyed: Why Love Hates Nyla Ghilzai."

I can feel my chin trembling as I pluck one off the shelf and flip through the pages. There are manipulated images of me with a fake baby bump, arrows pointing accusingly, and captions asking, "Mamma Mia! Who's the Daddy out of the dozen?" Another shows me leaving my apartment a week before my altar incident, exhaustion painted on my face, with a headline declaring, "Nyla Ghilzai's summer look: The Victim's Complex," followed by an extensive article on exactly what the title suggests.

I bite my lip hard, tasting the metallic tang of blood.

This isn't true. This isn't true. This isn't true—

The words blur before me as I read, a shadow hanging over them. Shahzad sidles up too close and snatches the tabloid from my grasp.

And every other one off the shelf.

"Maira, head to the car," he orders, tossing the tabloids into the basket, covering them with our snacks and a random car magazine.

Maira joins us from the aisle and tosses a pack of Hubba-Bubba in the basket. "Don't keep me waiting." With that, she heads towards the Nissan.

"What's going on?" My voice wavers as I watch him pay for our snacks, all five tabloids, and a big water bottle. Luckily, the clerk is an older man who moves at a sloth's pace, bagging the items one by one. "Will you please answer me?"

He stays silent.

Shahzad emerges, arms laden with tabloids and our snack bag, which he hands over to Maira. Busy with her phone, she tears open a bag of cheese puffs and starts munching.

I hover by the hood, murmuring, "Are you going to answer me?"

He presses the tabloids against my chest, trading them for the water bottle. "Just follow me, Troublemaker."

My heart pounds, and it feels like I'm about to face the principal's office all over again. The sneakers I've dusted off from my high school days scrape against the rough pavement.

Shahzad grabs my wrist, pulling me along like a flag fluttering in the wind. I have to jog to keep up with his long strides. He stops us near a small garbage bin by the self-wash for cars. "Dump it."

"What—?"

"You heard me. Dump that shit into the trash."

Anxiety nips at my skin as I throw the tabloids in, my nose wrinkling at the rancid smell, my eyes tearing up at the sight of those damning words.

Shahzad brings out a cheap plastic lighter, flicking the dial and passing it to me with a calculated look in his sharp black eyes. He doesn't need to say it aloud. His demand spears right through me.

I wet my lips, watching the miniature flames dance before me. *Burn it, Nyla. Burn it to hell.*

Closing my eyes, I gently place the lighter into the bin. The paper catches fire, edges curling, passing the torch from one headline to the next. My face disappears as the flames consume it, searing the harmful rumors along the way.

Water rains down on the fire, turning the outdated gossip and photoshopped images into smoke.

"Let's go," Shahzad says, his voice softer than I expected. Or maybe I'm just imagining it. I don't know. Everything feels distorted and overwhelming right now.

I watch the ashes a little longer before the scent stings my eyes. Although I'm crying, it's for an entirely different reason. "Yeah. Let's go."

Holding his hand, I follow him back to the car.

As soon as Shahzad unlocks his apartment door, a giant snow beast pounces on him.

I let out a startled scream and stumble backward, accidentally hitting my head on one of the sconces that line the corridor.

"You're scared of your own dog?" Maira raises an eyebrow, a judgmental look on her face.

"No!" I quickly protest. "No, not at all. M-My dog just likes to play peek-a-boo with Shahzad and me when we get home. And, well, I'm naturally jumpy."

Maira gives me a sarcastic, wide-eyed look. "Right. I guess Sky has her biases." She gestures towards the heartwarming sight in front of us.

Shahzad is crouched down, affectionately petting Sky's cream-white fur while she happily licks his cheeks. They're both showering each other with love. It's a sight that warms my heart and, if I'm honest, makes my lips creak up into a rusty smile.

When I step further into the apartment, Shahzad stands up and lets out a quick whistle, causing Sky to sit obediently. I hug the walls, trying to keep a safe distance from the majestic, azure-eyed beast tracking my movements.

"I'm a little scared of dogs," I admit quietly for Shahzad's ears only while Maira settles her carry-on in the corner of the living room. "No offense."

FAKE IT TILL WE MAKE IT

Shahzad tries not to roll his eyes but doesn't quite succeed. "Sky's not like other dogs. She's highly trained in security. You don't need to worry about her taking a bite out of your pretty little head while you sleep."

He thinks my head is pretty?

My cheeks flush with warmth. "Well, that doesn't change the fact that I'm still scared of them."

Meanwhile, Maira starts to scratch and interact with Sky playfully. "Good to finally meet you in person, girl."

Shahzad steps aside, extending his large hand toward me. "Come on, Alyn. Let's make amends with Sky for arguing in front of her last week."

Best act, his gaze speaks.

I give a small nod.

As I gently lower my backpack to the floor and cautiously approach Sky, she tilts her head to the side. She doesn't seem intimidating. Just her adult size makes my heart ready to leap out of my chest for her to chase.

"Hey, sweetie," I soothe, steadying my voice. "I missed you so much. Even more than your dad. Because he and I had a couple's quarrel last week."

Shahzad's calloused fingers wrap around my softer ones. He takes a knee, and I follow suit, staying close to his side. Sky manages to put on a pout and turns her head away. "Sky, give us a shake if you forgive us."

Sky extends her paw toward Shahzad, almost like a human gesture.

He accepts it and gives her a small kiss on her forehead. "Ny—"

I suck in a sharp breath at his little slip-up.

"Alyn," he stammers, a hint of anxiety in his voice. "Shake Alyn's paw if you forgive her."

Sky lets out an exasperated huff and extends her paw toward me.

I blink, then gulp, reaching out to take her paw in my hand. She sniffs and puffs out a breath with her tongue hanging out, tail wagging enthusiastically. "She likes me again?"

All of a sudden, Sky starts circling around me, and I end up flat on my ass with a surprised yelp. I hear Maira chuckling in the background as I sit frozen, silently pleading for some help from a useless Shahzad.

The husky sticks her snout into my hair, thoroughly exploring every inch of my face and clothes, down to my legs. Then she settles down beside me and lets out a soft whine. Is she hungry? Is she going to try and eat me?

I muster a nervous chuckle, feigning a sense of familiarity. "Oh, Sky. You really know how to keep me on my toes."

"Pat her," Shahzad whispers.

My trembling hand rises, giving her head a sequence of gentle pats. She rests down with two paws on my legs and her chin on top. "She forgives me?"

Shahzad raises an eyebrow, a faint smile playing on his lips. "Seems she does."

Getting a dog's seal of approval probably shouldn't light up my day, but Sky doesn't seem like your average pup. She's a big, lovable girl who thrives on pats and scratches, and she's just so overly friendly. The kind of companion I'd cuddle up with and spill my heart out about the last eight months. Animals just get it, you know? Maybe Sky's taken a liking to me because she feels sorry for me.

"I'll bring both your luggage up. In the meantime, give Maira a tour of the place," Shahzad instructs.

"Need a hand?" I offer.

Shahzad studies my face like I'm some kind of lab experiment that's delivered good results. "Nah. It's all good. I've grown a fear of you walking out on our place."

Our place. That was . . . sturdy fake-boyfriend dialogue. "Are you sure?"

"Don't be shy, Troublemaker. You've lived here for three months." Shahzad gives my elbow a reassuring squeeze, as if that seals the deal on our pretend romance, and heads out.

I stand up, dusting off my back. Sky nudges my legs, demanding her share of attention. I think I'm already head over heels for her. "Ready for the grand tour, Maira?"

Maira grins and gestures an arm out. "Lead the way, lady of the house."

Inhaling, I step into the shoes of my new role for the next month and start walking in them.

"It's not exactly a palace, as you can see," I say, motioning towards the small combined living room and kitchen area. "Uh, looks like Shahzad has been sleeping on that couch because of our big fight." I point to two neatly folded pillows and a blanket on the worn-out leather sofa. I skip over to the door that probably leads to a bedroom. "And this is . . ." Swinging it open, a twin-sized mattress reveals itself alongside a table and a closet. *Knew it.* "This is where you and I'll be sleeping. Cozy, no?"

"It's suitable."

I tilt my head towards the ajar door next to the shoe closet, revealing porcelain tiles. "Uh, that is . . . the bathroom." I keep my confusion to myself, muttering, "Right by the front door for some reason."

The hallways are narrow devoid of any colors or plants. There's a solitary large window leading to a balcony where I can retreat if I find myself on the verge of a panic attack. Or two. Or ten."

"That's pretty much it, honestly." I let out a relieved sigh, slapping my thighs lightly. "I know it's not quite like what you're used to back home, but doesn't it feel like we're our own little family? I mean, I— Sorry." I stumble over my words, and Maira chuckles, her laughter filling the space with its resonant, husky sound.

"Looks like we're off to a solid start," she says, lifting a finger. "But, why don't you and Shahz bhai take the bedroom, and I'll crash on the couch. You guys are a couple, after all, and I don't want to intrude on—"

"Oh, don't worry!" I chuckle, swaying back and forth on my feet. "Shahzad and I hashed out the whole housing thing after our little dispute. He's totally cool with the couch. Actually, he kinda loves it."

Maira arches an eyebrow. "Do you two fight a lot?"

"No! We're— *Pfft*. No, we're a really good match. We have our moments, but we're just *so* compatible. Twin flames. Our moons and suns and all that spiritual malarkey just click." I intertwine my fingers and give them a confident shake. "Two peas in a healthy, green pod."

"All right then. Glad to know I won't have to play referee." She grabs her backpack and heads into the bedroom, closing the door behind her.

Sky rubs her face against the side of my legs, demanding attention. I bend down and gently stroke her fur. She huffs and licks my cheek, catching me off guard.

This is a welcome change of scenery. This new, slightly worn-down setting and the company of good people. I needed a break from solitude; one month should hopefully do the trick. Besides playing the part of Shahzad's pretend girlfriend, I can make more progress in these upcoming months.

I'll figure it out.

4

F.C.K.

Shahzad

Sky has taken a *loving* to Nyla.

The two girls are down on the floor, showering my husky with belly rubs and chatting away, when suddenly Sky lets out a howl of pure delight, sounding almost human.

Meanwhile, I'm in the kitchen, slathering the pan with butter, ready to grill up some leftover spicy marinated chicken while the rice simmers away for a stir-fry.

I've always been one to cook in large batches, and I love sharing it with Jia and the rest of the kitchen crew. They've got a real appreciation for my skills when it comes to my cooking—always teaching me new tricks to up my game in culinary arts.

"Shahzad?" Nyla's way of saying my name always grabs my attention, even if she whispers it in a noisy room. She nails the pronunciation every time. *Sha-ha-zadh* instead of *Shay-zed*. "Do you need any help?"

"No . . . sweetheart." I focus on ensuring the chicken gets properly cooked on the other side. She doesn't say anything in response; just goes back to laughing at Sky's antics.

Later, the girls devour their dinner, including my husky, with her bowl of chow. They praise it and clean their plates before stacking them up for me to take to the kitchen and wash.

Dish-washing is what I excel at. It's my job at Jia's BBQ House. The dish boy. Even though Jia keeps pushing to promote me, I hold back. I'm not one to rush into commitment, especially with the fear of fucking it all up—both in my professional and personal life.

So, I stick to scrubbing dishes.

Each one's got its own story, marked by different stains and wear. Some are well-used, showing chips and scratches; others are kept spotless. Those plates piled high with leftovers? They drive Jia and me crazy. But if you asked me to pick a favorite? I wouldn't. No matter how beat up or brand new they are, they all get the same meticulous treatment, erasing their peculiarities.

What the fuck am I rambling about?

I rub my nose and grab my leather jacket off the dining table.

"Where are you going?" Nyla inquires, stepping out of my bedroom—technically, Maira's room—her hair pulled back in a ponytail, dressed in another oversized tracksuit.

"Out for a smoke." I glance at Maira, who's immersed in sorting out her internship schedule on the couch, headphones on. "On the balcony."

Nyla nods, licking her lower lip. My gaze lingers on the gentle fullness of her mouth. "Should we, you know, formalize our act in some way?" she murmurs, glancing over her shoulder.

Like a porcelain doll—that's how I'd describe her lips. Perfectly circular, with a pronounced cupid's bow, naturally poised and slightly pouted.

"Shahzad?" Nyla tilts her head to the side, her emerald eyes searching mine. "Can we talk out the terms, please?"

Shaking off the thoughts, I stride past her toward the balcony, aiming to clear the smoke from my mind and instead fill it in my lungs. "You don't mind the smell, do you?" I ask, sliding the door shut behind us and claiming the corner spot to light my cigarette.

"I've endured enough meetings with my father and his cigars to grow immune." Nyla leans over the railing and inhales the air of Koreatown. A smile spreads like warm butter across her mouth, suddenly capturing my interest. She takes in a dreamy sigh, resembling a sheltered princess. "How I've missed you, New York City."

I stifle a chuckle. *Man, she's theatrical.*

Nyla claps sharply, jolting my shoulders. "Time for the rules!" She lounges against the railing, elbows propped up, and locks her gaze onto me.

"You can go first." I take a leisurely drag.

Nyla hesitates for a moment. "I think my main thing is making sure I stay safe and my identity is protected."

"You *think*?" I tease.

"No, I know," she corrects herself quickly. "So, my rule is for you to keep me safe and protect my identity, Shahzad Arain."

I bite the inside of my cheek and stand a bit taller. "And what about our relationship? Any do's and don'ts?"

"Sex?"

"You sound unsure," I say with an amused smirk.

"No, I'm sure," Nyla replies, running her fingers through her hair. Such a subtle gesture, yet its impact on me isn't one bit ethical. "No sex. Just kiss my F.C.K."

"*Huh*?" I choke out, nearly dropping my cigarette. "You're *what*?"

"F.C.K.? Forehead, cheeks, and knuckles?" Nyla explains innocently. "No kissing except on my forehead, cheeks, or back of my hand."

"You can abbreviate that better," I suggest.

She glances upwards in thought. "K.F.C.?" A shrug. "Less of a shock factor. Kinda."

I raise an eyebrow and steer the conversation back on course. "Why the back of your hand?"

A shy grin spreads across her face as she fiddles with her fingers. "I discovered how much I love backhand kisses when I starred in my first Regency movie. They were all the rage in the eighteenth century."

"F.C.K. it is," I say, taking another drag. "Anything else?"

She shakes her head. "And you?"

I kick back, arms folded, letting the dart dangle lazily from my lips. Nyla gives me the once-over before dropping her gaze. "My rules are all about the living situation. You've got fifteen minutes max in the shower, or else you'll be chipping in for extra utilities. You've gotta handle your own dishes and laundry, pitch in on the housecleaning when it's your turn, and take out the trash. Point is, since you're not paying rent, you're on for half the chores. It'll make our setup feel more legit, you know?" I squint at her. "Couples do this stuff, right?"

"You're asking the wrong girl. I've lived on my own since I turned eighteen. Never been in a genuine relationship either, so."

We're so fucked.

"But the chore thing works for me," she concedes without much of a fight.

I study Nyla. The *real* Nyla. The one right beside me, tugging the sleeves of a thrifted sweater down to her fingertips, sporting bubblegum pink hair and a permanently somber expression that agrees with every one of my requests. She's undergone significant changes since her altar abandonment, and while I don't hold it against her, I'm taken aback by how she hasn't bounced back from it.

In the past, she always found a way to resolve things, whether a slip-up on the runway or a wardrobe malfunction that she effortlessly brushed off. Even the harshest press, she flipped off without breaking a sweat. There wasn't anything Nyla Ghilzai couldn't conquer.

Except worldwide humiliation.

"Want a job?" I finally break the uncomfortable silence.

"A job?"

"That's right." Because I know she's an ambitious woman. Deep down, despite who she is now, she enjoys earning her wage and spending it on frivolous bullshit. The taste of triumph, the awards, people singing her praises—it's in her blood. Or at least, it used to be. I've got a feeling that spark's still in there, waiting for the right moment to flare up.

Nyla tilts her head and—*stop thinking it's adorable.* It's just a fucking head tilt. "Where?"

"Downstairs."

"At the Korean restaurant?"

"Exactly. Jia's BBQ House. We've been searching for an extra hand, but Jia thinks they're all posers—her words, not mine. So, if you're up for it—"

"All right," she interrupts, pushing off the railing and closing the distance between us. Ambitious, this one. "Yeah, all right. Cool. I promise to do a great job."

"First thing in the morning, I'll talk to Jia." I take the cigarette from my mouth. "Any other conditions before we finalize things?"

"Oh, yes!" Nyla clears the grogginess from her throat. She looks me in the eyes. "I want you to know that just because we are in a fake relationship doesn't mean you're tied to it. You can go out and have fun, but make sure Maira isn't home, and I know in advance when you invite someone."

I hold her gaze, my fist tightening in the left pocket of my sweatpants for reasons I can't quite put my finger on. "That won't be an issue at all, Troublemaker."

The mischievous glint in her eye almost makes me smile. "You're really committing to this fake-boyfriend role, huh?"

I let out a resigned sigh at her antics. "One more rule," I say. "If you're stepping out into the world, I'll be right there with you. As your bodyguard, of course."

She nods. "Sounds good to me."

I scan her again and find pure intentions and a soul that the wrong hands can easily manipulate. A soul that *has* been abused and exploited countless times.

And if there's one thing I've learned in my expertise as her father's bodyguard, I know the importance of observation. A little twitch in the enemy's finger can almost always lead to a hostile attack. A flirtatious comment from a slimy bastard typically leads to trouble.

That's why I keep my eyes peeled, whether I'm on the subway or anywhere else. I assess who's just trying to get home to their loved ones and who might stand in their way.

"Can I try that?" Nyla asks, pointing at my cigarette. She looks unsure, a cinch of concern between her brows. As if Abe is watching, controlling her choices.

I hold up the cigarette. "Part your lips for me."

She creates a small opening in her mouth, and blood rushes to my lower region. Eye contact with this woman is no laughing matter. It's almost as if I'm suspended in the air, transported back to our one-night stand.

I steady my hand, placing the cigarette between her lips and holding it in position. "Inhale, slowly."

Nyla's chest expands.

"Hold it," I caution. She nods, blinking leisurely, her body becoming tranquil. I withdraw the cigarette. "Inhale." Another ascent of her chest. "Exhale."

Nyla's smartass blows through her nose, a cheeky smile laying out on her lips. "Gotcha."

My insides ignite on fire at her little act. "You've done this before."

"Which celebrity hasn't?" She clears her throat, allowing a cough or two to escape. "Although, it's been some time."

I raise an eyebrow, suppressing a smirk. "You're something else, Troublemaker." As I bring the dart to my mouth, I taste a hint of her sweet lip gloss.

God help me.

She swipes imaginary sweat from her forehead. "Good to know I can still act."

"Moving on. Are you familiar with the concept of fake dating?" I settle into a lounge chair and pull another one up for her. Our knees brush as she takes a seat.

"Isn't it pretty self-explanatory?" Nyla chuckles, her hand covering her mouth. Can you taste a laugh? Because hers is like freshly harvested honey. "I once played the lead in an action film with a fake dating storyline. Instead of confessing our feelings, he took a bullet for me. *Literally*."

I stare at her incredulously. "It's a miracle we're living in reality."

"Hey, weirder things have happened in real life, too. You are my bodyguard, after all. Taking a bullet for me is in the job description." Her confidence is almost unsettling. It's kind of amusing, oddly endearing, but also a bit frightening. "On a more subtle note," she continues, excitement detectable, "we won't be dealing with bullets. If there's any hint of jealousy"—she gestures toward my supposedly bruised knuckles, still wrapped in gauze—"a punch will do just fine."

"Why not just have a civil conversation?"

"Because every fake-dating situation ends up with the fake being *poof*! Gone. Out of sight, out of mind."

It takes a minute for her words to click.

I bark out a laugh, scaring her and probably the people walking on the street, too. Nyla stares wide-eyed as I lose my goddamn mind over her *ridiculous* statement. I mean, she can't be serious? Even if she looks dead serious. "Like the idiot characters in my sister's books? Sorry to burst your bubble, Troublemaker, but that *poof* part is all fictitious."

Nyla cocks her head back, lips parting. "You've read fake-dating novels?"

"Against my goodwill," I reply, exhaling a plume of smoke. "I get it. We have to play the part and act like we're really together. Which means I've got the toughest role here. You know, the whole alpha-dominant-growling-around-the-clock routine, just in case some idiot has a death wish waiting to come true."

"Shahzad," she murmurs, hands hovering over me like I'm some hands-off exhibit in an art gallery. "*You*, of all people, know about fake dating? I don't believe it."

"Is that so?"

"Duh!"

"Fine. See this?" I scowl. "I have to pull this face every time some guy tries to hit on you. Assert my dominance, or whatever you call it." I dip my chin. "And don't forget to lower my lashes and narrow my eyes. Make 'em look even darker, even though they're already fucking black. And, oh, the classic jaw-clenching as the finishing touch. By the end of it, I'll be owing a visit to my dentist."

Shivers crawl down my spine as I recall the numerous romance novels Dua made me read for our book club. I'd grind through those explicit 300-page nightmares during culinary school breaks or on the train back to my place in Switzerland. We'd hop on FaceTime and dissect the corniest moments and cheesiest dialogues or how Sebastian Blackthorne sold Blackthorne Security Enterprises for some klutz he met a month ago. I know Dua's ass SparkNotes'd the critically-acclaimed classics I chose for our club.

"Is this why you wanted to fake date?" Nyla asks, her tone pointed. "Because you know the recipe, Chef?"

"Not a chef, Troublemaker."

"Not yet, *Chef*."

Fine, yeah, I admit it. I like it when she calls me 'Chef.' No further explanation is needed.

"As for me," she drawls, tapping her chin, "there isn't much to do."

I scoff. "A little backhanded, don't you think?"

Her expression shifts, a flicker of hurt crossing her features. "I'm sorry, Shahzad. I didn't mean to sound backhanded. I just— I have solid acting experience, so I don't think I really need any tweaking. But please feel free to give me suggestions if I slip up. You're the expert."

Okay, well, there *is* that. After seeing how lovingly she stared at Whitehorn or whatever the fuck, I'm not too worried about her.

As long as Mustafa buys that we've been a couple for three months, including Jia and her staff, I have no issues practicing my expressions.

"Got it." I stub out my cigarette with a firm press of my boot. I join her side, nodding in appreciation. "Thank you, again, for helping me out."

The moonlight reflects off her smile, illuminating something dim and hollow inside me. "Let's be the best, healthiest fake couple ever flowered on this doomed planet." She extends her hand for a shake.

A light bulb flicks over my head.

I grasp her hand, gently kiss her knuckles, and witness her mint-colored eyes widen. "Maira's watching."

She turns—

"Don't peek," I murmur, pulling her close to my chest. Her grip tightens on my arms. A cocky grin plays on my lips as she gasps, discreetly squeezing my biceps. "Remember, your name is Alyn Inayat. We've been together for three months now." I run my fingers through her hair, keeping my hand steady on the back of her head. "We met at Pets-A-Lot while I was grabbing treats for Sky, and you happened to be the cashier."

"Why do I have to be the cashier? Handling money makes me anxious."

I raise an eyebrow at her. She's fixated on my throat, blinking rapidly. "Didn't you have those fancy accountants to take care of that for you, Nyla?"

"Baba handled all of that."

"Fine, you were there to check out the puppies or something."

"I do love puppies."

"I'm sure you do." I catch a whiff of her fruit-scented shampoo, my eyes instinctively shutting. "Wrap your arms around me. It seems Maira's very nosy."

Nyla embraces my torso, even resting her cheek on my chest. Fuck, I can't wipe this silly grin off my face. Hugs, man. They just hit differently when the person fits perfectly under your chin. I'm not big on hugs from strangers, except for my sisters. But Nyla? She's never been a stranger.

"Is she still watching?" she asks.

"Mm-hmm."

"So, are we officially adding hugging to the deal?"

"Mm-hmm."

"Okay." She lets out a soft chuckle, my left eye cracking open. "You're so huggable."

"Is that so?"

"Without a doubt."

I wake up and give her a firm pat on the back to signal a permanent break. She steps away, straightening out her sweater and fixing her hair. I jam my hands into my pockets, gripping my lighter tightly. "You should—"

"I should—"

"Yeah."

"All right. Cool. See you in the morning?"

I nod. "Sweet dreams."

She lowers her head and heads back to the living room, emptied by Maira shortly after I kissed Nyla's hand.

"Sweet dreams? Seriously? What the fuck are you, her father?" I repeat my stupidity to myself, pulling out a second cigarette to burn off the day's tension.

5

Mustafa's Calling!

Nyla

Since I was nine, I've been having relentless nightmares, a ceaseless cycle of waking up in cold, clammy sheets, desperate to escape my own skin.

There were terrors when Baba would force my head beneath the icy water of a bathtub filled with jumbled cubes. Then, there were instances when the paparazzi stripped me bare, capturing a thousand images for their scandal-hungry audiences. On occasion, one of the countless predators stalking me would breach my apartment, committing unspeakable crimes. There were even moments in my night terrors when I'd find myself jumping off of hotel buildings or overdosing, and Hollywood would grieve the loss of my beauty, not my character.

Except today.

I slept. Somewhat.

My eyes snapped open and took in the tiny, dim room bathed in golden light.

Maira slumbers peacefully beside me, unknowingly clutching my arm tightly—her lively, ebony strands cascading over her cheek. She snores like a fifty-year-old man with severe sinus issues, a small puddle of drool forming on my shoulder.

I gently free my arm from her grasp and sit up, running my hands through my hair. Maira and I share a twin bed, like Elizabeth and Jane Bennet—Maira, naturally, plays the role of Elizabeth.

The room is plain, with a small walk-in closet. A lone window is carved into the red brick walls of the apartment, offering a view of emergency fire steps leading down to a dingy alleyway. As always, no decorations adorn the space.

The front door rattles open, accompanied by Sky's muffled barks and Shahzad's whistle to calm her.

I adjust my hair and swing my legs over the edge of the bed, reaching for my bathrobe and cinching it snugly around me. Yet, as I catch my reflection in the standing mirror, I let it hang loose.

As I step into the hallway, Sky's gaze locks on me instantly. She stands in the center of the kitchen, next to her . . . shirtless owner.

My mouth dries on cue.

I've ogled Shahzad's intricate tattoo sleeve before, but his back is an entirely different masterpiece. A mythological tableau with a phoenix etched from his shoulder blade down to the curve of his waist. The details are so precise that when his taut back muscles flex, they breathe life into the mythical creature.

I've always longed for a tattoo, but Baba insisted it wouldn't suit a girl who shows her skin for a living. He demands perfection, limbs, and legs with soft tones. All of which I lost in eight months.

Shahzad turns as I step out, the floorboard creaking under my bare feet. His chest is a canvas, unmarked by symbols. I let my gaze shamelessly roam over the—*one, three, six*—eight pack he's sculpted. An eight freakin' pack. I thought these bodies were reserved for Men's Health cover models or professional trainers, but here it is before me. And that warm brown skin only adds to his beauty. It glows in the early May sun, sweat droplets glistening like morning dew on his abs. His long locks are pulled back into a half-bun, the rest clinging to his neck. In his rather large hands, he cradles Sky's food bowl—

"Nyla?"

Startled, I lift my gaze. "Y-Yes?"

"You didn't hear me call your name twice," he says.

"Oh." I gulp, my tongue moistened, a nervous chuckle escaping my lips. "Sorry. I just woke up, so I'm a bit disoriented."

He acknowledges with a nod, resuming his task of preparing Sky's breakfast. "You can shower first."

"No, really, you can go ahead—" I start.

"Nyla," he interrupts, turning to me, his gaze piercing through the layers of my being with a stoic expression. "Go shower."

I clear my throat, relenting. "All right, if you insist." I retreat to my room, filtering through my luggage for a towel. The majority of my clothes are various shades of pink, a testament to my stubborn affection for the color.

Locking myself in the bathroom, I carefully unwrap the towel concealing the weight scale. Yes, I brought the goddamn enemy with me because it's a constant variable in my life. My entire day hinges on the number it presents. *Let's go for eighty-five today, Nyla.*

The scale slaps me with a strict 90 kgs.

I'm going to *kill* myself.

I'm going to kill this wretched weight scale first, then myself.

Maybe I'll bash my skull with it until it stops at the forty-five like it once did.

I tuck it away in the cavities of Shahzad's sink cabinet and strip off my clothes, exposing my vulnerable form to scrutiny. My hands squeeze my two-ton breasts, tracing the contours of my soft belly, grappling with the stretch marks. They travel down to the ass that used to fit into double-zero jeans, a mere memory of what it used to be. Collarbones, once pronounced, are now lost beneath layers of flesh. A double chin that I conceal with practiced precision, tongue pressed against the roof of my mouth.

Frowning until my cheeks hurt, I revolve the shower faucet to hellfire level, wishing it would burn the extra fat off my skin.

After my shower, the type where I shaved every part of my body and almost fainted from the steam in the tight space, I eventually leave—

Shahzad stands firmly in the doorway, his grip tight on the frame. "One hour, Troublemaker," he growls.

I clutch the robe tighter around me, taken aback. "One hour?"

"*One. Hour.*"

Confusion clouds my mind. "One hour . . . ?"

"Do you have any idea how much your hour-long shower has cost us on the water bill?" He strides inside, forcefully shutting the door.

I stumble backward, only to be pulled against his chest. His chest. *God.* I grasp onto his inked forearm, my breath coming in ragged gasps. "I-I'm so sorry. I'll find a way to compensate you."

"With what money? Thought Daddy cut you off?" Shahzad still hasn't released me, his grip growing even tighter. "Speaking of, are you planning to meet him?"

Truth be told, the thought of standing before Baba, face to face, has crossed my mind. It feels futile because he knows I'm alive (I called him on FaceTime, my drunken rage spilling out, hurling every venomous word in the dictionary at him just months ago). Despite being aware of my whereabouts, Baba remains stationary, a voice in my inbox reminding me of my accident, urging me to return to First Class Faces so he can sculpt me into a masterpiece for the world to admire.

"No," I whisper, the words barely escaping my lips. "I don't ever want to meet him."

I'm just trying to shift gears from modeling to fashion design. It's been a long run, always living in my father's shadow, even though he's been putting me in the spotlight since I was a kid. But even in that flashy glare, all you really see is darkness. Once the cameras have done their due diligence, and the crowds scatter, leaving behind a confetti of fleeting joy, it's just me.

I've always been on my own.

Might as well *make* it on my own now, too.

I retreat from his hold, which eases as soon as I begin to move. "I'll make sure to be more considerate about showering next time."

Shahzad scrutinizes me from top to bottom as though I'm some kind of scientific abnormality. He's been doing this since last night. Maybe he's puzzled by the person I've evolved into over the past eight months, or maybe he's just appalled.

I embrace the spot where his arm had somehow completely encircled. Knowing that he can feel the protruding curves on my stomach makes bile rise in my throat.

"Mustafa's calling!" Maira shouts from the other side of the door.

Shahzad gives me another appraising look. He extends his hand, his fingers thick and scratched with lines that'll take a palm reader a century to decipher.

I slowly, shakingly, clasp his fingers, noticing the slight difference in the size of our palms. "Fake it till we make it, Chef."

"You'll do great, Troublemaker."

A gentle smile graces my lips in reaction to the silly nickname.

Following his lead, I follow him out of the bathroom and into the living room, where Maira is engrossed in a conversation with her brother over her laptop.

"Oh, they're here!" Maira exclaims, rising from her seat to make room for Shahzad. She scoots a chair over for me and gives me an encouraging thumbs up as I nervously settle beside him, tucking my bangs to cover my eyes.

"Shahzad!" Mustafa calls out with excitement. He's a good-looking man, sporting a thick, brown beard and wavy, dark hair that mirrors Shahzad's, albeit slightly shorter. His eyebrows shoot up to his hairline as he lays eyes on me. "And you must be Alyn."

"Hi, Mustafa," I greet shyly. "I'm Alyn Inayat, Shahzad's girlfriend."

Shahzad suddenly envelops me in a hug, planting a gentle kiss on my cheek. *Oh my.* "How you been, Mustafa?"

His friend gazes at us in wonder before his eyes settle into a friendly expression. "I must admit, Shahz, I'm absolutely thrilled for you," he says, clasping his hands on the table. "Where are you from, Alyn?"

"My mother is Pakistani, and my father is Afghan."

"Oh, wow," he murmurs to himself. "Do you speak Pashto?"

"And Dari," I respond, sitting up straight as if I'm in an interview with Kelly Clarkson. "I'm proficient in several languages. Traveling allowed me to expand my skill set to communicate with the locals without having my team translate for me."

"Your team?"

Shit.

Shahzad's hand finds my thigh and gives it a cautionary squeeze. *Shit, shit, shit!*

"My backpacking companions!" I burst out laughing, and Shahzad forces himself to join in. "I've been backpacking across various continents for some time before settling down in Koreatown with my wonderful boyfriend here." I playfully squish Shahzad's cheeks together, earning me a bemused side-eye. Anxiety causes my hand to retreat almost instantly.

"Adventurous," Mustafa remarks with a tiny smirk. "She's exactly your type, brother."

Maira groans, rolling her eyes. "Hate when he talks like this."

But Mustafa persists. "Shahzad, man, I'm so proud of you. You know the saying, "Good things come to those who wait"? Well, here you go. After all those wrongs, you finally have someone right." He exudes the pride of a doting parent. It's endearing.

Shahzad musters a smile.

"You know, Alyn, Shahzad had *the* worst taste in women," Mustafa muses. "Goriyan, you know? Blondes on weekends, brunettes on weekdays." *Oh god.* "It was so tricky telling them apart."

Shahzad scoots closer to the edge of his seat. "Mustafa—"

"Absolutely horrendous." Mustafa doesn't have a pause button or any self-awareness. "Every night, a new face would ring him up whenever *we* were on call. You can't imagine my relief when he left that modeling agency."

"Fuck me," Shahzad whispers, pinching the bridge of his nose.

I cringe in my seat. "That's. . . a relief, I guess."

"But you're nothing like them, Alyn," he reassures me. "I already believe you're perfect." *Because I'm culturally acceptable.*

"How did you and Shahzad meet?" I ask, trying to change the subject. Shahzad nudges my knee under the table. "Oh, I— Well, I wasn't given the specific details about the backstory of your friendship—about you, more. But Shahzad *always* tells me how he cherishes the time your families used to spend together."

Mustafa chuckles softly. "So he's sentimental about me when I'm not around, huh?" He absentmindedly brushes at an imaginary speck on his shoulder. "My father passed away when Shahzad and his family moved to Toronto. It left my mother in a deep depression, and Maira was still in elementary school, so I didn't have anyone to rely on except this idiot here. He slowly became a part of the family and took half the burden of my household duties off my shoulders."

I offer a warm, empathetic smile. "You should be incredibly proud of yourself, Mustafa. To have someone who you're not related to by blood take care of you like you're their family is . . . I can't imagine there was ever a rainy day."

I often considered the idea of relocating to Dubai with Mama to learn her fashion design mastery. However, the chance of dealing with my numerous step-siblings never sat well with me. I worried I wouldn't receive the attention I needed. Baba, on the other hand, is a different case.

"In hindsight, it was a bit challenging at first, but I've adapted to it. I even mustered up the courage to propose to my dream girl, Layla. You two would hit it off. She loves traveling, too," Mustafa shares, flashing me a smile that showcases his perfect teeth. It causes a blush to spread across my cheeks. "But thank you for your kind words. They mean a great deal to me."

I fight the urge to break into a foolish grin.

"How did *you* and Shahzad meet?" Mustafa asks. "He has yet to tell me the story he's been hiding for three months."

Shahzad pats my side; his side glance filled with caution. *Stick to our story*, they say.

"Uh, yeah, no, we met at Pets-A-Lot," I begin. "I was having a rough day, so naturally, I went for some puppy therapy to cheer myself up. Shahzad and Sky happened to be doing their little shopping. I think he was buying treats for Sky. Right, babe?"

"Right," he states like a robot.

"Right," I repeat timidly, caressing his back. "We started chatting for what felt like hours and had some . . . tacos. Right, sweetie?"

"Right. Fish tacos."

"Beef," I say. "I don't like fish. You should know that, babe." My fingers pinch his ear, eyes playfully rolling. "He can be *such* a forgetful boyfriend sometimes."

"She had beef. I had fish," he clarifies. "And crêpes for dessert. They were very . . . good. Good ratio of batter consistency and whipped cream filling. Did yours taste good, Alyn?"

"So good. With the little sprinkle of strawberries."

"And the hazelnut spread."

I groan, praising the sky. "Mmm, the hazelnut spread. It was . . . I mean, it was the perfect meet-cute dinner-dessert type of thing for a sweet, romantic couple like us. You know?"

Mustafa's smile is dangling by a thread as if he regrets questioning us, while Maira stifles a smile behind her hand.

Shahzad clears his throat. "Alyn, my lovely girlfriend, and I have some work to attend to. If that's all, we'll let you return to Maira."

"Yes, of course. This call has been going on for too long." It's only been in eight minutes. "Anyway!" Mustafa claps his hands once, giving me a slight head bow as if I were royalty. "It was a pleasure meeting you, Alyn. Let's make sure to stay in touch."

"There's no need for that," Shahzad interjects sharply. He catches my surprised gaze. "You should stay in touch with *us*."

Mustafa grins, hiding his smile behind his fingers, and gives an affirming nod. "Exactly, Shahzad. I'll make sure to keep in touch with you and Alyn. Does that stoke the flames of your jealousy?" He winks at me.

I pinch my lips together in a smile. "Of course, Mustafa. Nice meeting you, too."

Shahzad lets out a sigh and beckons for Maira to take our place. "We'll catch up later," he tells Mustafa, then stands up, our fingers still intertwined. He practically pulls me along before letting go. "Put on something professional. We're meeting with Jia."

I pout, adjusting my bangs. "Do you want her to know we're dating?"

"She's nosy. She'll figure it out if I don't tell her. And let's not do the whole taco and crêpes meet-cute story."

"*Never*."

"Ever."

I nod, shifting my gaze to Maira and Mustafa, who share a similar laugh. I always dreamed of a sibling growing up. Someone I could lean on when the pressure from my parents became too much. I had Alina, but she lived in Canada, and by the time she was at MIT, I was jet-setting for international shows, missing out on my adolescence.

FAKE IT TILL WE MAKE IT

Sky's head bump against my leg snaps me out of my reverie, and I find myself locked in Shahzad's intense gaze. My posture instantly improves, and if my cheeks aren't already warm from Mustafa's smiles, they're practically aflame from Shahzad's impassiveness. It's an attractive quality, that stoicism of his.

"What's going on?" I question.

He tips his chin up. "Mustafa's getting married."

I blink. "Uh—"

"He's engaged. To his best friend Layla. Their families gave their blessing last year."

"I'm aware. He just told me two minutes ago."

Shahzad shuts his mouth, crossing and uncrossing his arms over his chest. He takes a sharp breath, then opens the bedroom door, urging me inside. "Five minutes," he instructs before closing the door.

Body dysmorphia decides on twenty minutes instead.

6

Jia's BBQ House

Shahzad

Jia's place is a quirky haven of eclectic treasures, a mix of relics from her homeland and finds from Samuel's vintage shop just down the block.

As we step inside, we're greeted by a mesmerizing collection of ornate mirrors lining the entrance. The walls tell the story of Jia's life, from her childhood in South Korea to the bustling household of siblings she grew up in, her marriage to an American-Korean man, the move to the West, the whirlwind arrival of her children, and the genesis of Jia's BBQ House following her husband's passing. Amidst all these memories, you'll find snapshots of Tae and her, and strangely enough, Tom Cruise.

Yet, that's not even the quirkiest sight in her place. A collection of taxidermied mice that she forced Tae to murder lined like trophies over her fireplace mantle. Portraits of 17th-century monarchs peer out from the floral living room walls. Framed pictures of Tom Cruise share windowsill space with potted plants, and the pièce de résistance? A vibrant cherry-red latex couch that squeaks under the weight of Nyla and me.

"You've got quite the interesting hair, Alyn," Jia remarks after a few minutes of silence post-Nyla's introduction.

"Thank you," Nyla replies, shifting uncomfortably on the leather couch. I wrap my arm around her waist, drawing her closer. She carries the scent of fresh fruits and vanilla, a sweet and intoxicating fragrance that surrounds the air. "I've been thinking about going even brighter pink or—"

"Don't," Jia interrupts, turning to face me. "You never mentioned you had a girlfriend, adeul."

Nyla lets out a snort. "That's adorable. She calls you 'son'."

"You speak Korean?" Jia checks out Nyla with newfound interest.

She stumbles over her words. "I-I've traveled quite a bit. I've always enjoyed delving into new cultures and languages, making navigating a city easier."

Jia smiles. "Impressive."

She starts chattering in Korean, and Nyla nods, chuckling and replying effortlessly. Her accent is almost as flawless as Jia's. Impressive, indeed. "Well, anyway, you're more than welcome to stay, Alyn. I prefer you over the other girls Shahz used to bring home."

Not this again.

"Jia."

She flinches and clarifies her words. "Sorry, sorry. Don't worry, Alyn. It was a *very* long time ago when he first moved in."

"I see." Nyla chuckles nervously, giving my back a gentle rub. Her touch is soothing and comforting, a feeling I haven't had in a while.

"You two are adorable together. Remember to shower your girlfriend with plenty of kisses," Jia says, her lips forming a playful smirk. "That's how my husband won me over, the best kisser in Korea and America."

Jesus.

Jia blinks at us. "Well?"

"Well, what?" I ask, sharing a puzzled look with Nyla.

"Give the girl a kiss, pabo-ya."

Nyla giggles, using her finger to wipe the tip of her nose. "She just called you stupid."

Suppressing an eye roll, I lean in and plant a soft kiss on Nyla's round cheek. They flush pink, just like they did this morning when we were selling it to Mustafa. As for me, there's a strange fluttering in my chest.

"Your turn," Jia prods Nyla. "Love, it's not exactly autonomous, is it?"

"Of course," Nyla agrees, her voice soft. She takes a breath, and her doll-like lips meet my cheekbone. I shut my eyes, determined not to pull her onto my lap, and let her kisses wander down to my neck—

No, Shahzad.

"How sweet!" Jia's applause breaks the spell, and Nyla retreats, apologizing under her breath. "Now, let's talk about your work placement. Shall we?"

This time, Nyla appears more at ease, adjusting her bangs and those thick black-framed glasses she calls a 'disguise.' As if Jia has any interest in modern Hollywood. She's got a whole collection of old Hollywood films with Korean dubs. If she were a teenager today, there'd be a cut-out of Marlo Brando in the corner of her bedroom.

"Hmm." Jia tilts her head. "Would you like to be a hostess?"

I wasn't keen on the idea when Nyla first brought it up. Most of the men who come into Jia's BBQ House are the sort trying to climb the ladder, thinking every woman wants them and every smile is an invitation.

The word slips out of my mouth without hesitation. "No."

"What?" Nyla asks.

"No." *Why, Shahzad? It's not your decision to make, dumbass.* But I need her where I can keep an eye on her, preferably from the back kitchen. "Cashier works."

Nyla lets out an exasperated groan. "Oh, god."

Jia raises a brow. "We are not a grocery store, adeul."

I level her with a look that would leave me questioning myself if there were a mirror in front of me. "She will be a cashier, Jia."

"I can be a waitress—"

"No."

Nyla excuses us from Jia and speaks in a lower tone. "What's wrong? I thought we talked about how I get anxious handling cash."

"You'll have enough helping hands."

"Well, what if I want to be a hostess?"

"Our last hostess left because of harassment, and we're short on waitstaff for the same reason. You'll work as a cashier where Jia is. It's the safest option." *Plus, I'll have a clear view of the back of your head in case someone decides to make a move.*

Nyla's light-green eyes probe my dark ones, scrutinizing me from head to toe. This woman's eye-contact game is no joke, even with those bizarre glasses.

"Fine." She sighs. "You're my bodyguard. You know what's best."

Jia clears her throat. "Whispering is done?"

"It is," Nyla states, folding her hands on her lap. "I'll handle the cash register. Once you're ready to close up, I'll pitch in with the cleaning. It's the least I can do."

Jia shoots me an inscrutable glance, her lips curling slightly before I shift my gaze to the vibrant rug beneath us. "Very well, Alyn-ah. You'll be my cashier. But when things get busy, and they usually do, I'll need you to step in as a waitress. Clear?"

"Crystal!" Nyla nudges me, her eyes widening in a silent warning.

"Clear," I mumble.

"Excellent!" Jia claps her hands and rose to her feet. "Come along, Alyn. I'll show you around the place before we open."

"Will I be wearing a uniform?" Nyla's excitement surges suddenly. "If so, can I add my own touch? I used to bedazzle my outfits all the time. Chains on the skirt and whatnot. Super cute. My friends used to think a rich professional did it—"

"No uniforms," Jia cuts in, pivoting on her heel before Nyla can argue. I half-expect it, but she remains silent as we enter the back kitchen.

It's a steel fortress. Countertops gleam with industrial power, crowded with stacks of bowls, plates, and pans. Every tool needed for a Korean BBQ joint is at arm's reach. The floors, squared and polished, stand defiantly against the impending chaos that inevitably follows when lunch hour hits.

"And this is Shahz's station." Jia gestures towards the dishwashing section, where spacious sinks accompany a professional-grade dishwashing machine.

"Scrub Daddy?" Nyla snorts, grabbing my sponge.

"It was a gift from one of his many admirers," Jia chimes in, attempting a terrible wink. "I keep telling him to embrace his charm and attract more ladies, but he insists on hiding back here with the dishes. Stubborn as they come." She shakes her head at me, and Nyla nods in understanding. "More stubborn than an ass."

Nyla bursts into laughter, a delightful, genuine sound that captures my attention. She covers her mouth with her fist, revealing her gleaming white teeth peeking out from the corner of her lips.

"Let's go, Alyn. I'll walk you through the cash system. After that, we'll fire up the TV. I got Fast and Furious in Korean for my nephew. He's quite the talker, just like you."

Nyla shoots me a quick smile and a wave before heading to the front.

I step up to the sink, tilting my head to catch a glimpse of her head bobbing excitedly through the small window.

I can't help but smile.

Perfect.

In the end, Nyla ended up hosting.

No one's given her any shit yet because Jia's half-focused on Vin Diesel and my bubbly, fake-girlfriend.

"You've been staring at her for the past thirty minutes," Bao grunts as he sets down his grimy wok with the rest of my dishes. Meet our head chef, a hulking guy with a choppy black buzzcut and a silver left brow piercing. He's the powerhouse in the kitchen, ensuring everything runs smoothly with his gifted touch.

"I'm not staring," I assert, pouring the chicken stock from one of the filthy bowls. "She just happens to be in my line of sight."

"That's the definition of staring," Bao retorts, tilting his head to catch a glimpse through the window, where she's ringing up a takeout order with her radiating charm. "She's a beauty."

I wring the sponge mercilessly. "I think you forgot to turn off the stove."

Bao claps a hand on my back, letting out a laugh. "I was just testing you, Shahz. Just admit she's your girl instead of giving me a hard time. Jia already opened her mouth."

My gaze snaps to the side. "To whom?"

"Just me and Tae-hyung. He's her grandson, after all. They don't keep secrets from one another."

"She'd be in for a surprise," I grumble. "Keep it under this roof. Ny—" I bite my tongue. "Alyn values her privacy when it comes to us." Damn, saying that feels strange.

"Whatever you say, boss." He steals a glance and chuckles when I shoot him a glare. Bodyguard tendencies, that's all. "Could use a hand in the kitchen, you know. Tae can manage the dishes."

"Tae struggles with opening a soda can, Bao."

"True, but you've got more in your culinary arsenal than just scrubbing bowls. Your recipes are a taste of home. You've got a talent, Shahzad. Make use of it. Who knows, maybe Jia would be up for expanding the menu?"

Not a bad idea.

"I'll give it some thought."

"Think fast. Time doesn't wait around, not even for gifted guys like you." He claps my shoulder and heads back to his station, where a parade of incoming orders pours through.

I take a quick break from my post; just three small bowls left to wash.

Outside, I spot Nyla at a corner table, casually chatting with Tae. He's seventeen and a bit of a knucklehead, so I'm not too concerned if he tries to make a move on Nyla. Not that

FAKE IT TILL WE MAKE IT

I should be, at least not on a personal level.

Bodyguard tendencies, again.

I scrape back the chair next to Tae and drop down with a thud. "Tae-hyung."

"Dude!" he hisses. "Don't call me that."

"That's your name, no?" Nyla asks.

"It's Eric," he replies cuttingly.

"Maybe for the white folks," I say. "Here, you're Tae-hyung. We clear?"

He pouts, shooting a flushed look at Nyla. "Tae's fine."

"Eric—" Nyla pauses, then restarts her comment. "Tae here was just telling me how your touch has made this place even more popular, Shahz."

I shoot her a glance, unphased by the nickname slipping from her lips. It's par for the course when you're playing the fake boyfriend game with a seasoned actress like her. *Just a nickname, man.*

"I've been saying that," Tae chimes in, slinging his arm around my shoulders. "Best kimchi this side of the planet. But keep it lowkey. Halmeoni's already pissed at me for spilling the soju crate after this morning's delivery." He flexes his biceps. "Someone needs to help me bulk up a bit, right, noona?"

Nyla jabs her chopsticks in my direction. "You caught that, didn't you?"

"Muscles need fuel," I say, nodding towards the spread of fish, seaweed, beef soup, sticky rice, and marinated scallions that make up Nyla's meal. "Load up on this, Tae. It'll put some meat on those bones of yours."

Nyla's chopsticks clatter against her plate. Tae and I exchange a bemused glance and notice the ruddiness sneaking up her cheeks. She chews hastily, picking up the utensil and setting it down, dabbing at her mouth. "You've got the rest, Tae."

"You sure?" he asks, already snagging the spoon and a fresh pair of chopsticks. "Halmeoni prefers I don't eat on the clock, but who am I to turn down free food?"

"All yours, buddy." Nyla starts exiting the booth, smoothing down her sweater. I lean in and pluck a lone grain of rice from her sleeve. "Thanks."

A new wave of customers strides in, a family of four, and Nyla rushes over to greet them.

I examine the single grain nestled between my fingers, observing Tae devour her half-finished lunch with lightning speed.

Without a second thought, I swallow the tiny morsel.

"How was work, Alyn?" Maira questions as soon as we enter the apartment.

"Great!" Nyla replies, bending down to ruffle an overly enthusiastic Sky, who showers her with affectionate licks. "Easy there, girl. I need a shower first."

"Was Jia pissed you missed a week of work?"

She snorts. "Why would she be pissed?"

"Because you ran away?"

I internally sigh at her obliviousness to our fabricated story.

"Oh, right, yeah, no. We're good. I informed her before I headed to Rhode Island. She's pretty laid back about the whole thing." Nyla offers me an apologetic smile, too charming to be annoyed with.

I whistle, and Sky trots to me for a head pat. "You fed her, Maira?"

"Yup. She's a sloppy eater."

Nyla ambles into her and Maira's room, grabbing her toiletries and a pink towel. It's like a sea of pink in there; I've never seen her in any other color. But damn, she rocks it.

"Fifteen minutes, Troublemaker."

Nyla flashes a two-finger salute and a smirk as she breezes past. Glad to see her confidence rising since she started working. She handles the Korean language like a pro, nailing the greetings and farewells, fascinating every customer, regardless of age or gender.

Maira catches me staring at the bathroom door. "You're watching her like she's gonna run away again," she remarks.

I blink, quickly coming up with an excuse. "Nah, just making sure the lock's holding up. It's been acting a bit wonky—"

"Save it." She plops onto the couch and drags the coffee table closer to her laptop.

"What are you working on?" I ask, heading to the kitchen to whip up a quick dinner for myself. Nyla claimed she was still full from lunch, which was like, what, nine hours ago? Guess the industry has conditioned models to eat less. Although, I doubt Nyla's planning a comeback on the runway or the big screen anytime soon.

"Sorting out meeting schedules. A seven a.m. session for a three-hour goals review for Jelly Mobile's summer advertisement followed by a campaign meeting in the afternoon? Insanity!" She throws her hands up in frustration, then attacks the keyboard with rapid typing.

Sky trots into the kitchen and lets out a whine.

"I hear you, honey. We'll go for a walk in a bit, all right?" I scratch behind her ear while effortlessly cracking an egg into the pan. I tear off a small piece of pre-cooked chicken breast and let Sky enjoy it.

"Can I ask you something?" Maira voices, retrieving her headphones from her bag.

Dread overwhelms me at the heaviness in her voice. "Go ahead."

"Does Alyn have any family around here?"

I shut my eyes. "Just her father."

"Are they in contact?"

"No."

"So she's not planning to meet him for his blessings?"

"As far as I'm concerned."

"And how can you be so sure?" she interrupts, smirking over her shoulder. "Because you're her boyfriend?"

"Yeah, Maira. And because I know her as well as anyone." I switch on the stove fan; its loud hum fills the apartment. "Besides, they're not exactly on good terms."

"I understand," Maira says, sitting up on the couch, arms crossed, chin resting on top. "My dad was a hardass, too."

I flip the egg. "Her mother lives in a different country."

Maira sighs. "A neglectful mother. Seems Alyn and I will become best friends in no time." She picks at the thread sticking from the couch. "I can't imagine what she must've gone through as a child. To feel so unloved by your own blood."

I glance at her briefly, noticing the frown etched on her mouth and a deep crease between her arched brows. "Alyn needs to stop being a people pleaser."

Maira scoffs. "Uh . . . *what*?"

Ah, damn it. "Before we met. That was all before we met."

"Yeah, but it's still a dickish comment to make."

I sigh. "You're right. I'm sorry." I plate the egg and wipe the pan clean before adding the chicken breast. "What I meant to say was she lived to please her parents and the people around them."

"Well, I guess I better get started on a friendship bracelet for her," Maira mutters.

I turn around and lean against the kitchen counter, feeling the cold surface against my marrow. It's as if my mouth has a mind of its own, and before I know it, I'm caught in a verbal whirlwind. "Alyn's got this idea that her whole purpose in life is to keep everyone else happy. She thrives from their head-pats and false compliments. She wears that fake grin like armor, making damn sure nobody catches a glimpse of her true feelings about things that rightfully bother her." There's no rehearsed script, no carefully chosen words. It's raw, unfiltered, and I can't rein it in. "Just this shiny fucking thing that's on a pedestal, always smiling, even when the lights are out, because you can never be too sure who's watching."

Maira blinks, clearly taken aback.

I'm gasping for breath. Did I just . . . What the fuck did I just go off about? It's like my brain took a detour without giving me any warning.

"I can't decide if you're annoyingly perceptive or fiercely protective of her," Maira grumbles, sinking back into the couch and ending our conversation.

I rake my fingers through my hair, holding them there momentarily. This isn't my concern. I need to quit psychoanalyzing Nyla like I'm her shrink or something. Her actions and her style are none of my concern. I'll just keep an eye out and make sure no one messes with her while she's people-pleasing her ass off.

Sky re-enters the kitchen, Nyla trailing behind in a coral-pink hoodie and grey sweats. She shoots a brief, emotionless glance my way before disappearing into her bedroom.

7

Tae-hyung and Hye-jin

Nyla

A noisy blow erupts outside my bedroom, jolting me awake.

I scan for Maira, but her side of the bed remains untouched and tidied.

Voices gather, growing ominously close. What is happening?

I bolt upright, shivers coursing down my exposed skin. Stripped bare, I scramble for the closet, only to find it emptied out. The bathroom echoes with nothingness, and my suitcases are nowhere to be seen. "What the hell?"

BANG!

The door slams open, flooding the room with blinding flashes. White upon white, questions thrown like daggers. I shield myself as the paparazzi converge, their cameras mercilessly capturing my every naked moment.

Where is Shahzad?

"Please, just leave me alone!" My voice trembles as I beg, but I can't summon the strength to force the camera away. If it were to crash to the floor, the PR damage would be irreversible. Baba's outrage would be unimaginable, and the media would brand me a heartless monster. "Shahzad!"

Firm hands grip my legs, yanking me towards them. I scramble desperately, drilling my nails into the floorboards to stop them. They overwhelm me, their touch invasive and abusive. Men and women alike, their clammy fingers tearing at my skin.

I resist with every ounce of my being, but my struggles are fruitless. Their hands and tongues glide across my skin, smearing me with their venomous touch and terms.

They murmur, "Pretty doll," soft and sinister, as they pinch and prod, molding me into their vision.

"*Shahzad*!" I scream, the sound stabbing and hopeless, but it feels swallowed by the suffocating darkness.

My body jerks up, and a sudden skin contact startles me.

I swat it away, only to realize it's Maira. My skin is sticky, soaked in sweat, and I'm panting like I've just sprinted a marathon, my fingers digging into my flesh, scratching at my neck, pulling at my clothes.

Sky's frantic barking echoes in the background.

The door bangs open, and Shahzad charges towards me, cocooning me in his arms. I let out a whimper as sobs wrack through me, clutching onto him like he's my final lifeline.

"They were touching me." I gasp, my eyes fixed on the ceiling, trying to escape the nightmare that still ripples over my back. "Shahzad, they got in. They took pictures—"

"Shh, baby. You're safe now."

"They touched me and—"

"Sweetheart, it's all right." He cradles my head, pulling me closer against his chest. "I'm here."

"You're late," I murmur against his neck.

"I'm so sorry."

I inhale his familiar scent, whispering, "You promised you'd keep me safe."

"I know, Troublemaker." His fingers gently massage my pounding scalp. "I'm here now. You're safe with me."

"I'm safe with you," I repeat, holding him tighter. "I'm safe . . . with you."

"You're safe."

Sometime in the morning, I wake up on Shahzad's couch, my heart thumping in my chest.

No nightmare this time, just the warmth of his arms around me.

My ear rests against the steady cadence of his heartbeat. Sky's fur tickles my bare feet, and I realize our legs are tangled together like lovers.

I bury my face deeper into Shahzad's chest.

It stirs him awake, and our eyes lock in a tense moment. He retreats to the edge of the couch, pulling the comforter up to his hips. "What's wrong?" I manage to ask, feeling small and inadequate.

Then it hits me.

I'm what is wrong. I'm the damaged problem.

I disrupted his sleep and his neighbors' with my screams. He must regret agreeing to this fake relationship, to having me in his house. In his life. I should have stayed unwanted and isolated in Alina's vacation home.

"I understand," I whisper, defeated.

Shahzad continues to look troubled.

I sit up and hug my elbows. "I'm sorry for making this difficult for you."

"Ny—"

"It's all right, Shahzad. It's just my anxiety. You don't have to— It's fine. I'll figure it out on my own. I'm sorry." I brush away a tear that escapes, then hastily get up from his couch, desperate to escape the growing awkwardness. Pausing at the doorway, I turn back. "Thank you. For last night."

With a heavy heart, I enter Maira's room.

I've made up my mind.

Tonight, I'll slip away quietly, bound for Rhode Island. Mustafa's already met me and knows Shahzad is seeing a girl; he knows Maira is safe to live here. Even without me, she's under Shahzad's wings. She'll be fine and have one less screwed-up roommate. I'll miss Sky, though. Terribly.

Maybe I'll get a dog, too. A therapy dog.

"What's bothering you, Alyn-ah?" Jia asks, her usual spot behind the counter momentarily abandoned, undivided attention now on me.

I peel my gaze away from the numbers on the POS system screen, offering a fake smile that I've perfected through practice, thanks to Shahzad's claim last night. "I'm sorry if I seem a little off. I had a restless night."

Jia's head tilts slightly as she leans in. "One of the neighbors mentioned hearing a woman scream in the early morning on your floor. Was that you?"

I swallow hard, nervously peeling the skin around my thumb with my forefinger's nail.

"There was a cockroach. It was crawling on my face. I'm not really a fan of bugs . . ."

"*Bugs*? In my building?" Jia gasps, rising from her chair and touching her heart. "Bao-ya! Did you schedule the exterminators last week?"

Bao, briefly lifting his head from the stew he's garnishing, responds, "Yes, boss. Just a couple of apartments needed some touch-ups."

"What about Shahzad's?"

Shahzad and I lock eyes through the window. Heat rises to my cheeks, and I quickly avert my gaze, pretending to be interested in something else.

"Sky takes care of the bugs," Shahzad remarks.

A new wave of customers streams in, and I seize the menus, eager to escape the unpleasant bug discussion.

Among them, a trio of high school girls with their backpacks settle down. I silently thank Jia for her policy of allowing us to wear facemasks during shifts like these. Teenagers are the only demographic I fear might see through the façade, exposing the timid mole that I truly am. They're so wrapped up in pop culture and its drama.

As I hand out the menus, I can't help but eavesdrop on their conversation.

"The casting is *so* off," Pigtail Girl exclaims, flipping her phone and showing Freckles a picture of a stunning artwork featuring a fantasy prince. *Tyler Graham's still acting after his heroin scandal?* "Worst part is, they're keeping Tyler's pedo-stache. Where in the book was it mentioned that Lord Voctoral De Ashburn has a mustache? *Blagh*!"

Lee Hye-jin, who I've only seen in pictures from Tae, greets Jia before turning her attention to me. "We'll take the usual."

I hurriedly reach for my notepad and pen, attempting to catch the remnants of their previous conversation. "I'm new here, so I'm not sure what your 'usual' is."

She narrows her eyes, tilting her head thoughtfully. "Have we met before? Your voice sounds very familiar."

Wow, she's perceptive. "No, I don't think so. I just moved here from Canada as an exchange student at NYU." I take a moment to adjust my bangs, lowering them slightly, and lift my glasses and mask a bit higher.

"My bad," Hye-jin says, then rattles off her order at the speed of light. "We'll have three bowls of jajangmyeon, two servings of sweet and sour pork, a small bowl of pickled radish—the cubes, not the slices—and three cans of pear juice."

I'm fortunate to have a natural photographic memory. Sometimes, I don't even need this notepad, but I have to maintain the façade of a helpless waitress. And I need to excel because this is the last time I'll ever have to do it.

Once I hand over the order to the kitchen, I tidy up the tables nearby, taking the opportunity to eavesdrop. Backstage, I used to love listening to gossip before every runway show or movie set—who's sleeping with whom and who's the next target for Cancel Culture.

Spoiler alert: my name was in red ink.

"Dude, she's seriously gorgeous. Look at her abs! They're freakin' sparkling like Edward Cullen." Pigtail Girl seems to be the TMZ of the group, displaying pictures of one of Baba's models, Amari De Grandi. She was, or should I say, *used* to be, my competition for the longest time, considering we both belonged to the same agency.

Our parents constantly pitted us against each other regarding our looks, weight, and height. Who's walked in more shows, who's on the cover of Vogue's September issue, whose net worth is higher—an endless stream of comparisons.

And yet, Amari always remained second and simmering with jealousy. She despised that I was the frontrunner in our little rivalry, and I thrived from her frustrations, feeding my ego with her failures.

But now she's the highest-paid model and a full-time actress, sipping rosé with the Hadid sisters on their yacht in Bora-Bora. Meanwhile, I'm wiping tables in a Korean BBQ restaurant, secretly hoping each swipe of the cloth doubles as a calorie burn.

It's okay.

It's fine.

No one will see me again anyway—no one wants to. I've got zero to no support system left, and even if I crawl back to Baba, begging for redemption and a full-blown clean slate and the toughest fitness trainer in the universe, it won't be satisfying.

My happiness derived from the satisfaction of succeeding. I was an incredibly motivated young girl, always on her toes about a commercial deal, an early riser to complete her tasks, and sleeping on time to avoid under-eye circles. My fuel was—*is*—praise. I thrived knowing I pleased my parents. My fans. The universe.

"Alyn-ah!" Jia calls with a swish of her hand, pointing at the girls' food tray. I am by her side within seconds, loaning her my ear to whisper. "Tae-Hyung really likes Hye-jin. They go to school together. She's what you kids call the popular girl. And he's . . . well, shy. Very shy. It's sad, considering I'm his halmeoni." She discreetly gestures toward Hye-jin, who's laughing with her head thrown back, revealing those adorable dimples beneath her lips. "Put in a good word for my grandson, will you?"

"I—" *It's your last day here. It's the least you can do before you disappear.* "I'll try."

Taking the tray, I return to the girls and begin placing their bowls before them. I gasp and point at Freckles' lanyard. "You go to Lincoln High?"

She raises a brow. "Uh, yeah? We all do."

Pigtail Girl smiles awkwardly.

"Oh my god. So you three probably know Tae— or Eric?"

Freckles steals a glance at Hye-jin, who deftly cracks her chopsticks and rubs them together. "Yeah, we know Eric. He's, like, totally obsessed with Hye—*ouch*!" The table rattles.

Hye-jin's nostrils flare as she hurriedly devours a slice of sweet and sour pork.

"Eric is seriously the coolest guy I've ever met! The other day, some jerk snatched my friend's purse, but Eric didn't hesitate for a second. He chased that thief down and caught him in just thirty seconds flat. I swear, he's like the Spider-Man of Koreatown." I notice the pair's eyes widen, exchanging impressed glances. Hye-jin remains cold-blooded. "And yesterday, a whole line of girls asked if he was on shift. When I said 'no,' one of them literally had a panic attack."

"For *Eric*?" Freckles scoffs. "We're still talking about Eric Park, right?"

"I couldn't even begin to count the girls, honestly," I murmur, holding the tray close to my chest. "He says his heart belongs to someone else."

The pair sneaks another look at Hye-jin. She chews vigorously, on the verge of snapping her chopstick.

I head to the fridge, retrieve their drinks, and place them in front of them with an extra special surprise.

"Tae-hyung's personal favorite," I say, setting an orange Crush next to Hye-jin's bowl before returning to the cash register.

Jia gives me a thumbs up, a question in her eyes, and I respond with a solid, delighted answer.

8

Sun Tower Hotel

Shahzad

Hearing Nyx rev to life with her brand new engines sends a shrill down to my marrow. My Multistrada used to be a weary, worn-out bike from all those frequent late-night rides without proper maintenance.

But now, with her new high-end parts and that sleek, black finish covering up the old scars and rust from casual races, she's a beauty once again.

"I gotta hand it to you, kid. She was a fighter." Paul, my go-to mechanic, approaches me while I inspect Nyx's exhaust pipes, giving her another rev. The vibrations resonate in my chest, a feeling only rivaled by the joy Sky and my little sisters bring me. "Feels good?"

"Fantastic," I reply, running my hand over the leather seat. One for me and an extra for a passenger. Usually, I'd take Dua for rides when high school got the best of her or when she needed a break from home and keeping her relationship with Zayan a secret. Somehow, she powered through to senior year, and Nyx deserves a bit of credit for that.

"Hey, so, listen." Paul rubs his nape, a conflicted expression on his weathered face. "I'm gonna have to shut down our installment system. Our new boss has strict policies, and it's cash upfront from now on." He grazes his fingers over Nyx's handle. "I meant to send you a quote beforehand, but with the whole switcheroo, I forgot. Sorry, Shahz."

Well, shit.

"You quoted me six hundred earlier. I hope you haven't decided to jack up the price, or else I might consider switching to Terry's instead." I lock eyes with him, drawing on the intimidation I honed during my days as a bodyguard. It's all about the stare-down. The first one to blink reveals their defenselessness. And my role is to control that liability and slip through. "Losing a loyal customer, especially one who tips generously, wouldn't be in your best interest, would it? I'm sure your new boss wouldn't appreciate that either."

Paul licks his lips, casting a quick glance over my shoulder to where the office's main entrance awaits. He surveys his surroundings, taking in the hustle and bustle of the mechanics laboring away in the noisy garage. "Guess not."

"Good." I give his shoulder a firm pat. "I'll get you your six hundred and throw in an extra fifty for good measure."

He nods, offering me a small smile in return.

I secure my helmet firmly on my head and lift the visor. "If the kingpin gives you any trouble, I've got a couple of upper-class connections that could use your expertise. Bring your guys along, but only if things get rough." I extend my fist for a side bump.

His smile widens as he reciprocates the gesture. "Get outta here, kid."

I ignite Nyx's engine, feeling her pulsate with energy, welcoming me back after months of confinement. "Good to see you, too, sweetheart."

I lean into the throttle, and we shoot forward like a bolt of lightning.

Fuck ATMs.

They always feel like a slap in the face.

My savings aren't looking too pretty either. Five thousand dollars is peanuts in Manhattan—I'm practically scraping the barrel. And with my expenses and the situation back home, money is more crucial now than ever.

Savings mock me with a paltry $3,900, which will barely cover me for the next three months, especially now that I've got Nyla living under my roof. Maira's contributing to the rent, but I've kept it as low as possible because she's like a sister to me. I'd never charge my sisters. And with the utility bills stacking up along with Sky's vet bills, I'm on the brink of losing my mind to the cruel calculus of it all.

My phone buzzes in my back pocket. Speaking of sisters.

FAKE IT TILL WE MAKE IT

"Hey, Dua." I stride over and lean against my bike.

"I've failed you."

One sniffle sets off a chain reaction within me.

"Dua, what happened? Are you all right? Is Zineerah okay?"

"Everyone's fine except for me," she manages to say between soft, subdued sobs. Out of the three of us, Dua is the rock. She hasn't shed a tear since she came into this world, always the endless, optimist egg in the basket. Her dreams of becoming a sports journalist keep her on a steady course, along with her tight-knit circle of friends and her boyfriend, Zayan, the youngest of the Jafri siblings. My sister has never once displayed a hint of unappreciation or let storm clouds gather above her head.

Never, until now.

"Dua, talk to me."

"I-I don't know how to explain it without you being disappointed in me."

"Sweetheart, why on earth would I, of all people, be disappointed in you? Whatever's eating at you, let me know. Please?" I clench my jaw as sniffles and shudders echo through the line. More than a few times, I've felt the urge to book a one-way ticket to Toronto and live with my sisters again for the rest of my days, offering them support that goes beyond just financial.

"Okay, so," Dua starts, sucking in a sharp breath. "Okay. Basically. Do you remember when I applied for the David Rhodes journalism scholarship for SLU?"

"Yeah, I remember you telling me about it. What happened? You didn't get it?"

"No!" she exclaims. "They rejected me. My application didn't meet the requirements. They were selecting five applicants, and my essay must've been the shittiest thing ever written or something, and I didn't—" She stutters on her breaths, the sounds of her crying echoing as if she's sitting in a bathroom. "I didn't get it, Shahz. And Mama is paying for my spring term tuition right now because I told her I'd get the scholarship, which was so fucking stupid because I thought I would— I thought I would make her happy, and she'd pay for my second-year tuition, too, but I only made everything worse, and now she's m-mad at me."

"But she *did* pay for your first year and your current spring term, yes?"

"Yeah, she did. And I'm grateful for that, really, but what about the next three years? I can apply for government aid, but then I'll be shackled to student debts for the rest of my life. And who knows when I'll land a proper job while I'm stuck babysitting Zayan around the clock?" She breathes in a gallon of oxygen, repeating a slow, anxiety-relieving pattern.

"He said he'd pay for my education."

"And?"

"Obviously, I turned it down. The last thing I want is to owe a Jafri man."

"Good. Don't. He's a good kid, but don't take money from him. Maya's already covered your first year and spring term. I'll take care of the rest."

"No, Shahzad. Absolutely not. You're not paying for my education when you haven't even gotten yourself a new pair of sneakers since tenth grade!"

That's not entirely true, by the way. I wore my tenth-grade sneakers all the way through culinary school before some asshole in my residency swiped them during the graduation party. But the pair I bought the next day? I still use them for my runs.

"Have you been putting away some savings?" I ask, gripping the stress ball in the pocket of my jacket.

"Barely. It's mostly for rent and groceries. I don't want to push Zineerah into finding a job right now, especially since she's . . . you know, about to tie the knot soon."

"She hasn't said yes yet."

"She will. I'm sure of it. Professor Shaan is the one for her."

The imminent engagement of Zineerah is a subject that threatens to shred this stress ball to pieces. Not the time to delve into it, not when my little sister lacks the funds for her higher education.

"Go take a shower and get some rest. Put on some music or watch a movie," I direct, swinging my leg over my bike. "And if you can, apply for bursaries, anything that can at least cover your textbooks and supplies. Can you do that for me, sweetheart?"

"I'm too depressed to watch a movie," she mutters. The strain in her voice tells me she's pushed herself up, brushing off her shoulders. "I'll do my best, Shahz. I swear I'll pay you back every dime."

"Fuck no. Your education comes first. I'll do whatever it takes to get you there, you hear me? I'll live on the damn streets if I have to. You know I will."

Dua starts crying again, repeating, "I love you," like a busted record.

"All right, sweetheart. Send me the details of your tuition. I'll call you later once I've got everything sorted."

"Okay, Shahz. I love you. Take care."

"I love you, too, Dua. Get some rest."

"Okay. Love you again."

I crack a smile. "Love you too."

As I end the call, I lean forward on my bike, my head in my hands, feeling the weight of the world on my shoulders.

Parking Nyx in the alley between Jia's shop and a computer repair store, I remove my helmet and run my fingers through my hair.

"Good girl," I murmur, giving Nyx a pat before swinging my leg over the seat. "Let me feed Sky, and then I'll find you a safer spot."

Sighing, I make my way towards the back door, punching in the passcode and pulling it open just as someone pushes from the other side.

I hear a yelp, and as the woman falls to all fours, her oversized hat tumbles off, revealing a shock of pink hair.

"Nyla?" I raise an eyebrow, taking in the sight of her three hefty suitcases by the exit. "Going somewhere, Troublemaker?"

She pushes herself up, blowing on her bruised palms, the skin raw and bleeding.

When I extend a hand, she retreats, grabbing her hat and backpack before dashing away.

What the fuck?

My gaze lands on a crumpled piece of paper that had slipped from her hoodie pocket. I retrieve it, smoothing out the creases, and read her neat writing.

> I appreciate the kindness you all have shown me for the past couple of days, but I don't think I can stay here any longer, not with how bad my mental health is. I don't want to impose any longer and disturb the neighbors' sleep.
>
> Sky is such a good girl, and I'll miss her very much. I think I'll get a dog, too, to keep me company. Maira, thank you for being my friend. I wish you all the best with your internship and life in general. Shahzad, thank you for not laughing at me when you saw me again.
>
> Nyla
> Troublemaker
>
> p.s. sorry we couldn't fake-date.

I stand dumbfounded for a moment, processing the words and scanning the note over and over again.

What the hell was she attempting to do if I had been half an hour late?

My grip tightens around Nyx's keys, my mind racing with images and scenarios where Nyla's in some kind of danger, held hostage or worse. There's no one else right now who genuinely cares about her. It's just me, Maira, and Sky. And even though I may not have deep feelings for her, I'm still her protector. It's my job. She's my responsibility. Nothing more, nothing less.

Fucking run, then.

I relax the tension in my neck, swiftly turning around and securing my helmet in place before revving my bike.

Catching Nyla's ridiculous baby-pink hat bobbing through the crowd in Koreatown takes all of five seconds. But navigating through the traffic on the road is worse than on the sidewalk.

She barrels ahead, then makes a sharp right turn at the intersection, making it tricky for me to merge in at the last minute. Her stunt brings a reluctant smile to the corners of my mouth.

"That's how it's gonna be, huh, baby?" I mutter, giving her a bit of a head start as I keep pace with the flow of traffic. But as we reach the next stoplight, I smoothly merge and make a right turn onto a narrower street lined with rows of parked cars. It's a quiet residential neighborhood, mostly families and retirees.

I signed up as an extra chef at the soup kitchen—just passed it—aiming to gain some experience and build connections with the locals. They had stories to share, and I had the ears to listen.

Coming to a stop at the red light, I pull out my phone and quickly check Nyla's location. I've got her sharing it live with me, just in case things get rough. Who would've thought she'd be the one behind this chaos?

And she's playing it smart, making her way towards Sun Tower in the heart of the Financial District, moving at the speed of a four-wheeler heading straight there. Any major slip-up and she'll be spotted, especially with that unmistakable pink hair of hers.

Fuck, I hope her palms are okay.

Tucking my phone back into my pocket, I rev my engine and zoom directly for the hotel.

Half an hour later, I'm parking in the private lot that Azeer's given me access to. I check my phone, which shows her static activity. She's settled in a room, probably patting herself on the back for making a swift escape.

Seriously, I could laugh.

Taking the elevator up to the royal suites, I march down the luxurious golden-white corridor. Voice tuned to a higher pitch, I knock on her door, announcing, "Room service!" Why? Because I know she's a connoisseur of food and most likely ordered something to eat before her spirited adventure back to Rhode Island.

Just days ago, I caught her sneaking into the kitchen in the early morning and eating through a bag of potato chips. Then, last night, she was muttering, "It's fine," on a loop while finishing her box of Oreos. In fact, the groceries she buys from the corner stores are only junk food. I suppose she's developed a severe liking for guilty pleasure food, but locking herself inside the pantry at three in the morning while I'm trying to sleep on the couch has started to get on my nerves.

Then maybe you should leave her here.

Quickly, I seek my little polyester stress ball in my pocket and give it hard squeezes.

Nyla pushes the door wide open, a grin stretching across his face. "Hell—" But then it fades.

The door starts to close, but I wedge my body in, slipping inside and locking it behind me.

She takes a stumbling step back. "Shahzad."

"What the hell were you thinking?" I declare, taking a confident stride forward. "We had a deal, Nyla. You play the part of my fake girlfriend, and I keep you out of the limelight. That's what we agreed on, didn't we?"

She swallows audibly. Her body moves mechanically as she retreats into the opulent stretch of her bedroom. My eyes dart to the bed, every detail of our night together zipping through my mind. She notices and steps into my line of sight. "I'm sorry, Shahzad. I didn't mean to."

"Save the apologies, Troublemaker." I advance until her back is against the draped window. Her damp, pink hair is pulled up into a bun, and a satin bathrobe drapes over her curves.

"Look—"

"Don't give me a bullshit excuse. Admit you were running away again."

"I wasn't—" she stammers, delicately fiddling with her long, almond-shaped fingernails. Her gaze flits around the room, consciously avoiding direct contact. A lone tear broke free, sliding down her flushed cheek, leaving a shimmering trail. The tension in the air grew as she pressed her teeth into her bottom lip, a silent battle obvious as she fought to keep the unspoken words from escaping. A deep, shaky breath. "I was."

"Why?" I'm so close, almost pressing against her. "Do you think I'm incapable of taking care of you?"

"It's not that—"

"It sure as fuck seems like it, judging by what you wrote." I thrust the crumpled note towards her, letting it fall at her feet. "Do you really think I give a shit about you bothering my neighbors?"

"Stop cursing," she mutters. "I'm sorry if my note offended you."

"It didn't offend me. It infuriated me."

She arches an eyebrow. "Why? Why does it bother you? We're not even— We've only been around each other for a few days. You've barely acknowledged me, except when talking to Mustafa—"

"That's not fair."

"You're not holding up your end of the deal, Shahzad, and it's making everyone at work question our supposed relationship."

"It's called being professional. Just because you've retired early doesn't mean you forget how to behave in a workplace."

Yet that didn't stop you from sleeping with her this time last year.

"You called me a people pleaser," she whispers, her gaze fixed on the floor.

So she heard me that night. Great. Just great. I'm a fucking idiot for gossiping—something I never stoop to—with Maira, who's self-claimed as an anti-gossiper, especially in this cramped apartment where the topic of discussion was five steps down the hallway.

"But you're right, Shahzad," she says, her voice soft and measured. Her bathrobe sleeves slide down to her fingertips as if seeking comfort in their folds. The room carries a heavy silence, interrupted only by the beat of her slow, steadying breaths. And then, as if admitting defeat, a couple of tears manage to slip down her round, pink cheeks. "I've always been a people-pleaser, especially for my parents. It's been ingrained in me since I entered this industry. Be the good girl, recite lines that aren't mine, and pretend none of the media's garbage affects me because I'm a billboard for strong, young, independent women."

I notice her lips trembling, which she tries to hide by tucking them in. "I was just stating what I've observed, Nyla. If it hit a nerve, which clearly it did"—I gesture towards the room she sought refuge in—"know that I won't take back my words. I won't lie to you. Not when you've been lied to your whole life."

"I've never been apologized to either." She squeezes her eyes shut and wills out the last of her tears. They flow down her cheeks, marking a trail from her eyes to her chin, her head shaking in small motions like she's rejecting some unwelcome truth.

I bring my hand down from beside her head, gently cupping her cheek. "Nyla, I'm . . ." She turns her face away, leaving a hollow space in my palm. I clench my fist and return it to its place on the window. "What are you afraid of, Troublemaker?"

"You're too close—"

"And I'll only get closer if you don't give me an answer."

Her breath hitches. She avoids my gaze, and, being the stubborn bastard I am, I tilt my head until our eyes meet. It was her most potent weapon that shattered my defenses last year. Looking back, I might have even caved in if I had been sober.

She turns her head to the left. I do the same. She lowers herself, and I gently lift her chin, my fingers spreading over her jaw to hold her face. "Shahzad, please."

"Talk to me."

Her lips part just a little and form a small heart shape. She's such a distraction. I hate it. I hate that I can't—and could never—focus on my surroundings because of her. I'm willing to chase her down for thirty minutes, knowing damn well I can't afford to keep her for as long as we've agreed.

"I'm afraid of a lot," she whispers, and I feel the breath of her words graze my lips. "I'm even afraid of telling you what I'm afraid of."

"Why?" I raise my gaze from her mouth. "Do you think I'd use it against you?"

She nods firmly.

Something sharp twists inside my chest. "Why, Nyla?"

"Because . . ." Nyla presses her palms against my chest as if trying to push me back but denies herself the power to do so. She closes her eyes, shielding herself from my gaze. "I don't want to get hurt again, Shahzad."

Leaning in, I brush a kiss against her cheek, tasting the saltiness of her tears. "This is me abiding by your terms," I murmur into her ear. "Now be a good girl and stick to mine as well." I turn away before I can witness her reaction. "Get dressed. We're heading back home."

Nyla pinches the back of my shirt. "I don't want to disturb you, Maira, and Sky with my issues anymore, Shahzad." *Sha-ha-zad.* I almost dare her to repeat my name. "Let me go to Rhode Island. Let me deal with it on my own. I always have. It won't be any different—"

"No." I turn sharply.

"Sha—"

"I'm. Not. Letting. You. Go." *Again.* But that word turns to ashes on my tongue. "I'm not—" I clench my jaw, carefully choosing a tactic to convince her. "If you come home you can— You—" My hands rip through my hair.

Don't fucking say it, Shahzad.

"I can what?" she mutters, glistening, green eyes flickering and rich with fresh tears lining her viscous lower lashes.

"You can sleep," I breathe out, "with me."

"Oh. Like . . . in the same bed?"

"Couch," I correct. "It stretches out. You know that."

"I do." She glances at the master bed and then back to me. I can hear my fists tightening as I await her answer. *Say yes, say no, say yes, say no—* "It's inappropriate." No, it is, then. Disappointment isn't the emotion I should be experiencing. "And I don't want to ruin your sleep if I have another night terror. I'll keep sleeping with Maira."

A deep exhale of relief escapes me at her decision. *Why are you so relieved? Your expenses are only going to tank from here on out.* But Nyla has a job. *You can still back out.* She'll take care of her own costs. *Mustafa knows now that you have a girlfriend. Maira won't say anything.* No, it'll be good practice for when she's ready to step back into the limelight.

Besides, she's only here for another two months. After that, I'll drop her back in Rhode Island to do as she pleases with her life.

"Shahzad?" Nyla gently shakes my left arm, her brows knitting together. She takes a small step closer. "Where were you just now?"

"Nowhere," I assert, turning away from her. "Put on some clothes. I'll be waiting outside." As I steal a glance back, she's picking up the crumpled note.

Our gazes lock. Her eyes are so round and green, full of trust. Mine are brown and bland, grappling with an unexpectedly guilty conscience.

I avert my eyes and steel myself to step out of the door.

9

Nyx

Shahzad

"Nyx, Nyla. Nyla, Nyx."

Shahzad's sleek, black sports bike gazes at me, its single luminous headlight casting a bright white glow. It responds with what I assume is her resonant, purring engine.

"Hi, Nyx." I offer a wave to the monstrous machine.

"You don't have to wave at her," Shahzad remarks, handing me his helmet. "You can wear it for now. We'll make a quick stop at a nearby bike shop to find one that fits your head."

"You don't own a car?" I ask, instantly feeling regret for asking such a ridiculous question. "I'm sorry."

"Don't be. I prefer the subway or Nyx." He takes the helmet so I can secure my hair into a bun, his gaze unwavering.

I avert my eyes, momentarily overwhelmed by his eager stare. "When did you get Nyx?"

"My father bought her for me when I was sixteen. I borrowed a friend's bike to practice and earn my license. Guess he felt bad that I didn't have the same luxury as them, so a week after I passed my test, he surprised me with Nyx. I've kept her in top-notch, perfect condition ever since. She's the only physical reminder I have of him." He gently lowers the helmet and asks, "Is it comfortable?"

I nod, lifting the visor. "Thanks for sharing that with me."

"Weird, wasn't it?" He quirks an amused brow.

"What? Sharing your feelings?"

"Yeah?"

"Why would that be weird?"

"Exactly, Troublemaker." He pokes my forehead. "Whatever weird, nonsensical bullshit that's eating you up alive here, I want you to share it with me. I'm guarding not only your clumsy body against danger but also your mind. Instead of running away, stay. Can you do that for me?"

The cold loneliness threaded around my heart loosens from the warmth of his words. "If you're up for me sharing my feelings with you, I suggest grabbing two pints of strawberry vanilla ice cream and cozying up with weighted blankets. Oh, and I'll need your patient ears because I will talk a lot."

"And I'll listen a lot."

I taste the timidity lingering on my lips, though he probably can't see it beneath the helmet.

He secures the buckle, checking three times if I'm at ease and adjusting the helmet to my liking. "You look stupid, by the way."

I scoff at his comment. "It's too large. I can hardly keep my balance." My hands slip into my pockets to secure my phone—*Ah, crap.*

"What's wrong?"

I pat myself all over and check inside my backpack. "My phone. I think I left it in the room. I'll go grab it and meet you back here." I start to remove the helmet, but his firm grip catches my wrists before I can.

"I'll get it. Just pass me the keycard."

"Are you sure? I don't want to bother you."

"Keycard, Troublemaker." He opens his hand, and I retrieve my wallet from my backpack, handing him the keycard to my suite. "Don't move from this spot. Don't take that helmet off. And don't speak to anyone. Understand?"

"Understood."

He gives my helmet a gentle pat on the cheek and walks away, leaving me to stand there, taking in the moment.

I turn to Nyx, muster up some courage, and take three determined steps toward the bike. Somehow, I manage to swing my leg over the driver's seat. Thanks to my five-eleven height, my feet find solid ground beneath me.

"Woah," I exhale, feeling excitement shoot through me as I grip the handles, imagining myself cruising down an open highway.

Sure, I was in a movie where I had to handle a sports bike, but it was usually my stunt double, Rachel, pulling off all the flowery, complex tricks. I only hopped on after the adrenaline-pumping chase scenes were over.

So, I took training classes from Rachel. She accompanied me to my road test, and we celebrated afterward with strawberry cheesecake.

Baba scolded me for getting my bike license when I summoned the courage to confess, deeming it an "unladylike" hobby. In his eyes, women shouldn't engage in sports or build muscle. He prefers delicate matchsticks before they ignite. Little does he realize he burned me more deeply than anyone ever has.

If I show Shahzad my bike license, he would be proud of me. Maybe it'll even earn me some points in his eyes. It wouldn't suck to forge a platonic connection with him now that I've committed to staying and carving out a permanent place for myself. Quietly, in my own way.

I slip my hands into Shahzad's jacket pockets and find a set of cold keys.

Nyx's keys.

Drawing them out, I notice the tiny bike keychain swinging from the ring. "Cute."

Some mix of curiosity and impatience drives me to grip the clutch and turn the ignition key. I flip the red switch to bring the engine back to life and press the start button beneath the right handle.

"*Whoa*!" A burst of laughter escapes me as Nyx awakens beneath me. I grip the throttle and tug at it, the roar causing me to squeal. "My Vespa is a piece of junk against you, Nyxie-girl."

My left foot eases onto the shift, moving it from neutral to first gear.

A primal scream bursts from my throat as I lurch forward, my instincts kicking in as I slam the brakes with all my strength. The sudden halt sends shockwaves through my body, and I'm airborne for a brief moment before gravity claims me. The metallic screech of Nyx colliding with the parking column reverberates, echoing the chaos. I roll away, feeling the impact rattle my bones as Nyx crashes to the ground beside me, a loud bang signaling the end of my mistake.

Shit.

Shit!

"Shit!"

I scramble up quickly.

Summoning every ounce of strength, I lift her back onto her wheels, using my heel to prop up the kickstand. Nyx falls silent as I tuck the keys into my pocket, bracing myself to face the aftermath.

The front side bears the brunt of the impact—a brilliant headlight reduced to shards. Countless scratches, like scars etched into her metal skin, blemish her once pristine surface. Each deep dent feels like a dozen nails piercing into my chest. On the right, the side mirror dangles askew, teetering on the edge of complete collapse with a fragile touch.

"Holy shit," I murmur, my fingers clenching into fists as if trying to jolt myself awake from this cruel reality. "Oh, my God. Okay. Okay, I— God, what do I do?"

I unclasp the helmet, pulling it from my head and using the back of my hand to wipe away the burning tears. My heart dangles by a thin thread as I survey the extensive damage. Given the model of his bike, repairing my mistake will cost several organs. And because of Baba, I can't access any of my funds.

The elevator doors slide open behind me.

"Damn it," I mutter, sidestepping and frantically searching for a plausible excuse. If I try to shift the blame onto someone else—no, that won't pass. He'll review the security footage and catch me red-handed, joyriding on his motorcycle. If I admit fault . . . he might just run over me right here and now.

Shahzad saunters over, slipping his phone into his back pocket after a quick message. He raises his gaze and freezes.

He examines Nyx.

Then me.

Back to Nyx.

Back to me.

"Shahzad—"

He marches forward, nudging me aside, then crouches to gently inspect Nyx's wounds. His touch barely skims over the scratches as if afraid he might remove the chipped polish. His reflection in the side mirror shatters into ten fractured pieces.

"Shahzad, I'm sorry. I'm so sorry."

"Stop."

"I'm so sorry, Shahzad. I promise I will pay you back for it—"

"Stop talking."

"—even if I have to work another job or pick up extra shifts—"

"*Nyla!*"

My breath hitches, making me take an involuntary step back.

His grip on my arm keeps me firmly in place, fear coursing through me like an electric current. "Are you okay?"

In the blink of an eye, dread gives way to bewilderment. "W-What?"

"Are you okay?"

Am *I* okay?

"Jesus, come here. Let me take a look at you," Shahzad says, his touch gentle as he holds my face in his rough hands, tilting my jaw and checking for any scratches. He crouches down, running his fingers over the faint, dusty marks on my knees. "Fuck." He pulls out a tissue packet from his pocket and carefully dabs at the spots of blood seeping from my wounds.

Why is he being so kind to me? I *wrecked* his cherished motorbike—a gift from his father, no less—all because of my own foolishness. I don't deserve him tending to the bloody scrapes on my knees and blowing on them to soothe the pain. He should be yelling at me or pushing me until I'm backed into a corner, drowning in my own shame and guilt.

Shahzad straightens up, handing me the balled-up tissue, phone, and keycard. There's a discernible tension in his jaw, and his gaze remains intense and tenacious on my forehead. I keep my fists clenched at my sides, my lips sealed, half expecting him to lose his temper and lash out.

"I need some time alone for the rest of the night," he whispers hoarsely. "Go back to your room. I'll see you tomorrow."

I easily comply with his request and slip off his jacket, handing it back to him. "Do you need a ride home? Should I call Richard? Alina assigned him as my hotel driver."

Shahzad shrugs on his jacket and takes my hand, tugging me toward the elevator. He gives me a gentle nudge inside. "Text me once you're in your room."

"Okay . . ." My heart breaks into fragments as he walks away, and every fiber of my being shudders as his once steady and composed demeanor falters over the dents and scratches on his bike.

His grip on the handles turns his knuckles paper-white.

In an instant, he revs the sputtering engine and speeds away, and the elevator doors close on cue.

NOOR SASHA

I can't sleep.

Knowing I wounded Shahzad by damaging something he held precious to his heart is heavy on my conscience. I let him down by acting out of character, disobeying his instructions, and being a total ignorant idiot.

The past hour, I've poured over researching nearby mechanic shops or tutorials to mend the scratches on the motorbike and replace the side mirror. Each solution demanded more money than my savings could provide, and my financial situation is currently a house of cards. Relying on Shahzad for my safety and shelter only intensifies the worry.

Summoning courage and pushing aside my pride, I decide to call Alina. After three rings, she answers, slightly out of breath. "Hey."

"Hi. I'm sorry, is this a bad time?"

"Uh—Wait. Gimme a sec—Stop—" She mutes herself, though not before I hear a faint giggle. Probably not the best time to call her.

I hang up and send her a message: *I managed to figure out the recipe, never mind*.

But Alina still calls me back. She's well aware I wouldn't step foot in the kitchen to save my life, so I don't need to be perusing through recipes.

"Hey, angel," Alina's voice comes through, a trace clearer now. I catch the faint sound of a door closing in the background. "What's wrong?"

I nestle into the bed, surrounded by the extra pillows I had delivered from room service, and pull the blanket over me. "Lina, I *really* messed up."

"What happened? Are you okay?" Her concern sets off a whirlwind of anxiety in my head. I'm becoming a burden to her, too. Since the incident at the altar, every call has been me venting and her listening. I wouldn't blame her if she's considering tossing me off a cliff. "Nyla? Hello?"

"Nothing," I manage to squeeze out. "I broke a nail. It started bleeding. I didn't realize—"

"You're a terrible liar, Nyla."

I sigh. "I don't want to bother you if you're busy."

"Our family pillow fight can wait."

Oh, that's so sweet. "I'm sorry for the interruption. I'll be short, and you may not like it, but I've never been this desperate, Alina." I chew on my bottom lip. "I promise to repay every cent, but if you could wire me eight hundred dollars, I'd *really* appreciate it."

"That's all?" Alina snorts.

I blink. "You're not upset?"

"Why would I be upset? I'm the wife of a millionaire, Nyla. Eight hundred dollars to me is equivalent to dollar-store chocolate." Her laughter spreads through my chest like a warm, soothing balm. "If I'm going to spend my husband's fortune, I might as well do it to help you, my angel. That's what sisters are for."

"Sisters," I murmur, a smile gracing my lips. At times, I long to be an Azlan rather than a Ghilzai. Despite being treated as their own, as Alina and Fahad's sister, in the end, I'm still tied to my materialistic father and absent mother.

"What on earth do you need eight hundred dollars for, anyway? You better send me a haul video if it's for a shopping spree." She knows just how to make me laugh and somehow guide me in finding a spark of humor in grave circumstances. It's the Alina Azlan magic.

"I accidentally wrecked Shahzad's bike."

"What?" She gasps. "Are you okay?"

"I'm fine. I just . . . I hopped on it and shifted gears without thinking twice. It shot forward, and I hit the brakes too hard, losing my balance. It took a nasty hit against one of the pillars." I let the blanket fall, inhaling fresh air, and reach for the plate of mini chocolate croissants on my bedside table. "I don't even know if he has insurance on it."

Alina lets out a sigh, and I echo it. We sit in stillness as I chew away at the tension.

"You know, Azeer and I can assist you in finding an apartment here in Toronto if you're considering a permanent move away from the Hollywood bullshit. I recently bought an adorable house for my parents in the suburbs—"

"America is my home, Alina." I swipe the crumbs from the corners of my lips and lick the smudge of chocolate on my thumb. "I have no interest in locating up North. I don't want to keep running. Plus, the arrangement Shahzad and I have is beneficial for me. I'm gaining valuable experience in my role as a . . ."

"Waitress?" Alina's disapproval tuts in the click of her tongue. "You deserve so much more than playing the part of Shahzad's pretend girlfriend and wiping tables at some Korean restaurant. You're wasting your potential, Ny. You have a gift to make things—"

"Worse?"

"Beautiful," she insists. "You have a way of making everything beautiful."

I gently touch my protruding stomach, sighing. "I don't feel beautiful, Lina. So, I don't believe I can create beauty in anything or anyone."

Alina's voice takes on a more serious tone. "Remember who sewed clothes for my Barbie dolls when we were kids? Who did my wedding makeup and sketched out my lengha with those fancy watercolor markers and Faber-Castell color pencils for a custom design?"

"I understand—"

"Who the fuck stitched long sleeves onto my prom dress because it was too revealing?"

"Lina—"

"You, Nylana Ghilzai. *You* made me feel beautiful with your talent. And don't ever think you've wasted it by taking some time off this past year. You're still that same Nyla. You'll always be her. And you'll never change. Do you hear me?" Her words leave an indelible mark on me, like a gentle tattoo, like being cocooned in feathers or draped in satin sheets.

"I know you hate acting, angel," Alina whispers, a subtle smile in her voice. "But I know firsthand how much you love experimenting with fashion. And I want you to follow what you love, to chase it, and never fucking let go. Because if you lose the one thing you love, whether a person or a hobby, you'll spend all your years regretting why you didn't try harder."

In the background, Zoha and Azeer's voices fill the air.

"Go win your pillow fight," I tell her.

Alina chuckles. "Chase for me, okay?"

"I'll try."

"Damn right, you will. I love you. I love, love, *love* you!" She playfully kisses the speaker, causing me to giggle like we're children again, discovering the ticklish spot around my neck.

"Love you, too. And thanks again for wiring me the money, I'll pay you—"

"Never. You will never pay me back," she asserts firmly. "But if you *really* want to, pay me back by starting your fashion line. I'll invest every dime into it. Whatever you need, Ny. I'm here, okay?"

Tears well up in my eyes. I quickly wipe them away before they have a chance to fall. "Yes, I will. I promise."

"And don't worry about Shahzad. He'll come around. There's no way he won't."

I frown. "Yeah."

We conclude the call on a warm, affectionate note.

I tuck my phone under my pillow and select another croissant, rising to call room service for an assortment of colored pens and a stack of printer paper.

10

Abe's Deal

Shahzad

I step out into the alley for my smoke break, fishing for my lighter and cigarette from my pocket.

Yeah, I keep telling myself I'll quit, but it never sticks. Especially not after the day I had yesterday, dealing with my sister's tuition and Nyla's accident.

Nyx is over at Paul's place. He winced pretty hard when he saw how beat up my girl was. Didn't cut me a break on the bill, but he's decent enough to let me settle up after the repairs.

A rat scurries out from under the garbage bin, standing all twitchy with his nose crinkling and small arms pulled in tight.

I pull a granola bar from my pocket, rip it open, and toss it his way. The little guy latches on and starts nibbling, eyes darting around like he's expecting trouble. I grin and take a drag.

"Playing the gracious host to the rats now, huh?"

Fuck. Me.

I pivot my head, spotting Abe leisurely, making his way down the alley, clad in a sharp three-piece suit and sporting that all-knowing grin begging to be punched off his face. "You've got no business being here."

He spreads his arms wide and gives an indifferent shrug. "Neither should my daughter, yet here we stand. Oh, wait. She's probably all by herself at Sun Tower, right?"

Fuck, fuck, fuck.

His piercing green eyes lock onto me with a controlled anger, baldness reflecting the sunlight, and his snow-white beard impeccably groomed. It's ironic, really, how he dominates the modeling scene while standing on the shorter side. "Can I be honest with you, Shahzad?"

"I don't know. Can you?"

He chuckles from his throat, hand gliding down his tie. The grin fades just as quickly as it appeared. The bald bastard doesn't faze me, but there's still a feeling like a limo might roll up any second, and I'll be expected to open the door for him. "You've seen better days, son."

I clench my jaw and pull on a long drag of tar, blowing it away. "I'd rather not waste my ten-minute break listening to your bullshit. I suggest you take your leave."

"I have a proposition."

"I'm not about to work for you, Abe."

"No?" He circles around to face me, arms folded, imposing in stature. "You know Chinatown won't cut it for the long haul, right?"

"Koreatown," I correct him. "You ignorant prick."

Abe isn't the least bit bothered. Decades of enduring the media's nonsense and rivals trying to fuck him over have wiped out every trace of empathy.

He digs into his blazer and produces photos of Nyla leaving her Rhode Island house and sitting in my rented car. Pictures of Maira, Sky, Jia, and Tae—everyone I've interacted with since bringing Nyla on board—are in the stack. "I know everything."

Of course, you fucking do.

I grab the photos and extinguish my cigarette in the center, holding his mirthful gaze. "Tell your fancy PIs to retire. She's under my protection now. Given my credentials, you should know I can keep her and everyone around me safe. So fuck off."

Abe chuckles, clapping his hand and pointing both forefingers at me. "You? Capable of protecting my *only* daughter?" More condescending laughter. "All right, if you're so sure, why is Nyla holed up in a hotel room as we speak?"

I grind my teeth, crushing the photos in my fist.

"Here's the deal." Abe paces back and forth, his no-nonsense demeanor taking charge, hands slicing through the air, emphasizing his points. I can't stand this side of him. "You're going to come clean about why Nyla is living with you and that girl in Koreatown. And if I even get a hint of deception, which you know I can, I'll tear down everything you've worked for and destroy the lives of everyone you care about." He stops before me, a smirk playing on his lips, and tucks his ringed fingers into his pockets. "So, I suggest you start speaking."

"I can spot a bluff, Abe. Don't try to fuck with me. Take your leave while I'm still feeling nice."

"How are Dua and Zineerah these days? Is the middle one still recovering?"

I inhale sharply.

Abe knew about my sisters from the background check when he hired me. He knew their names and where they lived. What he didn't know was about Zineerah's recovery from domestic abuse. How he got that information terrifies me, making me wonder what his next move will be. Part of me wants to end it right here and now before he has a chance to make another move. End *him*.

"Time's ticking," Abe whispers.

The cigarette slips from my trembling grip, my lips parting on their own. The words spill out, choked yet unstoppable. Then, they take life on their own. I tell the details of my plan, stumbling over the words, my eyes squeezed shut as I try not to picture Dua blacklisted from her university and future jobs or Zineerah being stalked by Abe's private security while she's grocery shopping. In the cracks of my resolve, I catch Nyla, a specter of anxiety pulsing in my chest.

As I finish, I reach into my pocket and crush the stress ball.

Abe contemplates in silence; his lips pursed in thought. He casts a sidelong glance, his hum filled with a sense of objection towards me.

He claps his hands once, making me cringe. "I'll remove the private investigators from the equation and agree to any demand you make."

"But?"

"But, my boy, negotiations are a two-way street."

I moisten my lips, my forehead throbbing from the strain of my furrowed brow. "Name your price."

"Simple." He shrugs nonchalantly. "Return Nyla to me in June."

The muscles in my jaw tighten, and I fight to control my breathing as I clench my fists. "*Return* her to you?"

"Did I stutter?"

"Why?"

"In the first week of June, there's a show. I've had to pull a thousand damn strings to secure Nyla a spot. It's her comeback, and I need enough time to fix her before New York Fashion Week kicks in."

I narrow my eyes. "Fix her? What do you mean by *fix her*?"

"Physically, mostly. Her therapist will take care of the emotional rubbish. I'll get her to train with Billy again. You remember Billy? He's that dietary gym freak who could pass for your"—he circulates his hand around my torso—"Hulk-ness."

I scowl at his despicable perspective on his *only* daughter.

Abe continues, lost in his thoughts. "It's easy. Cut out the carbs. Sugars. Proteins. Make her eat her steamed veggies or ice cubes since we're on a time crunch. Five hours in the gym with Billy. The plan *was* to bring her down to exactly a hundred-and-six pounds in three or four months. But I'll make it work in four weeks tops. I can't suffer another major financial loss because of my reckless daughter."

I swallow hard, my jaw clenched, and my vision blurred, feeling the weight of the pain and pressure Nyla's endured for the past decade under his power.

"I'll cover the young girl's housing, so there's no need for you to keep up this charade with Nyla," Abe says, earning my undivided attention in an instant. "You like the sound of that, huh? Because I'm willing to make it happen. I'll secure her a top-notch apartment near her workplace and even throw in a Porsche or whatever you prefer. That works, right?"

I don't like the lightbulb that flickers over my head at his words. But I can't think straight through my spiraling thoughts at the opportunity that's miraculously presented itself at the right time.

Makes me feel like the many models who ended up in Abe's office, desperately seeking a second chance in the aftermath of irreparable scandals. After he humiliates them, using threats of putting their families on the street or blocking off other sources of employment by any agency as prominent as his or by a local CVS, he reluctantly offers them an opportunity to redeem themselves.

I've seen first-hand how many relationships he's destroyed, and now he's in a spot where it's his turn to plead, even if he's a pro at hiding his desperation.

So don't fuck it up.

"No, not Maira," I manage to say, my breath shaky from battling my conscience. "If you pay for her living expenses, it will raise too many questions that I won't have the answers to."

He exhales in frustration, a hand on his hip and the other wiping his forehead. "Listen, son. I don't have all day. Name your terms so we can wrap this up."

My knuckles itch for a brutal connection with his jaw, yet my stupid fucking mouth persists. "Pay for my sister's schooling, and at the end of June, your daughter will be back in your arms. By then, Maira will have found herself some roommates from her internship, and I won't need Nyla's help any longer."

Abe steps away, sizing me up as if I've just taken a battering ram. "End of June? You can't be serious. I have her scheduled for a show on the fifteenth—"

"Find another one."

"Another one? Son, do you know how this industry works?"

"I don't give a fuck." I straighten my posture, taking a purposeful step forward. "She's not the same girl from back then." Another step, closing the gap. "Her whole outlook on this industry has shifted, thanks to the people who tore her apart for their own goddamn amusement." His back hits the wall, grimy and probably stained with shit. "If she decides to return to modeling, it'll be on her terms. Got it? On her own fucking terms." I jab a finger in his face, locking eyes with him, cracking his arrogant front. "And if I find out you're pumping chemicals into your daughter's body or subjecting her to some military boot camp, I'll make sure your life goes up in flames."

"Are you threatening me after demanding I pay for your sister's education?"

"Don't," I say, giving a casual shrug. "I've got a Jafri *and* the Khans on speed dial." Not that my pride would ever ask Azeer, Sahara, or Zaviyaar for money. Maya and our shared relatives' brutal comparison has stacked on insecurities that refuse to topple down, especially when I stand next to Azeer. For now, bluffing is all I've got. "Follow my rules, and I'll keep Nyla safe. Cross a line, and I'll keep her forever." My lips curve to one end when he slices me a mean glare. "How's that sound, Abe?"

He takes a deep breath, clearly disgusted by the melange of scents in Koreatown assaulting his senses. I mirror his stoic expression, squeezing the stress ball and holding my breath.

"All right," he concedes, giving me a firm push on the shoulder. "I'll have my lawyer draft a contract tonight and cut you a cheque for your sister. We'll iron out the details at my office tomorrow."

"Nah," I say nonchalantly. "I'm not stepping into your plastic factory." He pivots on his heel, fixing his cufflink. "We'll meet at the deli shop across from it." I fit a brand-new cigarette between my victorious smile and light it up. "Get rid of the PI's tailing everyone."

Abe narrows his eyes, but then a slow grin spreads across his face. "You're on a time limit, son."

I take a long drag, savoring the taste of the smoke on my tastebuds. "You're free to get out now."

He turns on his heel. "Oh, one more thing." Faces me again. "Don't go falling in love with her."

I laugh the smoke out, shaking my head at his sheer stupidity. Sure, I'm a little attracted to Nyla, but I'm not about to fall head over heels. Not in my playbook. "That's not even a concern."

Abe gives me a once-over with those unexpectedly protective fatherly eyes. "Don't let her die." He strides his dramatic ass off to a waiting black limousine.

"Fucker," I mutter.

Once I step through the door, shoulders shaking and abusing my stress ball, I plunge into a deep dive of research into Nyla's glory days in the modeling world.

The photographs from past years show her in boy shorts and a sports bra, her figure lithe, towering, and sculpted. It's the kind of physique everyone envied, one that countless everyday women would strive for yet could never quite reach.

Abe wants to sculpt her back into that same form.

Fuck me.

My fingers jitter as I type out her name in the search bar again, chewing my lower lip while pacing around my kitchen. Sky whines as if she can sniff out the stress in the air.

Various fashion websites offer bogus versions of her dietary plan. There are medicines and supplements that probably cost a small fortune. Vegan meals—*Christ*. In my household, veganism is nonexistent. Why would I want to cook grass with coconut oil or some shit?

The most peculiar diet is the ice-cube regimen. Nothing but a cup of ice cubes twice a day for two straight weeks. Did Nyla *seriously* stick to this routine? Sweet fuck. I might just grab the gun from my closet and put two bullets in Abe's face for putting his only daughter, not to mention her immune system, through this.

The only semblance of normalcy is the exercise routine. It's a well-considered monthly cardio plan, coupled with light muscle building and pilates.

I close the app and sink onto the couch. My sister's education will be secured if I can keep Nyla safe and steer her back towards modeling again. If Zineerah and Dua knew about the contract I'd be signing tomorrow, they'd disown me, much as I did with our pathetic excuse for a mother.

Nyla's whole existence orbits around her father. Every damn thing she's ever pulled off is just to make him happy. He's the puppeteer, and she's his pretty, little puppet, connected by strings of silver and gold.

And once I . . . once I hand her over to him against her will, she'll lose sight of her purpose. Those little fashion sketches she does during her lunch break and the precise stitching of patches on her sweatshirt will fade into memory.

I scratch Sky's ears, wrestling with my conscience. "Am I a total dickhead for doing this, Sky?"

She looks up, letting out a low whine. *Yeah, motherfucker.*

"Yeah." I clench my jaw, giving my husky a pat on the back. "Let's go fetch your favorite human, honey."

Props to Azeer's connections for hooking Nyla up with a driver in New York. The surprise on her face was priceless when Sky and I showed up at her suite. Apologies gushed out of her mouth like a broken dam—from the hotel's elevator ride, car ride, and the second elevator ride up to my place.

Now, she's keeping quiet as we step into my cramped space.

Nyla inhales deeply and exhales, a smile playing on her lips. "Home, indeed."

I tighten my grip on Sky's leash.

She turns to me. "I really am sorry—"

"Enough. Go change. I brought your bags up to your room."

A curt nod. "Where's Maira?"

"Bunch of project meetings tonight with some phone service company. She'll be back later," I say, setting Sky free in the living room. Maira's cleared out a spot for Nyla's fashion setup. I eye it as I speak, contemplating whether it's the right time for a question. "By the way—"

Nyla's already in her room, door closed. I run my hands down my face, feeling the tension, and then head to the kitchen to fix myself a sandwich. Sky follows, and I toss her a little piece of ham. "Oh, come on. Don't give me those eyes. You've got your own food."

She whimpers a bit, enough to crack my tough exterior. I relent, giving her a whole slice to chew on.

Nyla emerges, clad in another oversized pink sweater and baggy sweatpants. Pink bangs pinned up with a curler, probably a gift from Jia, who pins twenty of those velcro curlers in her feather-light hair during work.

"Whatcha making?" she asks, eyeing my sandwich assembly.

"Lunch," I reply, spreading mayo on the bread.

Nyla sidles up, her soft sweater grazing my bicep. She's tall enough for her warm breath to tease my neck. "Mmm. Looks good," she murmurs.

"Can I get some space?"

"Sorry." She steps back, leaving a scent of flowers and what feels like a fucking candy shop in her wake. Sweet and tempting as hell.

Why the hell does Abe think this woman doesn't have the same alluring power she had before? In my book, it's even stronger now. Or maybe I'm just saying that because it's been months since I've been with anyone.

Nyla's eyeing my sandwich with a ravenous intent. I'm not about to deny her the pleasure of lunch. I'd toss myself out the damn window before doing something like that. So, I ask, "Want one, too?"

Her green doe-eyes lift, and I take a quiet breath as she locks onto my gaze. "Please?"

Damn it.

I ditch my sandwich and start whipping up hers. She's watching me the whole damn time, tilting her head or shooting me a smile when our eyes meet. It's like she's undressing me with her gaze, digging under my skin to unearth my darkest secrets. Hell, I'm starting to think she knows about my meet-up with Abe. Or maybe I'm just worried I'll spill the details by accident if she keeps staring like that.

"Here," I grunt, shoving the plate in her direction.

She takes a massive bite and moans. Yeah, no, that's great. *So* great. Just what I needed. A compliment that coaxed my dick to wake up. "God, Shahzad. This is amazing! You should seriously think about opening a restaurant." She looks like an adorable chipmunk.

Jesus, Shahzad. The fuck kind of observation is that?

"Eat slowly," I turn away to finish my sandwich, my gaze fixed on the spice cabinet as I start chewing away.

"Where's Nyx?" she asks.

"At the mechanic's."

"Which one?"

"Gary and Sons."

Nyla's humming beside me again. "I see." I let it blend with the background, ignoring her and those captivating eyes. "I know you'll want to murder me, but I *am* very sorry. I thought I could ride— Never mind. I'm not going to make excuses for my actions. You have every right to be mad."

"I'm not angry. Just disappointed. In who? Not sure."

"What do you mean?"

I take a deep breath—hints of vanilla and fruit in the air. "I owe you an apology," I admit. "Raising my voice last night was cowardly. I let the heat of the moment get to me. I witnessed what went down, and instead of keeping my cool, I acted out of character. For that, I'm sorry, too."

"Oh, my god! Don't worry about it at all. I didn't deserve your kindness after you were concerned about my knees."

"But you did," I insist, noticing the band-aids on her scraped palms from the escape attempt. "Your safety matters, Troublemaker. The bike . . . Yeah, it's a bummer about the damage, but as long as you're still breathing, so am I."

Nyla's shoulders slump, and her gaze drops to her plate. "I don't want to disappoint you again, Shahzad," she mumbles.

"Unless you decide to turn my apartment into a bonfire, I think you'll be fine."

Her playful pout brings a smirk to my lips. "Unless."

I clear my throat with a low rumble. "So, I wanted to ask you . . . " *Fuck.* How did I smoothly propose the topic of walking the catwalk again? "Um, do you— Okay." I set down my plate, brushing crumbs off my hands. "Good sandwich?"

"*Great* sandwich. Can I have another for later, please?"

"Of course."

Nyla chuckles softly, picking at a crumb on her plate. "I should probably hit the gym soon. Had one too many chocolate croissants last night."

My grip tightens around the bread knife. If she starts following Abe's diet routines, I swear I'll rearrange his face with my fist. "That's your choice, Nyla."

Her gaze snaps to mine, a mix of sympathy and dread. "Once this act is over, I'll confront Baba."

I hold my breath in place, giving a slow nod.

"And I'm quitting."

Yeah, holding my breath will kill me. Which, after her statement, is acceptable. "Quitting?"

"*That* is my choice." A roguish smile begins at her lips. Truthfully, I won't be mad if she flashes me that grin while confessing to murder. "I've been giving it a lot of thought lately and decided last night at the hotel. I'm ditching the whole model and actress gig and pursuing fashion design." Sandwich halfway in her mouth, she dumps the plate in the sink and starts munching on it with a twinkle in her eyes that I'd been waiting to see.

"Okay. That's great. Yeah, no, that's awesome. I'm cool with that," I reply.

Nyla snorts. "Thanks?" She starts pulling stacks of papers from her purse.

"You sure you won't miss the catwalk?"

"Why? You want me to leave?" she asks bluntly, flipping through pages as she walks over. I struggle with my words, running my fingers through my hair. "No, I never said that. I was only—"

"Relax, Chef. I'll be in the spotlight and all, but as a fashion designer, not a model."

Still part of the industry, so it's all good. She'll strut her stuff, come to a mutual agreement with her father, and return to her roots as a fashion designer, not a fashion model. All I have to do is boost that confidence in her—ditch the training wheels and let her ride off into the spotlight.

Nyla lays the papers on the counter with a wide smile that's starting to fill the gap in my chest. "I designed all of these last night," she says with a glint in her jade eyes. "What do you think?"

I flip through the pages, tracing the shaded lines and absorbing the colorful details. "Nyla, these are . . ."

"They are . . . ?"

"Fantastic," I state. "These are fucking fantastic." My gaze lingers on the long body shapes of the hand-drawn models and Nyla's original clothing styles. Her taste is refined and upper-class, yet infused with a firework of iridescent color. Christ, I don't blame her for leaving modeling behind to pursue this craft.

"You really like them?" Nyla whispers, leaning in. "Like, is the shading and stuff okay? I had to work with cheap office pens, so they might be a little bit off—"

"They're perfect. I don't know much about fashion design, but I'm glad *these* sketches are my introduction to it." I return the designs to her, and she clutches them to her chest. "What's your take on your work?"

"They could use some adjustments, like in the second picture, it's—"

"Forget the details, Troublemaker. What do you think of your talent?" I flick the top of the paper stack. "What was going through your mind as you designed these?"

Nyla blinks rapidly, struggling to find words. "They're pretty good. I like the structure I've created. It's cohesive."

"Good." I advance, and she moves back until her back meets the counter. I trap her between my hands on either side. Her eyes fixate on my neck. "What else?"

Her gaze remains on my neck. "Uh— I-I like that I could create these designs from my imagination. Didn't really think I had it in me, honestly."

"What else?"

She nibbles on her bottom lip. I pinch her chin, stopping the torment. "I have ham breath."

"So do I. What else?"

Her voice is barely above a whisper. "I think I can do this?"

I smile a little, matching her volume level. "You *think*?"

"Yes?"

"Or you *know*?"

"Not yet. I don't know yet. I don't want people to think I'm bad and hate me."

"No one's going to hate you, Troublemaker." I shake my head while she nods, absentmindedly staring at me with flaring jade eyes. "Confidently, tell me you know you can do this."

Nyla's chin trembles, lashes flickering. Her breath quickens, nostrils flaring as she clutches the papers close to her chest. "I . . ."

"Tell. Me."

"I can't tell you something I'm unsure of—"

"Tell me you *know* you can do this."

"I can do . . . this."

"One more time."

With apprehension, she mutters, "I can do this."

My hand cups around my ear. "What was that?"

"I can do this," Nyla declares in her soft, silvery voice. "I *know* I can do this."

I pause, my lips lingering on her temple. "If you want me to step back, just say the word." Her audible gulp only fuels my amusement, and I find myself chuckling against the strands of her hair. "You've got a hell of a lot of power, Troublemaker. I'm here to make sure you use it right. And it starts with your designs."

A shiver runs through her, noticeable enough to make me step back. I use my thumb to wipe away a tear from her cheek, and she stares at me, awestruck, with that lovely twinkle in her eyes. I gesture towards the open corner of the living room with a tilt of my chin. "That's your new workspace from now on." She turns her head, her gaze dragging from mine to the wall.

"Shahzad—"

"It's not a lot, so use it wisely. Turn it into something real. Just knowing you gave it your all makes it worthwhile, even if it turns out to be dogshit." I tap her papers. "*This* right here, it's worth the effort." I point directly at her. "And you, despite whatever those jobless fuckers online have to say, are damn well worth it."

Nyla sniffs, mustering a crooked smile that I mirror.

Swiftly, she wipes both eyes with the back of her hand and sets her papers aside. "Come here." She surprises me with a tight hug. Her arms grip my torso, her head fitting snugly under my chin. "You're worth it, too, Chef. You always have been."

Sky barks at the birds outside my window, prompting Nyla to draw back and chuckle. She takes her designs with her, embracing Sky as well.

I press my hand against my numb chest and *holy fuck*, my heart has never pounded this hard before.

All from a simple hug.

Or from tomorrow's meeting with Abe.

I don't know.

11

A Sexy Viking

Nyla

I'm wrapping up with a table when Tae walks into the restaurant looking a bit roughed up, his clothes disheveled, and his bottom lip bleeding.

"Hey, hey, hey." I stop him on his way to the kitchen. "What happened? Are you okay?"

"I'm never sticking up for an independent young woman again." He marches off but pauses at the door. Turning his cheek my way, he adds, "Well, except for you, noona. You're cool."

I chuckle, giving his shoulder a friendly grip. "Wanna talk about it?"

He nods toward an empty table. Since it's still early, business is slow until the afternoon rush.

"Okay, so you know how I like Hye-jin?" he begins.

"Yes."

"And Hye-jin likes this guy, Kyle Donovan, from a private school nearby. We're always competing with some of their popular groups. Just last week, we had a contest to see who could eat a can of tomato sauce the fastest," he says with a proud smirk, pointing at himself. "And your boy here won. Know what I'm sayin'?"

I look off into the distance with a drained look. "Sure."

Tae winces when he touches his bottom lip but keeps talking. "Anyway, I got into a fight with him because he called her a slut with his friends at Mel's Milkshake Shack near my school while Hye-jin was in the bathroom."

"Hold on, why were *you* there?"

"Getting a milkshake, obviously."

"But you're lactose intolerant?"

He shudders. "How the hell do you know that?"

"Jia's always complaining about you having a white man's disease."

His head sinks. "Jesus Christ, halmeoni."

Silence ensues us as I await the truth.

A defeated sigh. "Okay, I was following Hye-jin—"

"Tae—"

"But not because I was stalking her. No way. I'm a man. Only boys stalk. And ya' boy ain't a boy." He adjusts his collars, trying to show off his manliness, I assume. "Sure punch like one, though." He spreads his fingers, blowing over the bruises on his knuckles. "Anyway, I lost the fight because Hye-jin stepped in to break it up. Pretty sure the whole Manhattan school district is laughing at me."

A loud gasp comes from near the kitchen doors.

Jia, with her hand over her heart, stares at her grandson's bruised face. She rushes over and starts ranting in Korean about his misbehavior, stretching his face and holding his hands, going on about how he won't be handsome anymore if he keeps getting into juvenile fights.

"Halmeoni!" Tae sighs. "Maybe if you and Eomma fed me real food instead of powdered milk and cheddar fish crackers growing up, I'd be like Shahz." He gestures toward me. "Even Alyn eats better than me! Look at her muscles!"

I check my supposed muscles, a grin spreading across my lips. "In Halmeoni's defense, Tae, you're still a growing boy—man. Sorry. You're still a growing man," I say, scratching the back of my neck. "Maybe if you started eating all your meals now, you could reach Shahzad's level."

"I'd love to, noona, but *this* is my halmeoni," he retorts sarcastically, earning a light smack on his feeble bicep from his grandmother. "You know what? I'm done. My bones hurt. My face looks like the Kill Bill lady, and I need a seventy-two-hour nap." He walks away, halts, then turns around. "And I'm not going to school tomorrow."

"Yes, you are," Halmeoni asserts, prompting him to stomp away like a moody child, belching a low growl and forcefully pushing open the kitchen doors. "I don't know where that boy gets his temper from."

"Is that so?" I mutter, chewing on seasoned bean sprouts.

Shahzad emerges at that moment. "Woah! Watch where you're going, kid."

Tae scrutinizes him from head to toe, shaking his head. "God, I hate you for looking like a sexy Viking," he mutters before marching away.

Suppressing a giggle, I watch as Jia massages her temples and heads to the cash counter to queue up another movie.

Shahzad tosses a dishcloth over his shoulder, twirls his chair, and straddles it backward. "What was that all about?" he asks.

"Girl problems," I reply. "What brings you out here? No dishes left to scrub?" I cut him off before he can answer. "Oh, oh, oh. Wanna take a peek at the designs I made last night?"

Up tug the corners of his lips. "Show me what you got, Troublemaker."

Though Shahzad may be unaware, his approval means the world to me. He's the first man I've shared my designs with, and his excitement in that unmistakable Shahzad Arain way sends my heart into a joyful dance.

"Be right back." Without hesitation, I slip through the kitchen doors and into the back room, retrieving my sketchbook. My gaze lingers on Shahzad's leather jacket hanging gracefully from the coat hanger.

He set out on his morning run at the crack of dawn and returned later in the morning. I was already at the restaurant, immersed in my usual routine, assisting Bao in unpacking the morning's meat delivery and neatly arranging it in the industrial freezer. When Shahzad finally walked through the door, his demeanor was distracted and clouded with tension. Instinctively, I chose not to burden him with my questions.

My insatiable nosiness clashes with my unwillingness to poke around. The old me, the one I'm beginning to *sometimes* miss, wouldn't have hesitated to dive headfirst into such matters.

But times have changed.

As I walk out, my attention catches onto the scene beyond the kitchen door windows. Shahzad sits where I was before, engrossed in texting, his face illuminated by a radiant smile. His hand glides over his jaw as he pinches out a picture on his screen.

Hmm.

"I get it," Bao's voice startles me from behind.

"God!" I exclaim, my heart recovering from the surprise. "Give a girl a warning next time."

"My bad." He sidles up next to me to peer through the window. "Hmm."

"That's what I said, too," I mutter. "Well, thought. That's what I thought, too."

"Think he's cheating on you?" Bao, always one to entertain speculation, poses the question.

Oh, right. We're fake-dating. The make-believe dance we're winding through. Sometimes, I forget that this relationship we have is just a performance. With Shahzad, it doesn't feel like a play. *Maybe it's because you've still got a fat crush on him.* But shouldn't crushes summon a flurry of nerves? Sure, I get a bit jittery when he invades my personal space, but it's more about my insecurities—like my double chin or the irrational fear of having less-than-minty breath. Not that I actually do. I've been chewing a whole pack daily—Okay, I'm getting off track here.

"Shahzad's very loyal," I declare with unwavering confidence. "He's a committed boyfriend. That's who he is. My boyfriend. Shahzad is my boyfriend."

Bao gives me an incredulous smile and averts his eyes elsewhere. "Just double-checking here. Shahzad is your boyfriend, right?"

I playfully punch his shoulder. "You know, I think we can be really good friends."

"Yeah, I hope so."

"What do you mean?"

He chuckles nervously, hands finding refuge in the front pockets of his apron. "Shahzad's *pretty* possessive about you. Have you seen how he looks at you? It's like the man fantasizes about a whole universe with just you and him. Everyone else is just a waste of space."

To my surprise and vacant blinking, he continues. "The other day, he sliced himself washing dishes because he can't peel his eyes away from you. And when the guys and I tease him about scoring your number, he throws us those intense, super black eyes. And he makes sure your bibimbap doesn't have mushrooms because he apparently you get the runs easily or something like that."

"He *said* that?"

"Hey, I get it. Mushrooms make my stomach a little wonky, too."

My cheeks flush instantly. "I was on my pe—never mind. Whatever you've said is—" *Don't forget he's your boyfriend, Nyla.* "What you have said is *very* true. But Shahzad is aware you're one of his good friends, making you my friend, too." I extend my hand for a shake. "What do you say?"

Bao sighs, uncrossing his arms. "Co-worker friends. I don't want that idiot to hack my hands off with my favorite butcher knife. It's got my initials and all." He moves to shake my hand just as the kitchen doors swing open.

FAKE IT TILL WE MAKE IT

Shahzad's gaze darts between my face, Bao's face, and our clasped hands.

That's when I notice it—the glare in his super-black eyes. But it's just an act, right? What boyfriend isn't possessive? He knows what he's doing from all those fake-dating novels he's read. I've never had a boyfriend for more than a month. Or a genuine one. Publicity stunts stung like hell and messed with my perception of healthy relationships. Oh, and there's the whole family drama—*Enough!*

Bao swiftly tucks his hands back into his pockets. "I think I left something in the freezer," he says, lowering his voice just for me. "Make sure he doesn't lock me in, yeah?" A playful wink, and he's gone.

Shahzad tilts his head as he watches Bao disappear around the corner, then turns his attention back to me. "I didn't realize you two were friends. You rarely hang back here."

"I wasn't aware there was a rule against making friends at work." I stroll over to him, hugging my design binder close. Shahzad remains still, his gaze following me closely. My subtle, flirty side comes alive when we're alone in my comfort zone. "Jealousy isn't listed in our contract, Chef."

"Who said anything about jealousy?"

I shrug, casually flipping open my binder. "Mistaken observation, I guess. Maybe I'll give Bao a call tonight—"

Shahzad's hand grabs my shoulder. "He has your number?"

Ah-ha.

"Sure does," I reply, snapping the binder shut and giving him a raised eyebrow. "I even took a selfie for the contact pic. He threw in a crown emoji next to my name. Cute, right? Oh, and he's so thoughtful enough to skip the mushrooms in my bibimbap. Always had a soft spot for chefs, you know?"

Shahzad eases his grip, leaving a spicy, tingling sensation on my skin. He maintains a composed expression, and then a serious smile curves on his lips. "Jia needs you to restock the napkin dispensers."

Well, that was anticlimactic.

I let out a sigh and start to walk away when Shahzad grabs my arm and swipes my design binder.

"That's mine!" I protest, reaching for it. He holds it up high, and despite only being a few inches short of his height, it's still impossible to graze my finger against my weak portfolio. "Shahzad, what the hell? Give it back."

"Why? Didn't you want me to check them out?" His mouth is dangerously close to mine, and I almost lose my balance from the sudden movement. "Or were you saving it for Bao?"

"So, you *are* jealous."

"Seethingly." He rolls his eyes and starts walking toward his dishwashing station. "We'll talk about your designs at home. How does that sound?"

"Sounds good to me. Good luck with your jealousy, Chef."

He smiles. "Good luck with the napkins, Troublemaker."

Sucking it up, I reluctantly exit the kitchen and make my way to the supply room, knowing my binder is safe and secure with him, knowing that I'll be pleased to listen to his approval during our lunch break, knowing he's a shit actor.

After I finish work, I try to talk Shahzad into letting me buy design materials and a mannequin.

"No need for that," he says to the mannequin part. "I've got a guy who works at a department store. I'll get you one for free."

"But those are plastic mannequins. I need one made of cloth so I can poke it with pins. Also, no arms."

"Just pop 'em out."

"And the cloth part?"

Shahzad surrenders with a sigh and returns to pouring kibble for Sky. "I'm coming with you."

I sigh, too, not because I've lost but because I'm determined. "Look, the store's just down the block, and so far, I've been in the clear." I quickly knock on the wood. Sue me for being superstitious. "I think I'll be fine on my own."

"Wait until Maira gets back home. We'll go together."

"Maira won't be back until midnight. She's stuck in meetings."

I march over to him but take a step back when he stands up. He's so looming and broody, and . . . Yeah, Tae was right. I can *totally* see the whole sexy Viking appeal to him.

"You can't be trusted alone," he says, grabbing his old leather jacket. "And don't you want a second opinion?"

All right, he's got me there. Aside from Maira, he *is* the only person who's seen the designs I want to bring to life. Might as well bring him along.

I wear my heart-shaped sunglasses, shoulder my oversized coat, and cover my head with a baseball cap. "If you get tired fifteen minutes in, I'm sending you home."

He smirks. "Yes, ma'am."

Oh, Jesus.

Blubbering like a fish, I spin around and put on my sneakers, fumbling with the laces as I hop on one foot.

Shahzad snatches them from my hands and . . . kneels. My heart pounds in my throat and ears, and, well, it *has* been a desert down there for eight months now. "Permission to tie your sneakers on for you, Troublemaker?"

I offer him my left foot, secretly wishing I wasn't wearing socks. The touch of his calloused fingers against my bare skin is too much to bear sometimes. Sometimes, I'll accidentally bump into him while he's cooking or when his fingers linger over mine for more than five seconds while passing the salt shaker. Those subtle touches set off fireworks in my stomach.

I resist the temptation to run my fingers through his espresso-colored waves, which cascade down to his shoulders. When he opts for a half-bun, my legs lose all sensation, or when he goes for a full bun, I might as well bury myself beneath his floorboards. Yet, my favorite style remains the loose and shaggy look he's sporting right now. Paired with his thick, well-maintained beard, it triggers memories of our hookup a year ago with a side of hopeless fantasies.

As Shahzad finishes tying my laces, I gather the courage to meet his soft yet dark gaze for a whole minute, leashing my breath. How he conveys a touch without physical contact spellbinds me.

When he stands tall, my back presses against the front door. He reaches to cage me in between—

Click.

I blink and realize he unlocked the door latch conveniently right next to my shoulder.

Oh.

Three more clicks follow below.

Click. Click. Click.

I step outside, and Shahzad signals for Sky to join us. He kneels to put a leash on her, and she gives him a grateful lick on the cheek. "I know I said I'm scared of dogs—*was* scared of dogs until Sky—but I always wanted a one growing up."

Shahzad locks the door and pockets the key. "You had the money. Why didn't you?"

I shrug as we stroll side by side toward the elevator. "Baba isn't a fan of animals in general. He insisted I use the treadmill for walks or runs." A soft, pitiful chuckle escapes me. "I don't think he understood that dogs aren't exercise machines with tails and paws. They offer comfort, security, and free therapy. Plus, they make loneliness fade away."

He smiles down at his husky. "Sky checks off all those boxes."

The elevator doors reveal an elderly Korean lady, who retreats to the corner as Sky enters, clearly uneasy.

A warm, sizable hand rings my trembling one. Shahzad compels me to splay my fingers, intertwining his with mine and squeezing tightly. The roughness of his skin against mine sends my stomach into a flip-flop.

We courteously let the elderly lady exit first.

"Keep your head low, and don't point at every little thing you find fascinating," Shahzad advises as we stand outside his building. He adjusts the bill of my cap and straightens my coat collars. "Instead, you will whisper your excitement to me so it doesn't go unappreciated."

Gosh, my crush on him has grown tenfold its average amount. "I'll annoy you."

"I'll allow it." He chucks my chin up. "You trust me, Troublemaker?"

I flash him a smile. "I trust you, Chef."

12

Mannequin

Shahzad

Threads and Textiles is Nyla's personal paradise.

She peruses through the aisles, gasping at the rainbow wall of threads, squealing at the different patterned textures, calculating yards of materials in her notebook with a Paw Patrol pen that Zoha gifted her.

"Tulle is a must!" she declares, dropping fashion facts like a walking, talking fashion design encyclopedia. "And silk is the key to everything in design. People often mix up satin and silk, which is understandable, but satin is a weave, while silk is a natural silkworm fiber. My top pick, though, is cotton. It's a timeless choice. Humankind has been using it for seven thousand years, from Egypt to Pakistan to China. It's the mother of all textiles." She spins around to face me. "Did you know cotton was the first plant to grow on the moon?"

I rub my forehead, feeling a headache coming on. We've been in this god-forsaken shop for two hours, and all she has in her basket is a set of pins and three shades of pink threads.

"You do realize you can get more with your paycheck, right?" I point out, slightly frustrated.

Nyla looks at her meager purchases and shrugs. "I want to spend it wisely. It's my hard-earned money since . . . well, you know."

Fuck.

Just when I managed to push the contract signing out of my mind, it comes back to haunt me. And with a headache, too.

Abe had this cocky grin on his face when I strolled into his setup right after my run with Sky. She growled at him so much that he had to loosen his tie and park himself a mile away from me. I made sure she got an extra treat once we got back home after sealing the deal.

"Oh, Shahzad! Look!" Nyla excitedly points at the rows of her kind of mannequins. I make eye contact with my reflection in one of those pillar mirrors. A dumbass grin is on my lips that I quickly wipe off. "*This* is a cloth mannequin. Watch and learn." She removes a safety pin case from her bag and pokes the needle into the mannequin. "Ta-dah!"

Okay, I admit her adorable enthusiasm makes this situation light-hearted and less light-headed. "Is that the one you want?"

She frowns upon checking the price tag. "That's half my paycheck." But in a second, her radiance returns. "We can just ask your friend for the spare. I'm sure I can make it work. Let's go look at some sequins!"

As she skips away like Dorothy in Wonderland or whatever, I glance at the mannequin's price tag. Three-hundred bucks? The fuck is this mannequin made out of? Saffron and edible gold? Jesus Christ.

Ignore your heart, Shahzad. Listen to me—your head. Don't you dare do it. Utility and vet bills, remember?

I walk away from the mannequin, sigh, and then find myself returning to it, rechecking the price tag. I drop it again and push my feet to propel forward, but they seem stuck in quicksand. So I reel back, check the tag once more—

"Are you going to get it or not?" a monotonous voice cuts through the air behind me.

I turn around to find Hye-jin. She's wearing a blue apron with Threads and Textiles printed over it, her light-blonde hair plaited over her head. "You work here?"

"In this economy? Unfortunately," she replies, dragging her feet as she approaches, eyeing the price tag. "Yeah, that's *way* beyond your budget."

I roll my eyes at her remark.

"I had no idea you were dating Halemeoni's waitress," she mentions, crouching down to give Sky a gentle scratch behind the ears. "How long have you two been a thing?"

"A few . . . months."

Hye-jin arches a brow. "And you're already living together?"

I rub the back of my neck, quickly shifting the subject. "So, how's school and stuff? Heard Tae took a hard beating yesterday at Mel's Milkshakes for you—"

"For *me*?" She snorts, stepping away and shoving her fists in her pockets. "He was poking his nose in my business. If anything, he deserved that beating."

"He's a good kid, Hye-jin."

"It's Juliette."

I'm not going to argue with a seventeen-year-old. "Okay, *Juliette.* Tae was defending your honor—"

"My honor?" A scoff. "I'm not some damsel in distress, Shahzad. I don't need Tae-hyung or anyone to defend my freakin' honor or whatever the hell that means. I was on a date with a guy I've been crushing on for months, and Tae-hyung just—" Her head sinks as she swallows in a deep breath. "Just tell him to stay away from me, will you?"

Even if I tell Tae, he isn't going to listen to me when it comes to Hye-jin. She's everything he's ever wanted in a girl, and considering Hye-jin lives in our neighboring building, they've grown up together, too. She's probably grown out of their friendship, and he's still daydreaming about her shampoo's smell.

"Got it, kid."

Hye-jin nods and points at the mannequin. "Want me to use my discount on that?"

I glance at the mannequin once again. It's what Nyla wants. It's perfect for her. She's got her own money, so there's no use in me paying out of my pocket. She wouldn't have folded so quickly if she needed it. It's her choice to make. *Head not heart, Shahzad.* "Thanks for asking, but I'm good."

She shrugs and walks away to aid a group of elderly ladies.

Sky wastes no time sniffing Nyla's shopping bags the moment we're home.

I lug in the mannequin I snagged from Richard's sports store on our way home. He had a bunch of extras in his shop, where I usually grab my biking gear.

Nyla stayed quiet, sticking close behind me and pointing to the right one. Before Richard could get too flirty, I held the box of mannequin parts with my left hand and grabbed Nyla's hand with the other.

"Want me to assemble it?" I ask, planting down the box of plastic limbs on her workspace.

"I've got it, Chef." She gives my chest a pat that leaves something lingering. Fuck that nickname, but also *fuck*, that nickname. "Thanks for everything, by the way. I probably chewed your ear off with my fashion fun facts. Feel free to cut me off if I'm coming onto you too hard."

I raise a brow.

"Coming off—I meant coming *off* on you too hard!" she corrects. "Not coming onto—I'll just shut up now. Sorry."

The amusement stretches my facial muscles higher. "Don't be."

She shakes her head, muttering self-deprecating stuff as she puts together the lifeless mannequin. Man, she's a basket case.

"Hungry?" I ask as I enter the kitchen. Of course, Sky trots behind me with her tail wagging and her tongue hanging loose. "No more ham, sweet girl."

She whines.

"I'm not *not* hungry." Nyla begins arranging the pieces on the floor. "But I also need to keep the calories in check." She glances up at the ceiling, letting out a frustrated growl. "It's fine. I'll eat as much as I can at night so I won't be hungry tomorrow. Maybe I'll even tag along for a morning run?"

I moisten my lips and rest against the kitchen counter, its cool surface soothing against my warm skin. "Nyla, not that my take matters much on your body or looks, but I think you're wonderful just the way you are."

She snorts, absorbed in her task. "Your opinion does matter to me, Shahzad. My whole life, I've cared about what others have to say. It's just how I am." Her green eyes meet mine, and the golden hour casts a vibrant glow on her pink hair. "Also, you used the word '*think*.'"

"I *know* you're wonderful. How's that?"

"Now you're only saying it to ease your conscience."

Goddamn this astute woman. No way she'll believe me if I keep repeating she's fucking gorgeous. "What I'm trying to say is that you shouldn't focus on losing weight because you feel pressured to do so."

"Who says I'm being pressured?" She asks, with the white, plastic arm in her hands, giving me a narrowed look. "I'm not being pressured, Shahzad. Not by my father or anyone else for that matter. I want to lose weight for myself. I want to get back to how I looked before everything went south. I want to feel good for myself."

I straighten up, gripping the edge of the counter. "You don't think you look great as you are? Nourished and glowing?"

Another snort. "That's a polite way of calling me fat."

Jesus Christ.

I huff a breath, hands up in surrender. If she wants to believe her taunting conscience concerning her opinion of her figure, then so be it. I can't help her accept herself, but I can give her gentle nudges in that direction.

Eventually, she'll come to terms with a healthy mindset, not the one her father drilled into her brain.

At around eleven in the evening, Maira arrives home, drained and cracking her knuckles. "Hey."

"Hey. How was work?"

"It su— You know what? I'm not gonna complain. I worked my ass off to secure this internship and convince my brother to send me here."

I return to the stove, mixing the sauce for my cordon bleu recipe. Nyla's been sketching for hours, and her stomach's been singing the hunger anthem. A quick Google search revealed her favorite dish, cordon bleu with dijon cream sauce, giving me a good reason to flex my French cooking skills.

"*Agh.* Speak of the devil. Mustafa is calling!" Maira yells, almost dropping her buzzing phone. She props it against the tissue box on the table and swipes right. "Salam, bhai-jaan."

I turn down the heat on the sauce and wipe my hands on my sweatpants. Nyla yanks off her headphones, struggling with shaky fingers. Playing my pretend girlfriend isn't her strong suit, especially in front of the guy making us go through this whole charade.

"I've got you," I assure her, flattening the pink strands sticking out and brushing her bangs with my fingers.

"What's wrong?" Nyla asks quietly, noticing my slower movements. "And none of that 'nothing' nonsense. Your left eye and twitching lips give you away." Goddamn this woman and her masterful observation. "Did I say something to upset you?" *You didn't even talk.* "Did I do something—"

"Save your breath, Troublemaker."

"Yes, they're here!" Maira signals Nyla to join us with a wave. She pulls out an extra chair, but I push it aside.

Taking my seat, I pull Nyla onto my lap, wrapping my arm around her waist. At first, she protests in hushed tones about my lack of awareness. However, when Mustafa speaks nonchalantly, she eases into the situation.

Her sweatshirt exudes the scent of fresh mandarins and vanilla extract, and I can't help but close my eyes, taking a deep breath. She's like my personal, comfortable furnace. I want to rest my head on her chest. Memorize the song of her heartbeat. Feel the gentle touch of her fingers running through my hair.

And I *hate* to use this word, but goddamn, she's so . . . cuddly.

"Shahzad!" Nyla whispers, nudging me in the chest. I open my eyes to find that smug bastard behind the screen, grinning at me with a knowing look. "Mustafa wants to know if you've agreed to Bao's offer to cook."

I notice just then that I have both my arms secured around Nyla, and she's comfortably pressed back against my chest. No exaggeration, I want her glued to me like this. I'm not usually big on hugs or physical stuff outside of hookups. I have a zero-tolerance policy against kissing, and the last time I broke it was with this Troublemaker, currently sitting on my lap with a fake smile. Don't know why, but hugging her feels like munching on cotton candy or something. Her scent and skin are just melting into mine.

"Shahzad," Mustafa's aggravating voice interrupts me. He tilts his head, that smirk of his going strong. *I know, fucker. I'm weirded out, too.* "Did you accept the offer?"

"I did."

"You did?" Nyla and Maira exclaim in unison.

"Good for you." Mustafa claps once and points at me. "That's what I wanted. Explore the opportunity and build on it. Open your restaurant one day, you know? Just like your plans—"

"Thanks," I interrupt before he starts some sentimental, fatherly speech about my past achievements. Keyword: *past*. Present-wise, I haven't achieved much, considering everything.

Every time I give it a shot, I fail. I'm not a natural talent like Mustafa. If I were, I'd probably be kicking back in a four-bedroom pad, holding a chemical engineering degree, and engaged to a lovely woman.

And I know it all depends on the person to motivate themselves to achieve whatever the fuck they want, but when your will to succeed is running on a low-fuel tank, the ride will only take you so far before you sputter and spend out.

"How about you, Alyn? Are you planning on becoming a chef as well?" Mustafa throws at her.

"I like to . . . draw," Nyla mutters.

Mustafa leans forward. "What was that?"

"We done here?" I butt in, swinging the laptop towards me.

He sighs. "Come on, Shahz. You pull this every time I try to get to know Alyn. How else am I supposed to be friends with my future sister-in-law?"

"Oh, God." Maira groans, rolling her eyes. *Same, kid.* She marches over and whirls the laptop to herself. "We've got an early day tomorrow. Talk to you later."

"Maira—"

"Allah Hafiz." She ends the call and shuts her laptop screen down. "I'm *so* sorry, you guys. He can be such a nosy pain in the ass sometimes. It's his way of showing he cares, but I completely understand if it gets overbearing." With an apologetic smile, she hugs her device and heads inside the bedroom.

"I think it's nice," Nyla mumbles, playing with her fingers. "To have someone who cares about your future. All I've ever had are people who *plan* my future." She tucks a pink strand behind her ear, and suddenly, her expression changes. "Oh, my god."

"What's up?"

She looks back at me, tearing herself away from my lap. "I-I should've gotten up. Are your legs okay?"

I raise an eyebrow and stretch out my legs. "Seem perfectly fine to me."

She blinks rapidly, her cheeks turning bright pink. "I'm sorry again. I don't know why I just—I should've sat on the chair." She grabs the chair she pulled out for herself and nibbles her bottom lip with her teeth. Is she okay? "Your lap . . . it was comfortable."

Ah.

"Not that I would sit on it again!" Nyla's hands flail in front of her. "It was comfortable in a sense that—you know—I—forget it." She chuckles nervously, grabs her stationary and sketchbook, and turns to face me. Her lips open and shut twice. "Never mind." She hurries back into the bedroom.

Sky lifts her head from the couch, tilting it as if to ask, *what is wrong with her?*

I smile and stand. "I don't know. But I don't hate it."

13

Potato, Potahto

Nyla

"Do you have a mother, Alyn-ah?"

Jia surprises me with her question while I'm busy arranging soda cans in the fridge. She stands behind the counter with yellow curlers pinning up her hair, slapping the back of the remote to adjust the volume of *Vanilla Sky* playing on the television.

"Yeah, I do," I reply, grabbing a Sprite on cue—Mama's favorite for when she had terrible indigestion. "But she lives in another country."

"And what about your father?"

I nod, not wanting to get into details about where Baba is, fearing Jia might persuade me to meet up with him. "How about you? Apart from Tae's mom, do you have other kids?"

"They're in other countries too," Jia says, popping open the back compartment of the remote. "My oldest son is in Australia with his family. My second daughter is in Korea, teaching at an elementary school. And Tae-hyung's mother . . ." She chokes up and clears her throat, and I decide not to push her about it.

"I always wished I had my own siblings," I share, finishing the first crate of sodas and moving on to the soju bottles. Bao likes to take three shots in the early morning—one for breakfast, lunch, and dinner—to get through the day. "I do have lots of step-siblings, though."

Jia happily hums as she opens a fresh battery pack and pops it into the remote control.

FAKE IT TILL WE MAKE IT

"I grew up with seven siblings."

"*Seven?*"

She smiles warmly, securing the remote's cover and lowering the volume on the television. "We always used to argue." Now, her attention is on me, and I close the fridge door to spare her mine. "I have three little sisters in Korea. When they were kids, I used to cut their hair and do their makeup with baby powder and crushed cherries."

"Are you the eldest daughter?"

"Yes, I am. I also have three older brothers." Her eyes frown. "One of them recently passed away, and the other two are in Korea with their families."

I offer a sympathetic smile. "So, you're the only one from your family here in America?"

Jia nods. "My husband was born here but met me on a trip to Korea. I didn't like him at first, especially his Western ways. Did you know I had to teach him how to speak Korean? He was such a fool." She says this with a playful grin, gazing up at Tom Cruise's face on the screen. "He was a fan of this actor. When we got married, he made me watch all his movies. That's how I learned English—watching his favorite movies and listening to his favorite songs."

I sigh nostalgically, adjusting my weight on the crate I'm sitting on. My chin rests on my palms as I observe the wistful look in her brown eyes.

Jia shakes her head and wipes her hand over her cheeks. "Okay, enough with the stories. Finish the rest of the fridge and help with the dishes in the kitchen since Bao took my best washer."

I giggle behind my hand and do as she asks.

During lunch, or as we call it, rush hour in the kitchen, I move from table to table, jotting down orders and calling them back to the kitchen.

It's terrifying how hectic it is back there, worse than the lobby tasks. At least I can take breaks behind the cash counter and catch snippets of conversations.

Shahzad, Bao, and the other hardworking team members are busy, shouting "Behind!" and "Corner!" every time they, you know, walk behind someone or turn a corner.

Apparently, Shahzad implemented this rule he learned in culinary school to prevent collisions.

"Noona!" Tae calls me from the kitchen window. I quickly serve the stew, nodding goodbye to the customers. "It's your turn with the dishes."

"Got it!"

"Behind!" Marine calls out as she swiftly moves past Bao, carrying a tray of steamed vegetables.

Rather than diving into the crowded chaos, I hug the walls. The air is thick with the hustle and bustle of the kitchen. Bodies burn through the wind with ceramic stew pots and cold noodle bowls, fryers sizzle with battered pork and chicken, omelet batter is poured onto oiled pans, and sauces are expertly whisked and tasted by Shahzad. Three people diligently arrange the side dishes.

Retreating to the back room, I grab a fresh pair of dishwashing gloves, the clamor of the kitchen muted behind closed doors. I secure a hairnet over my hair, adding a clean face mask. It's not my preferred disguise, but you make do with what you have.

Taking a deep breath, I push open the doors. The noise shrouds me once again. It's been almost a year since I've been in such a calamitous environment, but it's one I'm not afraid of. Paparazzi and journalists have staked out my apartments, shouting bizarre questions. Fans have camped outside all night, and stepping out to my car meant enduring their screeches at the highest decibel. Red carpets were even worse—constant shouts about how to pose and more.

"Behind." I swiftly navigate around Ryan, the only white guy at Jia's place, and go to the dishwashing area. "What in the world?"

Tae hasn't touched a *single* dish. The sink is practically overflowing with soapy water and bubbles. Did he use up all the dish soap?

This is fine.

I've dealt with broken heels mid-way through a walk, accidental nip-slips, and tackling sexist, misogynistic, slut-shaming questions during press tours take the cake.

I roll up my sweater sleeves, plunge my hands into the water, and start scrubbing dishes, loading them into the massive dishwasher in intervals. I take out the freshly steamed and polished dishes, placing them on a large rack to dry.

Min-seok, one of the cooks, walks over with a tray of dirty dishes. "Aren't you supposed to be in the lobby, bunhongsaek?" If only they knew my hair isn't naturally pink but brown, maybe they'd start calling me galsaek.

"Tae and I are taking turns every two hours," I say, grabbing the tray and putting the dishes on the rinsing side.

"Do you think Shahz noticed you're back here? You know he likes to watch you from the window, right?"

This again.

"Well, if he did, he'd realize by now that I'm not a seventeen-year-old Korean boy waiting tables outside."

Min-seok shrugs and gives me a friendly pat on the back as a goodbye.

I scour through most of the dishes, and holy smokes, I'm sweating like a pig. My body hurts from all the bending and scrubbing, and I've lost count of how many times I've accidentally rubbed my eyes with the soapy gloves. Everything looks blurry, and black dots dance before my eyes due to an empty stomach.

During fashion week, I've experienced countless moments of dizziness and sluggish movements. My diet was strict, trying to fit into Baba's idea of the perfect body. I spent endless hours at the gym, my footprints marking the third treadmill in the fifth row. But I wasn't eating proper meals, just fruits and ice cubes.

I really hate ice cubes.

"Drink," says a low, husky voice from behind me.

A glass of water . . . with ice cubes is presented in front of me, held by a large, familiar, calloused hand.

I turn around, mumbling, "Thank you."

Shahzad's wearing a blue apron over a white t-shirt that shows off his muscles, and his long, wavy hair is tied in a low bun. His facemask is under his chin, sporting dry sauce stains. "You're not supposed to be here, Troublemaker." He watches me fish out the ice cubes and toss them in the sink. "Drink slowly."

I don't.

I've been stuck doing dishes for three hours straight, even though Tae and I were supposed to switch. I didn't want to bug him, so I powered through.

A heavy sigh escapes me as I place the glass in the sink and lean back. "I don't know how you do it, Chef."

"*Sous* chef."

"Potato, potahto."

"Potato, Troublemaker."

"See? You *are* a chef!"

He shakes his head, hand on his hip, a small smile playing on his lips. "Look, why don't you go sit down? Traffic died down a little while ago, and I don't mind making you an early dinner."

"Thanks, but no thanks. I've still got a pile—"

"*Nyla*," he whispers.

My heart skips a beat as his eyes, a deep, dark abyss, paralyze me in place. And the way he pronounces my name is so . . . perfect. Nyh-lah instead of Nay-la or, even worse, Nee-la. It might not be a big deal to others, but it feels like a huge deal when he says it. Ask any delusional girl with a crush.

I take off my hair net and face mask, gathering my courage. "Do you think I've done better with the dishes than you?" I slip the items into my apron pockets, swaying a bit on my feet.

Shahzad checks my handiwork, and I anxiously wait for his response. "Hmm." His lips tug low as he examines what I've done. Getting his approval is always thrilling because it's genuine. If he's not pleased with how I'm doing something, he'll let me know. "You've done a terr—"

"Give her a kiss," Jia says, popping up with a portable hand-fan and a playful grin. Oh my, here we go again. "My husband did it when I was doing the dishes." She waves her hand. "Come on, give your girl a kiss."

Shahzad shifts his gaze to me, the question of consent evident in his eyes.

I nod briskly, breathing in the soapy, humid air.

His lips touch my forehead. *Three seconds*. My right cheek. *Five seconds*. My left cheek. *Five seconds*. Then he slips off my gloves and gently lifts my hands to kiss my knuckles. *Ten seconds*. He never breaks eye contact, unleashing a flood of shivers and delightful tingles throughout my body.

Jia strolls away with a satisfied *hmph*.

"New plan," Shahzad whispers, turning to me with the exact smile I've held my breath for. "Considering I'm legally your superior in the kitchen now, I ask that you go upstairs and take a breather, then meet me back down here."

I lick my desert-dry lips. "So, did I do a good job with the dishes?"

"Certainly impressed me."

"Glad I did, Chef." Biting the inside of my cheek, I walk past him, letting that smile inside me break free.

"Okay, I'm off to a game," Shahzad announces as he emerges from the bathroom, his long, dark hair still wet and a gloriously naked torso for my eyes to feast on.

Surprise, surprise.

"What game?" Maira asks with a highlighter between her teeth and printed PowerPoint slides with bar graphs and numbers splayed out on her lap.

"If you don't mind us asking." I unplug my sewing machine and pack my threads into the containers Jia gave me from the storage closet. One biscuit container had a cockroach crawling inside that Sky almost ate.

Glancing up from his phone, Shahzad replies, "Just a local basketball game at my old high school. It takes place in the middle of May each year."

"When is it?"

"In about an hour," he says, heading to the kitchen to start dinner. I always try to guess what he'd cook, having only been right once when he made a simple grilled cheese with tomato soup.

Suddenly, he stops and groans, "Fuck," which, for my hormones, was not the ideal move.

"What's wrong?" I clutch the measuring tape hanging around my neck.

He gives me a heavy look and asks, "Will you and Maira be all right?"

"We can handle ourselves," I reassure him. "Right, Mai?"

"I believe in the law of every man for themselves," she says.

"Except we're women!" I say, hands on my hips, a playful smile on my face as I look at their vacant expressions. "We stick together."

"That's not the point." Maira turns to address Shahzad. "But your girlfriend is right. We can take care of ourselves. So go ahead, make your dunk shots."

Shahzad doesn't budge, however. "It's okay. I can skip this one. The guys have enough players on the team anyway."

"If you go, how will you get there?" I ask.

"I've got Sahara's jeep. It's parked in a public lot about a block down." He turns sharply to look over his shoulder and asserts, "But I'm not going."

"Oh. Either way, we can manage not to die while you go to the game."

"I mean, there's no guarantee one of my votive candles won't set your curtains on fire," Maira says.

"Mai." I groan. "You know he has a thing about his kitchen being set on fire. Now he *seriously* won't go."

"Yeah, I'm *definitely* not going now."

"As your girlfriend, I demand you go to your game and take some time out. What's the big deal, anyway?" I snort.

Shahzad studies my face, almost like he's searching for hidden damage or delving into the secrets of my pores—although if I had any secrets, a quick Google search would spill them all out like an open book. "Wanna join me for the game?"

I lift up on my toes, surprised. "R-Really?"

Shahzad pivots on his heel, opening the laundry closet door to grab a dark t-shirt. "I'll be way less stressed out of my ass if you're both there. So, yeah. Really."

Maira caps her highlighter. "I'm gonna change into something unapproachable and un-sporty." She disappears behind the bedroom door.

I tidy up my space quickly, wiping my clammy palms on my sweater. "What should I wear? Are we talking sundress with wedges or rugged booty shorts?"

"Wear this." He tosses me an oversized t-shirt with a Guns N' Roses logo. I bring it close to my nose as he searches the closet. Disappointing. It smells like fabric softener, not the rugged mix of firewood and leather. "And these." I quickly hide the shirt behind me as he finishes his scavenger hunt. "Given the circumstances, I suggest this shitty disguise to protect your identity. Style your hair however you want."

I give a little smirk, pinching my lips. "Just to be sure, no booty shorts allowed?"

"It's in a high school gym."

"Oh. True."

He gives me a lopsided smile that sends shivers crawling up my spine and bites the gooseflesh forming on my skin. "Five minutes, Troublemaker."

14

Rodney The Rooster

Shahzad

"This is, like, *so* cool!"

Nyla gasps as we enter through the doors of Theodore Roosevelt Secondary School.

Families are gathered in the narrow hallway, the brick walls decorated with murals of our mascot, Rodney the Rooster. Lockers, banged-up and green, decorate the corridor, fluorescent tube lights in need of a major fix, and little children—siblings, kids, or cousins of the players—buzz around playing tag.

"I went here," I whisper to Nyla, stopping by the framed yearbook photos from the '70s to now, especially the class of 2011.

Nyla gasps. "Oh, my god. Is that you?" She points to the twelfth picture in the second row. My hair was shorter then, with a fake silver-hoop piercing in my left ear and a crooked ass smile. "No joke, but if I ever went to your high school, let alone *a* high school, I'd totally have a crush on you."

"You never went to high school?" Maira asks, no judgment in her voice.

Nyla hesitates before answering. "I was homeschooled. My parents were my teachers. But I've always wanted the high school experience." She looks around with a childlike wonder. "This is the closest I'll ever get to it."

"High school was terrible," Maira says, shrugging casually. "Everyone's too caught up in the drama. Friends date each other's friends. Bullies are a whole 'nother level of torture. And the English teachers are always flirting with the football players. Plus, we had a stabbing during junior year."

Nyla and I stare at her in shock, mouths shut.

"It was a Catholic high school, so," she adds as if that justifies the stabbing.

"Stabbing or not, I still want to sit in a real classroom someday," Nyla says, peering at my picture again. "Although, if senior year Shahzad Arain was in my class, I'd have a hard time focusing."

"Add cheesy couples to the list of high school cons," Maira says, pretending to gag.

"Thanks for the compliment, baby." Thanks to Jia, I'm wired to lean my cheek in for Nyla's impending soft, tiny kiss.

She smiles, coos, "Aw, you're very welcome, love," and turns away to admire the murals.

"Ouch," Maira winces, walking off toward the gymnasium.

Yeah. Ouch, indeed.

As we stroll down the corridor, Nyla unknowingly swings our arms back and forth. Her adorable little gestures hit me like pink, glittery nails in my chest.

"Come here," I say. She leans in, and I adjust her pink strands under the Yankee's cap. "Good?"

"Great."

I leave her cheerful eyes, walking into the gym, which could easily be mistaken for a Tesla showroom.

"I'm guessing half the school's budget went towards the sports program," Nyla says.

I huff. "That's what I said, too. They've taken away the authenticity." Seriously, did we *really* need fifty fucking rows of off-white bleachers or an ultra-wide portrait of Rodney the Rooster in a basketball jersey, winking and flashing a single feathered thumbs-up with his wing? Nope. Total waste of money that could've gone to the arts program or, hell, even the infected cafeteria food.

"It's too white," Maira comments, face scrunched in disgust at the minimalist harshness of the walls. "Excluding half the families." She rolls her eyes and heads up the bleacher stairs, finding a spot in the middle.

"Last I played here was almost a year ago, but I keep in touch with the boys every now and then," I explain. "Let's stick to our story. Cool?"

She nods. "Got it."

I pull her towards the players. "Yo, Jones!"

Tyler Jones, my team captain, and center, breaks from the group. His arms shoot up to the sky, and he jogs over with those long, dark legs that practically fly from one end of the court to the other in a handful of seconds. "Shahzad Arain in the fucking flesh! How you been, brother? Haven't seen you since our last game."

"I'm good, Ty. Just been a little busy. You?"

"Better now." Tyler catches on and shifts the conversation to Nyla. He shoots a smirk my way. "Who's this?"

"This is Alyn," I reply. "My girlfriend."

The term 'girlfriend' hits him like a ton of bricks. Tyler, the guy who tied the knot with his high-school sweetheart Ariane, versus me, who had a history with half of Ariane's friend circle. He'd given me the settle-down talk after graduation, after Baba's death, but back then, I was too fucked up to drag someone into my chaos.

"Hi, I'm Alyn," Nyla greets, shaking Tyler's hand. He's in full-on airplane mode, processing the fact that I'm actually holding hands with a girl. His reaction matches Mustafa's perfectly.

"How long have you two been together?" Tyler asks, flapping his hand behind him to call Jackson, the power forward, Austin, the small forward, and Warren, the point guard. The rest of the boys are unfamiliar bench warmers.

"Three months!" Nyla chirps, hugging my arm. "We met at Pets-A-Lot."

"Who's she?" Jackson asks.

"Shahz's girlfriend of three months," Tyler mumbles, staring dumbfoundedly at Nyla. "They met at Pets-A-Lot."

"He's in a relationship." Austin clutches his chest and leans back on Jackson and Tyler. "Someone call an ambulance. Shahzad Arain is in a relationship."

"Your friends are hilarious," Nyla whispers, laughing at their attempts to revive Austin, who's now on the floor. "Why is everyone so shocked?"

"Alyn—"

"Because it's Shahzad 'I've-lost track-of-my-body-count' Arain," Jackson says, offering a hand for me to clap.

"You're supposed to keep a count?" Nyla cocks her head to the side in adorable confusion.

"Yeah, my thoughts exactly," I reply.

"Birds of a pretty feather flock together," Warren remarks with a sigh.

"Shut up." I laugh, moving around the group and exchanging greetings with each snickering bastard. They pull me in during our handshake and whisper, "She's gorgeous," or, "Where's the ring, man?"

"Enough," I command, reclaiming Nyla's hand.

They straighten up but keep shooting heart-eyes in our direction. It's either I've got overprotective dads or teasing brothers—no middle ground.

"Miss Alyn," Tyler says, pointing to the bleachers, particularly the front row where their wives and Austin's fiancée are chatting. "VIP seats for the first woman Shahzad Arain has ever brought here."

"I am?" Nyla asks blatantly.

The guys can't help but smirk, giving each other nudges as they wait for my answer.

"Y-You are," I mumble.

The annoying chorus next to us starts with their teasing about my stutter.

Nyla's cheeks tint the color of her hair, her doll-like lips stretching into a grin. "Oh, come on. I find it kinda cute that I'm the first girl you've brought to your games."

"You hear that, Shahz?" Jackson says, slithering an arm around my neck. "She thinks you're cute."

"Super cute," Austin chimes in, appearing on my left and giving my cheek a pinch. "Isn't he just the cutest, Alyn?"

"Totally," Nyla adds, pouring more fuel on the embarrassing moment. And the crazy thing is, she's not even being sarcastic.

"Children," Warren comments.

"Get your asses back in the circle," Tyler orders, pulling the two guys away from me to prevent me from decking them. "And you?" He points at me. "Grab a jersey. I need my best shooting guard on the court if we're gonna beat the Red Devils."

I observe the huddled group in flashy red jerseys, too serious and downbeat for a throwback basketball match. Fucking Red Devils. They've stolen every championship from us after our team graduated. "Got it, Captain."

"Good. And you, Alyn darling," Tyler says, shifting to a cheerful tone, "it was great meeting you. Feel free to join us sometime for drinks. You don't want to miss a drunk Warren."

"Jesus Christ," Warren groans. "You're never letting go of the J-Lo thing, huh?"

"Seeing you sing 'Jenny From The Block' on our booth table?" Jackson teases, throwing his arm around Warren. "Nope." Teasing our point guard never gets old.

Amid their laughter and the noisy crowd, the only sound I focus on is Nyla's sweet, silvery laughter.

Whoa.

I have to blink three times to understand what I'm seeing.

Nyla Ghilzai has a dimple on her right cheek.

She. Has. A. Fucking. Dimple.

A firm hand claps my back. Tyler's. "You good to go? Or do you wanna stare at your girl some more?"

I notice Nyla has moved to the front row of the bleachers, calling Maira over. They create space for them next to Tyler's wife and Austin's fiancée. Her jade eyes shine at me, and now that I've noticed her dimple, I hope she'll smile just for me.

After about ten minutes of going over our team strategies, Principal Fred steps onto the court and taps the microphone. "Is this thing working? Ah, there we go. Good evening, Thomas Roosevelt High!"

Fred hasn't changed his style one bit since I last saw him. Same old three-piece suits, that shiny blond wig, and those rosy cheeks that pop up the moment he drags his ass out of his fancy leather chair. I used to serve detention for what felt like an eternity in his office. Enduring Beethoven's never-ending musical torture during his classical music and opera club on weekends was the worst.

"Jesus, it's like they recruited the freaking Juggernaut or something," Jackson comments, nodding toward the giant Russian dude on the Red Devils' team.

"Roman Kozlov," Tyler whispers. Meanwhile, Frederick is going on about TRSS history in the background. "He was one of Lincoln Park High's top shooting guards and center when we were freshmen. Almost made it to the NBA, but got into a brawl with a board member over mocking his accent."

"Fair enough," Warren replies.

"Yeah, he just moved back to Hell's Kitchen. The Red Devils snagged him for these throwback games, so . . ." Tyler gestures towards me. "Good luck."

"'Good luck'? Seriously? What's the lowdown on his weaknesses on the court?"

"None, man. He's like the Thanos of basketball." Tyler snaps his fingers. "Inevitable."

Great.

I glance at Roman, and the grumpy giant is smiling like a massive puppy, waving up at the bleachers. Following his gaze, I see—

"Oh, fuck."

"What the—?" Tyler questions, and the guys shoot me strange looks because of the pregnant lady I just spotted.

I roll my eyes up to her and shake my head.

Jackson smirks. "Is that . . . Renée Gonzalez?"

"*Don't.*" I jab his knee hard and sneak another glance at Renée. She's rocking that pregnancy glow, her brown skin glowing, tight black curls in a high ponytail, and caramel brown eyes locked onto Roman and Roman only.

Talk about perfect timing.

My favorite high school fling, the one I thought I might've fallen for, who shot me down in front of the whole school when I asked her to prom after a big win, is now carrying the child of my current competition.

And if Warren chimes in with a "You're fucked," well, I'm officially fucked.

The buzzer interrupts, signaling us to get up and go through the last-minute details.

I check out Roman's six-eight frame from head to toe—man's an inch shorter than LeBron and a solid five inches taller than me. Not that height means everything on the basketball court; it's more about being quick on your feet and reading your opponent's moves. But I did get the shorter end of the stick.

No pun intended.

Our sneakers squeak against the polished court as we warm up for about five minutes. Usually, when I go on weekend walks with Sky, I always bring a basketball to shoot some hoops at the nearby public court. Sometimes, I'll even jump into games with strangers who are so damn skilled they could be pros.

I was on the path to going pro myself until Baba passed away. After that, I shifted gears and jetted off to Switzerland to chase my cooking dreams.

"Shahzad!" The exclamation snaps me out of my thoughts, and I turn around to face Nyla. Her enthusiastic waves cut through the air, her smile lifting to the skies as she fashions my leather jacket on her shoulders. Each time her infectious excitement is directed at me, it melts me out of my frozen state all the damn time.

I'm beginning to like it. A lot.

"You've got this!" she hollers, hands cupping the sides of her mouth. Maira has to yank her down to sit steady. Still, the woman is jittery, like she's drunk a bucket of espresso.

I chuckle and respond with a thumbs-up.

Almost involuntarily, *annoyingly*, my gaze lifts to the top row, immediately locking onto Renée. She blinks rapidly as if I'm a ghost. I swallow hard, yanked back to the terrible age of seventeen—dealing with Maya's abuse, Baba's declining health, laying low from Renée's

FAKE IT TILL WE MAKE IT

public humiliation, and facing college rejections. Fuck seventeen.

Breaking free from Renée's stare, I redirect my attention to the jade eyes observing me. Nyla offers a small, reassuring smile and falls into conversation with Tyler's wife.

Once warmed up, we form a neat line, all eyes fixed on the American flag as the national anthem plays. When we shake hands with the Red Devils, Roman's gentle grip feels like he could crush my knuckles. He really *is* the Juggernaut.

As we take our positions, Tyler addresses each one of us with his pointer finger. "Fun, boys. We're here to have fun. No need to break kneecaps and ankles; this isn't the NBA. It's just another throwback game at our high school. Drill that into your thick heads."

"You're saying that now," Austin says, making us laugh.

Tyler smiles. "Go to hell."

The referee stands in the middle, engaging in conversation with Tyler and Vince, the Red Devils' center.

My attention flicks to Nyla, who seems absorbed in watching the game rather than me. That's fine. Everyone's focused on the court. I'm not that special, not compared to the colossal giant that Roman is.

The sharp whistle pierces the air.

Scoreboards light up.

The ball ascends into the air.

Everything seems to move in slow motion as the excitement of the game settles into my bones, down to my knuckles still tingling from Roman's handshake. Tyler and Vince rise together, but our guy has the height advantage.

Everything transforms into an electrifying speed on the court.

The ball rebounds into Austin's hands. His eagle eye navigates the court with unimaginable speed, leaping three times faster than one would expect. Two Red Devils immediately screen him. With precision, he passes the ball to Warren, who in turn passes it to Tyler, finally reaching me.

Dribbling the ball twice, my focus narrows on the net. Locked in on my target, I leap onto my toes and take the shot—only to have a large palm smack the ball, sending it bouncing outside the court lines.

Roman fucking Kozlov.

He smirks down at me, striding confidently toward his teammates.

"We need to tighten up our defense against the Juggernaut if we want to score," Warren advises, retreating to our end of the court. "Limit it to two defenders on him at most."

"The second I pass the ball to Shahz, close in on him," Tyler adds, and we all nod in agreement.

The whistle sounds once more.

The basketball dances fluidly between teammates, swiftly traversing both ends of the court. The Red Devils secure the initial points with a precise shot, and moments later, Tyler elevates the excitement with a resounding dunk. The game unfolds in a rhythmic pattern, shifting from my typical three-pointers as we strategically opt for dunk shots, sizing up our opponents in the process.

Throughout the game, I notice Roman's vulnerability: his constant glances at Renée every three seconds. Three damn seconds will give me leeway to shoot from afar.

"Yo, Austin. Warren. Over here," I call as the Red Devils add more points to their tally. "Block Roman the moment the whistle blows."

"What? We can't cross the court that fast—"

"Understood," Warren cuts in decisively.

Austin sighs, and together with Warren, they position themselves at the court's midpoint, toeing the line of our territory. Vince passes the ball to Niels, the designated shooting guard who willingly gave up his role to Roman.

Niels dribbles towards our side, and Roman shadows him, dangerously close to the court's edge, his attention repeatedly drawn to Renée's enthusiastic support.

That's it, Gonzalez. Keep cheering for your guy.

Taking a deep breath, I see their entire strategy map out in my brain.

Pass to a distracted Roman. Roman scores a three-pointer. Vince grabs the ball under our basket. Vince dunks it back in.

"Austin!" I shout just as Niels throws the ball toward Roman.

Austin and Warren flash across the court and close in on Roman, who refocuses a shred too late. And the boys? They have already leaped into action, reaching up to block his shot.

I smile and leap forward with all my might, snagging the ball.

I take off running.

No, I *fly*.

I fly towards their basket and park myself in the position of a three-pointer. Austin and Warren are on Roman, Tyler's handling Vince, and Jackson and our youngest player, Dre, are holding off the Red Devils' defenders.

I dribble the ball once, locking onto my target like a sniper.

Jump.

Ready.
Shoot.
Set.
Score.
Let's fucking go!

Our crowd erupts as we score our first three-pointer. The guys celebrate by roaring their lungs out, pulling me into their huddle, and giving me a playful tousle of my hair. I'm pretty sure Jackson even slaps my ass.

"Great defense!" I compliment Austin and Warren. "Let's keep it up, okay?"

"Got it, boss," they reply.

I glance over at Nyla and almost trip over my own feet like an idiot. She stands there with intertwined fingers, tears glistening in her jade eyes as she cheers her little heart out. Her flair for the dramatic never fails to amuse me.

But fuck me and that deep-rooted insecure, seventeen-year-old shithead for raising my attention a little further up the bleachers and finding Renée applauding for Roman.

I don't know what possesses me to roll my eyes, but when I do, they land directly on him.

Fuck.

His eyes drag to his girlfriend, then down back to me. A slow, disapproving shake of his head destroys all the confidence I had in standing up to the bastard. He saw me checking out Reneé, he saw me rolling my eyes at her, and fuck, he even passed a look at an innocently smiling Nyla.

Yeah.

I'm so fucked.

15

Principal Frederick

Nyla

In the midst of the game, I secretly steal another glance towards the bleachers and spot Renée Gonzalez, all bubbly and cheerful for her Thanos-like boyfriend, better known as Roman Kozlov, my fake boyfriend's court rival.

Yeah, I got the lowdown on Renée and Shahzad's romantic tale courtesy of Ariane, Tyler's delightful wife. They were on and off in senior year, and apparently, Shahzad was head over heels for her just a week before prom. However, she didn't reciprocate those feelings and turned down his promposal in front of the entire student and teacher audience right here in this gymnasium.

Most of the students who've settled into family life or pursued their dream careers are perched in the bleachers, well aware of the history between Shahzad and Renée.

If I were in Renée's shoes, I'd have fallen for him the moment he suggested a no-strings-attached relationship, then strategically orchestrated it to become the opposite. I'd have said yes to a hundred promposals from him. Actually, I'd have such an embarrassingly huge crush on the boy that *I'd* be the one asking him to prom.

"What's wrong?" Maira asks, popping a kernel in her mouth. Where did she get it from? I have no clue. For all I know, she could've sneaked into the staff room and made herself a bag of popcorn. "Alyn?"

"Hmm?"

"What's wrong?"

"Oh, nothing's wrong. I'm just a bit exhausted."

"Popcorn?" She nudges the bag towards me. "I got it from the staff room. Can you believe they don't lock that door?"

I manage a chuckle, accepting the buttery popcorn, my attention half on the game and half on, well, not the game.

Roman's third dunk shot sends a shockwave through the gymnasium.

Across the court, the opposing crowd bursts into tears of joy. My eyes dart back to Renée, clapping joyously with her arms outstretched to the heavens. And Roman, sweet, love-struck Roman, blows her a two-finger kiss before snarling at Shahzad and the boys.

"*Devils, Devils, Devils!*" The opposing fans start their chant.

"They need a morale boost." I twist side to side, my eyes scanning the crowd until they land on Renée and her friend shouting their hearts out. "Goddammit. How can we be louder?"

"Alyn, this is a basketball game!" Maira exclaims. "Not a fucking chanting competition."

"Clearly, you've never experienced a FIFA tournament. Be right back." I separate myself from the lively crowd just as the buzzer signals.

Principal Frederick and the staff are cozily settled behind the scoreboard, socializing with volunteers. As I approach him, he's engrossed in checking what I'm certain is his wig in his phone camera.

He turns around as I tap his shoulder, eyeing me up and down as if I'm a lost child. "Can I help you with something?"

"I'm Alyn."

"An answer to a question I never asked."

"I'm Shahzad's girlfriend. He was a student of yours?"

Recognition flickers in his narrowed eyes. "Arain?"

I stand confidently, adjusting the thick-rimmed glasses perched on my face. "Yes, I am Shahzad Arain's girlfriend, and I'd like his favorite principal's help."

Frederick probes his ear with a pinky finger, drilling into its depths before withdrawing it and casually wiping it on his blazer. "Come again?"

Douchebag.

"I'd like our side of the chant to be louder than the opposition's. Could I possibly borrow your microphone, please?"

"Why would I help you?"

I pout at the sourness in his voice. "B-Because you're the principal?"

He lets out a subdued chuckle. "Allow me to clarify. Why would I help my worst student's girlfriend?"

"Shahzad wasn't your worst student," I remark, taken aback by his claim. Then again, how would I know? *Was* he your worst student?"

Frederick gazes off into the distance, where Shahzad is flying around the court. "In all my three decades of teaching at Thomas Roosevelt High, I've never encountered such a menace to the public school system." The whistle blows as Shahzad scores a three-pointer, sending a shiver down Frederick's spine. "Whenever that boy stepped into my office, I questioned God, 'Why me? What have I done to deserve this?' and the answers never surfaced."

Okay, I don't understand which version of Shahzad he grew up with, but the one I know is only a menace in bed. At least, he was. Not that I'm imagining if he still is a menace in the sheets. I mean, yeah, sometimes I get carried away with my fantasies—*Not the issue!*

"In his first month of senior year, we had a wildlife rescue visit with a baby jaguar, a pair of chimpanzees, and some terrifying pythons," Frederick recounts, his blue eyes fixed on the clock above the entrance doors. "Shahzad was the first to volunteer for the pythons."

Oh, no.

"What . . . did he do?"

His eyes linger on the sparkle of my curiosity. "He draped it over his shoulders." My heart tap-dances against my ribs as I catch the horror in Frederick's eyes. "Then, he sprinted down to my office with the reptile, unleashing it on my desk, fully aware of my herpetophobia."

"Oh my god." I stifle a laugh by clearing my throat. "That's horrible." But my smile slips out. "What happened after?"

"A week-long suspension." Frederick sighs, shaking his head. But there's a nuanced twist in his emotions, a frown carved with sympathy and guilt. He glances at me, scratching his left brow with his thumb. "He, uh . . . When he came back, there were bruises covering his arms. I sat down with him and asked where on Earth he got all banged up—if he got into a fight somewhere." His eyes shut, lips tightening. "Turns out, mothers don't always know best."

Maya.

Of course, Maya mistreated Shahzad during his childhood. Last year, at Alina and Azeer's dawat, it was evident that the two were actively avoiding each other. My curiosity got the better of me, poking me to ask Alina for the full story.

Turns out, Shahzad had cut ties with his mother shortly after turning twenty. Despite this, he maintains close contact with his sisters, providing financial support and stepping into the roles of both the father they lost and the mother they never had.

"Here." Principal Frederick hands me the microphone. "I regret the day Arain approached my office, yapping about his roster of female friends from our sister school. I had to toss my favorite stress ball at his head before the details started pouring out." He shudders for the fiftieth time. "A troublesome student but an exceptional basketball player. Surprisingly, an even better cook. Ask him to make you a grilled cheese sandwich—he used to bring it to me to prevent me from calling his mother to inquire about his punishments back home."

I grasp the microphone, pulling it close to my chest. "Thank you, Principal Frederick." My gaze shifts to Shahzad deftly passing the ball to Jackson for a shot. "He may have been a terrible student, but he's a terrific human. I don't think I've ever met someone so uplifting. His kindness is like a breath of fresh air."

Watching Shahzad immersed in his passions has me itching to rush home, yank out my sketchbooks and markers, and let my creativity flow onto the pages. His dedication to basketball and cooking indirectly inspires me. Maybe, one day, I'll gather the courage to confess that one of the reasons I'm pursuing fashion design is because of his belief in me. That no one, aside from Alina, has ever believed in me when there isn't a script or a set of instructions involved. That sharing the same tiny roof as him, in close proximity, isn't restricting or noxious, but . . . liberating.

Adjusting to a life where I'm no longer a mere plastic toy is a painful process, but the sensation of being truly alive hasn't been this real since my debut at Alexander Wang's show when I was nineteen.

I activate the microphone, tapping its top to test the volume. "Wanna do the honors?" I extend the baton to Frederick, who raises a brow, his lips curling into a smirk. "You're still his principal."

Accepting the microphone, Frederick enthusiastically shouts, "*Let's go, Roosters, let's go! Let's go, Roosters, let's go!*" The chant repeats relentlessly until our crowd joins in, establishing a rhythmic beat by stomping their feet twice and clapping once.

The Red Devils begin to fall behind.

Shahzad singles me out, shifting his gaze toward his principal. The two men exchange quick nods, and from his shorts pocket, Shahzad produces something—a crocheted ball in hues of blue and brown. I've witnessed him squeezing it a few times during work, particularly when Bao explains a new recipe intended for inclusion on the menu.

"My stress ball," Frederick murmurs, bursting into laughter tinged with sheer disbelief.

"That little snake still has it."

Ah, there we go.

I chuckle, bowing my head and extending a handshake. "I'll take care of your curse from here."

Frederick snorts and reciprocates with a firm shake. His eyes soften a bit as he studies me once more, a genuine, fatherly warmth stemming from him. "Best of luck with your endeavors, Alyn."

During the halftime break, the gymnasium clears out as attendees head to the cafeteria for snacks and drinks.

Conversations ripple through the crowd as families engage in small talk before filtering back to their seats on the bleachers. An irritating cameraman moves around, projecting live footage on the large screen, playfully comparing random faces in the audience to animated characters or Hollywood celebrities. Maira offendedly matches with JoJo McDodd, preparing her fists to knock the soul out of the volunteers.

Naturally, I speed walk to the bathroom, and *naturally*, because I've been condemned with the worst luck, I run into Renée and her friend Christine. They're in the midst of touching up their lip gloss, fluffing their hair, and engaged in gossip as I enter.

"Hi," I offer a greeting.

"Hey," Renée responds, returning to check herself in the mirror. Christine also mumbles a quick "Hi."

I proceed to wash my hands three sinks down, stealing glances at Renée's friend whispering something in her ear, followed by shared laughter. "How far along are you?"

Renée pauses mid-giggle, glancing down at her belly before meeting my gaze. "Seven months."

"That's wonderful. Congratulations."

"Thanks."

"Of course. Are you looking forward to motherhood?"

"Mm-hmm."

As they conclude their hushed conversation, I finish washing my hands, trying to eavesdrop on some of their whispered words.

"*So,*" Christine drawls, "are you really going out with Shahzad?"

I turn off the tap. "Who wants to know?"

She tilts her head. "Me. Clearly."

Smiling at Renée's reflection in the mirror, I reply, "Yes, I am dating Shahzad."

"Interesting." Christine runs her fingers through her sleek, straight hair. "How long?"

"What?"

"How long have you two been a couple?" she asks, sharing a sugary smile with Renée. "Can't be more than a week."

"Actually,"— I rip out the paper towel—"it's been a *year.*" Their movements freeze momentarily as they gawk at me. Swiftly, I turn to face the dispenser. "And frankly, it's none of your business."

"Well, then. I guess some men do grow out of their old habits." Christine ends the conversation, packing up her brush and smoothing her brows back with her fingers. "I like your hair, by the way. The pink is so cute."

"Thanks. I did it myself. Almost passed out from the smell of bleach."

"I can relate," Christine admits, twirling a strand of the golden highlight in her naturally brown hair. "I need to schedule some touch-ups ASAP."

I smile, and they reciprocate. "I apologize if I came off as condescending."

"It's all right. I apologize if I came across as a total bitch," Renée replies, accompanied by a remorseful smile.

"Oh, not at all. I can see why both of us might be a little upset," I reassure.

"Upset?" She raises an eyebrow. "Why would *I* be upset?"

I sense a growing tension between us. Tension that I do *not* want to confront. "I'm not sure either. Forget I mentioned anything."

"Just to clarify, we never really dated," Renée explains, closing her lip gloss and turning towards me. "We had a no-strings-attached arrangement throughout high school. He just couldn't keep his end of the bargain, so . . . "

I slide my hands into the pockets of Shahzad's jacket. "You never felt anything real for him? Not at all?"

Christine chuckles. "Sweetie, if you went to school with him, you'd understand why falling in love with Shahzad Arain was a waste of time and energy."

"I just didn't want to experience any pain," Renée confesses, approaching me. She spreads her open palms, signaling with a raised brow for me to hold them. I comply, admiring the softness of her petite hands. "A bit of advice from one woman to another: date a man you can see yourself marrying, not babysitting."

Christine casually strolls by, giving a wiggled wave, and Renée, after squeezing my hands, follows suit.

I return to the bleachers just before the game begins, observing Roman wiping a spot on the first bleacher for Renée to sit.

They share a sweet kiss, and she likely whispers words of "good luck" and "I love you," pecking his lips once more. It's endearing how he bends down for her, one hand on her shoulder and the other on her protruding belly.

I exhale deeply, gazing at my hands on my lap, my lips forming a resigned smile.

Shahzad and I are *fake*-dating. I constantly remind myself that with each passing day, we're getting closer to the expiration of our charade. The sight of Maira casually browsing through apartment listings signals the looming end of this make-believe plan—a fantasy I've been indulging in through rose-colored glasses.

The foundation of our relationship is built on deception, a web of false information entangled to maintain our act. Yet, the feelings I hold for Shahzad and his character are the unvarnished truth.

I like him. I *really* like him. It's akin to a school-girl crush, the type that would make me hide behind my locker door to steal glances at him with his jock friends or purposely enroll in a mechanics class just to witness him dipped in grease and sweat.

See, this is what happens when you skip the high school chapter of your life. You start developing whimsical daydreams about what could have been if you had embraced the experiences of a typical teenager.

But what Renée and Christine, and Shahzad's team players, have said about his perspective on romantic relationships has me questioning whether I should let this crush of mine dissolve or evolve—only if his feelings undergo a change.

If, by some miracle, he wants me to stay and give our relationship an honest try, then yeah, I'll stay. And if he's helping me move back to Rhode Island after playing house is over, then I'll let the idea of us vanish.

Easier said than done. Your attachment issues are your worst qualities. You'll have him running from you instead of towards you. No one wants to be with a burnt-out celebrity with cotton candy hair.

Shahzad's face comes into view.

I startle at the suddenness of his action. He steadies me by gripping my elbows, preventing me from toppling back. It's then that I realize he's crouched on one knee, his espresso-brown waves slicked back with sweat and a white towel draped around his neck. "What's the matter? Why aren't you playing?"

He leans in and whispers, "Can I kiss you?"

I'm taken aback. "*What*?"

"Can I kiss you, Troublemaker?" His eyes briefly shift to the projector displaying Shahzad and me, surrounded by animated hearts and the words "Kiss Cam."

My smile is on pins and needles. "Oh."

"F.C.K.?" he asks.

"I thought we agreed on K.F.C.?"

He straightens up to his full height. "I'd agree to whatever you say."

Oh, my.

I tilt my chin upward, and his eyes crinkle, a shade lighter than their usual deep brown. Shahzad gently holds my face, lowering himself to kiss my forehead. My eyes stay open, his closed, exhaling warm breath over each cheek. His thick, calloused fingers intertwine with mine, guiding them to his smooth, smiling lips.

A slight catch in my throat accompanies his kisses on every knuckle, even my thumbs, and he tenderly presses his lips to the undersides of both my wrists, inhaling the fragrance I've sprayed there. In this gymnasium, it's just the two of us—locked eyes, connected hands—floating on a cloud beyond the ninth.

With each touch of his lips and the brush of his skin against mine, he carves his name onto my heart and soul. As he places my hands back in my lap and hurries away at the buzzer's sound, leaving a lingering yearning in my erratic chest, I notice Maira's smirk and the admiration in Renée soft expression. It's then that I come to realize:

You're so fucking screwed, Nyla Ghilzai.

16

Family Trauma

Shahzad

Nyla's on her twentieth round of fussing with the textile on the mannequin. Meanwhile, I'm in the kitchen, as usual, tossing a dozen wings in honey-garlic sauce. Maira's beside me, spreading butter on garlic bread, discreetly feeding Sky's gluttonous ass my baked french fries.

"I think I have to return to Threads and Textiles and get that mannequin after all." Nyla brushes her brows up with the mounds of her palms. She smacks her lips and abandons her measuring tape onto the table. "I'm so sorry, Shahzad. I know you tried your best to get me this mannequin, but I can't. It won't work."

"All good." I dump the fried wings into a bowl and swat Maira's hand away before she can steal one. "I can take you back tomorrow morning. Hye-jin works there and said she can give us a solid discount on it."

"Really?" Nyla's face lights up as she grabs the bowl and sets it on the dinner table. All of this feels so normal. Like we're a married couple or some shit, with a dog, and Maira's our daughter. I'm getting *too* comfortable with this, especially knowing it'll vanish by the end of June.

"Yeah," I say, clearing my throat. "We're covered."

"Oh!" Nyla perks up after setting the fries and garlic bread down. "We should totally take Tae with us. He's got a *huge* crush on Hye-jin."

"Are we talking about Eric? The annoying teenager downstairs?" Maira slides into a seat next to Nyla, and I'm sitting across from them. "What's your plan?" She loads up her plate with wings before passing the bowl to Nyla.

But, surprise, she hands me the bowl instead. She always pulls this move when we eat—filling her plate last. It's like the unwritten rule that elders eat first. Maira couldn't give a flying fuck about that rule, but Nyla's conditioned to follow them.

Sighing, I take a couple of wings before giving her a go at it. "Our plan is simple. Grab a mannequin and head straight back. There won't be any matchmaking shit going down. We clear?"

"You're so boring," Maira mutters, sticking her tongue out at me. "You two should get your mannequin and *man-Eric-in*to asking that girl out. Tell me that was clever, Inayat?"

"Absolutely, Salman." Nyla gives Maira a quick low-five while tearing into a piece of garlic bread with her teeth.

"I'm not dragging Tae along for such a small task," I say, dipping the baked fries into the ranch sauce and taking a bite. "Hmm. Needs a bit more salt." I stand up to grab some.

"Come on, Shahzad."

"No."

"Please?"

"No."

"It's your classic popular girl and geeky boy story. I've seen plenty of movies with that trope to understand Hye-jin and Tae's relationship better," she says, adding, "He's the Patrick to her Kat," as an afterthought.

"Who are Patrick and Kat?" Maira asks the million-dollar question.

"*Ten Things I Hate About You*? Julia Stiles and Heath Ledger? It's a classic coming-of-age movie, guys."

Despite having two little sisters, I'm clueless about who she's referring to. Zineerah is all about music and doesn't bother with the recycled stuff Hollywood churns out every year. Dua's into chick flicks, but she kicks me out if I ask what's going on in the movie. Besides, I prefer people-watching with Sky from my window.

That's why I ditched the TV. Saves on electricity bills and pointless streaming subscriptions.

"Alyn's right, Shahz bhai," Maira complains, even though she's not joining us tomorrow. The month of June started yesterday, and she's been officially assigned to an advertisement project for some juice company instead of meeting-hopping at the crack of dawn. "Try to, you know, enjoy yourself and all. You're always so grouchy."

"I'm not grouchy," I state.

The two women stare at me with a no-nonsense look.

"I have a solid reason to be grouchy," I reiterate. "Tae's a big part of it. He's just plain annoying. Always poking me to check if my muscles are real. And the one time I invited him to the gym at Jia's request, he ended up spraining his wrists trying to lift a ten-kilo dumbbell."

"He sounds pretty lame," Maira comments. "But an appealing kind of lame. Geeky, tall guys are all the rage these days. And they seem to be the freakiest according to the girls at work."

I mentally note to make sure she's not out and about experimenting with these geeky, tall guys. It's not just Nyla I've promised to look out for.

Nyla shakes her head. "Can we just bring him along, please? I swear we won't get into trouble."

"That sentence"—I point my wing at her—"is a jinx."

"Please, Shahzad?" Nyla's light-green eyes somehow turn glossy and twinkling. She pouts her pink lips and whispers, "Please?" again.

I shut my eyes and erase the image of her begging with that same intensity as last year, pulling me into her. "Fine."

"Yes! Thank you, thank you, thank you! You're the best boyfriend ever." She bounces out of her seat, hugging my head to her chest. Her soft, *cuddly* chest. Cud—Jesus. I won't be able to get rid of that word if this woman unconsciously hugs me again.

When she returns to her seat, I clench my fists under the table and focus on the sound of her giggles rather than the faint scratch of Abe's pen when I betrayed her by signing the contract.

"Thank you so much for bringing me with you guys!"

Tae's practically shitting rainbows as we stroll down the crowded Koreatown street. Nyla matches his energy, and the two of them are hatching a plan for Tae to act like a gentleman when he sees Hye-jin.

I hang back, keeping a watchful eye on anyone who brushes past us. So far, I've counted three guys and a girl who bumped into Nyla. While I'm not exactly peeved at the girl, those jerks are starting to get on my nerves. Especially since Nyla's the one apologizing.

"Oh, here we are!" Nyla's fists wiggle as we stand outside the store's doors. "Remember Tae—"

"Eric."

I glare at him.

"Eric," she corrects herself. "Just act normal. Be yourself and chat about something that'll actually interest her. So, no diving into anime and Valorant, got it?"

"Then how am I being myself if I don't *get* to be myself?" Tae questions, scratching his head in confusion. "You catch my drift?"

"Drift caught, but maybe throw in some talk about what Hye-jin enjoys too," she suggests, giving him a comforting back rub.

I can't help but stare, my fingers itching to push him away.

"How'd *you* two start dating?" Tae wonders, glancing between Nyla and me. "You're like polar opposites, just like Hye-jin and me. What's your magic trick to getting along?"

I look at Nyla, expecting her to chuckle nervously, but she appears calm and ready. Maybe she's already cooked up the perfect story.

"What's not to like about me, right, babe?" Nyla laughs, elbowing me in the ribs. "When it comes to Shahzad, I love his cooking and the extra details he adds in the footnotes of his recipe journal. The mysterious stories behind his tattoos. And when he wears those black cross-fitted shirts with grey . . . sweatpants."

My eyes settle on the red painting over her round cheeks. That wasn't the answer I had expected out of her. So observant and detailed.

"Damn." Tae cocks his head and turns to me. "How about you? You gonna try to one-up that?"

Nyla's green eyes devour me.

"Uh." *Think, think, think.* If Maira asked me, or maybe one of my sisters, hell, even Nyla, I'd easily gather an answer. Not sure where my confidence fucked off to right now. "I like Alyn's passion for her . . . passions."

He raises a brow. "Passion for her passions? What does that even mean?"

Her brows scrunch up, probably apologetic for placing me in that position. She's constantly worrying about others, and even though that's something I don't *technically* like, it sets her character apart from anyone else.

"No worries!" Nyla laughs, giving my bicep a playful smack. "He gets *super* shy with these kinds of questions."

Tae shrugs and casually strolls into the store without a second thought.

"Sorry for putting you on the spot," Nyla whispers, absentmindedly rubbing my back. No doubt, her love language is all about physical touch. My sisters and I once took a quiz together, and it turns out mine is acts of service. Zineerah's into quality time, and Dua's is words of affirmation.

"Hye-jin-ah!" Tae calls out, waving an arm at the young girl working on restocking the rainbow thread wall. She pales and quickly averts her gaze as if she didn't hear him. "Didn't know you worked here?"

"Hilarious, considering you follow me *every*where during school like a lost puppy."

"Duh. We have the same classes."

"Whatever." She gives him a cold shoulder, hooking a pastel blue thread on the wall. "Back for the mannequin?" That question is directed toward me.

"If the offer is still on the table?"

Hye-jin gives Nyla a thorough once-over, her sharp eyes narrowing. If she's figured out Nyla's identity, I'm thankful she's chosen to keep it under wraps. She doesn't strike me as the gossiping type either. "Follow me."

Tae falls into stride with her as Nyla, and I linger back. "Hey, I was thinking maybe we could grab some pizza after your shift?"

"I brought dinner."

"How about milkshakes?"

"Mel's banned you."

"Candy store?"

"What are you, five?"

"Seventeen. I thought you were smarter than that?"

Fucking idiot.

Hye-jin stops in her tracks and turns to face Tae, causing him to stumble back into a bunch of yarn. "You ruined my date with Kyle, Eric."

"Well, to be fair, his name *is* Kyle. I might have done you a favor there."

She groans, rolls her eyes, and marches away down the aisle.

But before Tae can follow and overstep her boundaries, Nyla pulls him back by his arm. He immediately shrugs her off. "What the hell, noona?"

"No, Eric. I'm sorry. I know I brought you along with us to talk with Hye-jin, but I won't allow you to invade her space when she's clearly asking for it."

He opens his mouth to argue but thinks better against it. "You're right. Shit, man. You're so right. I'm an idiot."

"You're not."

"I am." He crouches down and runs his fingers through his hair. "I shouldn't have ruined her date with that asshole. You saw it, right? She hates me. We can't even be friends anymore."

"Get up, kid." I pull him back on his feet. "Listen to me. You and Hye-jin grew up together. You'll always be each other's first friends forever, even if it doesn't feel like it right now. Just, you know, give her a little breathing room to figure out what she wants or who she wants to be with. I'm sure she'll come to understand your feelings for her when she's ready."

"What if she doesn't?"

"Then you won't pressure her," Nyla says, rubbing circles on his back. "If she wants to be with Kyle, then that isn't your choice to make. It's hers. Okay?"

Tae looks between Nyla and I, shoulders slumped and eyes drooping like they're frowning. "Okay." He forces a smile and mumbles, "See you outside," before dragging his feet away.

"This was a bad idea," Nyla says quietly. "I'm sorry, Shahzad. I thought it would work out, but I didn't take into account how Hye-jin must've been feeling, too."

"Don't apologize." I almost caress her cheek with my knuckles. "They're teenagers. They'll fuck up, then figure it out themselves eventually."

Nyla sighs into a melancholic smile. "Honestly, I wish I went to high school. I wish I experienced those confusing feelings and detention periods and eating stale cafeteria lunch with a group of friends." She begins to walk, and I fall into step with her. "But unfortunately, my career took off right after middle school, so I didn't get to experience further education." She swings her arms back and forth and turns to me. "What'd you do after high school?"

The question takes me aback. Not that no one's *ever* asked me about . . . well, me. But who, outside of my family, has the time to care about my extended education? "Uh, yeah, I went through all the usual school stuff. Then did culinary school in Zürich right after high school."

"Yes! I remember you telling me that during our lunch break weeks ago." She stares at me with her adorable excitement. "Wow, Shahzad. That's *so* cool. I mean, Switzerland is just beautiful. Have you gone on a train ride there before?"

"Multiple times."

"Isn't it just magical? I've always wanted to retire there or at least have my honeymoon there." The tip of her pink tongue darts from the corner of her lips. "Actually, Mama always wanted that as her honeymoon spot, but because of their financial situation, Baba took her to a nearby Cheesecake Factory. She told me that story with such a *sincere* smile that I thought she was crazy. I mean, Cheesecake Factory? *Seriously*? Nobu would've been a wiser choice." She comes to a stop before a roll of pink satin fabric, gently running her fingers across its surface. "I wonder if she ever thought about him whenever she stepped into a Cheesecake Factory with one of her exes."

"Where's your mother now?"

"Dubai," Nyla replies with a sincere smile. "She's about to be married soon. Again. For the fifth time."

"Any plans of meeting up with her when you're ready?"

She shrugs. "I don't know. We haven't seen each other for a while. I did invite her to my sham wedding. Speaking of, did you see it?"

I raise a brow. "See what?"

"Me being abandoned at the altar. It's kinda hard *not* to see it since it was a viral spectacle for months."

"Will you believe me if I said 'no'?"

"Yes." No hesitation. The sudden pressure of Abe's deal pricks at the nape of my neck, making me rub my hand over the spot. "Oh, my God. You *did* watch it."

"What? No. No, I didn't. I never watched it, and I never will." I tuck back a loose strand from her forehead. She blinks slowly, watching me retrieve my hand as I slide it into my jacket pocket. "I promise I didn't."

She absentmindedly picks at a thread sticking out from a mannequin's t-shirt, lost in her thoughts. "I hope Mama didn't either."

Now I get why she's always striving not to disappoint. Her parents—especially Abe—fucked her over repeatedly during her childhood, teenage years, and early adulthood. She's shouldering their pain on top of her insecurities, crushing whatever confidence remained from our last encounter.

A neglectful mother hits close to home. All she ever cared—still cares—about is herself and preserving appearances. She never appreciated Abbu's kindness and adoration, even though they were arranged at a young age. At least he was making an effort.

He was exceptional.

Zineerah, Dua, and I made sure he knew that until his final breath.

Abbu was the knot that tied us together, and with his passing, the fibers snapped, tearing us apart. Maya relocated to Islamabad, inheriting Abbu's property as per his will. Dua and Zineerah moved to Toronto shortly afterward, and I distanced myself from the family right when Maya chose not to attend Abbu's funeral.

"You, too, huh?" Nyla murmurs, giving a subtle tug on the sleeve of my leather jacket.

"Hmm?"

She motions towards her jade eyes. "You've got that 'family trauma' glare in your eyes. I'm here if you ever want to open up about it."

"No, it's fine. I'm good."

Her lips set into a determined line. Delving into discussions about my family or emotions isn't part of our arrangement. I'm consciously avoiding forming a bond with the woman because of my terrible tendency to get attached to things I've been working on for some time now.

"We should probably get the mannequin now," Nyla whispers, clearing her throat. "Maira's requested I make a dress for her to wear at a networking event next week."

"Yeah, sure. That's what we came for, anyway."

"Cool."

I wipe my perspiring hand on my jeans before extending it toward her. "If you want to."

Without any hesitation, she intertwines her fingers with mine and gives three firm squeezes, guiding me ahead.

17

The Origins of Arain

Shahzad

Maybe I'm looking too much into my fake girlfriend's personality, but she's been acting strange lately.

Nyla's on a cleaning spree, handling all the laundry, studying YouTube guides on washing dishes efficiently, giving the living room and bedroom a thorough wipe and vacuum, and even asking me to teach her how to make toast. On top of that, she's been pulling double shifts at Jia's shop, all while expertly working on Maira's dress.

"I've got it!" Nyla swoops in, snatching the salad bowl from my hands. Our fingers graze, making my shoulders tense up. Her vivid green eyes, filled with a mischievous twinkle, briefly meet mine before she turns her attention to the dining table.

Control yourself.

I run my fingers through my hair, grabbing the duo of plates as Maira plans to dine out with her new friends. I made it clear she needs to keep her location services on and stay within the city. I don't want Mustafa flying in from Toronto, ready to cut off my neck for losing track of his little sister.

You did this to yourself, buddy.

"White or red?" Nyla asks, revealing her stash of red and white wines from Rhode Island. "Choose wisely."

"Beer."

She cringes and gags, producing a grin from me. It's a glimpse of the Nyla I used to know.

All that's missing is her teasing me about—

"I'd never touch something that looks like pee. Probably smells like it too." *There we go.* She hands me a can, and I catch it, setting it aside amid the surprise of her comeback.

"Red."

"For real?"

"Yeah. For . . . real."

Nyla lets out a delighted squeal and rummages for wine glasses, assuming I have any. I don't even have proper glasses. "Mugs it is." She effortlessly pops the cork with her teeth, pouring a quarter cup for me and a full, overflowing cup for herself.

I grab the bottle from her. "That's enough, Troublemaker."

"What the hell? I wasn't done pouring yet."

"Look, I know you love to drink, but last I remember, you've got a low tolerance." She's not exactly hitting the bottle like a seasoned alcoholic, or else she'd be pairing it up with every meal of the day. Though, I *did* catch her eyeing a soju bottle during her shift. "Can I trust you to drink moderately? One sip for every ten bites?"

"Five sips."

"One."

"Four."

"One."

"Three?"

"*One.*"

She sighs and nods, picking up her fork and poking her food around. "Ass."

"What was that?"

"Nothing."

"Sounded like 'ass' to me."

Nyla glances up from her lashes and mirrors my smile. "You're an ass."

"Yeah? Well, you'll be thanking this ass when you're not diagnosed with some rare liver disease."

She rolls her eyes and takes a bite of her food, a permanent smile on her lips and on mine, too. "You know, I've noticed you don't talk much about yourself."

"It isn't an interesting topic."

"To you, maybe. But not to me," she says. I slow down my chewing as I watch her play around with her food. "Like, you know everything there is about me—it's all one Google search away."

Been there, done that.

She continues. "It's vital information for every fake girlfriend to know about her fake boyfriend's origin story. And because we're friends. Right?"

I clear my throat, piecing together the fragments of my life in my mind. It's true I don't often talk about myself to others because the company I keep around has been with me for years. I don't actively seek long-term friendships, either—well, I've got a few exceptions with Jia and her team. Maybe the reason why I don't find speaking about myself an interesting subject is because no one's ever bothered learning about it, which is why I stopped caring, too.

"Shahzad?"

I break out of my thoughts and take the first sip of the red wine. It's disgusting, but I'll need it as support. "Right. So, a year after my father and, uh, Maya—that's—"

"Yeah, I know who she is. It's kinda hard not to." Nyla takes her first bite and listens intently.

"After they immigrated from Islamabad to America, I was born. Well, technically not born *here*, in Koreatown. It was in a one-bedroom apartment in East Harlem. My abbu was working as an electrical engineer in construction—entry-level, so we didn't have much in our pockets or on our plates. Then, two years down the line, Zineerah was born, and we just couldn't afford to live in America. So, thanks to Azeer's family, we moved to Canada, and as my eleventh birthday present, I got another baby sister as a gift, Dua."

"Aw," Nyla coos.

"You wouldn't be saying that if you had to wake up every school night taking care of her little hungry ass."

"Still. Aw."

I roll my eyes, smiling. "Moving on. We lived in a decent-sized apartment—two bedrooms, one that my sisters and I shared and another for Abbu and Maya. It was hell on Earth, but thankfully I had Zineerah to handle Dua's needs."

"What was Maya doing? Sleeping?"

"Yeah. Pretty much. She didn't really give a shit about us."

"Then," Nyla drawls, brows wrinkled, "why did she want kids?"

"Well, the first time, she wanted a distraction from her arranged marriage, but I wasn't good enough. Second time was familial pressure on Abbu and Maya from both their families. Third time was, shockingly, Maya's decision."

"Really? Why?"

I put on a smile and rub my fingers together. "Canada Child Benefit."

Nyla scoffs. "Of course."

"But fast forward to when I was thirteen, Abbu got a job offer in New York that was impossible to not accept."

I smile at the memory of Zineerah and Sahara baking Abbu a congratulatory cake while Mustafa, Azeer, and I cooked a feast for the celebration. Dua, Maira, and Iman, Azeer's little sister, played in the living room. Maya had decided to visit her relatives in Islamabad that weekend, so thank fuck she wasn't there to sour the mood as she did on every birthday or special occasion, and Abbu was coming back from work to a surprise.

"Anyway, we moved to Hell's Kitchen," I say. "It didn't take a lot to convince Maya after Abbu had shown her the big apartment we'd be living in. It was bigger than the pictures. There was a playground nearby where Zineerah, Dua, and I would spend all our evenings playing with the other kids. I even got banned from the community center's pool for cannon-balling."

Nyla laughs. "Oh, my god. That *is* something little Shahzad would do."

I smile lopsidedly, shrugging. "I *was* a bit of a troublemaker. Always getting into petty fights like Tae, and then when I was home, I had to deal with Maya's bullshit."

Her smile unwinds for a second, then she tucks a loose strand behind her ear. "Go on."

Nodding, I continue. "I did my senior year at Theodore Roosevelt, as you saw at the basketball game, and a few months after I graduated . . . " I tongue the inside of my cheek when I realize I'm at *that* part of my story where I wish the words didn't exist. "Uh, after I graduated, Abbu passed away from an aneurysm."

Nyla's mouth parts, and she lowers her fork. "Shahzad, I'm so sorry."

"It's fine."

"You don't have to continue if you don't want to—"

"No, I do. I want to talk to you and tell you these things. I don't know why, but I just do."

Nyla carefully considers my words. She lays her palm outward on the table. "You can hold it whenever you need to take a rest."

I stare at the softness of her skin, the three deep creases, and the smaller lines running across the surface. "Maya didn't show up to his funeral, but she did at the will reading." My fingers clench into a tight fist as I recall holding both my sobbing sisters' hands, with Azeer, Sahara, Mustafa, and Maira spending the next couple of hours in the graveyard with us until we were told it was time to go home.

But I came back the next day. And the day after. For weeks and months, sometimes with my sisters, sometimes alone. Just telling him stories about Zineerah singing their favorite songs in coffee shops or how Dua joined the girls' volleyball team. I'd even mentioned Maya's well-being in passing.

"At twenty, I decided I wanted to put my culinary talent to the test," I say. "I waited until Zineerah turned eighteen, and with the help of the Khan family, I had my sisters move back to Toronto. I permanently cut ties with Maya and took a one-way ticket to Switzerland, and spent two years busting my ass in fine-dining restaurants as a waiter. I lived in a shitty hostel with three roommates of all ages. One of the most skilled chefs I worked with, Chef Solomon, who could remove meat from a lobster in under five minutes, wrote me a letter of recommendation to a prestigious culinary school, and with a scholarship that cut my tuition in half, I was a student for a whole year."

Nyla takes a sip of her drink and smiles wide. "Were you the best?"

"Looking back on it, I was decent than most applicants. Working in different kitchens or food trucks since I was sixteen diversified my skill set. Sometimes I'd even cook without any measurements and still get away with a great grade."

"You do that now, too, and it's safe to say"—she holds up her plate—"it works flawlessly."

"Yet, you haven't eaten more than two bites."

"Hey, hey. I'm a slow eater, okay?" She squints an eye at me and takes a bite as if I offended her. Maybe I did. I don't know.

"Sorry," I say.

"Don't be."

I eye her hand on the table because the next part is just as bad as Abbu's passing. My fingers spread out, inches away from her rosy fingertips. "I got an apprenticeship at a three-star restaurant in France after I graduated in the high ranks. I was bat-shit drunk at the graduation party and missed a bunch of calls from Dua." I barely graze her middle finger, but the touch sends an electric shock through me. "Zineerah was in the hospital because of a boyfriend I never knew about." I take Nyla's hand without looking at her, and she squeezes hard. "I . . . *fuck*."

"It's okay. We'll stop here for tonight."

"No, I just—I wasn't—" I put down my fork and cover my eyes with my free hand, rubbing the top of my face back and forth. "At that moment, I didn't even care about the apprenticeship anymore. I dropped everything and took a flight back to Toronto the next day. For two years, I worked patiently with Zineerah's recovery and spent every second with my sisters. On the side, I was getting my license in security and thanks to Azeer, again, I started working at Sun Tower Hotel."

Nyla brushes her thumb back and forth over my knuckles and places her second hand over mine.

I run my fingers through my hair and take a larger gulp of the red wine. "Uh, I think Azeer noticed how miserable I looked working as a nightguard and offered to help me find a job in a fine-dining restaurant, but I was just . . . I was exhausted. I had fallen out of love with everything I loved doing. It was just all about the money now and supporting my sisters." My chest tightens at another reminder of the deal with Abe, at how I'm holding his daughter's hand, the woman I sold off without her knowing. "Long story short, Azeer pulled some strings, and I moved to New York to work . . . for your father."

She tries at a smile. "Mm-hmm."

"It paid well. I was educated enough in the role to lead a team of rookies. I think at that point in my life, it was all a means to an end. Whatever I earned went towards my sisters, and whatever was left of it was in my savings or for Sky after I adopted her. When I quit, I had a little remaining to get this apartment. Jia gives me an employee discount on my rent because I work for her. "

"That's sweet of her." Nyla's grip loosens on my hand. "Can I ask you another question? You don't have to answer this if you don't want to."

"No, ask me. What is it?"

"Did you . . . Did you quit because of what happened between us that night or because of something else entirely?"

I look at her and immediately understand the answer she wants. "I quit because of what happened. And it was my fault."

"It wasn't—"

"It was, Nyla. I was supposed to be your bodyguard that night and the day after. I mixed my personal feelings with my professional—"

"We were drunk, Shahzad. We were stupidly drunk, and we *both* mixed personal feelings with our professional. But I remember it was a mutual, consensual hook-up. Wouldn't you agree?"

I smile. "I do."

"And it was fun."

"It was." It *really* was.

"And we should probably never drink in close proximity again." She creates a distance between her dinner plate and mug, and I follow. "Thank you for sharing your life with me, Shahzad. I always knew you were a great guy." I shouldn't have signed that contract. *You needed the money for Dua's education.* "But I didn't know you were such a great son. A great brother." I shouldn't have signed that contract. *You needed the money for Dua's education.* "And a great, *great* friend. You're also a decent fake boyfriend, I guess." I shouldn't have *negotiated* with that conniving son of a bitch in the first place. *You. Needed. The. Money. For. Dua's. Education.* "I want to tell you something, too."

I swallow hard. "Yes?"

Nyla chews her bottom lip and holds my hand tightly. "Well, since we're being vulnerable with one another . . ." She scoots her chair closer and searches the scratches on the table before speaking. "I like you, Shahzad."

I don't think I heard her correctly. "What?"

"I like you," she mumbles. "Like, *like*-like you. Not as your fake girlfriend— Well, no, I like you as your fake girlfriend, but I also like you in reality. As Nyla. Kinda like how Tae likes Hye-jin, but not, like, I'd stalk you or something."

My heart's beating fast. It's never willingly beaten for a woman before. Only once. Only with her. Now, it's only *for* her.

And I don't know how to feel or what to do about it.

"I really like how encouraging and hardworking you are," she whispers, inhaling deeply. "I like that you don't judge me for everything that's happened. I like that you've given me a space to follow my ambition. I like that you're in my past, in my present, and . . . I'd like you in my future, too. If you want. Even as friends. No pressure."

In stillness, I think carefully about my response. Nothing arrives as she continues speaking.

"It's okay if you don't feel the same way about me. I know we're supposed to be pretending or whatever, but in private, I want you to know I'm not. I've liked you since last year, and I thought those feelings were buried by the weight of my humiliation, but seeing you again brought them to life." She chuckles in disbelief. "Honestly, I don't know what it is about you that makes me feel so alive."

Goosebumps prickle on my skin as she continues to run her thumb over the back of my hand. I fight the temptation to gaze into her eyes, scared I might say something she doesn't want to hear.

"But be warned, I'll purposely leave one of my pink sweaters here when I leave," she teases with a giggle. "You can donate it when you get a girlfriend or use it to wipe down your kitchen counters. Maybe you'll keep me in the back of your closet." She fades into a smile. "I'll always keep you in the back of my mind." Her eyes resemble fresh grass touched with dewdrops—curiously wide with lashes drawing low to my lips in a state of intoxication.

A storm stirs within me, pulsating through my trembling chest and numbed body. My fingertips quiver with anticipation to hold her, every inch of me ablaze with warmth because of her presence.

"Nyla..."

"It's okay," she whispers. "I think the wine kicked in earlier than I expected." Her hands leave mine, and I find myself reaching forward to grab them but ultimately surrender so she can *finally* eat. "Seriously, dude. You need to open your own restaurant."

I chuckle weakly. "It's on the back burner."

"Well, you know what happens when you leave something to cook for too long," she says, biting the chicken off the fork and pointing it at me. "You're a chef, Shahzad. And a damn good one at that. Remember the words of your favorite fashion designer the next time you visit the back burner."

"I will."

"Good." She smiles, and I do my best to mirror it. "Now, tell me how you and Sky first met."

18

Mr. Chewy

Nyla

As Maira delicately curls her short, dark-brown locks, I take a moment to make some final adjustments to her dress.

The gown, a navy-blue satin creation, boasts long sleeves that gracefully cinch at the wrist and a modest square neckline. Its corset-like bodice accentuates her petite waist, while the skirt flows down to the tips of her toes in almost a silky, running water texture, catching the light with every subtle movement.

Incredible how my first *official* design has transformed into a flawless success. Maybe it's a result of channeling all my time and energy into my projects, a needed distraction from the awkward confession to Shahzad just two nights ago.

He, too, has immersed himself in managing the kitchen staff alongside Bao. Our paths cross occasionally when he stops by the washing area to drop off dishes, but our interactions are to small check-ins and polite smiles. At home, he's focused on refining new menu items to propose to Jia with his back to me while I stick to my design corner. Sometimes, he'll call me over to taste test to get my opinion, and I'd be as critical as I possibly can.

Right now, Sky's hanging out in the kitchen with Shahzad, probably asking for some extra ham or bits of basil. She's really into basil these days.

"Done." Maira unplugs the curling iron and puts it down to cool. She runs her fingers through her hair, giving the curls a salon blow-out look, and flashes a dazzling smile. "How do I look?"

I meet her eyes in the bathroom mirror. "Extraordinary, love."

"If you say so." She reapplies a neutral brown shade of lipstick and fluffs up her curls a bit more. Her phone pings with a text message notification, and her eyes light up at the name on the screen.

I raise a brow, adjusting the zipper. "Who's Zaviyaar?"

"A friend," she mutters, typing out a quick text.

I notice a pink hue warming her high cheekbones. Amusement curls at my lips. "Do you like this friend?"

She stammers or chuckles, a mix of both—a truth she can't find in herself to deny. "That's the most disgusting thing you could ever say to me, Alyn. It's insulting. Zaviyaar—he's—I've known him since I was ten. Mustafa and Shahzad are some of his closest biking buddies. They practically adopted a prep-school kid when they were in high school."

"Oh?" I adjust her neckline. "Does your brother also enjoy biking?"

"He used to before our dad passed away. After that, he had to take on the household responsibilities that our mom couldn't manage alone. He was pretty good at it, but he never saw it as a career like Zaviyaar or a hobby like Shahzad. He just did it because it brought him joy." Maira picks up her earrings from the sink's edge. "Now he's got a lovely fiancée taking up his time. You know, priorities."

Priorities.

That's what I need to figure out. How long can I hold onto this school-girl crush instead of concentrating on my new career in design, rebuilding myself from the fire I was burned in? If I set my priorities in stone, I won't have to hide in the shadows any longer. I'll hash out a plan for my designs, maybe a small fashion line, dabble in a little research and development, and then present it to potential investors.

Oh, maybe I should start by renting the workspace I've been eyeing online in SoHo.

And maybe . . . I'll be able to move on from said school-girl crush? Yes, that's a question in the air for now.

"Are you okay?" Maira asks, brushing my bangs out of my eyes. "You've been quiet lately. Did something happen between you and Shahzad?"

"No, we're fine. I think I'm just a bit under the weather from working so hard. Who knew Jia was *this* popular?" I laugh off my nerves and pack up my sewing kit.

Maira shrugs and picks up her powder brush. "You can always talk to me, you know? Can't promise I'll offer much, but I can at least listen."

I've been pondering a question lingering in the recesses of my mind. "What was Shahzad like during your time in Toronto?"

Maira lets out a chuckle. "He was a tough-as-nails trickster who practically lived at our place. Of course, a lot of that had to do with his family's circumstances. He played the roles of both provider and caretaker, ensuring that Mustafa and I enjoyed good meals when our parents were caught up with work. At the same time, he took care of his own sisters. He'd go to great lengths for those two. Even now, with Dua's tuition challenges, he's putting in extra hours to cover the costs, not to mention dealing with Zineerah's medical bills . . . " She lets out a sigh. "Shahzad has always been our pillar of support, someone to lean on or shed tears with. But now, it's his turn, and you're the best thing that has ever happened to him, Alyn."

I force a smile. "Thanks, Mai. I'll keep doing the best I can to support him."

"Girlfriend of the century." Maira's phone chimes with another notification. "My ride's here."

I trail behind her as we leave the bathroom.

"Who's picking you up, kid?" Shahzad asks, turning around from his culinary work. "You look beautiful, by the way."

"Becca and Lori. We're in a project together, and it turns out they used to smell paint fumes and eat kinetic sand as children, too." She grabs her little satchel. "Trauma bonding forms great friendships."

Shahzad sighs and wipes his hands on the kitchen towel hanging from his broad shoulder. "I expect you back at ten sharp. Keep your lo—"

"Location on. Phone off silent. And use my pepper spray if I notice a creep. I know, *Baba*." She sticks out her tongue at him and heads to the alcove, lowering herself to wear her heels.

"Stop, stop. I've got it. The stitching is still a bit delicate." I take her silver strappy heels and crouch down to secure them on each foot. After fixing the hem of her dress, I stand and adjust the shawl around her shoulders.

"You'll make a great mother one day," Maira whispers, surprising me with a hug and a gentle kiss on my cheek. "I'll be back home soon."

I nod, a smile on my face. "Location and ringer on."

"Goodnight, Mama." She steps out, and I watch her until she's safely inside the elevator before locking the door.

Shahzad is already at the window, and together we observe as Maira enters a rented

FAKE IT TILL WE MAKE IT

limousine two minutes later. A red-haired girl pops up from the sunroof, letting out a cheerful "*WOO-HOO!*" as the limousine drives off.

A wave of nostalgia washes over me, morphing my lips into a grin. Amongst my so-called circle of friends, *I* was the sunroof girl. The lectures I heard from Baba the following morning about the repercussions of partying wild weren't pretty, but god, if those weren't the best nights of my life.

Sky barks, and I snap my head up only to meet Shahzad's eyes before he dashes towards the kitchen, where a pot threatens to overflow. A string of curses leaves him as he frantically wipes the stove and counter, activating the ventilator above.

"*Fuck!*" He growls, fanning his hand rapidly and dunking it under the cold sink water. Responding to the racket, I hurry over, gasping at the fiery red burn on the back of his hand. Sky's persistent barking adds to the chaotic environment. The noise from the ventilation only serves to heighten his already limited patience. "Sky, stay out of the fucking kitchen!"

I reel from his outburst, my back hitting the counter.

Innocent Sky whimpers and pulls back to the living room, seeking consolation on the couch.

A surge of anger torches within me.

I switch his stupid pan to a non-lit burner, ignoring his protests about the "temperature" or something, and turn the damn ventilator off. "Apologize to her."

Shahzad's eyes bore holes into my face, *both* his hands shaking.

"Apologize to Sky!" I command, pointing at Sky's guiltless face. "*Now*, Shahzad."

He turns off the faucet and wraps a towel around his burn, still clenching his stupid, chiseled jaw. Sky remains silent when he whistles. "I'm sorry, honey."

"Go to her." I push his back. He whirls around, but I stand my ground, draped in his shadow. God, he's such a Neanderthal. "*Make* her know you're sorry, jerk."

The black depths of his gaze flare bright and briefly set my lips on fire. I feel my protective resolve crumbling, but *no. You can't crumble. You won't.* He's in the wrong, and I'll be damned if I apologize for raising my voice at him.

He enters the living room with a slight scowl and plops down on the carpet. Sky turns away from him. She's so humane and intelligent—it makes me love her more.

"I'm sorry, honey," he says, placing his good hand on her back. Surprisingly, she doesn't growl or snap at him. "Sweetheart, I'm sorry."

I cross my arms. "You can do better."

Shahzad shoots me a dirty look and then breathes out a smile directed at his husky.

"Wanna go for a walk?"

Her ears twitch in interest.

"We can go to your favorite park with Mr. Chewy." Shahzad rises, picking up her precious, worn-out teddy bear, a victim of her eager chewing. "And we can get him a friend from the pet store. You can even meet Cookie there."

I don't know who this Cookie is, but one drop of its name and Sky perks up, wagging her tail. She lifts her head and barks. *Glad you're back, girl.*

Shahzad opens his arms, allowing her to initiate by resting her neck on his shoulder. He lifts her into his arms, showering her head with kisses. I think I shed a tear or two. There's just something about attractive men and adorable animals that tugs at my heartstrings, you know?

"Give me ten minutes, and we'll head out. Okay, honey?" He sets her down, and she affectionately licks the burn on his hand, whining. "I know, sweetie. I'll get that checked out, too."

Concerned about the burn, I offer my help. "Do you need me to clean that for you?"

"I've got it. Just get her leashed up. Please." He heads to the bathroom, closing the door behind him. It seems that his devotion and patience are exclusively reserved for Sky.

"Come here, girl," I call her over by patting my legs and clipping the leash around her collar.

By the time Shahzad's out of the bathroom, I'm already in loose jeans and a pinkish-gray printed sweatshirt.

"Here." Shahzad hands me his Yankees cap and a huge bomber jacket that practically swallows me whole.

Finally stepping out of the apartment complex, I take a deep breath. However, my moment of relaxation is short-lived as Shahzad grabs my hand, fingers intertwining. His expression is grave, eyes surveying the faces around us.

Oh, right. He's in bodyguard mode. Duh. That explains the hand-holding, but his thumb brushing over my knuckles?

You're overthinking.

Am I, though?

Yeah. You are. You're touch-starved.

I am.

Before a shoulder can bump into me, Shahzad pulls me in, shooting a rough look at the unsuspecting person. He quietly mutters, "Asshole," keeping a thin distance between us.

But hey, who am I to complain? In fact, let me take our little hand-holding up a notch. I loop my right arm around his bicep, sensing a slight muscle flex. A smile tugs at my lips. *Show-off*. Or maybe he's tense. Oh no, what if he's uncomfortable?

I try to pull away, but he uses his gauze-wrapped hand to keep my arm around him. *Phew*.

Glad to know he's okay with it. It almost feels like we're a committed couple strolling with our dog, creating the illusion of one big happy family. And to add to my delusions, our daughter, Maira, is hanging out with friends, giving us some alone time.

God, Nyla. Seek serious help, girl.

At the dog park, not too far from Koreatown, Shahzad quickly catches the attention of a group of ladies with their Pomeranians and purse-sized pooches.

After giving Sky some hushed instructions, he lets her roam freely, and we sit on a hill to observe as she enthusiastically jumps around the pre-set obstacle courses with the other dogs.

"Good to see you again, Shahz," says a petite brunette with a fair, slender face that seems to carry an air of grace. Her glossy, chestnut hair cascades down in perfect waves, framing her features like a carefully crafted painting. The overpriced workout gear clings to her figure in all the right places, accentuating the toned physique made from the world of personal trainers and exclusive fitness clubs. "Haven't seen you at the gym much lately."

I discreetly glance at Shahzad, noticing him sighing and forcing a smile in her direction. "Membership got costly," he explains.

"Oh, that's a shame," she coos, hands resting on her shapely hips. She's undeniably beautiful, but it irks me that she hasn't bothered to introduce herself to me. Do I not look like Shahzad's girlfriend? Is it the pink hair? "Well, you still look in great shape, so I won't complain too much about missing my favorite gym buddy."

The soft glow of the golden hour highlights the burnt umber strands in Shahzad's hair as he runs his fingers through them. Is he *seriously* flirting with her right now? Because that's a universal flirting gesture. Right?

"Thanks, Cass." *Cass*. They're on a nickname basis. They've definitely fucked. "How's everything going? Is your mom doing well?" He knows her *mom*? What, did she bring him over for Thanksgiving or something? Or worse, Christmas? Maybe they celebrated his birthday, which is fourteen days before Christmas. A double whammy.

"Funny you ask. We were reminiscing about how fun our Cancun trip was last year." *Last year.* Last year, when? When he abandoned me at the hotel after screwing me for hours? Or when he handed his resignation in and disappeared a week later? Probably just to go to Cancun with Cassidy? I'm sorry, I meant *Cass.*

Shahzad clears his throat. "It was."

Oh, they *did* fuck.

Sky, being the perfect timing expert, waltzes in with Mr. Chewy and plops him right at our feet.

Cass gasps. "Well, hello, Sky—"

Sky barks at her, causing Cass to stumble back with a yelp. *Good girl, Sky!*

Shahzad gives a sharp whistle, snapping his fingers at her. I push his hand away before calling my husky in for a hug. She licks my cheek and nudges her snout against my jaw.

"She's gotten . . . big." Cass composes herself with a skittish chuckle, straightening the creases from her jacket. *Polyester doesn't wrinkle, Cass.*

"Sorry about that," I pipe in with a high-pitched tone. "She doesn't take well to strangers. Isn't that right, honey?" I cradle Sky's delighted face and scratch her furry cheeks.

"Right . . ." Cass checks her watch. "Well, I better get going, then. But let's do dinner soon, yeah?"

"Mm-hmm," Shahzad hums.

I roll my eyes. *Mm-hmm*, my ass.

She waves bye to him, gives a disapproving look to Sky, then jogs her adorable bubble butt away.

I double-glance at Shahzad, who's watching me with a mirthful smile. "'*Oh, Shahz. Our trip to Cancun was super fun last year!*'" I mock her snotty voice and flail my hands around. "'*Oh, you're so fit and pretty, and I miss my favorite big, buff gym buddy!*' Give me a break. She doesn't need a gym buddy! She looks perfectly fine with her sculpted glutes and steel-hard kneecaps."

Sky huffs, dropping Mr. Chewy at my feet again. The stuffed animal is soggy and clammy, much like the look Cass gave Shahzad.

"We were *strictly* gym buddies," he insists.

I roll my eyes back to the expanse of the park. "If 'gym buddies' is the newly coined term for 'fuck buddies,' then I believe that's exactly what you two were."

He lets out a big sigh, grabbing Mr. Chewy and swinging him towards the obstacle course. "I don't see the reason behind your jealousy, if I'm honest."

"Oh, I'm sure you are." I pick at the grass. "Like, Cancun? Seriously? It's not the place to screw around with someone, trust me. Maybe Santorini. Even Iceland is a better option. And Italy takes the cake."

He raises an eyebrow. "You do realize you sound pretty hypocritical, right?"

"Whatever." I bump my sunglasses up my nose, shaking my head and feeling squirmish. "Did you meet her mom?"

"Why do you care?" He's watching Sky play with a lazy smile on his mouth.

"I just wanna know."

"Why?"

"What do you mean 'why'? I'm only curious."

"I don't see how it concerns you, Troublemaker."

"Fine. Whatever." I go back to picking at the grass and braiding stems into a flower crown for Sky. Alina and I used to make these when we played princesses, and we'd make some extra for our mothers. Mama preferred little flowers, but she settled for grass over her head because I didn't like plucking them from their roots.

I wonder if Cass and her mom get along well. They must, considering she talks about Shahzad to her. I don't even think I can talk about *my* mom without breaking into a million shards and endless tears.

Finishing the crown, I squint in the sunlight. "Sky!" I call, and she rushes over with Mr. Chewy.

"Good girl," Shahzad praises her, taking the toy, and I crown her with the finished product.

"Pretty girl," I whisper.

Her tail wiggles with joy, the crown bobbing up and down on her head.

"Is it okay if I can take a picture?" Shahzad asks, putting his phone on silent and taking a test picture.

My heart joyously vibrates from his gesture. "Of course." I throw my arm around Sky's neck and press my cheek against hers, smiling ear-to-ear. "Say, Mr. Chewy!"

Sky barks.

He captures the moment and smiles warmly at the image of me and Sky now preserved in his camera roll. "Should we go meet Cookie now?"

19

Cookie

Shahzad

"Cookie is a parrot?"

Nyla's puzzled gaze is focused on the cockatoo of Pets-A-Lot, perched on Sky's back as she roams around the dog food aisles.

"Technically a cockatoo," I correct.

"Oh, sorry," she mumbles. "It's kinda cute how she's best friends with a cockatoo. He's so adorable!"

"Cookie is a she."

"Oh!" She laughs in surprise. "I'm sorry."

"Don't be. I found out the gender from one of the store employees." I grab a basket and toss in a couple of Sky's favorite treats.

"How'd she meet you both?"

I stifle a chuckle as Nyla takes a whiff of one of the beef chew sticks, suppressing a gag behind her clenched fist. "Cookie was just a baby when she ended up crash-landing on my balcony." I take the stick and place it in the basket.

Her brows arch up. "What? How did a *cockatoo* crash-land on your balcony?"

"We didn't know where she came from, but Sky, who was only a puppy then, took a liking to her easily." I trail behind the delighted pair, earning "awes" from the customers and familiar workers. "Anyways, we rescued feather-face and learned that she loved eating cookies, hence—"

"Cookie," she interrupts. "Sorry. Go on."

"Don't be." I grin at the twinkle in her emerald eyes. "We couldn't keep Cookie because I didn't know how to care of a bird. Plus, they fly all over the house and shit everywhere. Sky was enough to keep me company."

"So you brought her here? This doesn't exactly look like an animal shelter to me."

"Pets-A-Lot works as a third party with local shelters to get the animals visible for adoption."

"That's so sweet—oh. My. *God*!" Nyla inhales sharply and bolts towards the enclosures holding rescued puppies behind a wide glass pane. This is the happiest I've ever seen her. She's skipping on the tips of her toes, hands pressed against the window, squealing for her life. "Oh my god, oh my god, oh my god. Look at the little one yawn, Shahzad!"

"That's the tiniest pug I've ever seen," I mutter, eyeing the small guy nestled in his oversized gray cushion with a blanket decorated with dump trucks. He lets out another yawn, prompting another squeal from his pink-haired admirer, before dozing off again.

"Rescued him last night," a friendly voice from behind says. Harriet strides away from the doorway she was leaning on to shake my hand. She's the one who had my back with Sky's adoption process, her food schedule, and playtoys. I even stepped up to volunteer for a few more local rescues. "You've never brought a girl here before."

I follow her gaze to a dumbstruck Nyla, stuck to the wall like a fruit fly, totally smitten with the pug. "She's a . . . friend."

Harriet shoots me a look that's calling me out on my bullshit. Honestly, I'm not entirely clear on what Nyla means to me. Am I attracted to her? Undoubtedly. Would I like to be friends with her? Sure. Friends with benefits? That's not something I can do to her. For now, she's just Nyla to me. Or Alyn to our friends.

"Interested, Shahzad's *friend*?" Harriet asks, slapping me in the face with humiliation. She opens the door and heads to the puppy's cage. Lifting the pug, she deposits him into Nyla's gentle hands. "Popcorn was born under extreme conditions, hence his state. He's the runt of the litter. But with a little love and nourishment, he'll grow into a big boy in no time."

Nyla sighs, carefully stroking from the top of his head to the tip of his little tail. "He's *so* adorable." She wipes the ends of her eyes. Is she *seriously* crying over the little puppy? "Sorry, I get really teary-eyed over cute things. And Popcorn is so—" A sniffle. "Cute."

Jesus, this woman and her heartbreaking dramatics.

"Would you be interested in giving him a home?" Harriet's throwing me quick glances as she poses the question to her. "Give Sky a friend? A little brother? I'm sure she could use the company in that apartment. Perhaps Shahzad could, too?"

I shake my head at Harriet's subliminal messages. "We don't have space. Isn't that right, Alyn?"

Nyla's wet, green eyes dart towards mine, growing to ten times their regular intensity. In an instant, the pet shop closes in around me, drowning out all the background noise and colors. "We don't?"

"We—" I gotta shut my eyes tight and shift my focus elsewhere. Otherwise, she's gonna drag me into her emotionally manipulating vortex. "We don't have space, and we don't have funds for a puppy either."

"You're right." Nyla surrenders with a sigh. Shoulders slumped, she turns to Harriet, giving the pug one last hug by pressing her cheek to his back. "Please give Popcorn the safest, happiest home in this world for me."

Harriet takes him and gives her back a few comforting pats.

"Go check on Sky, please," I tell Nyla. She's in autopilot mode, gaze fixed on Popcorn, dragging her feet forward.

Harriet locks up the cage. "If you don't propose to that girl with Popcorn, I'm banning you from entering my store."

"You're joking?"

"Am I laughing?"

No, she's not.

"Harriet, we're only friends. She's just crashing with me for a couple of weeks." I spy Nyla at the front cash, with Cookie casually perched on her shoulder. My troublemaker doesn't show a hint of concern. She's squeak-testing out the toys for Sky, sporting that *very* bright, blooming smile. *God, she's beautiful.*

"Friends, my ass," Harriet mutters. "Friends, Shahzad, don't look at each other the way you're looking at her."

I rake my fingers through my hair, a nervous habit that'll turn me into the poster boy for male pattern baldness if I don't quit. "And how exactly do I look at my friend, Harriet?"

She folds her arms and sizes me up. "Like you've been resurrected. You look at her with veracious, infinite happiness. And son, it'll damage you whole if you don't plan on doing something 'bout it soon." She gives my back a couple of hearty pats before striding back into the staff room.

Biting down on my lower lip, I rub away at the heavy burden on my chest, eyeing the dozing pug.

Stay rational, Shahzad. A puppy isn't in the cards. Not when you're going to send her back to Abe by the end of the month. She won't have time to care for it once she's busy. Be responsible, stash those bucks for smarter moves down the road.

Rationality wins once again.

"So, where's Nyx?" Nyla asks through a mouthful of strawberry-chocolate crêpe.

"At one of my cousin's residence buildings."

"You have a cousin here?"

"No, she's in Europe at the moment."

"Cool. What's she doing in Europe?"

I pause in the middle of devouring my fish taco, raising a brow at her evident case of clinical curiosity. Maybe she's genuinely trying to understand me because, well, she likes me. "She's the Chief of Marketing at Sun Tower Hotel in London."

Nyla's eyes pop open. "Wait— Sahara Khan, right?"

"You know her?"

She nods excitedly. "She's Azeer's adopted sister, isn't she? And we met at an after party that took place at Sun Tower in Europe. Briefly, though. But she seems very hospitable. Which makes total sense because she works in hospitality." A slice of strawberry slips from her crêpe and lands on her lap. She offers it to Sky, who's sitting by her feet, tongue sticking out at the sight of my taco.

We lounge on a bench in Madison Square Park, observing the lights of a nearby apartment building twinkle to life as half of the moon hides behind it.

"Are you and Sahara close?" Nyla asks.

"She's practically my third sister." I wipe the splotch of chocolate on her lip, then lick my thumb clean. "Azeer isn't the person she'd go to for advice. But then again, who would?"

Her pink cheeks flush as a sweet giggle escapes her. "He is a bit of a grump."

"Yeah, well, he was the fucking Grinch before he met Alina. Don't get me wrong, I love the guy like an older brother, but we're like oil and water. He was—*is*—studious and polished, and I was more rebellious and rugged. He likes an orderly system; I like creative chaos. Well, I *liked* creative chaos." I stare at my fish taco, stuffing the shredded lettuce back in its place. "But as you grow out of those childish habits, you realize that society functions according to a system. Hell, I work at a restaurant. I take *and* work on orders each day, trying to keep that system in check."

"Hmm." Nyla chews thoughtfully. "Can I tell you something, though?"

"Always."

"I'm proud of you for getting where you are today, Shahzad. For what it's worth, every stepping stone that's brought you here is remarkable. Even if you tripped and fell between the cracks now and then. What matters is that you're here, chaotically creative, and pursuing what you love." She seeks out my hand and gives it a reassuring, tight squeeze, causing my chest to constrict. "I've always seen myself as a soldier, never the commander. I thought I was. Closing high-paying runway shows, booking Vogue's September issues, even meeting Beyoncé— It always felt like I was the girl that . . . everyone wanted to be.

"Unfortunately, I was the girl that my father wanted me to be. From Dad to a dictator, his influence transformed me, turning me into a beautiful, obedient follower of his strict system and rules. And I went to war for him. Over and over again. Up and center at the frontlines. Hit after hit after hit until the pain became unbearable." A slight tension grips her jaw as she tucks a delicate strand of her pink hair behind her ear. "And I lost."

A sudden prickliness catches in my throat. With hesitation, my hand gently rests on her back. "Within your loss, Nyla, you gained a victory."

"And what might that be, Chef?"

"You, Troublemaker," I murmur softly. "Not Nyla Ghilzai, the highest-paid model in the universe, or the phenomenal rising actress in Hollywood, but simply you. Just Nyla." My hand deliberately glides up to the nape of her neck. "Nyla, the one who dyed her hair pink because it's her favorite color. Nyla, who finds joy in the scent of fabric softener and the sounds of water splashing in the washing machine. Nyla, whose excitement spills over into a river of tears. Nyla, who apologizes like it's her first language, despite my constant warnings against it."

My hand gently cups her left cheek, and suddenly, I'm controlling my actions, my continuous stream of words. "Nyla, who sees her perfections as imperfections. Nyla, who needs to believe that all her imperfections are fucking perfect to me."

For once, my brain is pin-drop quiet.

And the only thing I hear is the sound of her breaths matching the vicious pace of my heartbeat.

"Thanks for always listening to me, Shahzad," she murmurs, shying her eyes away from mine and onto her crêpe.

"Always." I gaze into the city lights, observing the ebb and flow of people, with apartment lights blinking on and off in the background. "What's one thing you've regretted not doing?"

"Oh." Nyla ponders, twisting her lips thoughtfully. "Grocery shopping."

I raise a brow. "Grocery shopping?"

"Yes. I've never been grocery shopping, let alone step into a grocery store. I don't know how to bag vegetables or fruits. I've never wheeled a shopping cart before or felt that warm gust of air when you walk in." She takes tiny bites of her dessert, smiling solemnly. A smile that doesn't sit right with me. "I sound stupidly privileged, don't I?"

I shove the final bite of my taco into my mouth, crumple the wrapper, and rise to my feet. "Let's go."

"Huh? Where?"

"To the grocery store." I grasp her hand, coaxing her to stand alongside me. "We're going grocery shopping."

"Right now? What about Sky?"

"We'll drop her off at home with her new toys and treats."

"Are you sure?"

"Absolutely, Troublemaker. I'll show you how to bag produce, read expiration dates, and maybe we can grab some snacks for a movie tonight or something."

Nyla's brows crinkle with concern. "You just did grocery shopping two days ago. Are you sure you want to spend money on more groceries?"

"For you?" I chuckle, holding her by the shoulders. "Absolutely."

"Shahzad."

"Nyla."

She dissolves into a sweet smile, catching my soul off guard. "Fine. Take me grocery shopping, Chef."

20

Grocery Shopping

Nyla

"Step one, Troublemaker." Shahzad inserts a quarter from his pocket into the cart's lock system. "Step two." He yanks back the chain and releases the shopping cart with a proud grin on his face. "All yours."

"What's the point of that?"

"Fuck if I know. America?"

Chuckling, I wrap my fingers around the cart's plastic handle and wheel it forward. "Woah. It's like walking Sky. If she was a metal, creaky trolley."

"Trolley." He snorts. "Did you have one too many martinis with the Royal Family?"

I smack his back, scoffing a chuckle. "I'll have you know that the Royal Family doesn't indulge in martinis. I've only ever had them with Meghan and Harry."

"Who's that?"

"Prince Harry? Meghan Markle? Oh my god, Shahzad. You lived in Canada! How do you *not* know?" I cover my gasp with my hand. "Do you at least know that the Queen is dead?"

"Why would I care about the Royal Family? I live in America now."

My body goes rigid as Shahzad's hand gently rests on the small of my back, guiding me into the store. The welcoming warmth fans against my face as I step inside, immediately met by the scent of fresh produce and the almost blinding glow of fluorescent lights.

"It's beautiful," I whisper, feeling like an alien experiencing Earth for the very first time, discovering where humans stash their basic supplies.

Shahzad leads us toward the fruits and vegetables aisle. "Tear that apart."

I shoot him a defiant look.

"Please," he adds.

I grab one of the loosely hanging, translucent bags from the roll. Shahzad does the same to demonstrate. "Now what?"

"These things can be a bit tricky. All you need to do is rub the center of the bag and create some friction until you find an opening to separate it. Exhibit A." He follows through, warming the bag between his fingers until a tiny opening appears, which he then splits open. "Your turn."

Rub. Friction. Open sesame.

"Great job," he praises, gently patting my cheek. *Oh my.* I flutter my hand in front of my warm face as he twirls around to grab some broccoli.

"Pick and choose whatever doesn't have plans of growing fungi on it in the next couple of weeks."

"Got it."

Our cart is soon filled with green apples, fresh baskets of strawberries, coriander, and romaine lettuce. As we wander to the dairy aisle, Shahzad lectures me on expiration dates, using a crate of omega-3 eggs.

"Since today's June sixteenth, ideally, we'd want something with a shelf life extending into the first week of July."

"Knowing you, this crate will be finished in three days, Rocky Balboa."

"Guilty." He picks up two crates. "Problem solved."

I share a laugh with him and stamp a friendly smack on his back. "What's next?"

"Snacks?"

"The key to seducing me."

Shahzad rolls his eyes, lips lifting high. He slips his fingers through mine and steers the cart with one hand, allowing me to choose our movie snacks. "What are we watching, by the way?"

"On the count of three. Ready?"

"Ready."

"One, two, three—"

I say, "Thriller," in unison with his "Comedy."

"A comedic thriller?" I suggest dropping a box of extra-butter popcorn and grabbing two bags of chips. "Pizza flavor or jalapeño?"

"Anyone who directs a comedic thriller wasn't loved as a child," Shahzad mutters, reading the ingredient list of some almond bar. "Jalapeño, please."

I'm mesmerized by his side profile. A pointed nose with a subtle crook along the bridge. Long, dark lashes that gracefully fan his cheeks with each blink. His soft, pink lips draw my focus every time he speaks, framed by a thick, impeccably kept beard. "You're pretty."

"Hmm?"

"You're pretty." I trace a finger around my face. "Your face. It's pretty. Beautiful. Or handsome. Whichever one you prefer. I'm trying to say that you're pleasant to gaze at."

Slowly, a smile forms on his lips. He places the almond bar in the cart and tugs my hood down, blocking my view of his face.

"Hey, what the hell?"

"I don't want you seeing me blush."

I swat his hand away and lift my hood again, readjusting my hair and framed glasses. Indeed, he's blushing. When our eyes meet, there is a faint pink hue on his cheeks and a shy flutter in his lashes. "Has no one ever complimented you before?"

He shrugs. "No one's called me pretty."

"Oh, yeah? And what have they called you?"

His left eye squints in thought. "Hot? Sexy? Buff? Delicious?"

Okay, fair.

"But I like pretty."

"Pretty, it is." I press my lips together and grip the cart handles, sandwiched between his arms as we move together, pushing the cart ahead.

"What other snacks would you like, Troublemaker?" he asks.

"I don't like most of these."

"Why not?"

"Trigger foods."

We stop—well, *he* stops—wheeling the cart. He tilts his head as if intending to say something to me. However, he remains silent.

"It's okay," I mutter. "It's mostly the scent that triggers it. Plus, I know which ones I like to eat."

Shahzad studies me for an extra minute, then grins, leading us away from the aisle. We stroll in silence, the warmth of his chest embracing my back. When he pauses to grab a box of spice or a can of soup, he rests his chin on the crown of my head, quietly reciting the ingredients to himself.

I'm thankful for his lack of questions and advice on my past eating habits. Instead, he asks me what I like to eat or what I've always wanted to eat. He believes that sharing intriguing facts about the history of specific spices will distract my attention from his genuine concern, but I'm aware of it. I'm always attuned to him. He's so present and constant and . . . Well, he's mine.

Shahzad Arain is mine to grocery shop with, to share all three meals of the day with, to bring our dog to the park and play with her, to hold hands with and kiss my knuckles, and exchange sweet-nothings as laughter echoes through our cozy apartment.

But everything present and constant, this—us—will soon become a past with the weather changing.

"I've been meaning to tell you something," I say, gripping the cart handle.

"Go on." Shahzad places the tomato sauce can with the rest of our organized items and stands at my side, hand on my lower back.

"I'm going to call Baba," I whisper.

His lips part as if to respond, but no words escape. The hand on my back moves in a comforting circle around my waist as though he's expecting Baba to be around the corner, ready to kidnap me.

I continue. "Maybe we could arrange a lunch meeting? I can explain that I've discovered a different purpose, and he needs to accept it. He really doesn't have a choice in the matter." My fingers nervously play with the ends of my hair.

"Do you, uh . . . Do you want me to come with you?"

"Not unless you want him to freak out. He still thinks I'm in Rhode Island. He'll use force if he finds out I've been rooming with his ex-bodyguard for the past month and a half." With a sharp sniffle, I face his kind eyes. "Thanks for offering, though."

He takes hold of my hand, gently placing it against his chest. The rhythmic thud of his heartbeat resonates beneath my touch, evoking a soft gasp from me. "Don't be so surprised, Troublemaker. At this rate, I'll be needing a pacemaker."

I burst out laughing, falling right into his arms. "That was *so* cheesy, Chef."

"Hey, it got you laughing, didn't it?" Shahzad tilts my face up, cradling my left cheek. I'm still chuckling when he plants a surprise kiss on my forehead, peering into my eyes as if he sees a sliver of sunlight through a cloudy sky. "Can I ask you a question?"

"Of course."

"Would you like to go out with me?" he whispers.

"Go out?"

He nods. "Go out."

What does that mean?

"Like, out of the grocery store?"

"Nyla, I want to take you out on a date."

The confusion crumbles, and soon, the audible sound of my heartbeat is in sync with his. "You want to take me out? On a date? Like a real, romantic *date*-date?" To be fair, no one has ever taken me out on a date. Which begs me to ask, "What exactly do people do on dates?"

He bumps his forehead against mine. "Whatever you want. We can go wherever *you* want. It can be in the city. It can be on the outskirts. Fuck, I'll even take you to dinner in a different country if you want."

"That's a bit extreme." I giggle softly, and he closes his eyes as if storing the sound. "Gosh, okay. I've never been on a date before. Maybe . . . No, that's boring. How about you cook us dinner?"

"Done."

"And we can get those crêpes again?"

"However many you want."

My smile deepens. "Can we take Nyx out for a ride? Oh! Maybe a romantic walk by the beach?"

He leans in, gently pressing his lips to the tip of my nose. I scrunch it in response to the tickle of his beard. "Done and done. Anything else? We'll have the whole day to ourselves."

"No. We have to be mindful of money."

"Fuck the money," he bites out, taking me by complete surprise. "I mean, I have enough money to spoil you for an entire day."

"Okay, then." I suppose frugal Shahzad has taken an early retirement. "You know, this is enough to make me happy."

"What is?"

"Being with you," I whisper, intertwining my fingers with his. He raises my hand, bridging soft kisses across my knuckles. "It's enough to make me happy."

"Come here." His hand rests on the back of my head, pulling me into a warm hug. I inhale the scent of firewood and leather, wrapping my arms around his waist. "On second thought, let's grab an extra egg crate."

FAKE IT TILL WE MAKE IT

Shahzad and I end up watching *Ready Or Not*—the perfect combination of comedy and thriller.

Sky rests her chin on my lap while I comb through her fur, casually munching on popcorn during jumpscares. Shahzad, on the other hand, hides behind my hair, repeatedly asking, "Did they kill her yet?"

"She's too clever," I reply each time. "Oh, watch, watch, watch."

"Is it another gory scene?"

"Nope."

Shahzad peeks out as the family members explode one by one. "Jesus Christ, Nyla!" he exclaims, burying his face in the crook of my neck.

I snicker, tossing a kernel into my mouth. "It's not even *that* scary."

"Not even *that* scary? Baby, are we watching the same movie? There's been nothing but murder for the past hour and a half."

"Oh, grow up."

Shahzad, shaking his head, plants a kiss on my shoulder. I brush him off and tell him to focus on the ending, which, in my opinion, is fantastical.

"Nyla?"

"What?"

He gestures towards something behind me, prompting me to turn my head. Swiftly, he slips his finger under my chin, shifting my gaze back to him. I feel a blush creep on my cheeks at how smooth he was with that little move. "I saw it on the internet."

"Aren't you a little too old for the internet?"

Mildly offended, he says, "I'm twenty-nine, Miss Ghilzai."

"Sounds like ninety-nine, Mr. Arain."

Shahzad wraps his arm around my waist, pulling me onto his lap. The popcorn bowl topples, spilling its contents onto the floor. Sky barks and huffs, disgruntled by us, then finds her bed in the corner, settling down. "Give me your eyes."

I gaze at him, closing my arms around his neck and fluffing his wavy hair. Stars shimmer in his eyes as he looks at me, blinking slowly as if on the edge of deep sleep. "I know you said never to apologize, but I am *really* sorry if I made you uncomfortable with my confession last week. Sometimes, well, *all* the time, I go to bed and repeat the things I've said in my head, and I just couldn't stop thinking how awkward you must've felt to be put in that position," I concede with a nervous chuckle. "However, I'm not sorry about liking you as more than just a friend. From the bottom of my heart, Shahzad, I really, *really* like you. And because you're taking me out on a date, is it safe to assume that you like me back . . . too?"

Shahzad threads his fingers through my hair and smiles tenderly. "Kiss me, Troublemaker."

I don't question it.

I gently hold his ruggedly handsome face in my palms, leaning in for a gentle, slow kiss. His tongue explores the contours of my lips, teasing and nibbling as I eagerly respond.

Drawing him closer, I drink in the warmth of his breath, savoring the sweet taste of Reese's Pieces on his tongue. His deep, guttural moans resonate through our close-knit embrace, and I sigh with pleasure as his hand sneaks beneath my t-shirt.

"Are you clean?" I whisper.

"Got a check-up months ago. Haven't been with anyone since." He cups the side of my neck, caressing his thumb across my jaw. "You okay without a condom?"

"I have an IUD." I peck his bottom, which he takes as an invitation for a kiss. "Also, I haven't been with anyone since you."

Shahzad pulls away, his eyes questioning, and murmurs, "Nyla, we don't have to if you don't want to."

"I want to," I say, pulling over my sweater to emphasize my point. "You, too. Right?"

"Damn right." He effortlessly lifts me with his arms under my thighs. "Where?"

"We can't do the bedroom because of Maira. I also don't want to traumatize Sky."

Shahzad licks the smirk from his lips. "We could shower together? Save water."

"We should shower."

"Yeah?"

"Oh, yeah. You stink."

He chuckles, changing our position by tossing me over his shoulder and giving my ass a playful smack. I retaliate with a firm smack, and our laughter mingles behind the closed bathroom door.

21

Thank You, Chef

Nyla

"Alyn-ah?"

"Yes, Halmeoni?"

"Are ghosts funny?"

I pause, setting aside my task of wiping down table four. The restaurant is relatively quiet today, considering it's nine in the morning. "Not unless you're talking about the ones in movies."

"Then why do you keep laughing? You sound like Tae-hyung when Hye-jin-ah texts him."

Ah.

Tae and Hye-jin have become closer since he started focusing a bit more on himself. He signed up for the tennis team at his high school and passed an invitation to Hye-jin when she came to the restaurant for dinner as she does every weekend. After the game, Tae told us they went for ice cream and talked everything out—he apologized for his actions and followed my and Shahzad's advice. She must've noticed the transformation because ever since the game, she visits almost every day, on staff dinner nights or to do homework with Tae, who conveniently pretends to struggle with algebra so she can tutor him as well.

As for me, I've returned to my sketching and the process of creating a dress for my upcoming date with Shahzad this weekend.

We're doing *pretty* great, which roughly translates to sharing kisses at any given moment or location. Whenever night terrors start to creep in, I'll get up, quietly make my way to the living room, and find comfort on the couch with him. Somehow, he always makes room for me, yet I always wake up nestled on his chest.

My delusions believe we're dating now, but according to my research and past experiences with pre-planned PR stunts, you need to have your first, second, and a couple more dates to be *dating*-dating.

Plus, I've never dated anyone I liked before, let alone gone on a real date.

Therefore, I need to be perfect and on my best behavior. One screw loose on my end will ruin *every*thing for the man I like. *Really* like. *You're going on your first date!*

The doorbell chimes overhead.

I turn around with a greeting smile. "Welcome—"

Baba stands at the threshold, adorned in his finest suit and a self-satisfied grin.

I inhale sharply, wishing the ground would open up and swallow me because *Baba is here. And he's going to take you away.*

"Can I sit?" Baba asks.

I blink away the biting tears rising in my eyes. My shaky hand gestures to an empty table far from the prying eyes of the kitchen window. I know Shahzad's supposed to protect me, but currently, I'm his guard. If Baba discovers the truth, he'll ruin the only man I've ever cared about.

"*Sit*, Nyla."

"It's Alyn," I whisper. "They don't know."

"That's absurd. I wouldn't be able to recognize you considering you've . . ." His eyes dissect me like a lab rat, and I shrink, forcing myself to appear petite. " . . . grown."

I bite my lip. "Why are you here, Baba?"

"Sit before you start drawing a crowd."

Perched at the edge of my seat, I face him, my knee trembling beneath the circular surface of the table. "Baba, please don't make a scene here."

"You lied to me. You told me you were in Rhode Island, eating your little feelings away when, in reality, you're out here breaking a sweat for minimum wage." His ringed hands slap the table. "Honestly, do you *know* how ridiculous you look right now? What the hell have you done to your hair? Where is *my* Nyla?"

"I'm still me, Baba. Freed from being Hollywood's prisoner. Your prisoner." I chew the inside of my cheek. A storm gathers in his eyes, and I find myself ensnared in the whirlpool.

"I'm not coming back. I want to stay here and work on my designs."

"Designs?"

"Fashion designing, Baba."

"So you're following in the footsteps of your traitorous mother?" He scoffs, running a hand over his gleaming, bald head. "Nyla, I *raised* you when that woman left us a decade ago because she couldn't handle the pressure of being my wife."

"You *slept* with Mama's friend, Baba," I grit out, knuckles burning paper-white at his transparent stupidity. "Mama left *you* because you're a cheater. A liar. And you never cared for her as much as she cared for you. All she ever wanted was to be seen by you, but you never *ever* looked at her. The real her."

"And since when did you start forming opinions about me, Nyla?" He smiles condescendingly. "I made you. I provided you with a successful career and countless opportunities to climb the Hollywood hierarchy. How could you be so fucking ungrateful after everything I've done for you?"

"You didn't make me, Baba. You manufactured me. You gave me a career I never wanted. You gave me opportunities that made me the laughing stock of the world and tarnished what little I had left of my dignity." I pinch my fingers together and crush it into a fist. "You were the one climbing the fucking ladder. I was just the boost you needed to make a name for yourself."

He exhales an irritated breath. I scan my surroundings to ensure I haven't attracted more attention than the businessmen who, after two bottles of soju, tend to create a scene in the late hours. "New York Fashion Week is approaching."

"So?"

"I've booked you a show with Marie Maurice. You won't be opening or closing it. You'll walk the middle portion."

"I'm not a model anymore, Baba."

"Yes, I can see that. But body inclusivity is all the rage these days, so I won't pressure you to conform," he says critically. I find an opportunity to sit without constantly sucking in my stomach or pressing my tongue to the roof of my mouth.

Rolling back my shoulders, I suddenly recall Maira's mention of Shahzad's financial support for his sisters and how he drained his savings to fund Dua's education. "How much can I expect to earn?"

"Five thousand at most."

I narrow my eyes and pull out my phone, opening the voice memo app.

He scoffs as I press the red dot. "You don't trust me. That's fair enough."

"Consider this recording as a contract since I don't want you coming back here again. And, yes, I don't trust you. You lost that privilege ages ago." I look him in the eyes. "State your name."

Baba exhales heavily and leans in close to my phone between us. "Abe."

"Full name. Not your stage name."

"You're both the same," he mumbles.

"Who?"

Instead, he says, "Abdul Ghilzai. Happy?"

"And this is Nyla Ghilzai speaking," I say. "Now, if I walk the *one* show during New York Fashion Week, will you transfer control of our joint account to me?"

Baba's gaze, resembling mine, narrows. He leans forward on his forearms, an imposing yet surprised grin on his face. "If you walk the show, yes."

"And you'll let me go afterward?"

"You ask for a lot, sweetheart."

"I *am* your daughter."

Baba genuinely chuckles, causing my lips to twitch. For a moment, I catch the man he was before power went to his head. "Who are you doing this for? Yourself? Or perhaps someone else you've grown attached to?"

Any stranger would see right through my admiration when I think of Shahzad's name. The face of a hopeless romantic, a girl whose crush confessed he likes her back and kisses her like he can't breathe without her. "I'm sure you know who, Baba," I whisper.

"What a terribly naïve decision for someone who claims to be *my* daughter." He reclines in the booth. "You will walk that one show. After that, the choice is entirely yours."

His offer propels me to the edge of my seat. "You're serious?"

"Dead."

I catch my breath, a goofy grin spreading across my face. All I need to do is walk one show, restore my bank account, and repay Shahzad by covering Dua's education, the remaining rent on his lease, and whatever Maira requires. I'll also settle my debts with Alina and Azeer, who supported me during my time in Rhode Island.

Baba rises from his spot. "We'll discuss your comeback further."

My heart pounds in my ears, making it hard to comprehend his words. "Okay," I barely whisper. "You can call me. I'll unblock your number. For now." I end the voice recording and tuck my phone into my apron, standing taller than him. "What now?"

Baba's brows are furrowed, almost as if he's concerned, an emotion he isn't well versed in. "Nyla." His eyes take in my environment again, and another sigh leaves him. How can a simple sigh make me feel so judged? "We'll talk soon."

I hug my elbows. "You can go now."

Nodding, Baba takes one last look at me and exits the restaurant.

"Nyla!" Shahzad's voice rings out from the front door. "You've got packages."

I quickly power down my sewing machine and rush to the entrance, where he stands holding two beige boxes. "Oh, wonderful! It's finally here. Thank you, love." I grab the boxes from him and place them on the dining table. Sky sniffs around, probably suspecting bags of cocaine or something. "Down, girl. It's just clothes."

"Clothes?" Shahzad questions, washing his hands in the kitchen sink.

"Online shopping. It was a fifteen and under sale." Because going to the mall is one of my greatest fears for several different reasons. The risk of accidental exposure, facing old advertisements featuring me, or, worst of all, stumbling upon a lingerie store.

Besides, my reliance on my fashion team meant I rarely set foot in a mall. Choosing outfits involved pointing at magazine photos or Fashion Week models, leaving me with a gap of missed experiences—no food-court indulgence, no kiddie coin machines, no trying on clothes with friends, and no impromptu fashion shows in narrow changing room hallways.

"Here," Shahzad interrupts my thoughts, handing me a pair of scissors. "Open it. I want to see what you bought, too."

"You just came from work. Go rest. I'll show them to you la—"

Shahzad cuts me off with a kiss. "Respectfully, no."

Chuckling at his antics, I slice through the cardboard boxes and unveil the layers of tissue within. A warm flush creeps up my cheeks when he envelops me in a hug from behind, resting his chin on the top of my head. Mini pleated skirts, lace cami-tops, cozy wool sweaters for winter, frilly blouses, and a classic pair of mom jeans spill out. In the second box, I catch a glimpse of satin and lace lingerie and quickly close the lid. "See? It's just pink and ordinary. Nothing special. Let's make some food now."

"No, no, no," he protests, pulling me back by my arm and gesturing towards the boxes with a lopsided, cocky grin. "I'd like to request a personal fashion show from Nyla Ghilzai."

My brows shoot past my hairline. "You've lost your mind."

He grins boyishly. "For you."

His charms break through my defenses, and I nod. "You're unbelievably cheesy."

"For you."

I snort, pushing at his chest. "Take the boxes to the bedroom."

"Yes, ma'am." He effortlessly carries both packages in one arm, smirking as he breezes past me.

Player.

I carefully arrange the clothes on the bed, stealing glances at him as I unpack the lingerie box. Fortunately, he remains focused on me, his crinkled eyes never leaving my face as his hands unconsciously pet Sky. Gathering the outfits I've selected, I scan the room. The bathroom is situated outside, and the closet is as cramped as a mole's burrow, leaving only the bedroom as a possible option.

"Um, do you mind?" I make a circular motion with my finger. Respecting my privacy, Shahzad turns his smile towards the wall, swooping Mr. Chewy off the floor and tossing him in the air for Sky to catch with her mouth.

Taking five minutes, I change into the first set of flare jeans and velvet blouse combo. Surprisingly, a sense of ease washes over my nervous system—a welcome change from the panic attacks that used to plague me before red carpet premieres and runway shows. I'd obsess over what people might say online, worry about looking too fat in a dress, or appearing awkward in heels despite being a model.

Thoughts would race: was I speaking too loudly during red-carpet interviews? Did I unintentionally roll my eyes? Was I stealing the spotlight from my co-stars?

These concerns would hit me like a bulldozer through a brick wall before the Range Rover door swung open, the fans' screams filled my ears, and flashes replaced my thoughts with a pounding migraine. Instantly, my fragile body would go on auto-pilot.

But not anymore.

I have Shahzad. I have our cozy sanctuary we call our kingdom. I have Sky as my reliable second support, along with a circle of friends I can depend on. *Even if you're lying to them.* But, in due time, we won't have to.

Grabbing my phone, I open YouTube and play any available royalty-free catwalk music.

"Ladies and gentlemen," I announce in a deep baritone, "Nyla Ghilzai!"

Stepping away from the bed, Shahzad turns, freezing midway to marvel. His pupils dilate, transforming the deep brown of his eyes into a golden hue.

Flipping my hair over my shoulder, I start my walk down the narrow path, channeling my inner model. While my walk draws comparisons to big names like Shalom and Yasmeen Ghauri, it's uniquely mine—a suave movement of hips, precise steps without faltering, head held high, and always a smirk. Stoic walks never appealed to me.

The end of my imaginary catwalk places me between Shahzad's legs. He smiles, completely smitten, his hands briefly on my hips before I pivot on my heel, returning to the closet door.

Shedding my blouse and unzipping my jeans reveals a cami top and shorts. Shahzad whistles, leaning back on his hands, absolutely relishing my figure. A second walk, complete with a spin and a wink, before returning to the starting spot. It's more exhausting than I expected, but the sight of Shahzad's constant smile and his admiration boosts my confidence to strip.

As Shahzad moves to turn around, I state, "Don't take your eyes off me."

"Never," he whispers.

I remove my top teasingly, leaving me in my pristine, pink lace bra. The audible gulp from him echoes in the room.

Cute.

A subtle smile forms on my lips, and I proceed to take off the shorts to reveal matching lace panties. Then, I begin my final walk down to him.

Shahzad seizes my hand, standing up to twirl me around, allowing me to complete the catwalk.

"And voilà, mon chérie."

"Millions all across the board!" he exclaims, applauding with enthusiasm. Sky joins in, twirling around me in endless loops. "Seriously, woman. You look incredibly beautiful. Do you realize that? You're *gorgeous*. You're—you're just— God, I want to kiss you."

I pinch my lips together, shy in the face of his astonishment.

"On second thought, I *am* going to kiss you." He strides forward, grabs me by my waist, and presses his smile against mine. I loop my arms around his neck, feeling my toes leave the floor during his sweet, dramatic kiss.

I pat his back. "No more," I murmur as I return to solid ground, "until you've seen every outfit."

He crosses his fingers. "Even the bras and stuff?"

I smile. "Yes."

"Yes!" Shahzad pumps his fists excitedly. "I guess I'll have to save space in my stomach for dessert. Let's finish the rest of the main course."

I welcome his kiss. "Yes, Chef."

Shahzad starts to prepare us dinner after my fashion show turned into an impromptu make-out-turned-sex session, which I saw coming from a mile away.

Stepping out of the shower, I am immediately hit with the smell of fried food. My mouth salivates, and my stomach growls with hunger. Placing my hand on it, I head to the living room. "Smells delicious, Chef."

"Thank you, Troublemaker. It's a lazy dinner." Shahzad holds up a plate of fried shrimp and sweet potato fries.

"I'll eat it later," I say, drying my hair with the towel.

Shahzad stops peppering the tray of fries. "It's eight in the evening, Nyla. Right now's the perfect time."

"Yeah, but it's, like, not late enough. You know what I mean? If I eat around midnight, I won't be as hungry until lunchtime tomorrow." I smile and enter the kitchen, grabbing the little box of gum to chew on.

Shahzad grabs the package and tosses it into the sink. "Nyla." He gathers his breath to say something but pauses to stare instead.

I arch a brow. "Shahzad?"

"I'd like to talk about your eating habits with you," he says, turning off the stove fan. He takes my hand and guides us to the living room couch. "Look, I've noticed a pattern."

"What pattern?" I ask, preventing my voice from breaking.

"It was in the first few weeks of your stay. You came into the kitchen at an ungodly hour to eat whatever was in the pantry," he speaks softly, patiently. "I'd caught you a few times, sitting on the floor, kind of zoned out. It's been concerning me, and I'd like to talk about it if you're comfortable with sharing what was going on, or . . . what *is* going on."

I wrap a throw around myself and huddle to ease the hungry cramps in my stomach. Shahzad moves closer, gently tucking strands of my hair behind my ear. "Just give me a minute to gather my thoughts."

"Of course, baby," he reassures.

I close my eyes.

And everything from last September flashes before my eyes.

When I escaped to Rhode Island after the altar accident, I'd spent a week without eating any fiber or protein-supported food. Alina filled the kitchen with groceries and even cooked me a meal that night, but I couldn't bring myself to leave my room. When she and her family finally left, I tip-toed down to the kitchen, crunching ice to stave off hunger.

God, I lost count of the amount of times I passed out from lightheadedness.

It hit me that I had no one to guide my eating habits, no one to control what I put in my body, or measure me, or comment on my figure.

Without my pathetic nutritionist who approved Baba's strict diets, I was on my own, with only the ocean sounds, a growling stomach, and a craving for potato chips.

I binged on three family-sized bags by the beach, willingly throwing up by shoving the end of my toothbrush down my throat. But I continued binging. Morning, noon, and night, wolfing down whatever was in front of me, ordering from whichever late-night restaurant was open for Uber deliveries, even the foods I despised. I thought eating a lot would make me happy, but that wasn't the truth. I ate a lot because I wasn't happy.

However, in the past month and a half, since moving in with Shahzad, my eating habits have changed. I still eat what I want, but now it's part of a thoughtful plan. Three delicious homemade meals a day, without the need to binge in the middle of the night.

Like, my mind and body teamed up and said, "*Hey, look, we don't have to raid the entire pantry like a raccoon anymore because we're eating what we had at midnight during the daytime.*" Finally, I felt in control of my overeating, but the cravings still pop up from time to time.

Today, all the progress I made in building a better body image crumbled when my biggest trigger strolled into my workplace with a confident grin. And now, as I'm about to step back into society with a Fashion Week show broadcasted to thousands, my fragile habits might waver.

A gentle caress near my eyes brings me back, and I see Shahzad's clear concern.

"Can you hold me?" I whisper.

In the blink of an eye, he fits in next to me, securing me tightly with his firm, protective arms. My face rests in the crook of his neck, my right hand traveling up his chest and resting in his hair.

"I trust you," I whisper, noticing the sharp intake of his breath and the tensing of his muscles. I might as well have said the three forbidden words. "Which is why I'm going to tell you this. Okay?"

"Okay."

I nibble nervously on my lower lip. "I have an eating disorder."

Shahzad doesn't react with shock or bombard me with questions like, "Oh my god! Are you okay? Do you want to get help?" Instead, he looks at me as if we're having our usual conversation, lying in each other's arms.

I continue, feeling at ease. "It's a binge-eating disorder, to be exact. It started back in Rhode Island. Alina connected me with a nutritionist, and after describing my eating habits and old modeling dietary plans, she gave me a proper diagnosis. I didn't take it well and started starving myself during the day and overeating at night. Then the guilt would set in, and the cycle repeated. It felt unbreakable, and the shame was overwhelming."

Shahzad kisses the top of my head and runs his hand up and down my back, purchasing me comfort.

"The day you showed up at my door with my cheese cappelletti . . . I didn't want you to see me like that, drowning my sorrows in cheap pasta. But you pissed me off, and I had no choice but to come out. And you weren't . . . You weren't disgusted or even surprised. It felt like I had just stepped off a runway and caught your eye." My head is pounding, and my heart rate is slowing down. The memory of the blackout episode in the kitchen darkens my vision, and sweat breaks out on my body. "Sorry, I have a migraine."

He perks up, hurrying to the kitchen and returning with a glass of water. "Drink this. I'll be right back."

I can barely hold the glass. Thanks to Baba, I skipped lunch and the little snacks in between, disrupting my usual eating routine, and now my body craves triple the calories.

But you can't go back to it, Nyla. You can't go back. You have the show in three weeks. You need the money for Shahzad and for Dua's education. Your account will be unfrozen. This is the only way.

Shahzad takes the glass from me. My eyes are half-closed, and I'm panting like a tranquilized horse. "Open up, baby."

I part my lips and bite down on the piece of shrimp he presses to my mouth. Small portions at a measured pace. He encourages me to savor each bite, diving into the origins of the recipe to keep me awake.

I have to mentally fight against my body to resist the urge for more, even when my plate is empty and my stomach is content. But if I don't indulge now, I might find myself reheating leftovers when the world is asleep.

"Nyla," Shahzad whispers, wiping the crumbs around my mouth with his thumb. "Did you like it?"

"So much." I smile lazily. "You're such a good cook."

He chuckles, placing the plate aside, and tenderly kisses my cheek. "If you're still hungry, you can always let me know. We could walk to the corner store and grab some ice cream bars."

"I'd like that."

"Yeah?"

I nod, cradling his face in my hands. "Thanks for always listening to me, Shahzad."

He draws me close for a hug, palming the back of my head. "I'll help you take care of yourself, Nyla. I promise. I'll do whatever it takes to keep that light burning in your eyes."

I whisper, "Okay," and promise to hold onto him for the rest of my life.

22

What Do You Love About Alyn?

Shahzad

"*NO!*"

Nyla jumps from where she's ironing her recently designed dress, and I hit the top of my head on the front shelf of the fridge. Sky starts barking, on high alert for danger in the living room.

Maira dashes out of her room in a panic. "No, no, no! You guys will kill me, but I forgot Mustafa and Layla were coming to visit! Well, he wasn't visiting me, but Layla's visiting her maid-of-honor, and I got so caught up in my projects, and one of our group members isn't responding in the chat—"

"Breathe, love." Nyla rushes over, soothing Maira's nerves by rubbing circles on her back as she panic-spills about Mustafa's arrival tonight. "But tonight . . ." Her worried green eyes lock on me, a curled pink strand falling from her updo.

Tonight's our first date.

And the Salman siblings royally fucked it up.

"I'm so sorry, you two." Maira runs her fingers through her hair. "I'm sorry, I know you two had plans, and now . . . I'm *really* sorry." She starts tearing up, and being around Nyla's constantly apologizing ass, I've become a soft-shelled man. She's also Dua's best friend and another little sister on the list. Yelling at her for being careless just won't sit right. "I don't mind taking them elsewhere to give you both privacy."

"It's fine," I admit, ruffling the top of her head. "Is he driving here?"

Maira's lower lip sticks out, her eyes becoming bigger and more animated. "He's on his way now."

Jesus Christ.

"Okay, that's fine!" Nyla's optimism kicks in right on cue. Honestly, that smile of hers could end wars and create world peace. "Maira, please get dressed and clean up the bedroom as best as possible if they're considering staying."

"Ny—Alyn—"

"Shahzad." She shakes her head, marking the end of my incoming complaints. "We'll take care of the living room in the meantime. Sounds like a plan?"

At approximately eight in the evening, Mustafa's at my doorstep. A man of impeccable timing.

"I've got it!" Maira rushes to the door, and Sky eagerly follows, swinging it open. "Hey!"

Mustafa and Layla stand there, grinning and holding hands like excited kindergarteners on a zoo trip.

"Welcome!" Nyla takes charge, nudging me back and inviting the party inside. She introduces herself to the duo, exchanging hugs with them, while I take Layla's bags toward the living room.

"You staying overnight?" I ask Mustafa.

"Don't get so excited now, brother." He pats my back and looks around the small space of my apartment. Sky sniffs him, then Layla and their belongings. "Well, having Alyn here has certainly added magic to your dungeon, Shahz."

"Oh, you're too kind. Actually, Maira's the interior designer here. I just take care of our plants and flowers on the balcony." Nyla grabs Maira by the shoulders and brings her awkward ass out into the circle. It's like I'm back at my house with Mustafa and Zaviyaar, who's missing in action, hoarding the living room, playing video games, while my sisters and Maira are relaxing upstairs.

"Anyone hungry?" I clap my hands and gesture to the dining table.

They dive into a conversation, mostly Mustafa grilling Maira about updates on her internship while she does her best not to punch him in the mouth.

"This is nice," Nyla says, coming to my side with a bowl of garden salad. "I've never hosted a proper dinner party before. Isn't it so exciting?" She wiggles her fists, her bracelets chiming together.

"Nyla," I whisper, "I appreciate you always looking on the bright side, but I really hate this." I set the bowl aside and take her hands in mine. "Tonight was supposed to be *our* night."

"I know, Chef."

"Do you? Because you seem awfully excited playing host for my childhood friends when I should be doing that shit."

She giggles sweetly and squeezes my hands. "Look, you barely see your friends due to your recent chef duties and playing my half-decent fake boyfriend and bodyguard—"

"Uncalled for."

"—so I need you to give them your attention tonight, okay?"

"How can I when you look so beautiful?" I check out her pink floral dress, the skirt reaching to her ankles and the croissant-looking sleeves falling off her shoulders. And then there's that smile of hers dipped in sunshine and glitter. "Yeah, I can't do it. You have every millisecond of my undivided attention."

Nyla's laughter fills my ears. This one's different from the rest filed in my memory bank. It's almost like a snort with bubbles of adorable giggles.

Jesus Christ, when did I start using these words?

Once dinner hits the table, our cock-blocking guests dive in right away.

Mustafa chows down like he's on the run from the law, throwing out compliments about my cooking with each satisfying bite. I'll cut him some slack—he always knows how to appreciate a good meal. The ladies are deep into their chats about hobbies, and Layla nudges Mustafa away when he tries to join in.

"You haven't touched your food at all, Alyn," Mustafa notes, pointing his fork at her neatly separated plate. While she was lost in conversation, I discreetly organized the veggies, proteins, and carbs. Just making sure she gets a taste of everything.

"I'm a slow eater," she replies, spooning up some rice. I watch, hand on her back for reassurance, as she takes a bite and happily chews. Relief washes over me that she's at least enjoying her meal in front of others. "Mm-hmm. Delicious as always, Chef." Her kiss on my cheek leaves me temporarily paralyzed.

"So, Shahzad, I know you're pretty shy about your relationship from all those video calls with Mustafa," Layla teases, aiming a smile my way. "But we're all *dying* to know this. What do you love about Alyn?"

Nyla quickly swallows her bite and chuckles nervously. "Oh, I wouldn't ask him that if I were you."

"What? Why?"

"Like you said, he's very shy—"

"I love each speck and particle of her kindhearted soul," I say.

Her eyes lock onto mine, and all I can see is a peaceful, green ocean. "Shahzad . . . "

"I love the way she laughs when she squishes a tide-pod, especially that one time it burst, and she couldn't stop apologizing. I love her clinical obsession with every shade of pink and how incredible she looks in it. I love the glow of her skin in the morning, as if the sun recognizes her as equal. I love how her smile is too big for her face, how her cheeks flush pink when I compliment her, and how her pupils grow in her eyes when we speak. I love the sound of her voice, silvery and sunny, especially when she shares stories of her childhood or asks me about mine. I love her ambitions, her passions, her dedication, and devotion to her craft." I steal in a breath when beads of tears appear at her waterline. "I love everything she fails to love about herself."

Nyla gives me a watery smile and kisses my cheek, squeezing my hands three times under the table. "Thank you," she whispers, kissing my knuckles.

Layla leans in, her gaze shifting to a grinning Mustafa. "You should have Shahzad proofread your wedding vows."

His eyes soften as they meet mine, a subtle nod carrying more meaning than words.

"There's hope for the male species after all," Maira mutters. "Congratulations, Alyn. I am officially envious of your cheesy relationship."

Nyla chuckles behind her first, and the warmth of her expression instantly brings a smile to my face. "I'm really glad you two decided to visit us. I've been curious about what Shahzad was like as a boy. He never shares those details with me."

"Unimportant details," I add, dismissing the subject.

"Loud," Layla recalls. "Like full-on Gordon Ramsey in Hell's Kitchen loud. I remember every time we hung out, he'd be shouting the recipe over Mustafa's head, rushing back and forth with ingredients, pushing us all out of the way. We were all forced to peel, cut, and boil the dinner we thought he was going to cook for us. And, oh, he *never* made Zineerah lift a finger. She's the baker of the bunch."

"Meanwhile, the rest of us poured our blood, sweat, and tears into the food," says Mustafa.

"Don't be ridiculous," I retort, stealing a cucumber slice from his plate. "I wouldn't allow you to contaminate my food with your bodily fluids."

Nyla laughs out loud, leaning into me, and my arm wraps around her shoulder, pulling her close. "Hey, at least you were all well-fed."

"Can't complain there." Mustafa props his chin over his fingers, chewing solemnly. "But in all seriousness, Shahzad was . . . well, he *is* one of the most nurturing people I've been blessed to know. You have no idea how lucky you are, Alyn, to have someone like him at your side. And from what I've gathered, the same applies to you, too, Shahzad."

I smile at Nyla as an answer. *I am.*

Her eyes vanish behind her smile. *I am, too.*

As Nyla hands out dessert to the Salman siblings, Layla and I stick to washing the dishes. Her lips sport a permanent grin, and each time I glance her way, that smile only widens.

"Spit it out, Lay."

She shrugs, drying one of the bowls. Nyla recently started eating acai bowls after Hye-jin brought an extra from a nearby café. I bought the ingredients on the day and taught myself the recipe to make her the bowl for breakfast. "Just wondering what you're doing dating Nyla Ghilzai."

Blood rushes to my head. "What did you just say?"

There's that conniving smile again. "What are you *doing* dating Nyla Ghilzai?" she whispers.

"How do you know?" I ask, gripping the sponge tightly.

"I've seen a couple of her movies," she replies, glancing over her shoulder. "It was difficult to recognize her at first when Mustafa mentioned it. But then I took a good, long look at the pictures you sent, and boom." One-half of her face scrunches up. "Also, Alyn is Nyla backward, so."

I exhale heavily, biting the inside of my cheek. Layla's always been sharp, even back when we were teenagers. Mustafa admired that quality about her; she could read his emotions and secrets better than he could. While he might not be into Hollywood's horrors, Layla brings the pop culture flair. Stable and eccentric, they somehow balance each other out.

"You should settle down," Layla says.

I snort. "I don't have plans of settling down."

"Well, you exceeded my expectations with your answer during dinner. Wouldn't be surprised if you're already dating."

"We're not officially dating. Also, don't tell Mustafa. It'll ruin everything."

"Of course I won't, dummy," she says with a shake of her head. "Does Nyla know that, by the way? That you're not dating?"

"Yeah, I think so." I scrub the stains from the fork. "Nyla and I, we're just . . . We're somewhere around that territory, but not in it. Know what I mean?"

She shrugs. "Your little speech sure made it seem like you are." A beat of silence and the sounds of the metal sponge against the pan's surface pass, then, "Do you see yourself marrying her? Maybe? Maybe not?"

Growing up, I bore witness to my parents' marriage—*arranged* marriage. My mother despised my father because she was separated from the man she loved. Still, she gave Baba children due to familial pressures, and he directed his patience and unconditional love toward us. He tried with her desperately, but she refused even after his death.

So, I say, "I don't know, Lay. It's a possibility, I guess."

Nyla's perfect. Far more perfect than me. She's got her demons and sharp edges, and I've got mine, forming a sense of relatability. But . . . we're on a time limit. An hourglass where she's at the top, and I'm the one showering in the grains. When it's over, she'll choose fashion design and make a comeback in the industry as a designer, and I'll support her from the sidelines, pushed farther back into the crowd as she grows.

It'd be selfish to pin her down in this apartment, in my lifestyle, when she deserves to be in the heart of the city. Fuck, she *is* New York City, and I've always been a small part of her. I didn't mind it then, and I don't mind it now.

Besides, I've got my ambitions that I'm working toward. I'm close to finishing my new refined menu for Jia with Bao and our team. I'm scouting for extra training at fine dining restaurants in the city and maybe my own little joint. The latter is still rough, but eventually, with time, things will smooth out. I've lived the bachelor life for the past twenty-nine years now. I'll be fine.

But who will take care of her, Shahzad? Who will take care of you?

The melodious sound of Nyla's laughter shakes my bones, causing me to look back at her and see her enjoying the pink sherbet. She meets my stare for a brief second and dissolves into a lovely grin.

Pretty girl.

"Word of advice," Layla mutters, stacking the last dish. "Either you get your shit together and put a ring on that woman." She dries her hands with a paper towel, a melancholic, serious expression written across her face. "Or you can watch her get married on the news again. Choice is yours. Though, I can't guarantee she'll be left at the altar this time."

She steps back into the party.

And I stand and watch Nyla from a distance again.

23

Phoenix

Nyla

The following day, Mustafa, Layla, and Maira head out to meet Layla's maid-in-honor in Greenwich.

Shahzad and I tidy up the house, give Sky a bath, and start working in our own areas. He's been quieter than usual this morning, not because his best friend left—he was thrilled not to sleep on the floor again—but there's something else bothering him.

"How are you?" I ask, plugging in my sewing machine.

He briefly glances back. "Fine. Yourself?"

"I'm great. Last night was fun, huh? Your friends make lovely company. I'd love to have them over again soon."

He hums in agreement, busy with the tweezers to add garnishing to the fancy-schmancy dish he's preparing. It definitely isn't for Jia's menu. *Maybe an original?*

I sling the measuring tape around my neck. "I don't wanna sound irritating or whatever, but did I say or do something wrong last night?"

He turns entirely now, concern on his face. "What makes you say that?"

"You seem annoyed. And I'm sorry if I'm assuming, but I don't know. Something feels off, and I want to know if I'm responsible."

Shahzad huffs a chuckle and washes his hands, wiping them with a kitchen towel. He approaches me, grinning, which is a safe sign. "Troublemaker, did you set the kitchen on fire?"

"Not as far as I'm aware."

"Did you sew your fingers together?"

"Rookie mistake."

He cups my face. "Did you make your bed this morning?"

I think briefly, and images of the messy sheets flash through my mind. "No. I can take care of that if it's bothering you."

Before I can step away, he stops me, gently kissing my lips. "Why would I ever be annoyed with you, Nyla? Even if you set my damn apartment on fire or forgot to make your bed—nothing can change how I feel about you." His dark brown eyes shift to my hands. "I would, however, be upset if you sewed these pretty fingers together."

"Then what is it?" I circle my arms around his waist. "What's on your mind?"

"You."

I sigh a smile. "*Who's* on your mind?"

"Always you."

Now I chuckle. "Where's your mind?"

"Wherever you are."

"*When* is your mind?" I pull back, knowing there isn't an ans—

A smirk. "Never not thinking about you."

Ah, shit. I narrow my eyes. "*Why* is your mind?"

He thinks for a second, holding my gaze. "If the *why* equals Nyla, then yes. Why *is* my mind."

I go up on my tiptoes and give him a kiss, my hand sliding to the back of his strong neck while the other moves up his chest. "You're cute when you're like this."

"Mm-hmm." He pulls the measuring tape from my neck to my waist, pulling me closer until our chests touch and our lips sync up. "Let me cook you that dinner tonight."

"Crêpes afterward?"

"Chocolate strawberries," he murmurs. "And then I'm going to take you on a bike ride and kiss the shit out of you at the beach."

I laugh as he showers my face with a hundred little pecks. "Whoa!" A yelp squeaks out of me as he lifts me off my feet, spinning me around with his deep laughter harmonizing with my softer one. He adds two sweet kisses to my cheeks. "You know, if we're hitting the beach, I need a bikini."

"You don't have one?"

Back on solid ground, I smooth out the wrinkles in his t-shirt, my joyful mood taking a dip. "I threw them out."

"No worries. We can get you new ones or, you know, skinny dip or something."

I raise a shoulder and smile. "Why not both?"

Shahzad tackles me onto the couch, covering me with a continuous stream of kisses.

"Time out, time out." I chuckle, pushing his shoulders back. He takes me with him as he sits, keeping me on his lap. I run my hands over his shoulders. "I wanted to talk to you about something."

"Okay . . ." He trails off with a pinch of worry between his brows.

"Right, okay. Um, Baba visited."

Shahzad muscles tense. "Abe?"

"Yeah, two days ago, before I did the fashion show thing for you and spilled everything about myself. You gave me the confidence to be assured of my decision, and so . . . " I tuck a curl behind his ear. Shahzad holds his breath, waiting for me to elaborate. "I'm going to do a show. It's next week." He remains blank-faced. That wasn't the reaction I expected. "It's just a one-time thing. Afterward, Baba said he'd let me do whatever I wanted. He said I'll have choices. And honestly, I could really get some industry experience with fashion design. Make connections again and immerse in the industry while remaining behind the scenes. I'm confident enough to make my comeback."

Shahzad's tough exterior breaks into a smile. He brackets my face in his hands and kisses my forehead.

"So, should I do it?" I whisper.

"You weren't forced, right?" he asks, his irises searching mine. "He didn't pressure you into something serious? 'Cause, no offense, your dad's a gigantic prick."

"You're funny."

"And?"

"And you can give the Gordon Ramsays and Jamie Olivers of this universe a run for their money." I press my forehead against his, noting the dark circles under his eyes, and when I take his hand in mine, I find cuts and faded burn marks from working in the kitchen. The brittle organ in my chest cracks into an infinite amount of pieces. "When's the last time you've taken a day off for yourself, love?"

Shahzad snorts.

I frown. "I'm serious."

He cups the side of my neck, tracing circles on my jaw with his thumb. "I care for myself by caring for you and my sisters."

"I want to take care of you, too."

By earning my bank account back so I can pay for your sister's tuition, pay you for taking great care of me, and save up enough for our future together.

"Okay," I state.

"What?"

"I'll tell Baba about my decision."

"Nyla—"

"Even if I'm going to make my comeback in Hollywood, I will always return home to you, Shahzad." I kiss his lips to silence him. "I'm nervous, I won't lie."

"About?"

"Modelling again."

He licks his lips and watches Sky harassing Mr. Chewy again.

"What?" I chuckle, turning his chin so he's looking at me again.

"Nothing."

"You completely spaced out there. What's wrong?"

"Everything's fine."

I narrow my eyes and pinch his cheek. "You sure?"

"One hundred percent." Shahzad cups the back of my head and hugs me tightly, rubbing my back. I wrap my arms around his neck, inhaling his familiar scent of leather and smoke. "You're going to do great, baby. You'll outshine everyone as always."

"Thanks, love. I'll save you a seat?"

"Mm-hmm."

"And it's just a one-time thing, again. We'll go right back to this. To us. I wouldn't have it any other way."

"Me, too." He draws my head back and smiles, grazing his thumb on my bottom lip.

"Your heart's racing again," I mumble, feeling the drum of his chest against my palm.

"As long as you're at the finish line."

"I love it when you're *this* cheesy."

He suddenly scoops me up like a bride and carries me to the bedroom, plopping me down unceremoniously. I scream as he leaps like a flying squirrel, arms outstretched, landing on my side. Sky joins the fun, hopping on and finding a cozy tunnel between us. She laps at my cheek, earning head scratches from her dad.

"What's the story behind the phoenix tattoo on your back?" I ask.

Shahzad takes in a deep breath and exhales a soft chuckle. "Pretty self-explanatory. I got the tattoo while going through a rough patch, battling things, and constantly coming up short. There were days when I felt like there was no bounce back. If I were clever like Azeer, I would've had a strategy. If I were ambitious like Sahara, I would be blowing ratings of my dream restaurant through the fucking roof. Then I got to thinking that maybe I was the problem. The issue was me. But I also didn't have the solution because it required money, and money required knowledge, and knowledge required time, and my time required healing." He smiles solemnly and presses a kiss to Sky's head. She huffs and whacks his hip with her tail. "But somehow— I don't even know how— I made it out. Rose from the ashes, you know?"

"I'm sorry, love," I whisper hoarsely.

"Don't be. If anything, I'm the one that's sorry. About a lot of things. Mostly about not spending more time caring for my father as he had with my sisters and me."

Tears spring from my eyes. I prop up one elbow and caress the bristles of his beard with the back of my knuckles. "You're more caring and stronger than you give yourself credit for, Shahzad Arain. You're unbelievably smart, with delicious skills that are helping with my recovery, and I know your father, bless his soul, couldn't be any prouder of his son. Pieces of him make up your soul, love."

He takes my wrist and kisses the underside of it, making his way up to the middle of my palm and each fingertip. "You know you've sewn my heart with yours, right?"

"I am somewhat of an expert with a needle and thread." I lean down and kiss his lips, savoring their softness and the warm sweep of his tongue over mine. My innards melted a while ago and some more afterward. Now, I'm simply putty in his palms. "Question?"

"Shoot."

"Do you want another private fashion show?"

24

Our First Date

Shahzad

Nyla's getting ready in the bedroom while I finish our dinner's final stages. I put together a platter of cheesy pull-apart bread with rosemary and basil, drizzled with olive oil for starters. The main course is her favorite—creamy Tuscan chicken with fettuccine and Caesar salad. Dessert? Well, that's covered with crêpes from the shop two blocks away, where I conveniently parked Nyx.

Maira decided to sleep over at her friend Raina's apartment under my strict instructions. No parties, location services on, ringer on, no wandering around the city after hours, and definitely no chatting with strangers.

Sky comes trotting into the kitchen and bumps her snout against my leg. *Give me ham, asshole.*

"I know, honey." Opening the fridge, I crouch down and search around the rows. Nyla has some trigger foods from her BED, such as bacon, sour cream chips, and frozen yogurt, and the only version of chocolate she avoids is in the form of milk. Because they are some of *my* favorite foods, I organized our main fridge according to her preference and bought a separate mini-fridge to store my snacks.

She's doing a great job on her journey to recovery, sticking to her portioned meals, snacking healthily, and enjoying three square meals a day instead of late-night binging. She's been sleeping on the couch with me, and her nightmares have pretty much disappeared. Or maybe I've taken them on because even with this incredible, strong woman snoring in my arms, I still find myself restless, without a map to guide my thoughts.

Is she going to stay? Is she going to leave? Is she going to return to Abe or Rhode Island? Will she find an apartment in the city? Will anyone find out that Nyla Ghilzai is back in New York? Will anti-fans swarm her? Will the paparazzi capture her at her worst again? Is she going to fall back into her binge-eating cycle? Will she drop fashion design if things get too rough? Will she ever want me when Abe tells her the truth? *Will she, is she, will she, is she?*

Suddenly, something wet licks my cheek. It's Sky, sniffing the ham I've been squeezing.

"Sorry, honey." I close the door, and there she is—Nyla, in the living room, hands behind her back, rocking the most beautiful smile the universe has ever seen.

And she's wearing . . . a *black* dress . . . made of a suede material she picked up last week. The straps are spaghetti thin, and the neckline is wide and heart-shaped. It's tight, almost like a second skin, with her breasts pushed up and her curves on a gorgeous display. Her pink hair is straightened out, parted through the middle, with the bangs tucked underneath on either side, displaying her soft, kissable forehead.

I lose my balance and accidentally drop the ham.

"That's a good reaction," she breathes out.

I don't let those striking emerald eyes wander off elsewhere as I wash my hands, dry them, and then pace toward her, careful not to ruin the masterpiece she designed. "Nyla . . ."

"Are you crying?" Nyla draws in a breath, her thumbs wiping away *my* tears. I *am* crying. "Gosh, Shahzad. Why are you crying, love?"

"You're so beautiful," I tell her, kissing her forehead and holding her close. "You're *so* beautiful."

She just brings me the kind of happiness that no one else can. And it isn't just her grand gestures that make me grateful for her. Things like doing the laundry, folding clothes, picking the crumbs from the table and piling them onto her plate, being my taste-tester and screeching excitedly about my cooking, *encouraging* me, listening to me, asking me random questions about her thoughts on aliens or some shit, and appreciating everything that's been given to her despite what's been taken from her.

Her dazzling smile and golden aura started to heal the emptiness in my chest the first time I saw her dance at a fashion brand afterparty. It continued when we made small talk on her father's private jet heading to Azeer and Alina's gathering and later in a hotel room where we both broke our no-kissing rule.

For her, I'd break all my rules.

"Hey, Chef," Nyla whispers, rubbing my back. "It's flattering that my mere existence has made you tear up. If I hadn't spent hours getting dolled up, I would've asked you to take me to bed now."

I chuckle into her hair, drawing back to study her face, fearing she might leave. Every detail of her is stored in my memory, though a delusional part of me wishes she'd choose to stay in this rundown apartment, but fuck she deserves *so* much better.

Closing my eyes, I kiss her forehead for a long time. "Hungry, baby?"

"Yes, please."

"Let's eat."

In the first stage of our date, Nyla finally gives in to my begging and sits on my lap to eat dinner. Compliments flow endlessly, and she even shares bits of chicken with Sky.

"Is it delicious?" I ask, adjusting the napkin on her legs.

She throws me a sour, sarcastic glare. "Now you just want me to feed your ego, huh?"

I kiss her shoulder. "Didn't hurt to try."

Her red lips peck my cheek. "Your cooking is drop-dead delicious and out of this world. Seriously, I can't eat anything else except what you cook. And I don't care if you won't have time to cook for me when you're Gordon Ramsay level. I'll force you." She takes a proud bite of a cherry tomato.

"I'll always make time to cook for you, Nyla. But that level is still a distant dream, maybe in the far future."

"I know," she chirps, sitting sideways on my legs now, arms around my neck. "Listen, I've been thinking—"

"Yes."

She blinks. "But I didn't get to finish."

"Yes." My blood pressure skyrockets because I know what she's about to say, and if this woman is secretly sadistic and enjoys watching me cry, I'll add an extra pound of salt to the food.

Nyla licks her lower lip, smiling shyly. "I'll talk to my dad. I'll make him understand that I want to stay." *Fuck, yes!* "And by stay, I mean I'm *staying*." *That you will, baby.* "Like, don't, you know, keep me as your girlfriend for a decade type of stay."

I raise a brow.

She squirms a bit on my lap. "What I'm trying to say is that, down the line, when we're settled in our careers, I'd like us to think about the future. You know, marriage?" She whispers the last part. "I mean, obviously, that's *too* soon to think about, but it's, you know, *some*thing to think about."

And I'm left feeling skeptical. When she's set in her career, she'll be jetting off to different countries, working long hours, following a schedule that might not align with mine. But that's far off, right?

"Right," I reply in a hushed tone. "Let's focus on the present. Where we are now, in our apartment, with Sky and our friends."

She snorts. "Sure, but we won't be here forever, will we? Eventually, we'll have enough money to move to a better place. Start a family . . . or whatever."

Honestly, I can't wrap my head around all that because I never envisioned it, not even when I looked into Nyla's eyes. All I saw was us, with Sky. This is what I want. This is our home. Somehow, I need to make her understand my views on marriage and children.

"It's okay," Nyla reassures, patting my chest. "It's all in the future anyway. I still need to find a proper design studio, and you'll want to work in a professional kitchen. We'll need to save up a lot before even considering moving out." She kisses the corner of my mouth and goes back to eating.

My lips meet the warmth of her shoulder.

Enough is enough.

I've decided to swallow my pride and ask Azeer for help in paying off my debt to Abe, once and for all.

We quietly enjoy our crêpes as we head towards Nyx.

My mind is a whirlwind, and I've been so lost in thought that I almost crashed into a cyclist, stumbled over my own feet, ran my fingers through my hair endlessly, and am now mechanically forcing my favorite dessert down my throat.

Nyla nibbles on her crêpe, equally deep in thought but with an apologetic expression. She *wants* a future with me. Willingly. Married and raising children in a bigger, grander home, with Sky running around the backyard. I have no doubt that she'll be a fantastic wife and an even better mother.

The problem lies within me.

"Here," I say, pulling off her hair tie from my wrist when she starts pinning her hair up for the helmet.

"You carry my hair ties with you?" she asks.

I smile. "Because you always leave them around the house for me to collect." Rolling up my jacket's sleeve, I reveal three pink-colored bands and a yellow one. "Sometimes, I use them to tie my hair back, too."

Nyla's bottom lip juts out. "You're a dream, Chef."

I push away the dinner talk and secure the helmet over her head and mine. After helping her onto the bike, I adjust the long overcoat around her legs, then settle in, starting Nyx.

When I took my bike to see Paul after Nyla had accidentally tipped her over, he said it was on the house for whatever reason. The tune-up and new coat of paint usually cost me eight hundred, but he waved it off, not even accepting a tip, and called me a "lucky bastard." I wasn't sure what that meant.

"Hold on tight," I call back to her.

Nyla's arms wrap around my chest, and a delightful warmth fills me. She's my adrenaline, coursing through my veins and always managing to stir things up with just her presence.

I rev the throttle twice, check for any oncoming traffic, then shift gears and speed away from the curb, heading straight for Cove Beach.

Thank fuck it's deserted.

But really, who goes to the beach at eleven in the evening?

Rather than sticking to the sand like most people, I discovered one of the many coves along the beach. It's a bit of a walk, but the spot is damn worth it. A lagoon is nestled into the ground like a hot tub, and the cove's opening reveals the sand and the sparkling shoreline.

"The zipper is a bit delicate, so be gentle," Nyla advises as I handle the small black zipper on her dress, lowering it down to her spine. "Thanks." She gracefully slips out of the dress, plucking out her bikini bra from her purse. Just as she's about to unclip her strapless bra, her eyes widen, meeting mine. "Look away."

"Nothing I haven't seen, touched, or kissed before, Troublemaker," I tease.

She rolls her eyes, smiling, but I respect her request, turning away as I remove my t-shirt and jeans and put on my trunks. "Okay, all set."

It's not like it's my first time witnessing Nyla Ghilzai in a bikini, but *my* Nyla in a black bikini, nonetheless, is S-tier, in my opinion. "Woman, you have ruined me."

She chuckles, and I take her hand, guiding her into the refreshing blue pool. "Jesus, that's cold!" Her teeth chatter, but as I draw her close, she melts against me like butter on a pancake. "Hmm. You're like my personal Baymax."

I'll pretend I understood her reference. "So, what's your verdict on our date so far?"

She lifts her head from my shoulder, pondering. "Well, the pasta was undercooked, my seat was extremely uncomfortable, the lack of strawberries in my crêpe was upsetting, and the bike ride here was too long."

"Nyla."

She smiles and swims ahead of me. "This date deserves a spot in the Guinness Book of World Records for being the best ever. No fancy five-star restaurant could beat the dinner you made for me. My seat was super comfy, although it did poke my back a lot."

I playfully splash water on her face. "You better start swimming, Troublemaker."

She yelps as I chase after her for minutes, round and round the lagoon. Her bubbly, sweet laughter ricochets around the stone walls, heating my body.

I dive and grab Nyla's ankles, pulling her underwater with me. With her waterproof red lipstick intact that she couldn't stop chattering about on our walk here, she smiles, concealing her perfect teeth.

Wrapping my arms around her waist, I bring her close, sharing my oxygen. We naturally rise to the surface, our lips moving in a rushed rhythm. Pressing against the lagoon's edge, I position myself as the first one seen if anyone decides to interrupt.

"Huh," I whisper, swiping my thumb over her lips and smearing her lipstick. "Label lied to you, baby."

She stifles a laugh. "Your lips . . . "

I touch my mouth and discover red staining my fingers.

"Shahzad." Nyla draws back and holds my shoulders. Her dilated pupils and hands sliding down to my chest speak volumes, the unspoken question hanging from her swollen, red lips.

"Yeah?" I whisper, already untying the strings of her bra.

"Please."

Ah, fuck.

I crash my lips against hers, gripping her jaw and exploring the soft curve of her neck. My hand finds its way to her breast, evoking a beautiful moan that torches my soul. Tracing my fingers down her chest, I groan as I reach past her underwear, savoring the journey from her jaw to her racing pulse. Such soft skin, so markable and remarkable. I could kiss her here for days and never get sick of it.

"Spread your legs for me, baby."

Nyla gasps as I fit my middle finger into her entrance. She claws my shoulder blades, a drunk smile on her lips, and probably a really fucking goofy one on mine.

I stretch her out by inserting my ring finger, rapidly thrusting them in and out of her. She's gasping, choking on coherent sentences, whispering my name when I hit the sweet spots that have her on the brink of a heart attack. Just the sounds she makes are enough to make me finish without being inside her.

"How do you want me, Troublemaker?"

"Eyes on me," she murmurs. "Please."

Sweet fuck.

I lower my trunks and let them swim elsewhere with her clothes. Our bare bodies pressed against one another, radiating the kind of heat that even the sun can't provide, but Nyla can. And when she smiles . . . *When she smiles.*

"Okay," I whisper, stroking myself slowly, taking my time to gaze into the deep, secretive flecks of her jade eyes. "Are you ready?"

"For you?" She wraps her arms around my neck, kissing below my ear. "Always, Chef."

I grit my teeth as I slide inside of her, a low moan guttering out of me from the tight fit. Her heavy, panting breaths fan against my right ear, pretty painted nails running down my spine with each forceful thrust.

Not wanting to risk her back getting bruised by the rocks, I draw her closer and grip her curvy, gorgeous hips to move her in a rhythm.

"You're taking me so well," I murmur against her jaw. "You always take me so fucking well."

"God," she moans out softly, gripping the back of my hair. Her lips connect with mine in a furious kiss, fueling my body to pump into her like a madman. I think she mistakes my bottom lip for hers and bites down hard, drawing blood. *Yup, my lip.* We wouldn't even be able to tell because of her lipstick, but fuck it.

It takes me five more minutes before I'm making her rasp out my name in strained breaths, making her bleed my back and my lips and my fucking soul. I gasp out her name as I spill every bit of myself inside of her, milling her back and forth on me.

I whisper, "Again," threading my fingers through her hair. "Give me at least three. Please."

Nyla blows a breath, chuckling with her head thrown back. Her devious green eyes narrow on mine. "Take all of me."

NOOR SASHA

I cut her off with a feverish kiss and take her again.

25

The Show

Nyla

So, here I am, sitting in the same worn-out Nissan that Shahzad rented to bring me to his home, and now, to take me to the runway venue.

Baba insisted on sending a limousine, but I declined, not wanting to attract attention in Koreatown and especially not wanting to reveal my identity to Maira and the BBQ house team. They all believe Shahzad and I are going on a trip, having booked time off and given Maira the apartment for the night.

While Shahzad fills up the gas, I'm on my phone, searching for vacant studio rentals in the city aside from the one in SoHo. I'm confident that my skills shouldn't be limited to a single corner of our apartment. Leasing a studio is necessary for preparing numerous designs before announcing my comeback. I know Baba will object, but I'm determined to prove that I can make a name for myself despite my background.

Jotting down potential addresses in the notes app, I stare at my phone screen, at the empty browser. I absentmindedly let my fingers type my first name, and the drop-down searches trigger a fearful shiver down my spine.

Nyla Ghilzai wedding video.

Nyla Ghilzai wardrobe malfunction videos.

Nyla Ghilzai boyfriend history.

Nyla Ghilzai leaked pictures.

"What . . . ?" I click on the leaked pictures search and open a link that reveals square rows of my face professionally photoshopped onto naked bodies. Some are clearly artificial intelligence, and others are pixelated enough to deceive dimwits who searched this disturbing rubbish.

Inhaling deeply, I click the 'x' and type a new search phrase: Nyla Ghilzai pink hair. So far, no one seems to have spotted me. *Yet.*

As I open Instagram, my heart sinks at the sight of my followers dropping by five million. The last post was a snapshot of the high heels I wore during my disastrous wedding.

Next, I search: *Glenn Jackson.*

He's thriving in the industry with my former assistant, Sandra—married and expecting their first child, sipping coconut water from a *real* coconut in their lavish Los Angeles mansion.

It's fine.

Once I secure investors and build a solid portfolio, I'll gradually return to aspects of my previous life. Not the extreme dieting, but indulging in shopping sprees, nail appointments, and occasional salon blow-outs. Maybe not as extravagant as before, but enough to support Shahzad with rent and save for our future.

I'm just about as done with the internet's bullshit when I start typing a new name: Rubina Ghilzai.

"God." I sigh as I scroll through my mother's latest wedding photos with the Palm The Atlantic investor. "Oh, Mama. You look so beautiful." Tears slide down my cheeks as I admire her in a mermaid-shaped white dress and a sixty-foot-long netted veil. Her husband, in a crisp white suit with Mama's classic tailor style, kisses her with a huge grin on his face. "I really hope this one's a keeper."

Shahzad jerks open the door and takes a seat. "All right, gorgeous, let's hit the road." He notices me wiping my cheeks and gently cups my jaw. "Hey, what's wrong? Why are you crying?" There's a slight tremor in his voice when he asks, "Did Abe call you?"

"No, no. It's nothing." I smile, tucking my phone away. "Just saw pictures of my mother's wedding a few weeks ago."

"Oh?" Shahzad breathes a sigh of relief, smoothing out the creases on his forehead. "Did you talk to her?"

"I don't have her number."

"Can you ask Abe for it?"

I let out a hollow chuckle. Baba's contact list mirrors his heart—there's no room for Mama or me. "It's okay. She and I never had a close relationship. Maybe that's why I stuck with my father. He was the only one who ever showed me any parental attention." Even if it was for his own selfish reasons.

Shahzad takes both my hands and gives them a kiss. "I know that you've always been on your own, Nyla, but you have done a wonderful job. Right now, your efforts may not seem like much because, let's be honest, no attractive woman would be living in a dinky-ass apartment in Koreatown, working at a Korean restaurant." He pauses to laugh alongside me. "Still, you've made the most of it. You discovered your passion for fashion design and brought peace to this dumbass chef of yours."

The tears drip down from my chin and onto my lap. "Thank you, love."

He smiles lopsidedly. "Come here, baby."

I lean in, kissing him and then embracing him. "I don't know what I'd do without you, Shahzad Arain."

"Me, too," he whispers, pecking the side of my neck and exhaling heavily. "Me, too."

Baba waits for me in the underground parking garage of Lincoln Center.

"My darling girl." He's so short that I have to bend down to reciprocate his hug. His eyes shift behind me, catching a glimpse of Shahzad. A smile briefly lights up his face, but my sweet, grouchy boyfriend looks away with a hint of irritation. "I have the team ready to take care of you."

I walk alongside him, hoodie over my head and glasses fixed over my eyes as a dozen or so security guards escort us into the elevators. Hugging my elbows, I crane my neck above the crowd. "Shahzad? Where's Shahzad?" Panic sets in when I can't spot him. "Sha—"

"Right here, baby." Shahzad's voice comes from my side as he squeezes through my father's guards to take my hand. I smile, intertwining our fingers and resting my head on his shoulder. "I'm here."

As we pace down the polished marble corridors of the venue toward backstage access, Baba updates me on all the arrangements he's made.

"Your position is number thirty. We'll do a quick measurement and some last-minute adjustments for your outfit and address any issues that need handling. Oh, and the pink hair will be hidden by a wig." Baba doesn't leave room for me to object; he continues, gathering his interns and team as we walk. They marvel at my appearance, exchange whispers, and are genuinely excited. "We're about to do a dress rehearsal in half an hour. Mingle with the team, immerse yourself in the environment, and for god's sake"—he lowers his voice for emphasis—"*don't* fuck it up."

The warning in his eyes screams that if I do happen to fuck it all up, I'm jeopardizing my end of our bargain.

"I won't," I assure.

Baba gives me a quick once-over, and the dressing room door swings open. The makeup and fashion team swoops in, guiding me toward the mood board featuring my outfit.

I spot Shahzad and my father engaged in conversation; Baba wears a hint of a smile while Shahzad scowls at him. Before I can intervene, I'm ushered behind a changing wall, where my limbs and waist are measured. Despite the team's supportive atmosphere, I can't shake the feeling of smallness and insecurity. One thing's for certain, I did *not* miss this traffic.

During the dress rehearsal, I nervously wring my hands as I join a group of fellow models I've partied with and celebrated birthdays. Cindy, with her bouncy, coiled hair, interrupts her conversation with Cassie and Valerie to give me an assessing look. She's signed to First Class Faces and never liked me much, especially after I snagged every ambassador deal from under her nose. Can't blame her. Despite putting in the damn work, I'll always be a product of nepotism.

"Welcome back," Carina purrs, walking straight toward me. She's still got a little wobble in her walk because of how much pressure she puts on her left ankle. My insecurities never liked her much, either. Honestly, past me never liked any of these women. I bet they were all celebrating together when I was left at the altar. "You look healthier, Ghilzai. That's a compliment, by the way."

Cindy and her clique giggle in the background. The rest of the girls pepper in with their soft, feminine chuckles. Sucks being the only mid-sized woman amongst the line-up of pretty, poised popsicle sticks.

"Don't break a heel," Cindy quips from the back of the line. Of course, she's closing the show.

I clench my jaw and roll back my shoulders, fixing the lilac wig, and confidently take the first three steps up to the runway.

Until I'm fully exposed from behind the wall.

In front of me, there's Baba, the First Class Faces team, the venue's crew, Shahzad—my gaze settling on him—and a bunch of nobodies that I couldn't care less about.

FAKE IT TILL WE MAKE IT

Strutting down the rectangular runway, I sway my hips with precision, keeping my steps light and tilting one end of my lip to the side. My arms hang relaxed at my sides, careful not to let them swing wildly and disrupt the magic of my walk. The lavender gown flows around me, silk fluttering across my arms, sending chills through my body. The adrenaline rush fuels me to stay sharp and maintain momentum. I sharply turn to the left and proceed along the width, followed by another left to cover the entire length.

The moment I'm backstage, I grab the worker's hand, release a deep breath, take a water bottle from Baba's assistant, and find a spot to sit and drink in large gulps.

Carina, who walked behind me, arrives a minute later, witnessing me on the verge of a panic attack. And this was just the rehearsal.

I glance up at her, slightly scowling at the condescending smile on her face. "What?"

"You've still got it, Ghilzai."

"I know."

"Good." She winks and walks away with her team.

Baba rushes up to me, grabbing my elbows and jumping around me like I'm Anna Wintour herself. "That was excellent, my darling. Add a little more sway with each step, and don't be afraid to loosen your shoulders and fists a bit." He kneads my shoulder blades, bringing some relief. "You've been practicing?"

"With Shahzad. I wouldn't be here if it wasn't for his daily encouraging affirmations." I notice Baba's displeased expression and twist the cap back onto the water bottle. "I get that my relationship status might catch you off guard, but it's something you'll have to accept if we're going to be working together at shows."

"Ah, yes. Your designs. How's that going for you?"

"I could use more workspace, but it's going well so far. I could show you some—"

"Later." Baba pats my cheeks and signals his team over. "Let's get her prepped for the official show."

I clench my jaw, letting out a half-hearted chuckle at my naivety in thinking I could have a heart-to-heart with a man who's always been *so* self-centered.

"Nyla," my home calls, navigating through the crowd, drawing sultry gazes from models and agents alike. His arms envelop my waist, mine around his neck, and we share a spin with our lips pressed together. "You killed it, Troublemaker."

"That was just the appetizer, Chef."

His fingers interlace with mine. "I love it when you speak culinary terms to me."

With that, we head back to the dressing room.

26

Nyla Ghilzai

Shahzad

"I'm out," I state, spotting Abe near the refreshments table in Nyla's dressing room. She's getting fitted in another section with the other models, finally giving me a chance to confront her dickhead father.

Abe sighs and dismisses the guards chatting with him, gesturing for them to leave and closing the door behind them. "Out of what, son?"

"The damn contract." I pull out a cash envelope. "Your ten grand for Dua's tuition is in here. Stay away from me and my sisters, and you sure as better stay the fuck away from Nyla if you want to keep your head."

He leans back against the table, stirring his coffee cup. "We had a deal."

"Fuck your deal."

"It seems you *are* fucking my deal, Shahzad." He sets the cup aside, creating a one-inch gap between us. A look at his clenched fists tells me I've hit a nerve. He picks up the envelope of cash. "Now, I don't know whose balls you had to lick to get this since the signing of the contract, but I'll have you know"—he pushes it at my chest— "I won't be accepting it."

"You're not getting Nyla."

He shrugs. "She's my daughter."

"She's your design." I scoop up the money and thrust it back at him. "You were never a father to her, so don't try to step into the role now that you know you've lost her for good."

"And you honestly believe she'll stick around with a dishonest guy like yourself?"

"Better than staying with a dictator."

Abe shoves me back, but I seize onto his collar, refusing to let go until a small vein bulges on his forehead. Still, the fucker grins. "You know who she'll come running to when she finds out that the only man she trusts is a two-faced bastard? Me, son. Her first protector. Her savior. Her father. Not some low-life bubble dancer struggling to keep his roof from leaking."

Raw anger consumes me, and my fist clenches, trembling with the hunger to pound his face until even his own reflection won't recognize him. But giving in to my emotions would only jeopardize Nyla's safety.

"Go on," Abe taunts. "Hit me."

I grind my molars, shutting my eyes tight. *Baba, if you're here, please help me.*

No response.

Not even a flicker of light in the storm.

Yet, a voice, not Baba's but a sweet, silvery voice, blankets me. *Being in your arms. It's enough to make me happy.* My Troublemaker's voice lowers my arm down and steadies my breathing.

So, I release Abe and take a big step back. "I love her, Abdul." My hand rubs at my beard as I catch hints of pink glitter on my shoes. Nyla's working on a headband for Sky and bought a shit-ton of pink and purple glitter. "God, I love her so fucking much. And I'm going to cherish Nyla. Protect her. Show her that she isn't alone. And once this is over, once you tell her the truth, it'll be her choice whether she wants to stay or not." I swallow hard, keeping my fists clenched at my sides.

Abe clasps his hands at his front, eyeing me up and down. "I suppose my daughter feels this way about you, too?"

"She doesn't have to say it yet, but yes. I know she loves me, too," I say honestly, remembering her confession and the countless signs she's given me. I've gathered each one without her realizing it, storing them in my heart.

He raises his eyebrows and tucks the envelope into his blazer. "Just so you know, your little fairytale won't have the happily ever after you expect."

As if I'd ever let that happen.

"Are you going to tell her?"

He shrugs without a care in the world. "Waste of time. You've played your part, and as for Nyla, well, you saw her. There's no changing her mind about her future."

I breathe out in relief. It's fine. I've paid him back the amount I owe him. I've settled my debt. Now, I can move past my stupidity and support Nyla and me with our endeavors. With our future together.

Abe claps me on my shoulder. Crow's feet deepen by the sides of his light-green eyes, missing the glimmer Nyla has. "Why don't we go enjoy the show now, hmm? Afterward, you, me, and my daughter can wind down about your relationship without any need for unnecessary hostility."

I could give less of a fuck about his blessing, but if it eases the pressure on Nyla, I'm in. But I won't lie about my uneasiness from how effortlessly he agreed to everything.

Backstage, Nyla's bizarre makeup is getting touched up in the lineup of models. Her lashes are snow-white, lips decorated with a purple-golden glitter heart, and her wig's bangs cut above her brows, the rest cascading down to her hips, practically hiding her face and curves. I look at the other models flaunting their ponytails, bob-cuts, and short dresses, and a strong urge wells up within me to steal my girl away from these shallow pricks.

"Shahz!" Nyla waves off the makeup team and strides toward me in six-inch heels, defying the laws of physics. She grabs my hands with her shaky, sweaty ones. "I look like an idiot."

"You're perfect in whatever the hell you wear."

"Even if I resemble the Red Queen?" She pouts, her heart-painted lips catching my attention.

"I always kinda had a crush on her, so." I may not know much about this Red Queen character, but if it eases her pre-show nerves, I'm more than willing to tell a little white lie. "I'll be right there with you, baby." I gently cup the back of her head, crowning her with a kiss.

Nyla clutches my shirt, breathing in deeply. "I'm scared."

I tilt her chin up. "Scared to walk in front of a crowd again?"

"Scared of everything, Shahzad."

"Then don't crush that fear, Troublemaker. Because from here on out, you'll go through passages of fear trying to get to where you wanna be. Do whatever you love, whatever you want, without feeling the need to apologize for your anxiety." I give her a flicker of a smile as tears form in her eyes. "What is fear, if not the voyage of bravery."

She sniffs, scrunching her nose in an adorable way. "When did you become so wise?"

And you honestly believe she'll stay with a dishonest man such as yourself?

I silence Abe's voice in my head and plant a kiss on her forehead. "Show the world what you're made of, Troublemaker."

My seat is reserved next to Alina's. It's easy to recognize her with the weird golden streaks under her natural black hair.

"Shahzad!" She leaps from the bench as I approach, opening her arms for a hug. Bending down for her makes me snort. I never have to lean down for Nyla. She's only four inches shorter than me. "It's great to see you. How have you been?"

"Good. Yourself?" I search around her. "Where's your lapdog?"

"I'm okay," she says timidly. "And he's in his luxurious kennel."

"You wanna talk about it?" I ask, taking my seat.

Alina nods, toying with the lace on her sleeve. "We're not talking right now, so. Well, we *are* in front of Zoha, so she doesn't get the wrong idea."

"What did he do?"

She chuckles, her charming dimples showing. "He, uh— I don't know, I'm probably just overthinking this, but sometimes I feel him slipping away during a conversation because of work calls and emails. The only time I have his attention is when I bring up . . . "

"When you bring up what?"

"Trying for a baby."

"Oh."

"Yeah. I feel like the topic of us *finally* consummating our marriage is at the forefront of his mind."

"You're holding off because of your health, right?"

"Yeah." She bites her lip and raises her lashes toward the ceiling. The spotlights catch her dark irises, turning them into a lighter shade of brown—similar to Zineerah's. "Yeah, I'm overthinking it all. Azeer's a fantastic husband. He's so patient and works on becoming a better person daily. I don't— You don't think he would, like, cheat . . . on me?"

"Fuck no," I state. "Azeer might be an idiot—a given from day one—but he's a loyal and committed idiot. He's been driven by success and living by the rules his whole life, even if it means self-condemnation for breaking them. What went down at Iman's wedding was him breaking every damn rule in the book. But marrying you and giving Zoha a kickass mother made it all worthwhile." I lay my hand on the top of her head, giving her hair a light tousle. "He's not slipping away, Lina. Honestly. I've never seen him love anyone so fucking hard aside from Zoha."

Alina sticks out her bottom lip and gives me a side hug. I wrap my arm around her for support. "Thanks, Shahz. You're a real one for listening," she says, drawing back and sitting up confidently. "I'll talk to him. We'll figure it out. We always do. It's the best part about us."

"Good. Let me know how it goes."

"I will if you spill the beans on how things are going with you and my darling cousin?"

I sigh, running my hands over my thighs, and observe as the crowd slowly fills in. Something bitter lingers on my tongue as I reply, "We're good."

"Just good? Her texts beg to differ. Lots of pink hearts and eggplant emojis." Alina lets out a gasp. "Please don't tell her I told you that."

I chuckle under my breath. "Nah, you're fine. Right now, I just want this show to be over so she and I can return home and relax. She'll probably work on her designs, and I'll cook us dinner. Same old routine."

Alina nudges my shoulder. "You're doing great. As long as Nyla is happy and healthy, I won't sharpen my knives."

The colorful lights point towards the stage, flickering as the first electronic beat pounds on the speakers.

"You're okay with the flashes?" I ask Alina, but she's too busy checking out a celebrity figure seated across from us. "Who's that?"

"Anzai Kei Winston." She chokes on her whisper. "He's *the* most famous actor in Hollywood right now. I watched *The Goldmine* last year, and it was fan-fucking-tastic. I'm not shocked he won Best Actor at the Oscars for it. And he's the only Japanese actor ever to win that award."

Abe's bald head quickly obscures Anzai Kei Winston's face.

"Damn it," Alina mutters, pretending to throw up at the sight of her uncle. "Forgot that asshole was present."

Ditto, Lina.

The show kicks off as the first model struts down the runway. Phones are out recording, heads turning with the model's walk and repeating as a new one takes the stage. Cameras are flashing, and I do my best to shield Alina's peripheral vision in case it triggers her epilepsy.

Nyla appears at the threshold of the stage.

I hit the record button on my phone, leaning forward in my seat. "There's my girl."

Murmurs ripple through the crowd when she takes the runway with a confidence fit for a goddess. Abe's locked onto her stride, nodding along as she passes him. The rest of the onlookers are too busy contributing to the gossip pool and filming her for an entirely different purpose.

Alina leans in and whispers, "She must really love you," just as Nyla turns down the width of the stage.

"Yeah? What makes you say that?" I stop recording as soon as she's backstage.

"Why else would she take on this gig if it wasn't for you?"

I raise an eyebrow. "Because she wants to get back into the fashion industry as a designer?"

Alina squints. "What?"

"What?"

"Shahzad . . ." Slowly, her eyes widen, and her lips part like she accidentally spilled some secret. "Oh, fuck. Fuck, fuck, *fuck*. Shit, Shahz. I wasn't—" She grabs her hair roots and pulls tight. "Goddamnit, Azeer and his stupid stress."

I take her wrists before her head can match with Abe's. "Alina, what the hell are you talking about?"

"Forget I said anything."

"What do you mean she took on this gig for me?"

Alina frowns harder and hides her face behind her hands.

I sit back with a thud.

Fuck.

I *knew* something was off about this whole situation. Why would Nyla, *my* Nyla, agree to strut down the runway for the one guy she swore never to have anything to do with again? It can't just be for industry experience. It would make more sense if she reached out to her mother, an *actual* fashion designer. It's illogical for Nyla to model in front of a crowd, exposing her status to the media, all because she wants to improve her sewing skills.

He's given me a choice.

Abe played her. That's the only explanation. He cornered her with an ultimatum, forcing her to accept his terms and gain her freedom. He's not planning to set her free. Not after she flawlessly owned the catwalk following a ten-month hiatus.

I bolt up from my seat and dash backstage, pushing past guards and workers. "Nyla!" I call out as soon as I spot her sipping water.

"Shahzad!" She kicks off her heels and rushes over, wrapping her arms around my neck. "Oh my god, Shahz! That felt amazing. I can't believe I got to showcase this body." She pulls back, cupping my flushed face. "Did you see the looks on everyone's faces when I strutted down? It was like they'd seen a ghost." She tongues her cheek, patting down her hair. "A sexy gho—"

"Nyla, why did you agree to walk?"

"What?"

"Abe's offer. Why did you do it?"

Her lips part but quickly close as her gaze shifts over my shoulder. "Baba." She moves past me and reluctantly accepts Abe's embrace. "How did I do?"

"Exquisite, my darling," he says, adjusting her bangs and gazing at her with stars in his eyes. Well, once my knuckles meet his money-hungry stare, he'll see more than just stars.

"Come, let's go to your dressing room and get this hideous wig off you." He wraps his arm around her shoulders, leading her toward the back door. "You can join us, son."

Nyla's buzzing with adrenaline, and I can practically see the wheels turning in Abe's corrupt mind.

Clenching my fists, I drag my heavy feet behind them.

27

People Pleaser

Nyla

We step into the dressing room.

Baba dismisses everyone, shutting the door and locking it. He turns sharply, arms wide open, grinning confidently. "Let's address the elephant in the room."

"We can talk later," Shahzad insists. "For now, Nyla and I are heading home." He extends his hand toward me.

I take it without hesitation, lifting it to kiss his knuckles. "We should celebrate with crêpes."

"That sounds wonderful!" Baba exclaims, hands sliding into his pockets. "Actually, I think you should treat Shahzad to something extra for the fantastic job he's done bringing you here."

I grin up at him, hugging his side and placing my palm on his rapidly beating heart. "Without Shahzad's words and reassurance, I wouldn't have had the confidence tonight."

As I was called to the stage, a wave of nausea hit me. Carina, among all the models, gave me a reassuring nod and rubbed my back at the last second. When the spotlight illuminated my face, and the murmurs broke through my mental barriers, all I could think of was Shahzad's advice. *What is fear, if not the voyage of bravery?* And the entire month of May and June crumbled down in the most incredible way, urging me to lift my chin, curve one end of my lip, and strut down the runway for the grand finale of my career.

Baba clears his throat. "I think now is the perfect time to repay his kindness. Don't you agree?"

I nod, taking both of his hands. He looks so beautiful and vulnerable, and my heart's bleeding through my ribcage for this man.

"Shahzad, I swear I didn't want to keep this a secret from you, but I also really wanted to surprise you." A toothy grin spreads across my face. "Baba is going to unfreeze my account so I can cover Dua's tuition and repay you for everything you've done for me." A laugh erupts out of me. "Surprise!"

He tenses.

That's understandable. Tonight has been a whirlwind, and we both need our couch, our Sky, a home-cooked meal, and a few hours of sex—before Maira returns home from work. We can even afford a television now, and I'll make him watch all seasons of Project Runway with me.

As my words are being processed through his buffering brain, I continue talking to untangle the confession. "That's why I agreed to go for a walk tonight. For your sister, for myself, but mostly for you. Your kindness and unconditional love have breathed life back into me, Shahzad. This is the least I can do for you after everything you've done for me." I embrace his torso, placing a kiss on his shoulder. *I love you*, is at the tip of my tongue, but I would rather take a bullet than publicly declare my affections in front of my father. "I'm so grateful for you, love."

Shahzad's arms remain rigid at my side. He must be truly taken aback if he's responding this way. He usually enjoys my hugs.

Well, maybe you should've chosen a more private moment to share this . . .

"There's no need for that, my dear," Abe interjects. "I've already covered Dua's tuition."

What?

"What?" I pull back abruptly, fixing a stern glare on my father. "Why? I told you I would take care of that." If this is some attempt at emotional manipulation to gain my favor, it's not working.

Shahzad stumbles backward, clutching onto a chair for support. "Abe."

"In the second week of May," Baba adds, "My memory is a bit hazy on the details. Shahzad, do you mind recalling our meeting?"

I turn around to confront Shahzad. "Meeting? What meeting?"

He can't meet my gaze. "Please."

"Please, what?" I scoff, laughing. "What's going on? Why did you meet with him, love?"

Shahzad blinks and closes his eyes as if in physical pain, his head sinking. "Nyla, please hear me out—"

"Ah, I remember now," Baba interrupts. "I approached Shahzad with a deal, my dear. He would return you to me for this show at the end of June, and I'd pay his sister's tuition. Of course, he was hesitant, but money always trumps love. Doesn't it, Shahzad?"

The walls of my chest crumble with each revelation.

"You sold me?" I whisper. Tears begin to burn my eyes, slowly streaming down my cheeks. "You *sold* me to him?"

"Nyla, I . . . I didn't—I wasn't thinking—"

"No, you're lying!" I retort to Baba, who's watching with a patronizing grin. Oh, he's definitely playing mind games again. He's trying to manipulate me. "You're saying all of this just to make me leave him. I told you I won't leave him!" My head whips in Shahzad's direction. But he avoids my eyes and turns his face away. "He's . . . He's lying, right?"

Baba pulls out a thick cash envelope and tosses it on the vanity, along with a folded piece of paper. Shahzad reaches for it, but I grab it first, quickly unfolding it to read the contents.

I find my name written on a blank page with First Class Faces' monogram logo at the bottom. I start reading the terms one by one.

My heartbeat . . .

Slows . . .

Down.

A contract.

It's a signed agreement.

A con—a contract signed by Shahzad. And my father. Inked two weeks into my stay in Koreatown. Dua's tuition is promised if Shahzad delivers me back into my father's control for a fashion show by the end of June.

"No, no, no." I try to decipher the clauses, but the growing black fog in front of my eyes makes it painfully difficult.

Shahzad legally committed to returning me to my father instead of letting me return to Rhode Island.

The man I love, the man I trust, the man with whom I shared my deepest secret about my eating disorder, didn't nullify the contract *even* after I swore I'd stay.

One way or another, I was going to be tossed into a lion's den, ready to have my flesh cut from my bones and those bones mended to Baba's ideals.

Stupid. You're so, so fucking stupid, Nyla.

And clingy.

Gullible.

Optimistic.

People fucking pleaser.

Shahzad's pleaser.

I was nothing, *nothing*, but kind to him.

I gave in to his extravagant ploy because I truly wanted to help him. I ate convenience store food to save the cost of groceries. I took a considerable loan from Alina to repair his motorbike. I used the money from my paycheck to get him a helmet engraved with his initials. I lifted his spirits even when my own were wilted. I praised him like he was my favorite movie in my mental cinema and built castles in the air about our future.

Was there something I missed? Was I so in over my head about him that I was blind to the signs? Deaf to the sirens? Defensive about everyone's opinion regarding his romantic life? Did I genuinely believe we could share rose-colored glasses and ride off into the sunset together?

I bellow out an empty, dry laugh.

I'm a fucking idiot.

Oh my god.

I'm a fucking. Delusional. Idiot.

"Ny—" Shahzad stops, and I realize this will be the last time I'll hear his voice. He keeps calling my name until he fills up my view. I used to love how he crowded me, but now I just want him far away. "Nyla."

His eyes meet a defenseless, enraged woman, covered in her snot and tears, holding a signed betrayal in her fist.

I don't need to ask if it's true or if this is another night terror, and I'll wake up in his arms to his kisses and sweet words.

The light in his face fades into complete terror, and darkness clouds his eyes.

It's real.

"I trusted you," I manage to whisper. "I trusted you." It's a broken whisper. "Do you know how hard it is for someone like me to trust anyone?" I push his shoulders back hard, repeatedly, punching and jabbing, and the bastard doesn't flinch one bit.

His eyes shut tight, not a single sound escaping those tightly sealed lips. Lips that used to be my sanctuary, the ones that whispered my name and had me at their beck and call.

The fight in me dissolves, and my pounding forehead meets his shoulder. "I trusted you,

Shahzad." Tears seep from my lashes and travel down my cheeks. "I placed every fragile piece of my shattered world at your feet, hoping you would mend it, and you did. You *almost* did. But instead, you . . . you cut right through my heart." Sucking in a sharp breath, I lift my head and cup his face, forcing his foggy eyes to open. My head shakes non-stop, and if I died now in front of him, I'd curse him from the grave. "Why?"

He pulls in his lips, and no matter how hard I try to make him meet my gaze, he remains stubborn.

"Why?" I murmur. "Why did you talk to him? Why would you do this to me?" My fingers grip his scalp. "Were you that desperate for money?"

Shahzad's eyes drop to the floor again.

Embarrassed.

Ashamed.

My chin trembles as he avoids looking at me. "Did you ever truly care about me?"

He nods, his head hanging so low it seems like it might detach from his neck. "I do."

"Did you ever—" I choke on my following words, but enough is enough. I'm going to ask everything I've overthought since May because fuck it. Fuck it all to hell. "Do you love—?"

"Yes!" He states with sheer determination, holding my face now. My arms hang lifelessly at my sides. "Yes, I love—" A shaky breath. "I love—I love you. I love *you*. I love you more than I love myself. You—you *are* myself. You take up all of me, Nyla. You are the only part of me that I love." His lips tenderly meet both my crying eyes.

"No. No, you don't get to do this. Not anymore. You—Get away!" I nudge him back when he tries to kiss me, unsure of where my emotions are leading me, and glance up at the ceiling. "If you love me, then do—did you see a future with me?"

No nod. No heartfelt monologue. He's not even breathing.

I force a smile and take a step back, releasing him. "Yeah, I wouldn't see a future with myself either." Grabbing my purse and phone, I meet Baba's perplexed expression with a scowl. "*You* are dead to me. Do you understand? I don't belong to you. And if I catch you spying on me again, I'll expose every bit of evidence I have against your twisted methods of torturing my body."

Tearing open the envelope, I find stacks of hundred-dollar bills. I pull out the cash and throw half of it at Shahzad's chest and the rest in Baba's face.

I storm out of the dressing room, texting Alina to pick me up from the parking lot with cold-blooded thumbs. The venue's security team surrounds me, but I choose two suited men to escort me, wiping away my tears, and shielding my eyes with sunglasses.

Suddenly, someone seizes my arm—a calloused, warm hand. Shahzad's.

"Step back!" One of the guards commands, shoving him away. "Jones, we need back-up—"

"Fuck you!" Shahzad spits back, pushing my guard so hard he crashes into the wall. "That goes for you, too." He points at my second guard.

I continue pacing down the hall.

Shahzad catches up to me and inserts himself in my path. His dark-red glossy eyes mirror the turmoil within him, and his whole demeanor is in disarray. My chin quivers, but I keep my head high. "Where are you going, baby?" His voice breaks, and the tears slip from my eyes.

"Home."

"You *are* home."

"Home, Shahzad, is anywhere but with you."

I shove past his shoulder, storming down the emergency staircase to the basement parking. Shahzad trails behind, a torrent of excuses rushing from his lips.

"Nyla, you have to understand. He only paid for Dua's tuition."

I refuse to waste another breath on him.

Alina is by her hotel driver in the parking garage when I arrive. "Hey, is everything okay? Why are you both crying?"

Shahzad steps in front of me once again. "Please, Nyla. Please, don't go." He drops to his knees with a painful thud, and my breath catches. "I borrowed money from Azeer. I paid it back before the show. Every fucking penny, Nyla. Please, just trust me this once."

I let out a bitter chuckle. "Trust."

His face twists into dread and disbelief. "Nyla."

I drag my eyes back to my cousin's worried face. "Get in the car, Lina."

"Nyla, *please*!" Shahzad's persistent pleas echo in my ears as he continues to chase after me.

My eyes remain motionless and unblinking, blocking out his noise until it's a pestering ringing in my ear. "Was any of it real?"

"What?"

I turn around slowly, my voice trembling. "Was any of it real? The conversations, the kisses, the trips to the grocery store, the private fashion shows. Was any of it real, or are you just a master of acting?"

FAKE IT TILL WE MAKE IT

Shahzad clumsily swipes at his eyes with the back of his fingers. "Everything I've ever said to you, done for you, given to you—everything, Nyla, has been from the bottom of my heart. I didn't realize when us faking it had become so damn real. You make me—you make *everything* so real. I just realized it after I... I'm... I should've told you, Nyla."

"But you didn't." I step up to him. "I'm not going to stand here and discredit you for being a great brother to your sisters and a great friend to others, but you're not great to yourself. You don't *care* about yourself, so why should I expect that you care for me?" My chin quivers, and I shake my head to ward off the impending migraine. "Honestly, I don't expect you to. You had me convinced that there was something real in our fake relationship." I start taking steps back. "I don't hold you responsible for your actions, Shahzad. Just understand that I would never have done this to you, even if we weren't... whatever I thought we were."

I slide into the backseat, forcefully shutting the door, blocking out the sound of his palms slapping against the window. His voice echoes like a distant ache at the back of my mind.

Nyla, please, don't go.
Nyla, I'll fix it.
Nyla, I didn't mean it.
Nyla, I'm sorry.
As the limo drives off, I start sobbing uncontrollably.

28

Rhode Island

Shahzad

"Shahzad bhai? I'm going to take Sky for a walk now. We'll be going around the neighborhood. If you can, maybe try to switch from the bathroom to the bedroom, please?"

I stare at the drainage.

"Um, okay, good talk. I'll grab some shawarmas on the way. See you in a bit."

Door unlocked. Shut. Locked.

I've strictly instructed her not to ask about my well-being. Jia and Tae tried, and I nearly broke down in the kitchen during rush hour. Bao tried to reduce my workload, but I've found it easier to distract myself in front of the burning stoves and boiling pots. *Very* little distraction.

Still staring at the sink cabinet, I flick open the lid of Nyla's colored shampoo and take a deep whiff of the rich, sweet berries scent. For the past week, I have found myself in the bathroom, or the shower stall, on the ground, hugging her shampoo, body wash, or the clothes Alina forgot to pack for her. In these quiet moments, I can almost picture Nyla right in front of me, her beautiful smile playing in my mind.

Not having her here, no stories, no sound of her sewing machine, no feeling the warmth of her body against mine—I might as well be a dead man without her now that she knows the truth and is out of my life for good. Her presence breathed life into this small apartment, keeping it alive, nourished, and warm. Now, it's faded and turned grey and blue. Even Sky's been whining, sniffing Nyla's side of the bed, and curling up in that spot. Maira, too.

I'm lost. I have no idea what to do. I don't know how to handle any of this.

I pull out my phone, brushing off the missed calls from Azeer and a couple from Alina. I begin scrolling through my camera roll.

Live pictures of Nyla sitting on our couch in her cozy pink sweater and my borrowed grey sweats, arm around Sky as she holds up peace signs, and when I hold down, her smile turns into a burst of laughter. Others are of us snuggled in bed, her lips meeting my cheek or my grinning face. Some photos are *strictly* for my eyes, showcasing soft, brown curves and flushed, dewy skin. Then, there are videos of me cooking and feeding her. She flips the camera, chews with a proud smile, and gives a thumbs-up.

"*Ramsay, you better watch out! My man's about to blow everyone on Food Network to another planet!*" She announces, then kisses my shoulder blade. "*More—*" The video cuts off. And I watch it endlessly until my phone dies.

I blink away the tears that catch me off guard. "Fuck." Sniffling sharply, I swing open the door of the sink cabinet, reaching for a roll of toilet paper—

CLANK!

Something square-shaped, wrapped in a pink shawl, tumbles out and lands by my feet. I pick it up slowly, feeling the poundage of it, and then unwrap it.

A weight scale.

I don't own a weight scale, so this must be Nyla's. Little battered, with faint cracks, as if she took out her frustrations on it against a wall, but the damn device was too stubborn to break.

Running a hand down my face, I drag myself out of the bathroom.

Opening the fridge door, I pull out a beer can stare at it, crack it open, and drain the golden liquid into the sink.

I head to the cabinet and settle onto the balcony with a bottle of red wine. Tastes like absolute shit, but it is her favorite, so it's *my* favorite, too. I silently hope she's not drowning her sorrows or slipping back into old habits, especially when she's been making progress in her recovery.

Where are you, my troublemaker?

I toss the weight scale aside and retrieve a hammer from my toolbox next to one of her potted flowers. Marigolds, I think. She liked their smell and how each petal had a light-to-dark orange gradient. Said it reminded her of a gown she wore at her tenth birthday party.

Gripping my hammer, I kneel and raise my arm back.

BANG!

I repeatedly smash the screen, the numbers in pounds flickering from high to low with each forceful hit. Glass fragments scatter, and I tilt my head to avoid it reaching my eyes. Again and again, I pound the machine until its inner workings are exposed.

My phone disturbs me once again. "God-fucking-dammit." I snatch it out, ready to toss it aside, but then I see that the caller ID belongs to the last little human I'd expect to dial my number.

"Shahzad uncle," Zoha greets, her tone as unhappy as Maira's been. I'm tearing up again. I feel a lump forming in my throat. The last time I cried this much was at Baba's funeral. Nyla's presence used to bring happy tears, I-can't-believe-she-exists tears, and after she left, I found myself crying almost every night, struggling to sleep without her on our couch. "Hello?"

"Hey, sweetheart," I croak, setting the hammer on the floor and leaning against the railing. "It's a school night. Why aren't you sleeping?"

"Because my favorite uncle and aunty are sad."

"How do you . . . Did your parents tell you?"

"No. I heard them talking in the kitchen."

This kid.

"Zoha . . . It's fine. I'm fine. Go to sleep before your dad finds out."

"It's okay. Mama and Abbu are sleeping. I'm hiding in my toy box so they can't hear me." She giggles quietly, then shushes herself. "How are you?"

I rub my forehead. "Not good, sweetie."

"Do you miss Nyla khala?" she mumbles.

"So much." I pull in my bottom lip. "I miss her so much."

"Do you want to know where she is hiding?"

My head snaps up. I've had a couple of theories about her whereabouts—Sun Tower, Toronto, a cabin on the outskirts of New York, a different state, or maybe Rhode Island. I intended to ride out the denial stage, as Maira described it, but if I could just discover her current location.

"Do you know where she is hiding, sweetheart?"

"Yup," Zoha chirps. "But you have to keep it a secret from her. I'm telling you because when she talked to me, she sounded sad like you. Mama says it's okay to be sad, but you shouldn't be sad by yourself. You need a shoulder to cry on."

210

FAKE IT TILL WE MAKE IT

How is she Azeer's daughter? Alina's, I can understand, kinda. But could I ever expect such innocent wisdom out of Azeer? Fuck no. He'd slap me on the back of my head and push me on my knees to apologize to Nyla. And while I'd dutifully perform that task, I know she deserves a *way* better apology.

"All right, sweetie. Tell me where she is so we can be sad together, okay?"

Jia stares disappointedly at the letter of resignation I hand her. "This better be a winning lottery ticket."

"I wish," I reply, taking a deep breath. Tae sits beside her, unfolding the paper and explaining that it's not a win but a loss. "The new menus got the green light from you, Jia. I've briefed Bao and the team on every recipe detail, and he knows he can reach me anytime for extra insight."

Jia's lips tighten, wrinkles forming around her mouth as she chews on a dried mango slice and snatches the paper from Eric, reading it herself. Without lifting her eyes, she asks, "Are you bringing Alyn-ah home?"

"It's Nyla, Halmeoni," Tae mutters as a reminder. Yeah, everyone at the restaurant knows because I couldn't keep the lie rotting in my brain any longer. Maira was initially dumbstruck, but she decided to join me in my suffering instead.

"No, I'm not bringing her home, Jia," I reply honestly. "I'm going wherever she goes."

"Wait, what? You're moving out, too?" Tae asks, sharing worried eyes with his grandmother. "Your lease isn't up until next January."

"I know. Maira will hold down the fort here, and we'll both keep paying rent even when I'm away." Leaning forward, I take Jia's hands in mine. She frowns, her gaze softening. "Thank you, Jia. For everything you've done for me. For giving me a home when I had nowhere else. For providing opportunities in the kitchen. Letting me learn from your incredibly talented team. Working alongside this . . . family. But it's time for me to make my own."

"Shit," Tae whispers, smiling. "You better visit."

"I will."

Jia's hand cups my cheek. "Be a good boy, adeul. Make sure to eat your meals on time.

And to take good care of yourself." Her eyes water, and I am there with her. "You are like my son. I want you to be happy with yourself and with Nyla-ya. That's all a mother wants for their baby."

I nod in a loop, rising from my spot and crouching beside her. Pulling her into a hug, I breathe in the scent of rose powder and fresh butter tarts. "I promise, Jia."

"And I want a wedding invitation," she says.

"Of course."

"A baby shower invitation, too."

"I won't forget."

"Also, I want to be one of the first customers to dine at your restaurant."

"I wouldn't have it any other way."

She leans back, gripping my shoulder. "And don't forget to have us cater your kids' birthday parties. We've got the best bibimbap in town."

I join in the laughter, nodding in agreement. "You'll do great, Jia. I'm sure of it." Standing up, I tousle Tae's hair. "Be a good man and look after your halmeoni."

"Sir, yes, sir," he says, giving me a tight hug around the waist. "Can you feel the muscles? Hye-jin noticed."

"You're making progress, kid," I assure him, hugging his head and patting his back. Grabbing my duffle bag and whistling for Sky, who's busy people-watching, I kiss Jia's cheek goodbye and exchange hand slaps with Tae. "Let the team know I'll catch up with them soon."

Maira's lounging by the Jeep I borrowed from Sahara as I make my way over. "You're really going through with this, huh?"

"Yup."

"I'm so proud of you." She closes the trunk, securing the rest of my bags, and lets out a sigh. Her thumb brushes the corner of her right eye. "God, sorry. It's just—I don't know. I wish you had been honest with me from the beginning. I could've helped you out or something."

"Get over here, kid." I extend my arm, and she wraps herself around my side. "Ground rules?"

"Location services on. Phone off silent. Pepper spray in hand. No wild parties. And no boys."

I grin. "Good."

She steps back. "What do I say to Mustafa?"

I open the passenger door, motioning for Sky to hop in. "The truth. Start to finish. If he wants to beat the shit out of me for leaving you here by yourself, let him know I'll give him a call when I'm ready."

"Got it, boss." Maira opens the driver's side for me. "Take care and keep yourself safe."

"I will."

"And make sure you *grovel*-grovel. No boom-box outside her doorstep or gigantic cue cards telling her how much you need her like the losers in Dua's chick-flicks." She jabs her finger in my chest. "I'm talking on-your-knees, patient, but intense, sweat-breaking groveling. For *however* long it takes her to forgive you. Don't lose her this time. Okay?"

"I'd die if I did, kid."

"Go get your girl, Chef."

Hoisting up in my seat, I shut the door and start the ignition. "Ready to bring back Mom, honey?" Sky barks twice. "That's the spirit." I slam the shift gear into drive and hit the gas, heading back towards Rhode Island.

Sahara's call comes in as I make a quick stop at the gas station.

"Good news only, sweetheart."

She sighs. "I've got the keys."

Fuck, yes!

"God, thank you, Sahara. Thank you so much."

"Anytime," she replies. "I had them delivered to the house this morning. They should be under a blue pot, according to Roberto."

I drag my hands through my hair, a shit-eating grin on my mouth. "It's right across, yeah?"

"Yes, it is. Try not to catch a stalker case, please. It'll place my real estate reputation into muddy waters if people found out I bought a vacation home for my cousin, a clinical stalker for Nyla Ghilzai out of all the women."

"I won't. I promise."

Sahara lets out a quiet chuckle. Compared to Azeer, I find myself closer to her at times. She values the fact that I'm not always trying to pry beneath the mask she puts on for the rest of our family. Around me, she lets her guard down and shows her true self. Why? Well, once, we got bat-shit drunk at her place, and in her intoxicated state, she confessed that I reminded her of her deceased father before passing out. Ever since that moment, we've had a special connection. On top of that, she's my adopted little cousin and Zineerah's closest friend.

"It's none of my business, but whatever the fuck happened between you and Nyla, I hope it all works out for the best," Sahara says as I finish pumping gas into the Jeep. "You two are alone and miserable without each other. You, more so."

"Great talk."

"Debatable. I allotted three minutes out of my schedule for this. Keep me updated through emails. I hate text messaging." She ends the call on her own accord.

My vacation house mirrors Nyla's, conveniently built just across from her.

I pull the Jeep into the driveway, keeping my eyes fixed on her house through the rearview. "Try not to make too much noise, honey."

Sky huffs.

I hop out, slam the door, and gaze at her place—four windows with curtains drawn. The driveway's clear, and all the lights are out. Well, it is pushing midnight.

True to Sahara's word, her assistant left the key under the blue pot. I slip it into the lock, turn it, and enter a fully decked-out residence.

The fuck did I buy an air mattress for then?

Sky bolts ahead, exploring the main floor with its spacious kitchen, bland, minimalist living room, guest bathroom, leisure room complete with a pool table, and a mini library.

Upstairs are four bedrooms—two masters and two guests, each with its own bathroom. The first main bedroom provides a direct view of Nyla's house across the way.

Yup, this is where I'll be sleeping.

Heading to the basement, I find a fancy homemade theater with expansive double doors at the back that open to a swimming pool, rows of lounge chairs, and a barbecue grill.

"Home sweet home," I mutter, hands on my hips. Sky barks in the background, weaving through the lounge chairs, her tail wagging with uncontrolled joy. At least someone's having a good time. Hopefully, that joy extends to the possibility of earning Nyla's trust.

I spend the next couple of hours unpacking and jotting down a grocery list. It includes Sky's food and additional ingredients aside from the ones already stocked in the fridge and pantry courtesy of Sahara and her assistant.

The distant hum of a car's wheels catches my attention, cueing me to kill all the lights in the house with the dumbass app Sahara forced me to install on my phone.

I sneak a glance through the living room curtains, spotting a white Mercedes parking in Nyla's driveway. My woman is stepping out from the driver's seat, clad in a blush-pink pant-suit and rocking high heels.

Her hair . . . isn't pink anymore. It's black. Stark black. Like the starless sky above us. She's still got those adorable bangs, though.

And she says she doesn't look great in black.

Nyla's speaking to someone on the phone as she walks up the steps of her house, a black file tucked under her arm. Fuck, she looks gorgeous in her little business suit.

She ends the call abruptly and pivots on her heel.

"Shit." I duck down, signaling to Sky to stay quiet by pressing a finger to my lips. Tilting my head up, I catch Nyla surveying my house and the Jeep parked in the driveway, a thrown-off look on her face. Then she shrugs and heads inside. "Missed you, too, baby."

29

Independence Day

Shahzad

July 4th

It's been a few days since I landed at the vacation house, and the one drug keeping me sane in this unfamiliar territory is Nyla's existence.

Here's what I noted.

She kicks off her mornings with a jog around the neighborhood and the beach, then swings by her place for a bagel or a muffin. After that, she heads off to the bustling town full of retirees and vacationing families, making her way to a compact studio space. Right next door, there's a café where she grabs whatever's on the lunch menu, and then she dives into her laptop.

Occasionally, she zones out, people-watching with a slight frown, and I try my best to blend into the scene. She wraps things up, packs up, and heads back to her studio. Late in the evening, she returns home, and the whole routine kicks off again.

And then there are her two assigned bodyguards, Mickey and Grayson, always stationed in a different booth at the café or surveying in their SUV parked parallel to her studio. At night, they clock off to a nearby motel. I recognized the bastards immediately; they were rookies back when I worked as a night guard at Sun Tower Hotel in New York. Of course,

FAKE IT TILL WE MAKE IT

Azeer and Alina provided them, and for that, I'm grateful.

Tonight, however, is America's birthday.

The entire neighborhood flocks to the beach for games and fireworks. Yeah, that beach right behind Nyla's place. Our streets outside are a riot of red, white, and blue, with families strolling down the two-way street, pumped with the Fourth of July spirit. Wouldn't be shocked if it started raining lollipops and cupcakes in this little state.

I'm holed up inside for obvious reasons, mapping out meals to give to Nyla and cooking up a variety of lunch and dinner dishes for the upcoming week, all packed with her favorite foods, along with snacks she can munch on in between.

Sky barks as an alert.

I kill the stoves, wipe my hands, and jog to the living room. Turns out, all I have to say is, "Alexa, turn the living room lights off," and the whole place plunges into darkness.

Technology, man.

Nyla steps out in a 1950s-esque sundress she'd shown me on her phone. She's like a rare gem, with her—*huh?* Her pink ponytail sways as she descends the porch steps. The black hair must've been a wig, I guess.

Lost, but not forgotten.

My attention shifts to a baby-blue Mustang convertible parked at her curb, packed by four unfamiliar women. The one with black braids throws her arms up in excitement, the others wolf-whistling and making Nyla blush as she twirls in her dress. I watch sneakily through the curtains, wearing a shit-eating grin as my girl hops into the back seat with her friends. Cheek kisses and side hugs are exchanged before the party cruises off, the radio blaring.

"Good for you, Troublemaker." I push off from the wall by the window, hustling back to the kitchen to double-check that everything's turned off and secure. "All right, honey. I'm going to go guard your mother from danger. When I'm back, we'll play fetch with Mr. Chewy?"

Sky barks happily and licks my cheek.

Locking my door, I start jogging down the street, keeping an eye on the sluggish movement of cars on the busy streets. Horns are being blared, cheers are being cheered, chants are being chanted, disturbing whoever *isn't* in the mood to celebrate. Spoiler alert: *everyone* is in the mood to celebrate.

Honestly, if it weren't for Nyla and her friends deciding to hit the town late at night, I'd probably have stayed home and continued prepping her meals.

And it's a damn miracle I tagged along because, surprise, surprise, they've parked near a crowded bar.

The patriotic party exits the convertible, sticking together as they enter the intoxicated vicinity. Not only am I safeguarding Nyla, but also her lovely friends. I'm just *really* glad she's had company to rely on for the past week.

I dish out five bucks for a budget-friendly cap sporting the American flag and get my cheeks painted in the national colors. Maneuvering through the bodies entering the bar, I make my way to the dimly lit corner where the jukebox is, avoiding the bright spotlights trained on the live band belting out a Bon Jovi track.

The girls are settled down in a booth with a pair of guys—Blondie perched on the lap of one dude, cackling like crazy as he ravages her neck with his tongue and teeth. A third guy shows up with red and blue shots and a plate of nachos. Better not be any fucking olives in there; Nyla hates them.

Nyla knocks back two shots and makes room for Nacho Guy to join. His arm immediately snakes behind the seat—right behind her.

My nails dig into the stress ball Nyla crocheted for me. It's the exact replica of the one Frederick gave me. "Fucker."

When I glance at my woman, she's throwing her head back, laughing at his jokes, her beauty painted by the colorful lights in the bar.

She's so . . . happy.

And if she catches sight of me, that happiness will vanish.

She doesn't want anything to do with me. I betrayed her trust. I killed the love she had for me. What she deserves now is pure, genuine happiness—even if it comes from within herself.

I mean, fuck. Look at her. She's thriving. Enjoying nachos, downing shots, and sharing giggles with some finance guy who probably pulls in eight figures and uses an excessive amount of gel in his hair.

But you won't give up on the one you love.

I make my way to the bar and order a Corona, casually leaning against the counter. I survey the crowd gathering in the middle for an impromptu dance party. Billy Idol's musical influence on these intoxicated souls isn't exactly a treat for my ears.

Nyla and her crew are up from their seats, blending into the crowd. She clings close to her girls. Blondie's getting cozy with her vampire in a KC jersey, Redhead and Braids are coupled up, and then there's Nacho Guy making a move on my girl.

A woman slides up to me, pressing her chest against mine. "Do you want to—?"

"I'm married."

She eyes my left hand and scoffs. "Yeah, nice try. Where's your ring?"

The fucker slips his arm around Nyla's waist. She startles, bumping against his chest.

"Hello?" Red fingernails snap in front of my eyes, pulling my attention away. "I'm talking to you—"

I hand her my beer and make my way into the pulsating crowd.

Just as I'm about to grab his shoulder and yank him away, Nyla pushes off of him. I turn around swiftly, lowering my cap.

"Fucking tease!" I hear him shout over the crowd, shoving people aside as he storms out of the bar.

Nyla's friends break away from the dance floor to accompany her to the bathroom. Good. She's safe with those girls.

In the meantime, I step outside and follow the prick as he heads into the alley between the bar and a boutique. He leans against the wall, lighting up a cigarette and muttering curses about Nyla under his breath.

I approach him with a casual smile. "Hey, man. Mind if I join you? It's getting a bit stuffy in there."

He shrugs. "Sure." He pulls on extra cigarette from his pocket, offering it to me, but I decline. "You a local?"

"Nah. My wife and I are just visiting some friends from Manhattan."

"Why the hell are you here then? Go find your girl before some jerk swoops in." He gestures towards the bar with a raised brow.

I glance through the window, hoping to catch a glimpse of a certain pink-head, but no luck. Hopefully, those girls are looking out for her. "I trust her."

"Three words that'll come back to bite you in the ass."

My gaze locks onto his. "Sounds like tonight didn't go your way."

He scoffs, lowering his cigarette. "City girls, man. They play too much."

"Yeah? What happened?"

He gives me a once-over, as if questioning my seriousness, mutters, "Fuck it," and launches into his story. "My friends and I just wanted to have a good time, but one of them decided to invite his situationship, and she brought her squad." He clenches his jaw. "Naturally, one of the girls, pink hair and shit caught my eye. Well, no, it was those tits and ass." And that's how he just sealed his own fate. "I tried flirting with her, and I'm pretty fucking sure she was flirting back. I mean, look at my smile?" He grins with a set of crooked, yellowing teeth. "It's one of the best parts about me."

It's the ugliest fucking smile I've ever seen. "And it didn't work?"

"Of course, it fucking didn't. Next thing you know, she's fucking pushing me away on the dance floor like the cock-teasing bitch she is." He points a finger in my face. "Moral of the story. Fuck. City. Girls."

I smirk. "Pink hair?"

"Yeah." He takes a drag. "Why? You know her or something?"

"I think I'd recognize my wife." I make a show of punching him, and he goes staggering back into the wall. I'm itching to break his nose in half, but because of the public and Mickey and Grayson hovering by the front entrance, I resort to grabbing his collars and slamming him back into the wall with a satisfying *oomph*. "That's for speaking to my wife." I shove him into the side of an industrial-sized garbage bin. "And that's for looking at my wife."

Turning him around, I press his cheek against the lid and deliver a swift kick to his shins. He drops to both knees, growling curses at me. I seize his wrists, giving his fingers a bone-crushing squeeze. Over the celebration of America's birth, no one can hear this fucker.

"If you ever lay a finger on my wife without her consent or any other innocent woman, I'll break all ten of your fingers, yank out all thirty-two of your decaying teeth, and stuff them so far down your fucking throat you'll be shitting it all out the next morning. Clear?"

"Whatever, man! Just let me fucking go!"

I release him with a forceful shove, sending him stumbling. My foot connects with his groin, producing an agonizing groan. What a satisfying sound.

Leaving him curled up in the alley, I tuck my fists into the pockets of my jacket. As I turn the corner, I spot Nyla exiting the bar and heading toward Mickey's blond, buzzed head and Grayson's curly one, the idiots devouring hotdogs by the stand.

She starts talking to her guards, scanning the area frantically, while the pair shake their heads at her questions.

That's my signal to make my exit.

I pull down my cap and the hood of my jacket, blending into the crowd surging toward the beach for the fireworks. Nyla's focused on the bar as I smoothly glide past her. The air carries the scent of fruits and vanilla from her.

"How could he just vanish?" I catch her silvery, sweet voice saying before disappearing into the crowd with a smirk.

The next morning, I wake up with a whole new perspective about myself.

If I can't be what Nyla wanted me to be in the past, I can at least be her friend. Start from scratch and build my way up; that's the whole reason I'm here. Because I want to take care of her, cherish her, and make her smile and laugh.

It's just shy of six a.m. when I throw on my workout gear. No more hiding. I want this woman to know I'm here and committed to staying as long as it takes to earn even a fraction of her trust back.

Wringing my hands, I peek through a peephole, jogging on my feet. Sky's waiting patiently, tail wagging.

Nyla steps out in her tights and sweater, poking in her Airpods and stretching.

I tighten my grip on the door handle, still hesitating. I should probably push it down. I should step out. I'll do that in a second.

A minute.

Two minutes.

Three.

She isn't even there anymore.

I groan, dragging my hands down my face. "Shit." Sky gives me a questioning look. "Yeah, I know. I'm a coward. Your mom's too damn pretty and too damn pissed."

Whatever. She's gone now, so my body decides to take itself out.

Sky barks loudly and dashes away.

I chase after her. "Hey! Hey—"

Nyla emerges from behind the Jeep.

Sky leaps over her and scores scratches behind the ear. Those piercing emerald eyes, though, are latched onto me.

Anxiety shoots down my spine, causing me to jerk back. I'm ready to retreat and never resurface, but she's here.

She's here.

So real and beautiful, and when those eyes spot the house behind me, she's furious. Still stunning in my eyes.

Her chin lifts slightly, eyes traveling over my body, a cold, stoic expression on her face. Meanwhile, I'm freaking out like a fucking schoolboy because she just checked me out. She can throw all the shades of bitterness she wants, but that hint of pink on her cheeks whenever she sees me gives her away every time.

Now, confidence trades places with anxiety, and I find the strength in me to step down. I whistle for Sky to return to me, but the stubborn husky remains circling Nyla.

Goddammit, Sky.

Nyla's gaze flicks up to meet mine. She rolls her eyes to the side, pushes in one of her Airpods, and jogs away.

The fuck?

Sky attempts to follow, but I whistle for her to sit while unapologetically staring as Nyla's perfect ass disappear down the street.

"Think she's challenging us?"

Sky barks. *You're delusional.*

"Maybe," I mutter. "What's the difference when you're in love with Nyla Ghilzai?" Patting her back, I stand and stretch, cracking the muscles in my neck. "Ready, honey?"

Sky speeds ahead, and I run behind.

Now that Nyla knows I'm here, I can start delivering my meals to her.

In a fashion that she absolutely cannot deny.

After keeping pace with her during a jog, with, to my surprise, no complaints from her end, I decide to call it a day and head back home.

I whip up two breakfast sandwiches and toss in some snacking bars, neatly packing everything into a paper bag and placing it in a charming woven basket.

"Okay, remember. Take this to Nyla's porch when she's there, and make sure she accepts it," I instruct Sky. She wags her tail and gives a huff in agreement. "Good girl." I carefully place the basket handle in her mouth, and she chomps down gently.

Five minutes later, Nyla returns, and I swing the door open wide. Sky confidently trots out, effortlessly crossing the road. She grabs Nyla's attention before she even makes it to the porch.

I lean against the doorway, arms and ankles crossed, a proud smile on my face as Nyla grabs the paper bag and peeks inside. She extracts the 'I love you' note I wrote and takes a moment to read it.

Eyes locked on mine, she crumples the note in her fist and tucks it into her jacket pocket. I count that as a victory. She didn't toss it out, even with the recycling boxes outside.

Ha. You still love me, baby.

Taking the paper bag, another sign that she still loves me, she gives Sky a ruffle over her head and shuts the door behind her.

I pump my fist, trying to contain my excitement.

Letting out a breath, I praise Sky for her efforts, promising her a shit ton of treats.

30

A Garden For Her

Shahzad

August 10th

We're a month in.

And I'm overflowing with determination.

Every day, I've got Sky delivering meals, each accompanied by a new note that my future bride crumples but hides away for herself. Nyla even waits an extra minute by the yard in the morning, by the porch for my husky to arrive with her lunch, then lingers in her car when she gets home until Sky's out and running.

Obviously, I made Sky late on purpose to test this theory.

Nyla likes this little gimmick. Who wouldn't? She's a sucker for romantic gestures, and I'm here to serve. Plus, ditching the processed junk from the café and opting for my home-cooked meals has given her this gorgeous glow. When I'm undercover, body-guarding her through town, she doesn't leave a morsel on her plate. She licks it all clean, and it's my kind of satisfaction.

God, I love her.

I've made it a thing to try something new for her on top of sticking with whatever I did the month before.

"Flowers?" I ask, tapping the whiteboard on my lap.

Sky doesn't bother lifting her head.

"How about cinnamon buns?"

No response.

"Noted. Butter tarts?"

Still nothing.

"Books? Girls like books, right? Azeer built an entire library for Alina, and . . . " I sigh, staring across at Nyla's house. "And I fucked up, so books can't solve shit."

A small white car pulls up by Nyla's driveway. My troublemaker steps out in a floral dress, looking pretty, and greets a short middle-aged lady in jeans and a white t-shirt. They exchange pleasantries on the porch.

"Showtime, honey," I say, opening the door for Sky. She rushes out with the lunch basket. The short lady, who turns out to be the housekeeper, given the supplies she's unloading from her trunk, yelps and staggers back. "Sorry, ma'am!"

She glares at me.

Nyla takes the paper bag but doesn't bother checking the note. Without making eye contact, she shoves the lunch into her purse, clearly distressed about something else.

Now, who's got a death wish?

After thanking the lady, Nyla gets into her car and drives off the street. I close my door and jog up the porch steps before the lady can retreat inside. When I see the cleaning supplies, a light bulb goes off in my head.

"Miss? Hey. Hi. Listen, I'm that woman's close friend, and I was hoping I could assist you?"

She eyes me up and down, arching a brow. "You're a friend of Alyn?"

My brows shoot up, and I hold back a chuckle. "Yeah, Alyn and I, we're good neighbor-friends. Actually, it's a bit more than that. I really love that girl, and I messed up big time. So now, I'm doing whatever the hell I can to hold her hand again." I take another step up. "If I can lighten your workload, maybe—"

"Are you Shaza?" she interrupts.

"Shahzad, yes."

The lady smirks, smacks her lips, and lifts her supplies. "Lady of the house said no Shaza allowed."

My patience is wearing thin. She went out of her way to ban me, which I get. "Well, okay. Can I at least help with something?"

She tilts her head, emphasizes, "Get a job," then slams the door in my face.

Begrudgingly, I take a seat on the porch steps. Sky whines, licking my cheek. A defeated sigh escapes me. "Maybe I should've just stuck to buying her flowers." My eyes scan the white picket fence, the overgrown grass, and the weeds. Not a single hint of color that reflects Nyla.

Fuck the lightbulb.

A lightning bolt of realization strikes me to stand.

Why bother with buying flowers every day when I can create a whole damn garden for her?

I've got the grass, fresh soil, a generous dose of free vitamin D, and some landscaping skills from the countless hours with Baba in the backyard of our family house.

Genius!

Homes for Gnomes conveniently sits a block away from Nyla's design studio.

Grabbing a cart, I navigate the gardening aisles, mentally ticking off items from the checklist I compiled from an elderly lady's YouTube video. She recommended potted plants instead of directly planting seeds in the soil—water them, tap your watch, and watch them bloom over the weeks.

And so I grab two hefty pots for her porch, along with a big bag of fertilizer, some flower seeds that should thrive in August, and a couple of pre-bloomed hanging flowers.

Depositing my purchases into the jeep, I head to the café across from Nyla's workplace, where the love of my life sits. She unveils the lunch I prepared for her, lifting it to her nose for a sniff. I swear, I *swear*, she smiles.

I roll down the passenger side window, and Sky starts barking eagerly. Nyla's head jerks up, and her eyes blink as she spots us. Even from a distance, with the glass between us, I can see the golden flecks in her sweet, forest-green gaze.

My head tilts, and I gesture with my chin toward her lunch. I give a thumbs-up, silently asking if it's good. Not that I really need an answer—she always returns the empty boxes to my porch in the early morning. I've thought about stepping out when she does, but I always veto that idea.

Nyla continues to glare at my smile.

She stabs the fork into the sliced chicken breast and stuffs it into her mouth, followed by a scoop of brown rice layered with teriyaki sauce. She grabs the chopped steamed broccoli from a separate container and bites the head off.

Nyla gives me a thumbs down.

Holy fuck, she spoke to me.

Okay, technically, she didn't. But I'll take it.

I burst into laughter, shaking my head at her adorable antics. Pulling out my phone, I type "I love you, too" in big, bold letters and flash it in her direction.

She strikes me with a heartbreaking expression, abruptly packing up her lunch. Wait, what? *You haven't finished eating.* She shoves everything back into the bag and walks to the other side of the café.

I hold my breath, clutching my phone.

As she goes about reopening everything, her back turned to me, I relax in my seat. My fingers absently scratch behind Sky's ears, and she whines, probably questioning something I already know. "Don't worry, honey. I'll get her back soon."

⁂

The cleaning lady's small, white car has vanished from the curb by the time I get home.

I start unloading my gear onto the driveway, beginning with the pots and peeling off the price tags. Then, I fill them with fertilizer, patting them down with my gloved hands.

"Hey, hey, hey!" I caution Sky before she can taste the soil and risk getting a stomach bug. "It's not for dogs."

She huffs through her nose. To cheer her up, I toss the tennis ball across my yard, keeping her playful and distracted.

Following the same YouTube tutorial, I plant the flower seeds in their designated pots and press them down. Filling the watering can from my kitchen faucet, I pour the liquid over the fertilizer.

My jaw is killing me from the grin on my face. *Fuck, she's going to love this.*

It's pushing dinner time by the time I've rearranged the pots on her porch. Hammering a few nails on the edge of her canopy, I hang up the pre-potted gardenias and step back to check out the greenhouse I've put together for her. *Yeah, she's definitely going to love this.*

Dusting my hands, I tidy up the gardening mess, set a daily reminder to water her plants before our early morning runs, which are silent and miles apart, and then get started on making dinner.

Nyla's home later than I expected.

As she exits her car, I escape to my yard with Sky and her basket for Nyla's dinner.

Her ballet flats come to a sudden stop, eyes taking in the vibrant scene of her once dull yard.

"Go on, girl," I whisper to Sky, and I watch as she pads over to Nyla, bumping the basket against her leg and breaking the spell I've cast on my woman.

Nyla's wide-eyed when she spins around and meets my gaze. I lean against my porch pillar, mouth curving up. She checks behind her as if imagining the flowers, then returns her focus to me.

Remember those daggers she was shooting at me hours ago? Yeah, they've been rusted and replaced by happiness. She doesn't have to smile for me to know that.

Sky bumps her again.

Nyla's lashes flicker as she breaks eye contact, reaching for the brown paper bag. She digs in for the note and unfolds it. She stares at it for what feels like hours. No annoyance. No frustration. Only a blank expression.

And guess fucking what?

She doesn't crumple it.

The note gets neatly folded and tucked into her purse. She grabs her takeout box, gives Sky a playful pat on the head, and heads indoors, lightly brushing the tips of her delicate, soft fingers over one of the hanging pots on the way.

And when she grins, my heart lodges itself in my throat, and I feel like I might vomit out a mix of glitter and all kinds of pastel shit.

You made her smile.

I made her smile. I fucking did that. She didn't look at me when she did, but that's cool. I won't be an ungrateful prick because *I made her smile.*

Containing my excitement, I throw up a fist as a victory and escort Sky and myself inside.

More smiles to come, Shahzad.

31

Caffè di Matilda

Shahzad

September 20th

We're officially two months in.

And I realized I *do* need to get a damn job.

Might as well find something productive to do while I'm out here grovelling for my life. Armed with a printed resumé, I try my hand at an Azeer Khan-esque appearance. A dress shirt rescued from the depths of my carry-on and repeatedly ironed. Dress pants that I didn't even know I owned—also given a serious ironing treatment. Since I lack fancy Italian leather, I settle for my combat boots, adjusting the pants' hem around them.

I slick back my hair, letting the dark strands fall loosely over my shoulders. Nyla likes my hair this way, so it's the way I like it now, too.

"All right, honey. Wish me luck."

Sky barks and leaps out the door the second I open it, Nyla's breakfast basket swinging back and forth as she walks over to her yard. The potted flowers are looking fresh and well-kept. I usually catch Nyla tending to them through my window with a tiny smile on her lips.

Mental note: build your future wife a greenhouse.

"Morning, neighbor!" I wave a hand as Nyla emerges from her place.

She glances up and misses a step.

My protective instincts kick in, and I bolt towards her like never before. Luckily, she grabs the railing to steady herself. Still, any excuse to make physical contact, even if it's just as subtle as holding her elbows, is good enough for me.

"Are you okay?" I crouch down, gently brushing my fingers over her ankle. "Did you twist it? I've got some medication if it's sprained."

Nyla gazes down at me, breathing steadily through her nose. Her eyes wander everywhere but my face.

"Wait a minute." I smirk. "Are you checking me out?"

Instantly, she breaks out of her trance and speeds toward her car, deftly unlocking it. But not before grabbing her breakfast from the basket.

I tap her window. "Read the note."

She keeps her gaze straight ahead, plunging her hand into the brown bag. Retrieving the note, she responds with a middle finger and fires up the engine.

I laugh my lungs out as she reverses and jet-sets down the street.

If I didn't already love her enough.

The place I've applied to is none other than Caffè di Matilda—Nyla's favorite café.

Sure, I could have opted for a fancy restaurant or a diner, but I've got to hone my dessert-making skills, and a café celebrated for its bakery goods is the perfect spot.

As a bonus, I'll get to see Nyla every day.

A win is a win.

"Yeah, you're hired," Donald declares, skimming over my resumé without bothering with an interview. The young girl beside him, Matilda, can't seem to take her eyes off me.

"But I haven't even described—"

"Don't care. You're a good-looking fella. It'll attract the ladies to walk in. My daughter here also mentioned that you resemble her favorite fantasy character," he says, turning to her. "Victor, right?"

"Lord Voctoral De Ashburn," she whispers, licking her lips. "He's a five-hundred-year-old vampire who slaughtered his enemy's court when they kidnapped his mate."

I shift uncomfortably in my seat. While I'd prefer a proper interview, I can't afford to slip up and risk jeopardizing my chances of getting this job. "Well, that's great news. When can I start?"

"Today. I'll email you the paperwork, schedule, and clock-in code. Fill the legal crap out by tonight and email it back to me ASAP." He squints at my resumé again. "Shaza, is it?"

"Shahzad."

"Yeah, no, that's a tongue twister. Victor, it is."

"Lord Voctoral De Ashburn," the daughter whispers.

"Tomato, tomahto," Donald grunts.

"You're a café owner, Papa. You should know the correct spelling of tomato."

Her papa looks mildly offended. "Do not lecture me on the spelling of tomato, Mat—"

"Another question," I interrupt. "What's my station?"

"Ah-ha!" Donald slaps his thighs, getting up and extending his hand. I quickly follow suit and give it a firm shake. "Cashier, Victor."

"Cash— You sure you don't want to interview me? I can *seriously* help out in the back kitchen, sir."

"I won't let these good looks go to waste behind a stove, son." He claps my back and leads me out of his office and to the breakroom. "Your locker." Green and rustic. Classic.

"Apron," Matilda mumbles, handing me what I'd like to call a piece of cheap cloth. "We don't have any . . . *larges* . . . at the moment." She's speaking to my chest, by the way. "Only small and medium sizes."

I check the tag. "This is extra small."

"Is it?" Matilda walks out of the breakroom.

Nyla, you owe me a thousand kisses for this.

I barely tie the apron, head to the back kitchen, and wash my hands. The place is a busy, organized chaos, with sizzling pans, chopping boards, and the clatter of dishes creating a symphony of culinary activity. My chest clenches thinking about Jia's BBQ House—the year I put in scrubbing dishes, sitting in the shadows at staff parties while Bao made a drunken spectacle of himself, and just as I decided to step up and commit myself to chef duties, I fucked it up. I've lost track of how many times I've sabotaged good opportunities due to my single-minded belief that I don't deserve them.

During the peak of my high school basketball career, tragedy struck with Baba's death. Just as I secured an apprenticeship at a prestigious three-star French restaurant, I had to abruptly leave for Toronto. After that rough detour, I returned to America and worked at Sun Tower Hotel, where constant comparisons with my cousin fueled my pride-driven decision to quit. Then, I began guarding that dickhead Abe, a choice that led to a colossal mistake.

The rest is history, never to be repeated again.

But placing a momentary pause on my ambitions to chase the girl of my dreams is worth it. Nyla's fucking worth it, and I'd be damned not to fight for her after everything she's done for me.

As I replace the girl at cash, my eyes lock with Nyla's lifting ones.

Oh, shit.

My face lights by a thousand watts. She tightly clutches her phone, looking at me from head to apron, *mostly* at the fitted apron, and back to my eyes. See, when she does it, I'm not creeped out.

"Greet the customer," the front supervisor, Amelia, whispers. A short young girl with blonde hair tied high into a ponytail and a perfect customer service grin.

"Morning, beautiful," I greet Nyla with a lopsided grin.

"That's not ethical," Amelia whisper-shouts, nudging me away from her hip. "I apologize for that, Alyn. The regular?"

"Beautiful name," I comment, crossing my arms. Her jade eyes briefly inspect my tattoos. "Is it short for something?"

"Just the regular, Lia," Nyla mutters. Amelia rings up a latte with oat milk and three pumps of vanilla. I make a mental note of her order to prepare it for her later.

Before Nyla can tap her phone to the payment pad, I beat her to it with my card, earning a disapproving glare from Amelia. However, my woman huffs and snatches the receipt I hand her.

"Have a beautiful day!" I say.

Amelia pulls me aside. "What was that?"

"What?"

"That thi—*Ugh.* Look, I know today's your first day, but you sure as hell don't want to make it your last. So, go crack open the ethics binder in the backroom and memorize it before you scare off all our regulars."

"First of all, kid, I am *very* regular with that regular, all right? She and I are . . . She's, you know . . . " I trail off, trying to gather the correct sentences.

"Girlfriend?"

"Not exactly."

"A friend?"

"Not at the moment."

"Just a woman you're attracted to?"

"I fucked up our relationship in New York, okay?" I drive my fingers through my hair. "And now I'm doing everything in my power I can to bring her back to me. I moved here for her. I got this job for her. And I'm sure as hell not leaving here without her."

Amelia shoots me a disapproving look, her gaze shifting to Nyla as she gets her drink.

"Either way," Amelia interrupts my ogling. "This is your new workplace. Others don't know about your situation with her. It can come off the wrong way. Mostly creepy. Do you understand what I'm saying?"

I nod. *You're not immature like Azeer.* "Yeah, no, you're right. I apologize, Amelia. I didn't mean to do any of that. Next time, I'll address her politely."

Amelia pats my bicep, her eyebrows raising in surprise. "Firm." She smiles kindly and heads back to the cash register.

Green irises hold me in an inquisitive, almost deadly grip. I find myself swallowing hard. She's the most beautiful statue, crafted from pure gold and polished marble. In my mind, she's the eighth wonder of the world.

I offer a smile in return.

Nyla remains focused on her laptop screen, but the tension between her brows doesn't fade away.

Caffè di Matilda is a small place with a maximum of eight workers.

Amelia, my trainer, has been glued to me for the past two weeks, coaching me at the register and helping me perfect my customer service smile. Matilda has me practicing the art of coffee and tea-making. She's a bit abnormal with her not-so-subtle touches and requests for me to cosplay as Lord WhateverTheFuck for her twentieth birthday.

As much as I'd like to keep my distance from her, I recognize the value of learning the ropes of barista-ing, a skill I plan to implement in my own restaurant's drink menu.

In the back kitchen, Roger handles the fryers during lunch, his twin Graham keeps an eye on soups and sandwiches, and Devon, the head baker. I bond a bit more with him, partly because he's the only person of color on the staff and also because I'm eager to sweeten my baking skills.

Then there's Harry, the new teenager responsible for tackling the dirty dishes. I've shared a few pointers with him about the soap-to-liquid ratio, the scrubbing angles, and the industrial dishwasher tricks. Despite his lanky frame and curly hair that sometimes blocks his vision, Harry is a good kid who shines at keeping those dishes spotless.

Donald, our pot-bellied, bald, and stereotypically aggressive Italian owner, would move mountains for his sweet Matilda if she so much as hinted. Probably a distant relative of Buddy from Cake Boss. I don't know whether that's offensive—I've never actually watched the show.

Then there's me, apparently the crowd-pleaser, especially with the ladies, as Donald predicted when he hired me. It's kind of impressive how our list of regulars keeps growing day by day. Mostly mothers, so.

My favorite regular, however, is always seated in the far corner booth, donning a different outfit each time. Pink hair, either let loose or pulled up into a ponytail, lips adorned with red lipstick, eyes defined with bold black kohl, and those soft, kissable fingertips relentlessly tapping on her keyboard.

But something isn't making sense to me as I scan the busy café.

How has no one recognized Nyla Ghilzai? Where are the paparazzi? The pestering fans? How come, Matilda, a young woman well-versed in pop culture, doesn't recognize her, either?

Checking my Donald-free surroundings, I pull out my phone and Google Nyla once again. As I navigate through the images, I am unable to locate a single photograph featuring her pink hair or any snapshots from the day she walked the runway. Shifting to the News section, I find a void in updates for the current year—only encountering ludicrous, outdated rumors dating back to her altar incident.

How is this possible? She doesn't have the power to control her privacy from leaking. That's something Abe would—

A small hand pushes at my back.

Amelia points her chin in Nyla's direction. "Go get her glass. Maybe strike up an *ethical* conversation?"

"She won't talk to me."

"Well, can you at least get the glass, please?"

I nod and tuck my phone away.

"All done?" I ask, approaching her table where only the foam remains in her now-empty latte glass. "I'd be more than delighted to treat you to another drink."

Nyla pauses from her sketching.

"I know you don't want to speak to me, and I won't force you to, but know that I miss you every day," I murmur, lifting her glass. My grip tightens around it. "I really miss you, Nyla."

She closes her eyes, signaling the end of our one-sided conversation.

Later, during closing time, Donald gathers all of us in the breakroom, playing the role of a coach rallying his team before a big game.

"Firstly, I'd like to thank Victor here for skyrocketing our sales through the damn roof!" He barks out a booming laugh, giving my back several hearty claps. The staff joins in with genuine applause. "All thanks to me, of course. If I hadn't hired him, most of you wouldn't even be here, and I'd probably have to declare bankruptcy." He mutters those words, thinning our trust in the idiot. "But that's all in the past!"

I'm shoved forward, and Matilda grabs my arm, pulling me down to sit beside her.

"You smell good," she whispers. "Like The Blood Woods after a brawl with the Fangvettes."

"Good to know." I slide down the bench, getting closer to Devon and Harry.

Amelia takes the stage, delving into sales projections for the Christmas season, new Halloween menu items, and the need for additional booth seatings (Donald hollers, "Boring!" from behind, but it falls flat, and nobody laughs for obvious reasons: he's just not funny), and lastly, customer feedback.

At the end of her spiel, Amelia asks, "Any questions?"

I raise my hand.

She sighs. "Yes, Shahzad?"

"I'd like to address the team if you don't mind."

Amelia nods and switches spots with me.

I wipe my sweaty palms on the sides of my jeans and say, "Hey, everybody. How's it going?" They respond with tight smiles, except for Matilda—she looks like she's ready to pounce. "Firstly, thanks for the kind words about bringing up the sales and stuff. I believe it's a group effort and not just me by myself. We're all in this together, you know?"

They look like they're ready to go home.

"I'm in love with one of our regulars." I drop the bomb.

Amelia groans, face-palming herself. Devon smiles because I indulged him with my mistakes on the first day and vice versa. Turns out, having younger sisters makes for great bonding material. Matilda is appalled, of course. Harry, Graham, and Roger exchange subtle smirks. Donald's grimacing, naturally.

"*Who?*" Matilda seethes.

"Alyn . . ."

Amelia's groan grows louder.

I continue speaking. "Back in New York, I fell in love with Alyn. *Hard*. Crash-landed. Then because I'm a man, I fucked it up. Boom. Just dust and nothing. I let her walk out of my life because I'm a coward. Because she wanted a future with a guy who lived in his past. So, I followed her to Rhode Island after a week of self-loathing. Not that the self-loathing has passed. Not yet." There's a scratchy feeling in my throat as I remember Nyla's face the day she left. "It's been two months of me trying, and while I am beginning to doubt my groveling skills, I won't give up on her. I'm going to get her back . . . and I'm going to follow my dream wherever the hell she wants to go."

Silence settles in, making things a bit awkward.

Sky was much more encouraging during my practice session this morning than my team's response now.

"*So,*" Matilda drags out, "you basically joined our team to what, use us to win her back?"

"Yes and no," I reply. "Look, I've never been much of a team player up until recently—until I met Alyn, and she taught me there was more to my talents than what met my eye. I'm—I'm a great cook. A damn great cook. I can knock out a hundred dishes in the first half-hour, handle the rush hour chaos, work the lobby, clear tables—whatever needs doing, I'm in with a hundred percent effort. And, most importantly, I want to learn from all of you—baking, tea making, soups, sandwiches—while also getting to know each of you better. This isn't just about Alyn. It's about me, too. Does that make sense?"

"Well." Matilda scoffs, a frown away from throwing a tantrum. "I guess I've read enough romance novels to help you out or whatever." She rolls her light-blue eyes, glaring at the lockers. "Not that I want to."

"Count me in!" Harry adds with a grin. "Can't promise much, but I'd love to repay you for your lessons."

"I appreciate that," I reply. "But really, you've already done enough by listening to me. You don't have to pitch in. However, if you ever catch me giving extra attention to that regular—" I nod towards an exasperated Amelia—"or throwing out some, let's say, unethical compliments—" I turn back to the audience—"just let it slide. That's my future bride, and I'll be damned if I don't tell her she looks beautiful every morning, at least ten times per second. No exaggeration there."

"This is beginning to sound like a horror movie plot," Devon comments.

I roll my eyes. "Thanks, buddy."

"Whatever." Amelia pulls out a blank page from her clipboard file. "Write down all the unethical compliments you plan to shower on your future bride, and I'll filter out the ones that won't fly in our business."

"Emphasis on 'unethical,' Amelia," I say, amused, grabbing the paper and pen.

Bumping her glasses up, she retorts, "I have a boyfriend, Shahzad. I'm well-versed in those 'unethical' compliments."

Donald claps his hands once, making the room jump. "I'll allow it!" He rushes over, slinging his arm around my shoulder. "It's been ages since we've had any action in our business. Well, unless you count those siblings who couldn't keep their hands to themselves. Fucking crackpots, am I right?"

"Just because Jackie and Niall had blond hair and blue eyes doesn't mean they were siblings, Donny," Graham points out.

"And they were married," Roger chimes in.

"We even attended their wedding, Papa," Matilda adds. "You got them a fifty-millimeter tequila bottle as a gift."

"Did I?" Donald scratches his brows. "Doesn't matter! We've got a new case on our hands—"

"Goodnight, everyone!" Devon stands up first, and the rest quickly follow, grabbing their stuff from the lockers. The guys pat me on the back, and the girls roll their eyes for various reasons.

I stand there alone in the room, staring at the blank page. A snort escapes me. "Unethical compliments."

32

Pride and Prejudice

October 31st

For almost ninety days straight, I've been on meal duty for Nyla.

On top of that, I've been busting my balls at Caffè di Matilda, sweating it out to boost up those sales. Now, finally, we're at a point where we can set aside a budget for some special events like karaoke, paint and wine, and trivia nights.

Tonight is Halloween.

Our so-called spooky decorations in black and orange are slapped all over the place, taped, cornered, and planted. The whole crew decked out in top-notch costumes.

Amelia is Wednesday Adams, draped in dark, gloomy colors and sporting creepy pigtails. Matilda, on the other hand, embodies Lady Merriweather De Ashurn from her erotica vampire fantasy, wrapped in a tight, white corset and a gown swiped from a medieval times museum. Roger and Graham take on the roles of Tweedledee and Tweedledum from *Alice In Wonderland*, rocking matching brown suspenders and striped shirts. Harry transformed into Chef Linguini from *Ratatouille*—a pretty fitting choice, if you ask me. Donald, true to his Italian roots, opts for *Scarface* vibes, portraying a cheap, low-time gangster. And then there's Devon, the center of attention at the café, strutting in as Deadpool without the mask, earning every woman's gaze as he expertly arranges his spread of baked goods on the buffet table.

As for me? I'm Mr. Darcy, the wealthiest and grumpiest guy in Derbyshire, straight out of *Pride and Prejudice*. Nyla's crazy about that book and movie, especially since she was an extra in one of the ballroom scenes at the age of twelve.

Matilda, my partner in crime, helped me score the Victorian-ish, medieval getup from a nearby thrift store. She tried to convince me to go all in as Lord WhateverTheFuck, but there's no way I'm passing up on a sweet opportunity like this.

The café echoes with the chaos of kids yelling, "Trick or treat," every time they hit our main door. Inside, a bustling crowd has already gathered. The air is alive with the beat of music from our brand-new speakers, and *Corpse Bride* is playing on the projector. Karaoke is going down in one corner, and booths and tables are packed with families, couples, and friends. Wherever I go, there's a symphony of lively conversations and laughter.

Devon smacks my bicep repeatedly with the back of his hand. "You gotta check this out, Arain."

I drop a tray of appetizers on a table and pivot, following his eyes to the front entrance.

My gaze cuts through the crowd like a knife, and there she is—Nyla, my beautiful woman, entering the scene.

She's draped in a long, white cape cascading off her shoulders, which she hands over to Roger for hanging.

Elizabeth. She's dressed as Elizabeth Bennet. As in the other half of Darcy's soul. *My* soul.

She's in a moon-white muslin gown, skimming her ankles, with netted short sleeves and a square neckline. Yeah, I've picked up a few fashion terms from Nyla.

She gracefully floats through the sea of people, exchanging polite smiles with those she passes. Her pink hair is carefully pinned into a curly updo, a simple braid bridging her crown, with white beads like morning dew scattered around and beneath her hair.

She's wearing a feather-light touch of makeup—no heavy kohl or smoky eyes. Just a hint of pink blush on her soft, round cheeks and glistening gloss on her doll-like lips.

It's a costume from one of the ballroom dancing scenes. The name escapes me—Notting—Neth—*Damn it.*

"Elizabeth Bennet's Netherfield ball gown," says Matilda, standing by my side with a glass of punch. She examines Nyla from head to toe. "Not bad at all." Her eyes meet mine. "Well, you and Mr. Darcy certainly have one thing in common."

I raise an eyebrow. "And what's that?"

"Fucking up." She smirks over the edge of her glass and gives a wink. "But you do know how the book ends, right?" With her weird cryptic charm delivered in a horrible British accent, she sways away.

I clear my throat, adjusting my dark coat. The Mr. Darcy getup I've thrown on is straight from the finale. His white tunic is unbuttoned, and his coat jacket majestically flows back with the wind as he strides towards Elizabeth Bennet with his heartfelt confession. It's the scene that had Nyla snuggling up to my chest, giggling like a maniac.

So, I take the lead.

Nyla glances around, fidgeting with her fingers, on the hunt for an empty seat.

But when she catches sight of me—

"Hey, Victor!" Donald interrupts my stroll and thrusts a bowl of jelly cups into my hands. "It's your candy shift. Remember, one cup per kid. These little bastards think the Devil's birthday is their personal piñata. Well, not on my watch. 'The only thing in this world that gives orders is balls.' Got it?" His attempt at a Tony Montana impression makes me cringe.

Once Donald is out of sight, Nyla has disappeared.

I turn my head, scanning the sea of party-goers. Mick and Grayson are seated at the corner table, wearing sharp, ironed suits—or *Men In Black* costumes. "Of course, they're here."

I spot a glimpse of white by the booths.

There she is, my girl.

She's joined her usual group of friends, the same ones from two months ago. I've learned their names. Nova's the blonde, Cassie's the redhead, and Rita's the one with the black braids. They're all in their mid-thirties, living as roommates in a local neighborhood, running a little business that crafts custom sweaters and mugs. They're caring, reliable women, almost like older sisters to Nyla.

Speaking of my angel.

Nyla's smile is radiant, heavenly, and utterly captivating. I'm frozen in place, soaking in the song of her laughter amid the Halloween chaos. Fuck, I can't even imagine how I'd react if I saw this woman in her wedding dress.

Let her have fun with her friends tonight, Shahzad.

I exit the vicinity to hand the kids a pair of jelly cups, figuring we've got a boatload stashed in the back kitchen. Donald decided to stock up, claiming it was a backup for our trick-or-treat supply. When Harry took out the trash from his office, he discovered fifty empty jelly cups in there. But no need to clue him in on that.

"Trick or treat!" a young woman in a Jason mask and a blue one-piece suit shouts, holding an empty grocery bag.

We're not technically supposed to give candy to adults but fuck it.

I grab two jelly cups and toss them into her bag.

"What about a trick?" she asks.

I squint my eyes. "Wait a minute." *Why does her voice ring a bell?*

The girl yanks off her mask. "*Boo!*"

My face lights up with the biggest possible smile. "Dua!"

I place the bowl on the ground and whisk my little sister up in a hug. She laughs throughout the spin before I plant her down and cradle her cheery little face in my hands. Words fail me instantly. I mean, my sister is here instead—*instead of Toronto?*

How? What? Why?

"Happy birthday, Shahz!" she exclaims.

"It's Halloween, Dua."

"What's the difference?" She squeezes the life out of my torso. "I've got the weekend off and decided to drop by to visit one of my favorite living demons on this planet. After Zayan, of course."

I respond with a series of kisses to her head. "Missed you, too, kid. Why didn't you call me before coming here?"

"That's the whole point of the 'trick' in 'trick or treat,' dumb-dumb." She grabs her Jason mask, fitting it over her head. Her brow raises in question as she looks at my costume. "Let me guess. Pretentious, regency douchebag who probably invented the patriarchy, hierarchy, and every 'archy' possible, and believes women are inferior leisure activities. Only to then blindly, madly, hopelessly fall in love with one who defies all his laws and ideals?"

"Yeah."

She winks. "Looks great. Where's Nyla?"

"Alyn for the public." I nod towards where she's engrossed in a conversation with Nova.

"Elizabeth Bennet at the Netherfield Ball." Dua whistles. "I know *many* women who'd kill for an exact replica of her costume."

"She made it," I state proudly. "It's obvious from the fine precision of the stitching and her love for the tulle and satin texture. The neckline is classic Nyla style."

Dua looks at me with amusement, hazel eyes mirroring our father's. "Who are you, and what have you done to Shahzad 'I only like denim and leather' Arain?"

"Vegan leather," I clarify.

She snorts and grabs the jelly-cup bowl. "I'll pass these out on your behalf." Adjusting the lapels of my jacket, she pats my chest. "Go chat with your Elizabeth and make sure you don't piss her off, okay?"

"You sure? I don't wanna make you do free labor."

"I'm Zayan Jafri's girlfriend *and* assistant. Free labor is my first name."

I lean down and plant a kiss on her forehead. "We'll talk at home."

She nods and begins handing out the treats.

Meanwhile, I slide back into the lively party and snatch the tray of Halloween-themed drinks from Amelia's hands just before she reaches Nyla's table.

"Jesus, you almost made me drop that, Shahz!" Amelia scolds, landing a punch in my ribs. Instead of pain, it just brings out a laugh. "Gosh, you're unbearable. Don't make a scene, got it?"

"You got it, mia Lia."

Rolling her eyes, she takes her dreary, dark Addams Family self back to her Spiderman boyfriend.

"Evening, ladies," I greet as I approach the table. All four pairs of eyes, including my favorite set of emeralds, focus on me—some hungry, others shy, and one downright glaring. "Let's talk costumes. What are we all wearing tonight?" I start placing the drinks down one by one.

"Daphne," Cassie says, "from Scooby-Doo." Natural ginger, purple dress, and the headband straight from the cartoon itself. She's nailed the look, no doubt.

"The Bride from Kill Bill," Nova declares, pointing to her yellow jumpsuit with black stripes. Dried blood stains her costume, streaks of it in her blonde hair and on her cheeks. "Rate it?"

I tilt up one corner of my mouth. "Solid ten across the board." Ignoring the giggles from Nova and Cassie, I shift my focus to Rita. My eyes narrow as I dissect the details of her costume. She sits a bit taller, subtly stressing her chest. "Help me out, would you?"

"I'm one of DC's famous anti-heroines."

"Huh." I run my tongue along the inside of my cheek, tucking the tray under my arm. There's not much I can decipher from the uncomfortable black latex, an eye mask, and those pointy ears. "I'm drawing a blank."

Rita rolls her eyes and slides out of the booth, ensuring her chest brushes against mine. Pinning me with a sultry gaze, she pulls a whip from her purse. I'm fixated on her face, but she clearly wants my attention elsewhere.

"Oh, for god's sake, I'm Catwoman!" she declares, crossing her arms. "You're a guy. How do you not know who Catwoman is?"

"I don't watch children's movies."

"Then what the hell are you supposed to be?" Rita asks, returning to her seat. "Jack Sparrow?"

"Mr. Darcy."

Cassie lets out a gasp and points at Nyla, who's tucked away in the corner, interested in studying her fingers on her lap. "She's Elizabeth Bennet!"

"I noticed." I lean in, planting my left palm on the table. Nyla lifts her dark lashes slightly, catching the mischievous glint in my eyes. Her cheeks flush a deeper shade of pink, and her square teeth nibble on her bottom lip. I gently take her hand, pressing a soft kiss on her knuckles. "Miss Bennet, would you grace me with the honor of a dance later tonight?"

"Say yes," Nova whispers, then turns to me. "She's a bit shy."

"Is she?" I tilt my head, letting my gaze drift down to the outlines of her breasts, rising and falling with every breath. *Fuck, she's out of this goddamn universe.*

Rita nudges Nyla with her elbow. "Girl, if you don't say 'yes,' I will."

"Come on, Alyn," Cassie encourages.

"What a lovely name," I muse, still holding her hand. There's a beautiful, almost frightful frost in her green eyes as if I'll out her in front of her friends. "Is it short for something?"

Nyla shakes her head, and her perfect curls follow in response.

Resuming my role as their waiter, I ask, "Should I go with Elizabeth during our dance or stick with your real name?"

"I don't dance, guys," Nyla lies to her friends.

"Neither do I," I say, tilting my head so she's looking at me. "But you must know, Elizabeth, *Alyn*, I'd go to great lengths for you."

Her brows scrunch up, and the greenery in her eyes flicker like grassy fields in the wind.

"Wow," Rita whispers to me. "You're, like, super committed to your character."

"She'll dance with you later!" Cassie chimes in with an infectious grin, her eyes into dark crescents. "We'll make sure of it, Mr. Darcy."

"Please do," I say, nodding respectfully as a goodbye to the ladies. The moment they start handing out their drinks and I move to another table, I catch Nyla unfolding the pink sticky note I slipped to her while kissing her hand. She takes a deep breath and folds it back, tucking it into her cleavage.

The perfect spot for my unethical compliment to belong.

Amelia, against all odds, swaps out our games and puzzles section for a dance floor, thanks to my begging.

It's a miracle her boyfriend Kevin was listening in and convinced her by saying, "Babe, you know I've always wanted to take you out dancing." That was all it took to thaw her cold, icy heart and make her agree.

I sidle up to Harry, who's handling the DJ booth and equipment. None of us are spring chickens, and curating a playlist of the latest pop hits isn't our forte. Plus, Matilda and Amelia were focused more on decorations and the schedule. "Play the greatest fucking slow song you know."

He rests his headphones around his neck. "Modern or classic 80s?"

"Classic 80s."

"Right now?"

"Please."

Harry shoots me a cheeky wink and turns down the pop music, grabbing his microphone. "All right, all right, ladies, gents, and non-binary friends, can I kindly ask you to make your way to the middle of the dance floor for some smooth swaying?"

I shift my gaze to Nyla's table. Catwoman makes a beeline for Devon, and Daphne and The Bride pair up. My Elizabeth remains seated with a small, pitiful smile. *Stubborn woman.*

Harry raises his eyebrows at me, and I nervously lick my lips. "Whoa, whoa, whoa!" The kid points out Nyla, and all eyes turn to her. "Now, we can't have sweet Miss Elizabeth Bennet hanging out solo, can we? Where's her Mr. Darcy, y'all?"

Goddammit, Harry.

I take the opportunity to shield her from everyone's view before another idiot decides today is his last. "Dance with me, Nyla," I whisper, extending my arm. "Please?"

Nyla dips her head and reaches for my hand. The gentle touch of her fingertips stroking down my calloused palms sends a shiver through my jaw and clenched teeth. Such a cruel, tempting sensation.

The moment she agrees, I pull her up and into the shadows of the crowd. They've all resumed their paired dances, focusing on the correct steps and hand placements.

Nyla rests her hand on my shoulder as I hold onto her inviting waist. Our arms outspread, and our palms find each other in the darkness.

"Time After Time" by Cindy Lauper, one of Zineerah's favorite songs, filters through the speakers. She's a classical rock junkie, which is why I deeply appreciate the music and its underlying romantic messages.

Nyla and I move to the steady rhythm, our eyes locked onto each other. In my mind, there's no one else around us. Just a mirror ball casting its fractured light across the floor, adding a rare, delicate glimmer to her jade eyes.

Every inhale, every exhale, every deep shudder that passes through her when I pull her closer to my chest, I notice. I notice and study and plant a garden of her quirks in my memory.

Even as I whirl her around, she doesn't escape my focus. My right-hand glides over her lower back, and her left-hand finds its place around the nape of my neck. The touch of her skin against mine causes my eyes to briefly shut, savoring the feeling of her closeness growing intentionally deeper.

"I want to dance with you for the rest of my days," I say, my words hanging in the air as I get lost in her flickering gaze. The button of my tunic steals her attention. I wish her soft cheek to rest against my bare chest, to kiss it until she falls asleep on it.

"Did you like my note, Troublemaker?" I ask.

Nyla's cheeks turn crimson, and her body tenses. If she gave me the green light on what I wrote, I could ease her tight muscles in just a couple of minutes.

I get close to her ear, my lips brushing over the curve. "I may be dressed as a gentleman, Troublemaker, but seeing you in this stunning dress is stirring up anything but proper thoughts."

Her nails dig into my flesh, the feeling triggering memories of our nights in the shower, on the couch, on her bed, in that cold lagoon. It almost seems like she's intentionally pressed herself close enough to sense my hard-on. A slight shiver.

I chuckle into her hair. "Let me know you feel me."

She nods.

"Say it. From those pretty lips of yours."

She shakes her head.

I smile and plant a light kiss on the side of her swan-like neck. "As long as you know."

Nyla draws her head back, irises darting at a rapid speed. Her breasts are pressed to my chest, and our breaths fall into a unified tempo.

I edge my lips near hers, watching as she closes her eyes. A smile curls at my mouth. Good to know she at least wants me to kiss her. And kiss her I will, but only in the privacy of our home.

The song fades away, replaced by applause that snaps Nyla out of her daze. I quickly button down my coat, covering up the undeniable reaction her close presence triggers in my body. She adjusts her dress and wipes her palms on it.

Taking her left hand, I begin with a kiss.

"I." Forehead. "Love." Cheeks. "You." Knuckles. And a fourth kiss to the tip of her button nose because fuck it. When's the next time I'll get to dance with my future wife this way? "Thank you for the enlightening dance, Miss Bennet."

Nyla scurries back to her table, her cheeks flushed and a flustered air about her.

I smile like an idiot to myself and head to the bathroom for a cold water face wash.

33

Caramel

Shahzad

November 2nd

Dua's in the kitchen, spreading butter on toast with the scrambled eggs she cooked when I stomp downstairs, towel drying my damp hair.

"Are you planning to get a haircut soon? You know, before Zineerah's wedding?" she asks.

"Fuck her wedding. It's not happening."

Dua chokes on her bite and gives me a solid smack on the back. "What the hell's wrong with you? How can you say something like that?"

"And how can she accept Maya's decision to marry your professor?"

"Professor Shaan is a good man. Yeah, he's a tough grader and unforgiving about late assignments, but anyone—*anyone*—would give up a lung to sit in his class. He's that knowledgeable and considerate, an all-around sweet, introverted guy. A perfect match for our sweet, introverted sister."

"He's eight years older than her."

"And?"

"*And?*" I mock her voice, shutting the fridge door after gathering ingredients for my and

Nyla's breakfast. "The man who stole her voice was just as old. Do you honestly believe our sister would revisit her trauma by *marrying* another old douchebag? Think rationally, Dua."

Dua places the butter knife down and pins me with a hard look. "You know, Raees is the reason she agreed to it."

"What do you mean?" I ask.

Sighing, she takes out her phone and starts showing me pictures of Zineerah with a cold, hollow-eyed expression while Raees appears to be smiling. "He *really* seems to care about her, Shahz. Seriously. During my first year, I joked that he should marry my sister just to get his mother off his back about the whole thing. Mama says it took him a split second to accept Zineerah's proposal. Well, before our sister made him wait twelve more months."

"And he still . . . agreed?"

"Yup. I showed him this picture of Zineerah." Dua reveals a candid shot of our sister in a green field, wearing a straight black skirt, a grey sweater, and her long, jet-black hair flowing in the wind. She isn't smiling. "He barely glanced at it and said, 'I'll tell my mother, and we can set up a meeting,' and the rest is history."

"He said that?"

"Yup!"

"Does he know about Zineerah's history?"

Dua shakes her head. "Mama didn't want a wealthy proposal like that to slip away by being honest."

"So, we're lying to the guy?"

"Zineerah made it clear she doesn't want to bring it up. She put that chapter behind her a long time ago, and Raees is okay with her silence. They're comfortable with each other. No need to stir things up." Dua gives me a timid, dimpled grin, resting her head on my shoulder. "She'll be all right, Shahz. You know she's a fighter."

Raees is a moron for believing that Zineerah would *genuinely* accept him as a husband. She's sworn off relationships after her incident, let alone *marriage*. But she can't stand the pressure from Maya. No one can. Maybe that's why my sister gave up so easily; she's in flight mode rather than fight.

We're halfway through breakfast, chatting about Dua's university life, when Sky starts barking from the living room.

"That's my cue." I wipe my mouth with a napkin and grab Nyla's breakfast basket.

"I can't believe I finally get to witness this." Dua snorts as I fit the basket in Sky's mouth.

Leaning against the doorway, she adds, "I'm surprised your grand gestures haven't won her back yet."

"She's not some carnival game prize, kid." I give Sky a pat on the back, ushering her out the moment Nyla's front door swings open. "I'm not here to win her back. I'm going to earn her back, starting with her trust."

Nyla grabs the breakfast sandwich and the note.

"What did you write?" Dua whispers.

"None of your business. Morning, neighbor!" I wave my arm, trying to divert Nyla's attention. "This is Dua, my little sister. She came down from Toronto to visit."

Nyla courteously smiles and waves at Dua.

My diabolical sister exclaims, "I wouldn't forgive my brother if I were you!"

I put her in a gentle chokehold, covering her mouth. "Don't pay attention to her. I think you should forgive me on your own terms."

Dua chews down on my hand and makes a break for it, rushing over to her. The two start chatting by her car, with Sky getting all cuddly under Nyla's ear scratches.

Never thought I'd feel this jealous of my little sister and my dog.

Dua bursts into laughter, shooting me a sardonic look over her shoulder, shaking her head in mock disappointment. What the hell is Nyla telling her?

They share a hug and swap numbers before Nyla hops in her car and drives off to town.

"Man, she's drop-dead gorgeous!" Dua squeals with her fists rattling. "Not gonna lie, I could barely recognize her. And I mean that in a great way. The last time I saw her was at Alina's dawat. I've never seen her glow like this before."

"Yeah." I exhale, getting lost in another daydream about Nyla and her radiance. All I need is for her to return home to me after working her Fairy Godmother magic in her studio. I'll set the table with her favorite dishes, stock the fridge with her go-to dessert, and have the TV set with her guilty pleasure, Regency movies.

It's my bedtime medication, and I envision this scenario to put myself to sleep. And, okay, maybe I've got one of her pastel-pink sweaters in my grip, like a kid clutching his special stuffed animal.

"You know what could amp up your groveling game?" Dua suggests, arms crossed with a mischievous smirk.

"Please?"

"Get her a dog."

I arch a brow. "A dog?"

"Yeah. Give her a furry companion. I mean, she's clearly whipped by Sky's charms despite her not-so-charming owner—*ow*!"

I release her cheek from my criminal pinch.

She pushes me aside and walks back into our house. "Look, all I'm saying is she's probably feeling pretty lonely in that house all by herself. Maybe when she's at work, you can look after her puppy, and she can return the favor," she suggests.

"Sky's big enough to take care of—"

"Oh my god, Shahzad! Do you want Nyla to talk to you or not?" she interrupts.

I shove my fists into my jacket's pockets, giving a nod.

"Well, then give her reasons to. Dogs somehow manage to bring even the fiercest enemies together. Trust me, I'm giving you some solid advice." Dua bends down, hugging Sky around her neck and pouting like a baby. "*Pwease*, Shazoo?"

Christ.

"Don't, Dua."

"Won't you *pwease* get Sky a *wittle* sib*wing*?"

I crouch down, eye-level with my husky. "You want a sibling, honey?"

Sky's tail starts wagging. She lets out a bark, marking the end of my decision.

I drop Dua off at my old apartment to hang with Maira after catching up with Jia and the team. *What is taking so long, adeul? It's been four months now, adeul. Ah, whatever. There's a lot of fish in the sea. Why don't you come back to my kitchen, adeul?* They seemed to assume Nyla was with me, but her absence only earned me a dismissive wave from Jia.

Meanwhile, Bao fills me in that Tae is out on a date with Hye-jin. Apparently, they made it official three weeks ago. Kind of a slap on the face, but never have I ever been so proud of that kid.

Stepping into Pets-A-Lot, Cookie flaps her wings and lands on Sky's back, cawing in greeting.

"Where the hell have you two been?" Harriet exclaims, clearly surprised to see Sky and me alive and breathing after four months of being off the grid. "Do you know how worried I got when you didn't show up for Sky's food and toys? You could've left a note, kid." She peers behind my shoulder. "Where's Pinky-Pie?"

I offer a brief rundown of my situation with Nyla and the efforts I've been making just to hear her say my name, to have her smile in my direction. To have *her*.

"Jesus," Harriet mutters, adjusting her reading glasses. "I can't believe it. A few months ago, you were so insistent that this girl was just a friend, and now you're fighting tooth and nail to make her your wife."

"You were right during my last visit," I admit, intertwining my fingers over her office desk. "She brings me veracious, infinite happiness. The kind of happiness I haven't felt in a long, long while. I'd be damned to let go of it."

Harriet smiles lopsidedly and rises from behind the desk. "Very well, kid. Follow me. Bring Sky, too."

I do as asked, giving a sharp whistle to call my husky, who's being petted by the employees, Cookie perched and cawing, "Friend, friend, friend," on her back. Sky trots over, nudging my hand with her snout.

"Is Popcorn still up for adoption?" I ask.

"Unfortunately, no. He found a loving family of five last month."

We step into a separate room where all the rescued animals are kept. Cats rest quietly in their cages, curled up and dozing, but the dogs start barking with enthusiasm. Sky's tail is wagging.

That's a good sign.

Harriet comes to an abrupt halt in front of a cage, arms crossed, wearing a smug grin. A grin that's completely warranted because *holy shit*. "He's a ten-week-old Siberian mix. Rescued last week from behind a graveyard near a Catholic church. Workers heard his howls, found him with his head stuck in a fence, and brought him straight here. Looks like someone heartlessly ditched this little guy." She sighs, shaking her head at the unfairness of it all.

I remember finding Sky in a beat-up box in an alley during one of the stormiest nights in New York City when she was just eight weeks old. She was practically freezing in the December chill as I was taking out the trash from Jia's shop. Without a second thought, I took her in, gave her some ham, and brought her straight to Harriet. But little Sky insisted on clinging to me like a baby being burped after a meal.

This little man, though, resembles Sky's long-lost brother, wearing a coat of caramel-colored fur and those same ocean-blue irises. Brown circular lenses frame his eyes, with two lines running from his forehead down to the tip of his snout. He blinks slowly, waking up from his nap and letting out a big, hearty yawn.

Man, I might just tear up at how adorable he is, thinking about all the love Nyla would shower on him as he grows up.

Sky's excitement mashes her face against the cage, trying to get a sniff of the shy puppy. Her tail's on the verge of breaking from all that furious wagging. Meanwhile, Cookie leaps off Sky's back and onto my shoulder.

"I hear you, honey. But let's introduce you properly first, okay?"

At my nod, Harriet opens the cage.

Stepping in cautiously, I hold onto Sky, preventing her from leaping at the puppy. I crouch down, offering my hand for the husky to sniff. He licks it before retreating to the corner. "How's he with others?" I ask.

"A bit reserved, I'd say. We're not sure about his past home, but it seems to have rattled him a bit. He just needs some time to adjust to the right owner," she explains.

Nyla's patience is next level, and her love knows no bounds. I'm confident this little guy will warm up to her charms in no time, probably within a week.

Sky sits calmly, patiently waiting for the puppy to come over. As he approaches, giving her a lick on the cheek, she begins to play with his wagging tail.

I settle back on the floor and affirm with my head. "We'll make sure he's well taken care of."

Before picking Dua up from my old apartment, I make sure to feed Sky and Caramel at the store.

Yeah, I'm calling him that due to his fur, but if Nyla prefers another name, that's her choice. A little something in me, call it wishful thinking, says that she'll definitely stick to Caramel.

"Okay, buddy. Time to get you settled in here." I drop a treat into the basket, a bigger one to accommodate his size, alongside Nyla's breakfast. *This* is the basket I'll be delivering.

"Hey, you?"

Dua turns from closing her duffle bag on the passenger seat. She's catching a flight to Toronto in a couple of hours for Zayan's winter volleyball championship game. "What?"

"Stay right here and record every bit of her reaction. I'm going to watch it tonight before I go to bed."

She throws a 'pathetic' my way and grabs my phone, hitting the record button.

We exchange a determined nod before I slam the car door shut.

I cross the street to Nyla's place with Sky. Caramel sits obediently as I stroke him between his pointy ears. Holding the basket up at eye level, I give him a pep talk. "All right, little man, listen up. The woman about to take care of you has a soul woven from gold threads and sparkles. I need you to keep her happy while I'm away and look after her as she'll look after—"

Caramel licks my nose.

"—you." I grin and run my hand down my face, tousling the top of his head.

Stepping up to her porch, I press the doorbell and take a deep breath, my leg shaking with impatience. The anticipation of her reaction hits me hard. Will she greet me by throwing her arms around my neck and showering me with kisses? Maybe she'll invite me inside, and we can goof around with Caramel and Sky. *Caramel and Sky Arain.*

Delusional. I'm incredibly delusional.

I consider a second ring when the door opens wide. "Morning, ba—"

An older version of Nyla stands in the doorway with curious eyes uncanny to my favorite green pair. She's got height, almost matching mine, clad in a sharp cream pantsuit. Lifting a perfectly arched black brow, she questions, "Shahzad Arain?"

"Y-Yes." I stick out my hand. "Are you—"

"Nyla's mother, Rubina." She shakes my hand. Soft yet firm. "Don't you even dare call me aunty."

"Rubina, then."

She motions with her manicured finger toward my basket, a smirk playing on her crimson lips. "I prefer felines."

I pull the basket close to my chest. "For N-Nyla."

"Why the stuttering?" She advances, siren eyes scrutinizing me from head to toe. "She never showed you pictures of me, Shahzad?"

"No," I whisper, cautiously stepping back. "I'm sorry, is Nyla home?"

"She's in the shower." Rubina possesses the gaze of a wild cat—formidable and intimidating. She sizes me up, not with hostile intent, but more like, 'Is he suitable enough for my precious gem of a daughter?'

"Mama!" Nyla's voice echoes from behind. "Who's at the door?"

Rubina's smirk gains a questioning edge as she steps aside, showing me.

Green flares within Nyla's eyes, as if catching me interacting with her neglectful mother is a crime. She rushes over, ushers Rubina inside, slams the door shut behind her, and rests her forehead against it.

Caramel's whines make Nyla's shoulders loosen up, and she pivots on her heel.

"For you," I say, exhaling, and lift the basket. "He's for you."

Disbelief. Pure, genuine disbelief takes over her face.

She stares at the puppy.

At me.

At the puppy.

At me.

And her eyes begin to water, the tears slipping down her cheeks.

"Baby, he's yours." I chuckle, lifting her tiny husky out with one hand and holding him out for her. "I named him Caramel because of his fur, but you can call him whatever you want."

Nyla's hands tremble as she reaches out. When Caramel is nestled in her arms, and his tongue gently licks away the tears on her cheeks, Nyla dissolves. She cradles him like a baby, running her hand through his fur, and her enchanting eyes shine in sync with mine. So what if I'm crying watching Nyla cry with her brand-new puppy?

"Your breakfast," I croak, setting the basket by her feet. "And his bag of food for the week, along with treats and some toys, are all in there too. If you need anything, anything at all, I'm just ten seconds away." I delicately brush my knuckles against her wet cheeks. "When you're ready to forgive me or talk, I'd like to know if you've made amends with your mother."

Nyla puts Caramel back in his basket and closes the distance until our chests are practically molded together. I sure fucking hope she can feel the rapid thud of my heart against her.

With her right hand, she reaches up and gently wipes under my eye with her thumb.

I suck in a sharp breath.

Nyla's touch lingers for one electrifying second before her fingers slip away. She turns, grabs the basket, and heads back into her house.

34

Happy Birthday

Nyla

December 1st

Something is practically painting my face with their saliva.

I peel open my heavy eyelids and find myself jolting awake to Caramel's face inches from mine. Laughter bubbles out of me naturally as the little husky tickles my face and neck with his licks. I pull him close to my chest, sitting up to peck his forehead and give him belly rubs.

The sweet sound of a sewing machine fills my ears.

Mama.

I cradle Caramel in my arms and make my way out of the bedroom toward my home design studio since I stopped renting the one in town.

Ten mannequins stand like soldiers, showcasing finished projects. Mama's back is turned to me as she sews together a netted sleeve. The loud, rhythmic hum of the machine causes Caramel to hide his narrow, small face in the crook of my neck.

I hurry over to Mama and place my hand on her shoulders.

"God!" She startles, turning off the machine and pulling out her Airpods. No, my Airpods. "My love, give me a heads up next time, please."

"I'm sorry." I set Caramel on his feet and receive Mama's kiss on my cheek. "Thank you for completing the sleeve. It means a lot. I promise I'll find a way to repay you for your hard work."

"I don't want a single cent from you, do you hear me?" She stands, enveloping me in a hug where my head fits snugly under her chin, and my arms wrap around her. "I really wish we had more time to spend together."

"I wish that too, Mama."

The morning after Halloween, an unknown number had messaged me. I initially thought it was some trick-or-treat prank, but when I reluctantly answered the FaceTime call, it turned out to be Mama. She'd gotten my new phone number through Shaiza khala after a lengthy parental lecture from her older sister.

Mama explained how she sent out a wedding invitation for me, but Baba got hold of it and tossed it aside. Despite her attempts to make time for me, Baba had such a tight leash on my schedule that he practically dictated every day of my week, denying her any chance to visit.

Eventually, she waved a regretful white flag and got caught up in the whirlwind of her life in Dubai.

But I'm going to make an effort to be here for you, my love, Mama said during our call, *I'm going to come visit you this week if you'd like me to and catch up on the years we missed out on. I promise I will make up for it all.*

I cried all the way to the airport to pick her up, then we cried together *at* the airport and continued to cry when we arrived at my house.

Do I believe she could have put in more effort to be there for me earlier? Yes. Do I believe that I should've reached out after attending three of her weddings to catch up? Yes. Should I have believed my father's blatant lies about my mother? Never.

"I love you, my baby," Mama whispers, a hint of a smile in her voice. She cradles my face in her hands and showers my forehead and cheeks with kisses, repeating the gesture thirty million times until I gently pull away. Even then, she holds both my hands and presses kisses to my knuckles. "I'm going to support you in achieving this beautiful dream of yours. Okay, Nylana? I'm going to invest every particle of my soul into this."

I release a contented sigh that transforms into a smile. "Thank you, Mama."

"Absolutely, my love." She playfully pinches my cheek. "Why don't you go for your morning run while I wrap things up here? We'll go through the final details of your designs before sending them off to my team for mass production. By next year, your name will be stitched in the fashion industry, and I'm confident you'll achieve even greater things."

"Love you, Mama." I give her one more hug and scoop up Caramel's attention-seeking butt in my arm. "And if, by some unfortunate miracle, Baba finds out you're here—"

Her green eyes turn into sharp glaciers. "That abomination of a man can't control me, Nyla. Not anymore." She lowers her lashes and points at me. "He will never touch you or harm you again, even if I have to lay down my life to protect you."

Oh, Mama.

My chin quivers, and I rub my left eye, sniffling. "Let's go out for breakfast when I get back."

"Isn't your boyfriend delivering that for us?" Mama's question makes my cheeks heat up. "He's very *hot*, by the way. H-O-T. Like in a sexy Viking manner."

"Ew!" I gag at her mischievous snickering. "Mama, that's, like, so— *Gah.* Please don't ever call him that again."

"Hot or a Viking?"

"Both!"

She gives an innocent shrug as if the fifth diamond ring on her finger doesn't even register. "Just saying, you know. You can't let your dad's mess ruin everything between you two."

"Mama, he signed a contract with Baba just a week into our charade. He knew about my nightmares surrounding the industry, and yet . . . It's unforgivable. He's a grown man who knew exactly what he was getting himself into."

She lets out a sigh and slides her arm behind my shoulder, guiding me to the window with a clear view of Shahzad's house. "Answer me this. Do you believe he signed the contract because his overprotectiveness for his sisters, for Maira, for his loved ones got the better of him?" She pins me with an amused expression as if she's already predicted my response. "I'm not trying to dismiss your feelings, Nylana. Put yourself in his shoes for a second and just think."

Being in Shahzad's shoes . . .

Being in Shahzad's shoes, I'd probably be desperate for help from someone I knew I could trust and also shared a small, intimate history with. All because my best friend's little sister needed a reason to stay there until she could find a decent apartment with trustworthy roommates.

Being in Shahzad's shoes, I'd be pissed out of my head that a woman he's come to know again managed to damage something that had been a constant in my life for a whole decade.

Especially if I were dealing with financial struggles, trying to support my little sisters' health and education, caring for a dog, *trying* to care about myself, and the only solution I could come up with was—

Mama grabs both my shoulders and looks directly into my eyes. "My love, do you know how deeply ashamed I felt asking my own sister for money when your father and I split? Especially since I'd been compared to her my entire life." She tucks a strand of my pink hair behind my ear. "The boy had no other option, Nylana. He had to provide for you, Maira, and Sky, and his desperation to help his family led him to the wrong door."

My peripherals catch sight of Shahzad exiting his home. He's in another black, compressed shirt and dark gray sweatpants. His burnt umber locks are tied back in a half ponytail.

"No man will ever keep your cold shoulders this warm, Nylana," Mama whispers from behind, her arms wrapping around my shoulders. She showers the top of my head with repeated kisses. "We've all made foolish mistakes that have hurt others. Like my absence in the last couple of years."

I hug her forearms.

"But I'm here to make up for it at any chance I get," she murmurs, tightening her comforting embrace. "Believe me, my love. You'll eventually forgive him when the timing's right."

"And when is that?" I look up at her.

Mama's gracious smile appears. "When his sweet notes taped to your bedroom wall stop growing. When you gaze into Caramel's eyes. When you water your potted plants. When you finally learn to cook the meals he delivers to you each day. When you walk into your favorite café and pay for your latte. When he leaves with a piece of yourself with him." Her lips meet my crown. "Do whatever your heart tells you."

Mama leaves the room.

I press my hand over my chest, feeling the racing beat of my heart against my sweaty palm. Caramel licks at my jaw, and I cuddle him closer, burying my nose in his cream-white and brown fur.

I started forgiving Shahzad after seeing the amount of effort he's constantly putting towards mending our relationship, and surprising me with Caramel was just the cherry on top. What can I say? I'm a simple woman. But my silence now is me trying to figure out a way to communicate that I have forgiven him and how we can work on our relationship from hereafter.

FAKE IT TILL WE MAKE IT

I'm not on board with *just* being his girlfriend for the next seven years. Someday, I want to be his wife, have children together, and be laid to rest next to this big buffoon. A future with him is what I need, but that's not possible if he's still tethered to his past.

I mean, what if he proposes just for the sake of my forgiveness and later decides on a common-law relationship? What if these grand gestures are just a ploy to draw me into an uncommitted game? I can't risk my heart being shattered again.

He's not a heartless dickhead, Nyla. What if he sees a future with you, too? What if you just talked to him?

Planting sweet kisses on Caramel's cheek, I steal a lingering glance at Shahzad, stalling his stretches in high hopes of my arrival, before retreating to my bedroom to kickstart my morning routine.

***

Seated in the cozy corner booth of Caffè di Matilda with Mama, I watch as she multitasks efficiently. Emails and calls flow seamlessly as she coordinates with her design production company, catching up on her private clients' gown requests and managing global advertisements for her upcoming spring-summer haute couture line.

With the last drops of my latte disappearing, I heave a sigh of relief. "The world is about to discover that Nyla Ghilzai is alive in just a few short months."

Mama chuckles, fingers dancing on her keyboard. "Are you excited, love?"

"Well, let's see. I might have paparazzi lining up outside my doorstep every Friday night, the few remaining fans I've got left, and journalists desperate for the scoop on why I disappeared from Hollywood again and why I chose to return as a fashion designer." I crunch the cinnamon cookie between my teeth. "Excited is an overstatement."

"Goodness, Nylana. Why do you care what some underpaid journalists have to say about you?" She lowers her laptop screen for yet another heart-to-heart. "The only person you need to please and keep happy is yourself. Got it?"

I take her pointed finger and kiss the top of it. "Crystal clear, Mama."

"Are you finished with that?" Shahzad's delectable, melted chocolate voice adds a lick of sweetness to my anxiety. Curse that tight-fitted apron and his charming, smug grin. It's unbelievable how he's transformed from a grump to eternal sunshine while I seem to have taken the reverse route.

"How sweet of you," Mama chimes in, resting her temple on her knuckles. She shoots him her signature wicked smirk. Never a good sign. "Say, Shahzad?"

Shahzad shifts his gaze from mine to my mother's. "Yes, Rubina?"

First-name basis. Just great.

"You seem to care a lot about my daughter, and I genuinely appreciate your efforts on Nylana's behalf," she says. I can't make head or tail of where this is going, but it's making me *pretty* uneasy. "You see, I'll be leaving tomorrow morning, and I'd like you to keep looking out for my daughter—"

"Mama!" I hiss, my cheeks burning at her direct request. It's like she's completely forgotten that I'm still giving him the cold shoulder until I'm ready to talk. But, as usual, my mother couldn't care less.

"That's a non-negotiable commitment I've made to myself." Shahzad throws his blue dishcloth over his shoulder. "Your incredible daughter can keep pretending I don't exist, and I'll still believe she's the reason I do."

My heart gallops out of my chest. Gosh, when did he become like *this*? I don't mind it, but I also . . . No, I don't mind at all.

After a lengthy, understanding gaze, Mama returns to her laptop. "Interesting," she mumbles with an endless grin.

Shahzad swipes up my glass, drops a note on my lap, and whistles as he strolls away to tidy another table.

I discreetly unfold it.

Come over tonight. Bring Caramel.

"What's it say?" Mama asks, her eyes fixed on her screen.

Even with her attention elsewhere, she's somehow always watching me. She mentioned tracking my life through fan accounts on social media and news articles, ignoring every rumor. She even had emails and text messages as proof, recalling the days she cried when Baba denied her the chance to see me.

"He's asking me to go to his place tonight," I say, folding the note and tucking it into my purse. "But I'm not going." *Right?*

Mama raises a brow. "Why not?"

"Because we have our wine and sketch night planned. I won't let anything disrupt our plans."

"Nylana."

"No."

"My love, how long do you plan on dragging this out?"

I look up. "Dragging what?"

She shoots a glance at Shahzad, busy taking a customer's order at the cash register.

"Until I'm ready to forgive him."

"And when is that?"

"Not tonight. End of discussion."

Mama's hand reaches for mine, giving it three reassuring squeezes. "I understand seeing a man on his knees begging for an apology is a sight for sore eyes, but eventually, you'll want him to stand tall and proud by your side."

"Baba didn't," I mutter, immediately regretting my words. "Sorry."

"He isn't a real man," Mama responds, holding onto my hand, and I reciprocate, seeing her green eyes crinkle with affection. "I've been married five times now, Nylana. Abdul was degrading. Terry, well, he was kind but easily swayed by the next pretty thing. Mansoor was the best of them all, but his ex-wife was a world-class bitch, and I just couldn't handle it. That one was on me."

"You left before she could murder you, Mama."

She chuckles from deep within. "Sweetie, my fourth husband was a wrestler. He would've broken her nose after getting my permission, believe me."

I sigh. "Yeah, I never really understood why you eloped and got married to *the* William Warrior in Vegas."

"It was my forty-fifth birthday. I deserved a little present." She quirks up a shoulder and smiles so infectiously that I'm under its control in a second.

"How about now? Are you happy?"

Mama twirls her wedding ring, nibbling on her bottom lip as a rosy hue touches her cheeks. "Did you know Mark has been interested in me since I was with your father?"

I blink. "No way."

"Yes way. He was invited to one of your early runway shows, back when you were just a tiny baby, as a potential investor for First Class Faces." Mama pinches my cheeks, making cooing sounds.

"I was nineteen!" I chuckle, taking both of her hands in mine. "Tell me more about Mark and his infatuation."

"Well, we somehow always ended up in the same room but never spoke because Abdul never involved me in the business end of his nonsense. But Mark said the only reason he invested was because of me." She fakes a dramatic hair flip over her shoulders. At fifty-one, she doesn't look a day over thirty. "He even teared up mentioning how he's seen me get married over and over again an hour before he proposed to me."

My jaw aches after hearing her story. "He cried?"

"Bawling, Nylana. Right in the middle of one of his restaurants."

I tilt my head. "Mark's a chef?"

Shahzad is a chef, too—Oh, shut up, brain!

"No, sweetheart, Mark's an investor. He likes to put his money where he sees value. Restaurants, malls, and even an aquarium. He rented it out on our first date." Mama starts rambling about their first kiss at the jellyfish exhibition, but my attention drifts to Shahzad getting scolded by Amelia over a spilled tea.

Our eyes briefly meet as he heads to the register. Fireworks shoot down my spine at his lopsided grin and wink. Then, Amelia smacks his back for being distracted and makes him grab the mop and bucket.

I stifle a chuckle—

"Meet him tonight," Mama cuts through.

"But—"

She rises and eases into the seat beside me, her arms surrounding my shoulders. "My love, I don't want you to go through the same trials and tribulations I went through to find my one true love."

I sink into her hug, inhaling a deep breath of her fruity, floral fragrance. "I'm very happy for you, Mama. Having you here means a lot to me. And I *really* want to meet Mark and thank him for bringing life into my mother's eyes."

Mama attacks my cheeks with kisses. And just like before, I can't help but burst into giggles. "As your mother, I demand you to go to his house tonight." She takes a sip of her frappé, winking and moving her laptop next to me. "We'll have a chat over wine when you're back."

I rest my head on her shoulder, hugging her arm close to my chest, and gaze at my empty vanilla latte glass.

FAKE IT TILL WE MAKE IT

Shahzad

I tuck my lighter away once the last wick of my candlelight dinner flickers to life. Nyla's a little soft-hearted with her mother around. The pair are clearly attached at the hip, and if there's one thing I've learned from binging *Gilmore Girls* with Dua, it's that mothers always know best. Not in my sisters' case, though.

Noticing Nyla hasn't left her place yet, I steal a glance out my bedroom window while getting ready.

"She'll show up," I mutter to myself, a familiar mantra. Maira swears by this whole repeating what you want to the universe until it happens. She calls it manifestation, I call it bullshit. Five months of manifesting Nyla's forgiveness every night before bed, and the universe hasn't done me any favors.

Finally, Nyla exits her front door.

I drop my hairbrush on my foot.

The pain is momentarily muted by her presence descending her porch steps. She looks up, not at my house, but at the delicate snowflakes falling from the night sky. Dressed in an oversized pink turtleneck, a white tennis skirt, white stockings, and her pink hair tied high in a half-ponytail, she resembles bubblegum candy. And little Caramel in her arms is just the icing on the cake.

"Goddamn," escapes my lips in a whisper. Peeking at her in that preppy-polished getup, a smile playing on her glossy, pink lips, and flushed, round cheeks, has me counting my breaths. If I've taken any at all.

Shaking my head, I turn to the mirror, fixing the collar of my dress shirt and scowling at my jeans. Jesus Christ, I knew I should've splurged on new dress pants. This outfit seemed fine in my head, but the more I stare in the mirror, the more I despise it.

Chimes of my doorbell echo through the house. I rake my fingers through my hair and pop two mints, chewing aggressively as I dash downstairs. Sky barks from the living room, alerting me.

"Come here, honey," I call, and she rushes to my side, anticipating the door's opening.

Gripping the knob, I swallow a deep breath. *Don't fuck this up, Shahzad.* "Cool. Okay. Let's do this."

Nyla's admiration for my porch comes to a halt the moment I swing open the door. I'm already feeling weak in the knees, on the verge of yelling, "I love you!" at the top of my lungs. She's just . . . *so* ethereal. With the snow falling as the backdrop and Caramel's puppy face tilting side to side, the whole scene is like a perfect picture of her.

"Hi," I whisper, my voice cracking. She raises an eyebrow. I clear my throat, lower my voice, lean in the doorway with my arms crossed, and flash a smile that brightens those pink cheeks. "Hey, beautiful."

Nyla sighs, and white fog swirls from her doll-like lips. I figure this woman's already scheming to avoid talking to me tonight—

"Hi."

I stumble backward.

Caramel jumps out of Nyla's arms, and she reaches forward to grab him but hooks onto my hands instead, making me lose my balance.

I know I'm falling backward.

I watch it unfold in slow motion.

Her eyes widen, lips parting in a yelp, and my arms cocoon around her as we both tumble onto the hard wooden floor.

THUD!

"Fuck." I groan, the back of my skull pounding from the impact. Does it hurt? Kinda. But the ache takes a backseat to the vision in pink stuck to my chest, breathing heavily after our joint tumble. Paradise. "*Aw*. Thanks for trying to save me, baby."

Reality hits Nyla, and she quickly scrambles off my chest, grabbing the doorway for support. "You *ruined* my outfit!" She irons out the creases in her skirt with her hands and fixes the collar of her turtleneck.

"I'm sorry—"

"I knew this was a bad idea." She composes herself and calls for Caramel. He lingers, intrigued by Sky's hopping antics. "Caramel, come here."

I prop myself up on my elbows. "You didn't change his name?"

Nyla ignores me. *Tries* to ignore me. The subtle flare of her nostrils and the tension in her clenched jaw reveal the fight against asking if I'm okay.

I get up, dust myself off, and say, "You caught me off guard, Nyla. It's been five months since you last spoke to me in person." I sling my arm around her waist and usher her inside, closing the door. She leans back on the frame, gripping my shoulders without thinking. *She's here. She's actually here.* "How cruel would it be if this was all a dream?"

Even her short, quick breaths seem in harmony. A wildfire blazes within the depths of her jade eyes. She digs her fingernails into my skin, and I have to gather every ounce of strength not to take her right here and now.

"Step back."

"Yes, ma'am." I take a step back and gesture with my arm. "After you, baby."

"Don't call me that," she grumbles, kicking off her heeled boots in different directions and following the dogs into the kitchen.

I let out a chuckle, running my hand over the back of my head as I bend down to organize her pink boots neatly beside my darker, muddier ones. *Perfect.*

When I find Nyla in the kitchen, she's gazing at the dining table decorated with at least twenty candles, the soft scent of white gardenia and spruce filling the room, casting an orange glow over the furniture, and her favorite bouquet of marigolds and pink carnations resting on the island bar.

Quickly, I scoop up the bouquet and hide it behind me. Without any smart-ass remarks, I offer it to her with an encouraging nod.

Sighing, Nyla takes it, cradling it in her arms like a baby. She follows me into the kitchen, and for a moment, I'm transported back to our small apartment. "How long is this going to take?"

"I don't know, Nyla," I reply, flinging the kitchen towel over my shoulder. "How long *is* it going to take?"

"I meant this dinner thing."

"As long as it took for you to get all dolled up and beautiful for me."

"For *myself.*"

I smile. "Even better."

Nyla's gulp travels down her throat. I want to kiss the constellation of beauty marks on her neck and connect the dots with my fingers. "Why did you invite me over, Shahzad?"

Sha-ha-zad.

Thank fuck I wasn't holding a knife or reaching into the oven for the chocolate cake I baked for us. "Want the truth?"

She nods.

Leaning against the counter, I say, "It's my birthday."

"What?"

"It's my birthday. I was born today."

"I know what a birthday is," she mutters impatiently, reaching for her purse and pulling out her phone. Her skin pales when she realizes the truth of my words. "Shit."

Birthdays have never been a big deal in our family. Baba took my sisters and me out to dinner and bought us small presents. Having him take care of his wild children was enough of a gift itself. The rest of the family would send messages, and distant calls from Islamabad would express how much we were missed.

After cutting ties with Maya, everyone distanced themselves from me for the sake of my mental well-being. Now, the only birthday wishes that come my way are from my sisters, the Khan family, Sahara, the Jafri siblings, and Mustafa and Maira. My inner-circle; my family.

And I've spent every birthday sitting by Baba's grave with a chocolate cake that I eat on his behalf. Sky joined me after I adopted her. It's as if Baba sent her to me as a special gift, knowing how badly I wanted a dog growing up.

"Happy birthday," Nyla mumbles, returning to the kitchen and handing me the bouquet. "I thought it was on the eleventh. My mistake."

I tap my cheek. "May I get a birthday kiss?"

"No."

"I tried." Turning to the stove—

Nyla grabs my shoulder and yanks me back. Her soft lips brush against my cheek for a split second, though it felt like a century to me. "Hurry up. I'm hungry." She strides over to the table and takes a seat.

I rub my chest, hoping my heart can catch a goddamn break from its marathon every time she's around. Dying on my birthday isn't how I want this night to end.

Plating a replica of a fancy steak dinner, I present it in front of her by standing behind and leaning low, my lips inches from her jaw. "Chef's special for his very special guest."

"Shut up," she mutters.

"As you wish." I run my hand down the back of her hair, catching her by surprise, and sit across from her.

She pauses just after her first bite of steak. "Damn it and damn *you*." Her eyes shut, head shaking in disbelief. "Damn your cooking, too."

I'm going to need a very cold shower every time she curses. "Do you like it?" I ask, scooting down five seats until I'm diagonal to her again.

Nyla's lashes open slightly. She regards me with a no-nonsense glare. "Why don't you decide that for me, just like you decided to stab me in the back, Shahzad?"

My playfulness flatlines at her question.

I run my tongue over my lower lip, trying to focus on my plate, but my thoughts are a jumbled mess. I know she's hurting; otherwise, we wouldn't be here, wrestling with our struggles to speak up about where our relationship is headed and where we want it to head. It eats at me, knowing that I'm the one who left scars on her heart that loved me with every beat.

Five months is enough time for me to figure out my wants, and I want—*need*—Nyla if that wasn't clear enough. As my friend, as my best friend, as my girlfriend, my fiancée, my wife, the mother of our children, the woman I'd grow old and gray with. My future is bleak and cold without her in it, but I also need to make it warm and comfortable for her before she's a part of it. I'm still figuring out how I'm going to do that without screwing it up.

Something warm bumps against my mouth.

I open my eyes, and there's Nyla, holding a piece of my steak with her fork. My lips automatically part, and I take the bite, savoring it slowly. She follows it up with a scoop of mashed potatoes and some sautéed vegetables.

No words are spoken, no shots fired.

She continues to feed me and eats from her own plate that I portioned up for her.

There's a certain calmness in the air. Or it's her fruity, vanilla scent she carries that makes each breath a bit easier. I used to take deep whiffs whenever she cuddled up to me at night, or just laid on my chest, telling me stories from her past.

That's one of the many reasons I love Nyla. Her history is a story to her, not a looming gray cloud or a vengeful ghost. To her, it's a stepping stone leading her to the future. The woman is a *firm* believer in what she wants for herself, refusing to let anyone, even a sore loser like me, interrupt her.

And it's taken me five months to realize I'm ready to fulfill all her needs and wants. Because all I want is *her*. All I need is *her*. I can't form any other coherent, solid goals or ambitions until I have *her*.

We finish our dinner in silence.

I handle the rinsing of the dishes while she loads them into the dishwasher. Clearing the dining table is my task, and she takes charge of extinguishing the twenty candles, giving each one a satisfied whiff.

After an hour of quiet, I break the silence. "They're yours."

"The candles?"

"Yeah. All yours. I'll pack them in a bag for you to take." I don't give her a chance to object, immediately moving to the oven where the chocolate cake is cooling. "Want a slice?"

Nyla stays just outside the kitchen, eyeing the dark sponge. "It's one of my trigger foods."

Fuck. What the fuck? How did I forget such an important—goddammit, Shahzad.

Without a second thought, I put the cake back in the oven.

"What are you doing?" she gasps. "It's your birthday. You should at least have your cake."

"The café team can enjoy it. How about I whip up some pan—"

"Shahzad." Nyla takes three steps forward. "Enough worrying about me, please. Don't try to stop yourself from enjoying the little things because I can't. Put a candle in that cake, make your wish, and eat the damn thing."

"I like worrying about you," I whisper. "I want to enjoy every little thing with you and avoid the little things you can't." She reels in a sharp breath when I hold her face in my hands. Her lashes flutter close as I skate my mouth over her left cheekbone. "My wish, Nyla, is a future with you."

"Shahzad—"

"*Please*," comes out of me like I'm being strangled. I stop and step back, dropping my hands at my sides. "All of my wishes now have you in them. And I want every single one to come true, Nyla. Do you understand me? Every. Single. One."

She lifts her lashes, and the sharp look in her green eyes sends a cold chill down my spine. "You're not just pulling words out of your ass, are you? Because it's *very* difficult for me to trust you after everything that's happened."

"I fucked up, Nyla. I fucked up badly, and I promise I would never dare to do anything like that ever again. I know it'll take you a while to trust me, and I want to give you the space you need—"

"Yes, you've been doing a fantastic job at giving me my space."

"I'm sorry, Nyla. I think we've established by now that I'm a gigantic idiot."

"You are."

"I am."

"But it's also your birthday. And the last thing I want to do is argue about a topic that we should have a long, civilized conversation about." She steps forward until her chest is pressed against mine. She's fully aware of the effect she's having on me when her pink tongue slides across her lower lip. "For now . . . I'm going to kiss you."

"Y-You are?"

"Is that okay?"

"Yes. Yes, of course. It's more than okay. By all . . . means. Please."

Her arms wrap around my neck as I hold onto her waist. She scoffs a smile. "'By all means.' God, you *are* a gigantic idiot." She reaches up and presses her soft lips against mine.

My eyes remain half-open just to double-check I'm not caught up in some fever dream. I'm not.

But seeing my Nyla's flushed face, her eyes tightly shut, and our lips in sync, I smile. And

I pull her even closer, running my fingers through her unruly, pink hair, imprinting her sweet scent onto my skin.

I kiss her eyes. Her forehead. Her cheeks. Her neck. Each kiss is a remedy for the five months I've been without her touch. The sensation coursing through my body combusts me. Blows me into bits and pieces. No point of recovery.

"God, Nyla," I whisper between kisses. "It's killing me not being able to touch you all the time."

Nyla pulls back abruptly, her hands pressing against my chest, her flickering green irises cutting through me. "Thirty seconds for turning thirty."

"Thirty minutes?"

"You want to kiss me for thirty minutes? Are you out of your mind?"

"I could kiss you forever."

Nyla's fists tighten on the front of my shirt. Her thoughts are at a battle with themselves. Mine have already tossed their shield aside, leaving me entirely vulnerable at her mercy.

"No."

"That's fine. I'm happy with what I got." I lick the strawberry taste on my lips. "Did this one come with a water-proof label?"

"Shut up. You missed a spot."

"So no."

Nyla shakes her head, wiping clean her smeared lipstick from my chin. "I'm gonna go now."

"Or you can stay? We could watch a movie. Sit two meters apart, separate popcorn and snacks?"

"Not tonight." She grabs her purse and turns on her heel, calling for Caramel, who's deep asleep with Sky in the living room.

"What about tomorrow night?"

"Work."

I sigh and drag my feet behind her. "You haven't forgiven me yet, have you?"

She slides her feet into her boots, answering my question with something else. "I'm sorry for forgetting your birthday."

"That's not what I asked."

"Caramel, come on."

Nyla's fighting her emotions, but I threw in the towel the day I took the plunge and asked her out. It was the day I silenced the voices in my head and started listening to hers.

Caramel pads over, accompanied by Sky, and stands on his hind legs, paws resting against Nyla's knees. She bends down, picks him up, plants a kiss on his forehead, and welcomes the friendly licks on her jaw.

"We'll talk when I'm ready, Shahzad. For now, I'd like some space to focus on my work and rebuilding my relationship with my mother. That's all I'm asking."

I push my hands into my jeans pockets, giving a nod. "Understood."

"Thank you." Her eyes soften as she looks at Sky. "Goodnight, honey."

I watch Nyla leave my home, which, for a minute, felt like ours.

35

Flirt With Yourself

Shahzad

January 10th

Christmas fucking sucked.

I spent all of December working night and day at the café, suffering in silence at the couples who shared hot chocolates and kisses under the mistletoe.

And if that wasn't bad enough, every staff member miraculously decided to find a partner and rub it in my fucking miserable face.

Devon betrayed me and started dating one of Nyla's friends. Donald's got a regular, single mom of two who comes in to see him in his office and leaves with an earring missing. Matilda went to a cosplay convention and met a boy dressed as Lord WhateverTheFuck. Amelia's fucking engaged to Kevin? I mean, when the fuck did that happen during my neverending Great Depression period? Harry ended up kissing his long-time crush during our holiday event and feigned sickness to go home with him. I took that as an opportunity to hole up in the back and wash the dishes.

But since the spirit of Christmas has come to an end, I've become a thousand times better at doing my job by spending the extra time fretting over Nyla's decision to do something productive for myself.

Matilda and Amelia were impressed by how I didn't need their help handling the front of the shop anymore. I can manage ten orders at a time, curate unique drinks that these girls pull off the dark web or some shit, and wait multiple tables with ease.

"Your drink will be on that side." I gesture to the left, where Matilda is handing tea to a different customer before she begins this order.

Nyla's next in line. She glances up abruptly from her phone, doing a double-take when she notices me.

I punch in her order. "Six-fifty, please."

She takes a second to process before clearing her throat and tapping her phone onto the pad. A part of me is guilty of refusing to buy her a drink for the very first time, but the other is immune to *any* guilt. I've already decided I'm going to stop with the grand gestures and stick to delivering her meals or shoveling her driveway in case she forgets.

I've even stopped with the notes. That one took every last bit of my willpower to decide.

"Drink's on the left," I tell her while making eye contact with the customer behind her.

Nyla walks away, and I release a little breath.

"Shahz?" Matilda walks up to my side with a glass. "Want me to make a heart on her latte again? Or a smiley face?"

"Whatever you want, Matilda. Thanks."

"Huh? You sure?"

"Yes." I let her scurry off to her station and plaster a smile for the customer. "What can I get you started with today?"

During my fifteen-minute break, I sit out in the back on a crate, gloved fists in my coat's pocket, watching an ant struggle with a crumb. Each time the little fella gets the piece on his back and starts walking, it falls off. I don't get it. It's wintertime. Aren't ants supposed to be hibernating and shit? What the hell is this one doing out here on his own?

The back door opens up with Devon lighting a dart. He sees me and raises a brow. "The fuck's wrong with you?"

"Life."

"No shit." He drags a crate over and sits down next to me, offering me the cigarette. The temptation is very much there, but I've been clean for six months now. Can't fuck it up because of Nyla's lack of . . . everything. "Talk to me."

I shake my head. "I don't know what the fuck I'm doing wrong. For the past six months, I've made sure she's—I've done so much to make up for my mistake. I mean, I get it. I get that I fucked up. I'm putting in all my effort to fix this—to fix *us*, but it's—I just feel like we're going in circles." I purse my lips to prevent them from quivering. "I hate myself for questioning if any of this has been worth anything at all."

"Hmm." Devon blows out a thick cloud of bitter smoke and relaxes back against the wall. "If I was her, I would have forgiven your ass the day you got her that puppy."

A hollow sound escaped my throat, barely resembling a chuckle.

"But I do respect that she knows her worth," he continues. "She isn't the type to fuck around with your feelings. She knows she's worth fighting for, and you're the strongest soldier. So what if she didn't want to sleep over at your place that night? Take into account how awkward it must've been for her after five months of . . . mouth celibacy? Is that a term?"

Now I *really* chuckle. Laugh, even. But as the reality of his words sinks in, I hate myself further for acting like a dickhead this morning. For even thinking I should pack up my bags and move the fuck on. That's impossible with a magnetic force like Nyla in my life.

"You know," Devon drawls, pinning me with a mischievous look, "you can always try to make her a little green around the gills."

"What the fuck does green around the gills even mean?"

"Make her jealous, dumbass. Flirt with a girl in front of her. Get a reaction out of her to calm yourself down. Believe me, man, it'll work like a fucking charm."

I narrow my eyes at his stupidity. "That'll drive her away further."

"Or pull her closer when she realizes that the only man who's ever given a *genuine* shit about her is moving on."

I shake my head. "That's stupid. She's very—she'll start comparing herself to the woman and spiral into this whole thing that I'm not gonna get into."

"I'm not asking you to take someone home with you. Flirt with your daily admirers or accept a compliment by complimenting them back. But just make sure your girl's watching. How do you think I got with Rita?"

I arch my brows. "Who's Rita?"

Devon smacks me over the head. "My girlfriend, asshole."

"Jesus, sorry. I'm just—I'm all over the fucking place right now." The little ant tries for the sixth time. "That's not an excuse."

"Look, Shahz, I don't know what else to tell you. Clearly, you're at a crossroads here. You want to keep your girl happy by doing the most any of us ever could, but your mental health is also taking a tank simultaneously." Devon's cheeks pull in with a long puff that swirls out through his nostrils. "Hmm."

"What?"

He purses his lips in thought, side-glancing at me. "Screw flirting with other girls. I've got a better idea."

I blink.

"Flirt with yourself."

I smack my lips and sigh. "Fuck off."

"I'm serious, Shahz. When's the last time you took care of yourself? Treated yourself? Gone out to a bar with the boys and me? Shaved your pirate-looking ass beard? Trimmed your dead-ends? Read a book? Made plans to open your own restaurant in the city?" His questions shoot through me like bullets made of logic and sense. "Come on, man. Think about it."

Last time I treated myself . . . I don't have any recollection. Maybe when I took Nyx out for a ride? Last time I went to a bar? When I was guarding Nyla on the Fourth of July. I *do* need to trim my beard and hair. Probably should start buying cooking books and form a business plan for my restaurant, or at least apply for jobs in the city.

"See, that's the face of a man who knows he's worth it, too," Devon says, pointing the end of his cigarette bud at me. "Trust me, man. Before anyone starts caring for you, you gotta start caring for yourself. And do it *for* yourself. Not because you want her to look in your direction with hearts in her eyes or some shit."

I nod. "Okay."

"Okay?"

"Yeah. Okay."

"Good." He stands and crushes the cigarette under his foot, tossing it into the garbage bin. He points down at me. "Act on it. If you need any help, I'm here for you."

"I know."

We clap hands and hold them tight before he disappears inside.

As for the ant, he's long gone with his crumb.

First place I go to is the barbershop.

It's sparse as fuck, with only a couple of elderly gentlemen occupied with other barbers and—oh, great. Matilda's cosplayer boyfriend is one of the team members.

How exciting.

He sees me and stands from his chair. "Yo, Shahz!"

I don't remember his name. Only the fact that he got Matilda's name tattooed on his chest on their second date. Aside from that oddness, he's a good-looking guy. Lean build, firm shoulders, dark, monolid eyes, and short, silver-cropped hair. Yeah, he's right up that girl's alley.

"Hey . . . Uh, I'm sorry. I'm blanking right now."

He sighs. Smiles. "Lucas."

I cringe from my lack of knowledge on the one man Matilda gushes to me about. "Sorry, Lucas."

"No worries. Have a seat."

I sit down on the leather chair while he stands behind me, smiling with a boyish charm in the mirror. Then he starts running his fingers through my hair. "Uh, so, I want to trim the ends of my hair. Cut down my beard close to my jaw as well."

"Okay, I see." He checks a bundle of strands from my scalp to my end. "Your hair is brittle, Shahz. Do you use a conditioner?"

"What's that?"

Lucas looks terrified. "You— *Wow*. Okay. What kind of shampoo do you use?"

"It's one of those all-in—"

"*Don't* finish that sentence." The dramatic alter-ego in him pinches his nose bridge and takes deep breaths. "All right, here's what we're gonna do. I'm gonna cut your hair—"

"Nope." I'm out of my seat.

Lucas pulls me back down with a surprisingly strong force and keeps me rooted to the seat. "I'm going to cut your hair up close to the nape of your neck. A little long but wavy and pushed back. Think Patrick Dempsey in Grey's Anatomy."

My worried eyes lock onto his delighted ones.

"The greatest trust you can ever put is in your barber," Lucas says, squeezing my shoulders. "Permission to Dr. Derek Shepard-ify you? They call him McDreamy for a reason."

I don't understand a single reference, but seeing the magnificence of his own middle-parted, blond hair that would have Dua fanning over, and the full jar of tips on his work counter, I firmly state, "I trust you, buddy."

Lucas drags me to the shower bowls, where he starts rambling about how he and Matilda met at Comic-Con in the city over the winter break. While he's snipping my hair, he lists all her great qualities, like her dedication to costume design and her clinical perfectionist barista personality. During the blow-dry, he gushes about how pretty she looks when they argue over stupid little things and how much her cuddles warm his soul. When he trims my beard down, he asks me, "How are things with your girl?"

I take a deep breath. "Not good."

"How come?"

"I don't know." I inch my neck up for him to buzz around the jawline. "I'm beginning to think I'm just being a nuisance to her, and it's best to just—to move on."

"Her from you or you from her?"

Moving on from Nyla is impossible. I know I won't love anyone else like I love her. And I won't string someone along either, knowing I don't see a future with them. It'll be back to waking up alone in my cold bed and working my wage.

"You know, Matilda and I had this fight—"

"Lucas, I appreciate you, I truly do, but I really don't want you rubbing salt in my wound."

"Too bad. I'm telling you anyway." He shuts off the machine and squares me with a smile. "I never expected Matilda to like me back. She's got itineraries, and I'm spontaneous. She's a multi-tasker, and I'm just very fucking lazy. She's the type of girl to ask for the ketchup packet on my behalf because I get anxious asking for things." His lips purse in thought. "The only time I've ever wanted something for myself was when I saw her. In her stunning, elaborate costume, surrounded by fifty Lord Voctoral De Ashburns asking for her number and pictures. And Matilda, out of all the boys there, wanted a picture with *me*."

My lips naturally curve up at his lopsided grin and sparkling blue eyes. "What's the moral of your story, kid?"

"Does every love story need a moral?"

"No," I mumble. "No, I guess not. Some stories are not meant to be lessons. Especially not about some teenage cosplayers who have a more profoundly sweet relationship than most adults I know."

Lucas rolls his eyes, chuckling. He turns on the electric shaver. "Let's finish lining you up."

FAKE IT TILL WE MAKE IT

Sky leaves the basket of dinner for Nyla at her doorstep and races back to me.

"Good girl." I usher her inside and shut the door. Usually, I'd wait until Nyla walked out and secured the goods, giving Sky a little pat on the head, but now witnessing all of that just feels unnecessary.

I take my dinner to the living room, tempted to peek out the curtains to see if the basket has disappeared.

But I veto it.

I've decided to leave in July. A complete full year of living in Rhode Island, where I've made new work friends, sought a spring of motivation for my future career and did all that I fucking could to earn Nyla's apology.

Yes, I could do more and get her to forgive me, but I can't force it anymore. I got her to smile at me. I somehow got her to touch and kiss me. I got her to talk to me—to say my name.

Wanting more is selfish. If she isn't on board with *us* anymore, then it's not my place to tie her to the wheel and captain our relationship. She's a beautiful, clever woman who truly deserves someone on the exact wavelength as her. Not a sore, greedy fuck-up with his head stuck so far up his demons' asses.

However, I don't see myself as that anymore.

First thing I did when I returned from the haircut was look in the mirror for a good ten minutes. A new record since I discovered the purpose of mirrors. And I wasn't ashamed.

Instead, I saw a man with the will to try again but on his own terms, by his own judgment. I will take Devon's advice and utilize this time to work on myself.

I'm going to look into some fine-dining, sous-chef postings in the city. I'm going to experiment with my cooking and curate my own menu for my restaurant someday. I'm going to accept invitations to the bar or campfire parties by the beach.

And I'm going to buy more dress pants.

36

Ketchup Packet

Nyla

February 14th

Valentine's Day may as well be coined as the day Nyla Ghilzai announced she's alive.

"You'll be great, my love," Mama whispers through our FaceTime call. It's currently eight in the morning, and I'm about to post ten slides on Instagram with pictures of my past two years.

First slide: Dying my hair pink.

Second slide: The beach that's my backyard.

Third slide: Standing outside Jia's BBQ house in my waitress uniform, pointing up at the sign.

Fourth slide: Sky's eyes.

Fifth slide: Shahzad's famous ham and cheese sandwich.

Sixth slide: Maira and I's matching friendship bracelets.

Seventh slide: A screenshot of Alina, Zoha, and me on FaceTime, laughing our lungs out over another stupid video of the girls pranking Azeer.

Eighth slide: Shahzad's phoenix tattoo.

Ninth slide: My home design studio with all fifteen mannequins dressed in my upcoming Spring collection. The neon sign on the wall reads *Nylana*.

Tenth slide: Caramel.

"Two minutes!" Mama squeals. "Did you proofread the caption?"

"Doing so right now." I clench and unclench my trembling fists, muttering the words I've written out.

Hi.

It's me.

Nylana Ghilzai, or Nyla, depending on my mood.

Where have I been for the past almost two years? Wallowing. Hiding out in Rhode Island. Dealing with my mental health issues and wondering if the next day was worth the pain.

Spoiler alert: It was.

Over the course of my hiatus, I met some amazing new people. I made new friends. I worked as a waitress. I helped those friends when all I felt was helpless. And most importantly, I fell in love.

I fell in love with a new morning. I fell in love with doing laundry. I fell in love with the little bubbles that leave the liquid soap when I washed the dishes. I fell in love with eating again. I fell in love with making true friends. I fell in love with a human who completes my soul. I fell in love with my passions that I buried a decade ago.

I didn't know I was capable of fighting after what had happened to me. But I'm happy I didn't do it alone as I sit here, ready to post this with a glass of red wine and my mother on FaceTime.

If there's one lesson I've learned from all these years of taking hits left and right, it's that in my losses, I gained victories.

And I'm not stopping here.

Happy Valentine's Day from me to you.

Nylana.

I exhale into a smile and press post.

The upload takes ten seconds before it's live on my empty feed. I archived every image and changed my profile picture to Caramel's cheek pressed against mine for a selfie.

"I'm so proud of you, my love," Mama says as I exit Instagram and return to our call. She wipes her fingers below her eyes. "I'm so proud of you."

"Mama, stop . . ." I start sniffling and calling Caramel onto my lap. He's grown in size and love since he was brought to me in a little woven basket. "It'll be fine?"

Mama can't contain her wavering smile. She kisses the camera and wipes the blurriness away. "You'll be fine, Nylana."

"Mother knows best," I say. "I'll call you later. I'm gonna clean up the place and watch a rom-com."

"Take care and have lots of fun, baby."

Ending the call and shutting off my phone, I shower Caramel with a flurry of kisses and head upstairs to change into my workout attire.

Sky's bark is the first sound I hear when I step out of the bathroom. My feet instantly travel toward my bedroom window. She's got the breakfast basket in her mouth that she delivers to my doorstep, then runs back to Shahzad.

Shahzad.

Gosh, his hair is slightly shorter and pushed back instead of his usual middle part. The rough edges of his beard, now trimmed into a stubble, make him look younger and more baby-faced. I swear, he's like a human adrenaline shot for me.

I hurry downstairs with Caramel and leash him up.

Opening the door, I expect Shahzad to be stretching on his driveway, but he's jogging off with Sky. Again.

I take the basket and bring it inside. There's no sticky note attached to the brown bag, either. He's stopped writing them since the shit show that was his thirtieth birthday.

In fact, ever since, he's closed himself off entirely. And he's happier that way. I see him joke alongside his co-workers, handle his tasks like a pro, leave work on time even if I'm still sitting in the café, and go out into town with his work friends. Maira, Tae, and Hye-jin would send me pictures of their hang-outs in New York with a "Wish you were here" tagline.

The attention I received up until December has vanished into thin air. All I have left now is his three meals a day deliveries and an occasional neighborly smile when I'm leaving my house and he's entering.

Well, glad to know you're taking care of yourself, Chef.

Sighing, I head out for my run with Caramel and let the wind blow away my thoughts of him.

The most efficient part of living in this gated community is that the paparazzi can't get through without TSA-type checkups from the security team and valid identification or visitation cards.

But that doesn't mean the residents aren't curious.

Most of the neighborhood are retired folks who forget the password to their emails everyday, but they've all got teenage grandchildren who are *very* much aware of my existence. And Mick and Grayson only clock in when I call them. They know I've got Shahzad's protection after I informed them of my intrusive neighbor. The duo struggled to contain their laughter at the antics of their former trainer.

When I step outside my house with a group of girls standing by the curb, squealing at the sight of me, I feel . . . pretty great, actually.

"Can we get a picture, please?" One of them asks.

"Sure!" I go around the group taking pictures and basking in their compliments about my hair and Caramel and how they've always supported me since everything. They even give me Valentine's Day candy and friendship bracelets with pink hearts.

Then they flutter off like excited butterflies.

I get in my car and start chuckling at my steering wheel. "God, I love girlhood."

The workers of Caffè di Matilda are surprisingly relaxed when I enter.

All except the owner, Donald Caruso.

"Move, move!" He ushers aside the young couple that finish taking pictures with me and kindly guides me to my designated booth seat. "You know, Miss Ghilzai, I didn't want to believe my daughter when she said you look a hell lot like, well, yourself, but here we are." Wiping the seat with his handkerchief, he sits me down. "Now, what can I get for you? All on the house."

"Please, treat me like you have before, Mr. Caruso."

"For you, I'm Donny."

I can't help but smile at him. He's a good dad from what I've observed sitting idly in this café. His daughter, Matilda, is the shiniest, sweetest apple of his eyes. I wouldn't be taken back if he threatened her boyfriend with a gun to treat her like the royalty she cosplays. Good to know they are great fathers out there.

A feminine laughter followed by a pair of deep chuckles, one that makes me sit straighter and hold my breath, enter the café. Shahzad and his cooking buddies, Devon and Matilda, carry bags of groceries inside.

"Oh!" Matilda squeaks, leaving her duties on the floor and rushing over to me. "Oh my gosh, you're here. You're actually here. I mean, you've always been here, and I always knew you were Nyla and *not* Alyn, which, by the way, is *so* genius? Reversing your name? Legendary." She snorts and skips on the tips of her toes, hugging her father's arm. "Told you she looked familiar."

"Yo, Mats! Let's pick up the pace, girl. These fruits aren't gonna put themselves in the freezer," Devon says, then winks at me and adds, "Looking great as per usual."

"Bye-bye," Matilda mutters and flutters away with a goodbye wave, squealing all the way to the kitchen with Shahzad, who didn't even bother to spare me a glance.

"What can I get for you, Miss Ghilzai?" Donny asks, hands intertwined and a featherbrained smile on his mouth.

I tilt my head. "For you, I'm Nyla."

He bursts out laughing, and I join him halfway.

The staff is incredibly sweet throughout the day, making sure I'm not bombarded by fans. Especially Amelia.

She's been monitoring the groups of girls, couples, and singles who enter the café to order, and right as they catch sight of me writing emails or sketching, they'll gasp and ask for a picture. If I'm overwhelmed, Amelia would sweep in and politely ask them to allow me space.

Close to five in the evening, I pack up my belongings and finish the last sip of my ice-cold latte, bundling up in my plaid overcoat, cream wool scarf, and a black peaky blinder.

"All done?"

I swirl around from sipping my bag and bump chests with Shahzad. The greeting dies on my tongue. Up close and personal, with his new brushed-back hairstyle and stubble, my knees weaken, and my fingers twitch to run through his dark strands.

Shahzad stretches his arm and picks up the glass behind me. "Get home safe."

"Wait." I seize his bicep. His eyes drop there for a moment and flick up to mine. "I was—I wanted to ask if—" *you wanted to come over for dinner?*

"If what?" he prompts.

I let go of his arm. "If . . . you wanted to drop Sky off at my place? Caramel's been missing her a lot."

"Sure." He checks his phone, and I catch sight of his wallpaper. It's his sisters and him at an amusement park. "I'm going out with friends tonight. I'll drop her off with your dinner."

My chin quivers, chest tightening. I'm not upset that he's made friends. I'm *incredibly* proud of him. He's always been a bit closed off and doesn't bother opening up about his interests unless pushed to. It brings me immense happiness that he's out and about, laughing with his . . . friends.

I smile. "Where are you all headed for dinner, if you don't mind me asking?"

"The Barrel."

"A bar?"

"Bar *and* grill."

I nod. "Well, have lots of fun. Make sure you've got a designated—"

"Do you wanna come with me?" He asks with a cinch between his dark brows and a faint smile. "You don't have to drink or anything. I'll make sure no one hassles you for another autograph—"

"I'd love to," I blurt out, fidgeting with my fingernails. "The dogs?"

"We can let them relax at my place. Sky's police trained, so she'll protect Caramel." He pulls out his phone and shows me multiple security screens of his rooms. "Precautions."

God, I wonder if he watched back the clip of his birthday dinner.

I clear my throat and nod. "I'll go . . . get ready."

"You look—You look great, Nyla." His lips twitch into an adorable grin that has butterflies ravaging my insides. "But I know firsthand how much you love dressing up, so I'll drive you to your place. Make sure the dogs are settled in, too."

I nod. "Okay."

Shahzad shoves his fists into the pockets of his leather jacket and steps past me. The heat radiating from his body barely brushes against mine, but the damn effect it has on my nerves is barely tame. And when dark brown eyes meet my green, fascinated ones, I have the sudden urge to give him all my oxygen.

I'm definitely drinking tonight.

The Barrel is packed with singles taking advantage of the Valentine's Day happy hour.

Couples are off in the corners, dancing in each other's embrace, where a live band sings a lively rendition of pop, romantic ballads. The lights are dawned in soft pink and red colors, and decorations of hearts and Cupid are stuck to the brick interior. Love shots are being shared, and drunk, romantic declarations are being shouted from table-tops.

A shoulder bumps into me, the tipsy woman apologizing ten times over.

Shahzad's hand covers mine and tugs me closer to his side. His scent of mossy woods and spicy cinnamon radiates from the dark-brown leather jacket that I pinch from the back.

"Woah, woah, *woah*?" I hear from the long, narrow table we approach, filled to the brim with Shahzad's co-workers and their partners. It's Devon who stands and points at both of us. "War's over?"

"Shut the fuck up." Shahzad chuckles and drops my hand to bro-slap with Devon and the rest of the guys around the table, already making small talk and stealing a shot.

I idly find a seat next to Matilda, who's already bat-shit drunk and is kissing her boyfriend Lucas's jaw. Thank God her father isn't here to witness this.

"Shot?"

I glance across the table at Amelia sitting on her fiancé's lap, holding up some sort of pink liquid. "What is it?"

"Tequila."

"I have an *extremely* low tolerance," I say, rejecting the drink.

She shrugs and scarves it down. "Best to maintain your reputation anyway."

Thing is, I didn't announce my existence on social media to "maintain a reputation." A reputation that my father clearly crafted. Going forth, I own the narrative of my journey as a fashion designer and a prominent name in the fashion industry. No more toxic diets and unhealthy amounts of workouts. I am my *own* person now.

But why do I feel like I'm missing half of myself?

"On second thought." I take the second shot from Amelia's fingers and down it, hissing through my teeth. *Shit, that's harsh.* My throat burns, but not as worse as my eyes do watching Shahzad sitting far off with his friends, sipping beer and sharing stories.

I take a shot from the fresh tray that's brought over.

A second.

Fourth.

Seventh.

I don't know how many I consume in the dark corner I sit in. Some taste like jellybeans, others like a bitter pill to swallow. I'm hoping it cures the throbbing ache growing in my chest.

"We should, like, *daaaaance*," Matilda slurs, head dropping on my shoulder. Her eyes are closed as she mindlessly chews on a french-fry.

My cheek drops on her head. "We totally should."

Giggles leave her and then she's ushering me out the booth and stealing my hand. "Let's dance the fucking night *away*!" She climbs up onto our table while Amelia moves everything out of the way, scolding her to sit her ass down.

But Matilda is lost in the music, swaying her hips and shimmying her shoulders. She drags her Lucas up as well, but he's smart enough to bridal carry her down and whisk her into the rowdy crowd instead.

"Can I get a picture, Nyla?" A young woman's voice squeaks from behind me. "Sorry, I know you're busy, but I've always been such a huge fan of your style and your movies. My Pinterest outfits board is mostly you, actually." She chuckles nervously. "But you totally don't have to—"

I grab her face in my hands, hiccuping. "You're adorable. Let's take a thousand pictures." Taking her phone, I wrap my arm around her neck and snap relentlessly. She's hugging me tight, squealing when I kiss her cheek, and rambling about how proud she is I'm coming out with my own fashion line.

"That's enough for now."

The phone is plucked out of my hand and returned back to the young girl. Shahzad sends her rushing back to her group of friends and pinches my chin.

"Go away," I grumble, swatting his hand aside. A snort pops out of me. "I'm gonna *dance*!"

"I'm taking you home. Let's go."

"No!" I thrash against his grip on my wrist. He releases me instantly and huffs. "You're so bossy, Chef. So chef-y. You're chefy. Chefy, chefy, chefy." My fingers poke his cheek and *boop* his straight, sharp nose. "So pretty, too."

"Nyla, please don't make a scene here, all right? Let me get you home—"

"It's Valentine's Day." I sling my arms around his neck one by one. My mouth brushes against his in the slightest of ways. I shiver when his hand presses against my lower back and pulls me flush against his rock-hard chest. "Aren't you going to give me a sweet kiss, Chef Arain?"

"My kisses are the least bit sweet, Troublemaker."

I giggle. "Don't lie. You're such a sweet kisser. In fact, I like all kinds of your kisses." My eyes travel up to his watchful, amused ones. "I like *you*. I like you *sooooo* much. I can't—it's hard not to like you, Shahzad." Hiccup. "It's hard not to forgive you, either."

He smiles. "Let's go home, Nyla."

"Do you like me?"

Shahzad sighs and rakes his long, large fingers through his hair. I want them to trace stars on my spine or explore my insides. There's no in-between. "I love you, Nyla."

I gasp. *Oh, my.* "Wait, really? You love *me*?"

He chuckles at my child-like amazement. "God, you're stupidly drunk."

"Say it again."

"I love you."

"Again."

Shahzad's fingers thread through my hair. "I love you, Nyla." He presses a gentle kiss on my forehead. "I love you." Both my cheeks. "I miss you." My jaw. "I will always love you even on the days you don't love yourself." He takes my hand from his chest and kisses each knuckle with delicate, featherlight precision. "You are my love. You're my beautiful first love. My only love." Then he pecks the tip of my nose and whispers against my temple, "Can I ask you something since you're insatiably drunk?"

"Always."

"Would you get me a ketchup packet if I was too scared to ask?"

I cock my head back. "*Huh*? Ketchup packet?"

"Mm-hmm."

"Well . . . considering *I* am super-duper anxious asking anyone for anything, I'd carry an entire ketchup bottle with me for us. I'll buy a ketchup company. No, no, no, I'll build us a time machine and find the inventor of ketchup, right?"

"Right."

"And I'll pay him a trillion, gazillion dollars to give me the patent, and then when they ask me how I invented ketchup"—I hiccup—"I'll say that the love of my life in the future was too scared to ask for a ketchup packet so I bought the rights. Easy-peasy. So now, every time you ask for a ketchup packet, just say, 'Oh, my girlfriend actually invented the ketchup.' Isn't that just *so* genius?"

Shahzad's eyes disappear into the widest grin I've ever seen on his face. "You'd go through all of that for me?"

I boop his nose. "Only for you, my gargantuan puppy."

Shahzad observes me, his irises flickering back and forth as if I've slapped him with a revelation or something.

"Gosh, you are so *cheesy* giving me that innocent schoolboy look, you dirty, dirty man." I pinch his cheeks and stretch them. "So squishy!"

He takes my wrists. "And another thing?"

I hold an invisible microphone up to his mouth. "Speak, Ketchup Man."

I *feel* his smile against my skin as he says, "I'm very proud of you for the step you've taken today and the steps you'll continue to take from here on out, Nylana."

Melting. I'm melting against him. My head rests on his shoulders, and my arms belt around his strong waist. Every laugh, every kiss, every particle of intimacy in the air reduces at the sound of his rapid heartbeat beneath my ear. I'm on cloud nine.

"I love you, Shahzad," I mutter. He sucks in a sharp breath, belting an arm around my waist. "I wanted to stay with you on your birthday and kiss you for thirty minutes or hours, or however long. I wanted . . . I wanted to sit super close to you and watch another comedic thriller and eat popcorn from the same bowl." The line between soberness and drunkenness blurs, and now I'm just saying whatever I've been mulling over since December. "I'm sorry if I broke your heart that night."

"Hey, hey, hey." He tips my chin up, genuinely taken back as if my words caught him off guard. "It's not your fault, baby. You weren't comfortable with where we were going, and I wasn't going to force you to do anything you didn't want to."

I bury my face in the crook of his neck. "You're so sweet, you know that?" Somehow, we fall into slow-dancing to a fast-tempo pop song. "Can you write me your little love notes again?"

"Is that an order?"

"It's a demand."

His calloused, warm hand runs down the back of my head and cups around the nape of my neck. "Yes, ma'am."

I fall into a soothing darkness.

37

Talk

Shahzad

March 10th

Zineerah calls me on FaceTime right as I punch out of work.
I control the madness brewing within me regarding her impending *arranged* marriage and swipe right, using sign language and my own voice to speak with her. "Glad to know you didn't forget about your brother."

Zineerah doesn't smile. She hasn't smiled since everything that happened to her. Her face remains deadpan, dark brown eyes hollow and hooded from mental exhaustion. Her knee-long, black hair, which she's been growing long since high school, is tied into a side braid. And she's in a black sweater, with her headphones over her head, sitting inside the comfort of her closet.

It is raining, she signs. *I miss you.*

My sister despises the rain. Always has since we were children. She thought the raindrops pattering against the window were gunshots and thunder, frightening the living shit out of her. She'd always end up hugging me in bed until I left the family.

"I'm sorry, sweetheart. How have things been?"

Surprisingly okay.

"Yeah? Is Maya giving you any shit?"

No.

"And your . . . fiancé?"

He is fine. We only spoke verses during our— She pauses and thinks. "Nikah," she mouths, holding up the golden band with tiny diamonds encrusted in the octagon in the middle. *I wish you were there.*

I frown. "You know my stance on Maya's decision, Zinnie. I would've torn the place apart if I saw you consenting to a marriage forced upon you."

Zineerah chews her bottom lip. *He's not him, Shahzad.*

"Better the fuck not be, or else I'll shoot his brains out before he can even think of hurting you."

Normally, there'd be an appalled reaction, but Zineerah sighs and nods. *This is good for me despite what you think. I needed an excuse to get away from Mama's clutches.*

"She doesn't even live in Toronto, sweetheart."

She would control me even if she was in hell, Shahzad! Zineerah huffs and fidgets with the end of her braid, chin quivering. *Raees is a good man. Dua always compliments him and praises his personality. He is a bit talkative and smiles too often, the complete opposite of me, but he is the only key I have to freedom.* She holds up her ring finger again. *This is the key, Shahzad. Deal with it when you come to my wedding.*

"Zin—"

You will come to my wedding. She ends the call.

I sit back with a thud and rubber-neck at Nyla casually strolling down the street with Caramel. She's gotten more comfortable chatting and taking pictures with her fans while Mickey and Grayson trail behind her.

Ever since Nyla made herself public to the media with an array of pictures of her hiatus, one of which was Jia's BBQ House, the restaurant's sales have skyrocketed, according to Tae. They've made me take a vow to visit as soon as I'm forgiven for extra marketing and also because Bao and the team miss Nyla and me.

Besides, I've been recently under fire from everyone about keeping Nyla's identity a secret when we lived above the restaurant.

A text notification from—*Alina?*—pops up on my phone. I click on the Twitter link that she sent me with a smirk emoji.

"Ah, fuck."

Blurry, noisy pictures of Nyla with her arms locked around my neck and mine around her waist are being spread like a virtual plague across the internet. It's *so* obvious it's her with the pink, wavy hair and the fact *everyone* knows she's currently in Rhode Island.

Fucking A.

Either way, I'm not pissed. Sooner or later, I will be pulled into her spiraling A-lister lifestyle. Might as well get a head start on it now.

I stare at the pictures a little longer, ignoring the tweets below saying, "*Who's the lucky lumberjack?*"

I scoff. "The fuck? I don't look like a fucking lumberjack." Checking the rear-view mirror, I notice my beard has grown out again.

Fuck, I do.

The tweets aren't negative, though. At least not towards me. Regarding Nyla, they're a horrendous wildfire. Incoming bullet shots that pierce through my chest.

@gionikolas: Not surprised that the serial dater has come out of hiding with her next target. One word, buddy: Run.

"Oh, fuck you, dickhead." I go to block him but realize I don't use Twitter at all. So I make an anonymous account, similar to the one I have for Instagram, to report *and* block the fucker.

And I do that to every misogynistic, sexist, body-shaming tweet I can find. I spend an hour digging under news articles slut-shaming or using derogatory terms toward my woman and reporting whoever dares to even tweet: "*Eh, she's okay.*"

Of course, I follow the die-hard Nylatrons (unfortunately, that's the best they could come up with), along with fan sites that update every breath she takes with heart emojis and a lot of: *ASFDHFJFKDLS.*

I don't know what those chunks of letters stand for, but yes, I agree.

"You know what? Fuck it." I grin as I change my default icon to a picture of Nyla. One that I stole from a fancy magazine article she recently interviewed for. Her pink hair is braided like a crown above her head, her jade eyes are sparkling, and her sandy-brown skin is glowing and dewy. She's in a pink pants-suit and leans against a window of an empty studio in New York, grinning ear-to-ear. "Hmm. Pretty girl."

In my bio, I write: *Nylana's #1 fan.* And I change my username to: *@Nylana4life0416.* The sixteen is because her birthday is on April 16th.

Which is coming up soon.

Something pink flashes in my peripheral.

I catch Nyla speed-walking back to her Mercedes, clutching her stomach. My first

FAKE IT TILL WE MAKE IT

instinct is to race out of the driver's seat, but I sit alert instead, not wanting to cause a scene in public.

The guards escort her in the backseat and drive her back to her place.

Naturally, I follow.

I park in my driveway just as the Mercedes does and rush over to Nyla exiting the back. Her facial muscles cringe, and she physically grunts, still clutching her gut.

"Hey, hey, hey." I take her face in my hands. "What's wrong? Are you all right?"

Nyla nods. "Take the rest of the day off, boys."

"You sure, Miss Ghilzai?" Mickey asks.

"I'll call you tomorrow," she says.

I stare at the pair, who continue to linger, but again, they're just doing their job. "Go. I'll take care of her from here."

Mickey and Grayson clear their throats and return to their Ranger, driving off down the two-way street.

I safely take Nyla inside her house, unleashing Caramel. "Did you eat?"

She groans, struggling to take off her shoes.

"Stop." I take her heel and slip it off her foot, followed by the other. There are red lines all around her skin from the discomfort. "Want me to bring you your sandals?"

"Please." She shrugs off her coat and hooks it onto the hangar by the door, followed by her beret and scarf.

I open the shoe closet and pick out her pink house sandals. Then I crouch and slip them onto her feet.

"Uh, I'm good now, so. You can head back home," Nyla says in a hurry and slips past me in a jiffy.

"Not so fast." I trail after and find her ravaging her pantry for a box of oatmeal cookies and then her fridge for whipped cream. My blood runs arctic. "Oh, fuck. Are you pregnant?"

"*Ow!*" Nyla hits the back of her skull, trying to stand up from scouring the fridge. "What the fuck kind of assumption is that, Shahzad? We're dat— Never mind." She scoffs a million times over and sets her food down on the counter. "I got my period. So no baby." She pouts.

"Not yet."

I breathe a sigh of relief that seems to piss her off further. "I'm sorry. I don't why I just—" I stop speaking at her ferocious yet attractive glare. "Let me help."

"You can *help* by leaving." She sprays a tall mountain of cream over the cookie and shoves

291

it into her mouth, deflating into a whimsical smile. "So, *so* good."

I approach her slowly, whisking Caramel's needy ass from the floor and into my arms. Sky's probably having a nap back in my bedroom, so I'll wake her up later after handling Nyla. "Do you need me to get you something from the store?"

She shrugs, half asleep and chewing.

"Nyla?"

"Hmm?"

"Do you need me to get you—"

"I don't know," she snaps, green gaze narrowing on me. I smile. She softens and rolls her eyes. "If you *really* want to help, and I'm only saying this because I want you out of my hair."

"Impossible. I love your hair."

She groans.

"Sorry. Continue, please."

"Pads," she states. "With wings. It'll be in a purple and green packaging. And *white* chocolate. If there's a heating pad, grab that, too. Oh, and Advil. Two hundred milligrams is fine." Grabbing her oatmeal cookies and whipped cream, she drags her sandaled feet across the floor and toward the living room. "Fifteen minutes, Chef."

I finish the task in twelve minutes.

I park in my driveway, grab Sky, and take the bag of her items back inside. Caramel's already scratching at my legs for attention, so I pick him up, too, and enter the living room, letting our dogs play around in their toy corner.

Nyla's sitting up on the couch, chewing a licorice stick, and watching . . . *Pride and Prejudice,* obviously. She's changed into her pink pajamas with black stars, and her hair's high up in a tangled bun.

"I brought your essentials," I say, taking everything out of the bag and lining them up on the table.

She pauses the movie. "That was fast."

"There's ten kinds of white chocolates—one of them has to be your favorite." I place the pads on the coffee table. "With wings." Then the sweet and salty treats. "Snacks." And the heating pad. "I'll go fill this up with hot water."

"You're a saint." Nyla continues to chew on her licorice and dismisses me with a wave.

Grinning at her behavior, I enter my natural habitat and warm up the sink water in a pot over the stove. I wash the heating pad with precision, then pour the scalding hot water from the depths of hell inside.

Cap twisted close, a shawl wrapped around the pad, I walk back to the living room and sit down next to her on the couch.

"Lift your sweater for me," I say.

Nyla curls up the hem of her sweater, fixated on Darcy's first appearance. I tuck the heating pad there, and she pulls down her sweater.

"Can I feed you?" I ask, cracking the white chocolate pieces into singular cubes. "Please?"

Nyla nods and sticks her tongue out.

Excitement overtakes me in an instant in a lot of different areas of my body. I sit straighter, placing it on the pad of her pink palette, and watch as she savors the sweet, creamy taste. The tiny bob in her throat rises when she swallows and drops when she sighs.

"Is it good?" I ask.

She nods. Five times. Adorable.

I continue feeding her the snacks, getting comfortable under the throw I spread out on both our laps. At every contact of my fingertips with her soft lips, I crumble. It takes every restraint in me to not steal a kiss on her cheek or hold her for eternities.

Soon, Shahzad.

"Why are cramps *so* much worse the second day?" She winces, hunching over and gripping her stomach. Her legs buckle together, and a small whimper follows.

"I know, baby." I run my hand over and down the back of her head. "What can I do to make it easier?"

Her head shakes. "Nothing."

"That word doesn't exist in my vocabulary when it comes to you, Nyla." I open my arms. "I'll carry you to the bathroom."

"No," she breathes out, digging her nails into her gut. "Advil."

"On it." I twist open the cap of the medicine bottle and place a tablet on her palm. She pops it and drinks it down. "Lay your head on my lap."

"No."

"Nyla, please. Just for today, give in to me. Tomorrow, you can give up on me."

With a pout, she hugs the blanket closer and plants her head on my lap. "Don't say things like that."

"Have you forgiven me inside that pretty little head of yours, Nylana?"

"Shut up. Only my mother is allowed to call me that."

I lick my lips and stretch my arms behind on the couch. "I've been meaning to ask about your reunion with her. Everything sorted out?"

Nyla remains silent, eyes trained on the movie she's seen a million times now. She even muttered the dialogue under her breath before the characters said it. "We're sorted."

"Okay." I tuck a strand of her pink hair behind her ear and slide my hand behind her neck. "Is she staying?"

"I said we're sorted, Shahzad. What part of *we're sorted* do you not understand?"

I contain my smile at her adorable outburst. "Apologies, baby."

"Don't call me baby," she grumbles.

"You don't mean that."

She glances back at me. "I mean *every* word I say to you, Shahzad."

"Even the ones under the influence?" I raise a challenging brow at her silence and shying cheeks. "They say there are two types of honest people, Nyla. Children and drunkards. You were both on Valentine's Day. A drunk child."

She sits up and glowers at me from beneath her lashes. "Yes, Shahzad, even the ones under the influence. What are you gonna do about it?"

"You keep giving me those eyes, and I'll find a hundred different ways to make them roll back to your skull."

Nyla's breath hitches, her fists curling at her sides. "Gosh, you're *so*—you're just so—"

"So what?"

She grumbles, "Charming." Her small hands press against my chest and take a trip up to my neck. She relaxes her forehead over mine and brushes her button-nose against the tip of my straighter one. "I wish you hadn't done it."

I cuff her frail wrists, keeping my eyes open on her behalf. "Me, too."

"Then why did you?"

"I don't know, Nyla. I should've known better than to bargain with Abe," I explain quietly. "I knew I couldn't afford to pay a stranger to act as my girlfriend, nor could I lie to Mustafa and risk Maira's ambitions, so my selfishness drove me to you."

"Because I was the easier option."

"At the moment, yes. You were an easy option. I knew you somewhat. We shared a tiny, intimate history together. If I felt comfortable with you, I knew Maira would, too." My lips curve up at the memories of our time together at our shabby apartment. "Though, your smile does make it *very* difficult for me to act properly around you."

Nyla remains blank-faced and focused on investigating the answers. "If you couldn't afford me, why didn't you just tell me? Why didn't you ask Azeer to pay for Dua's tuition? Anyone except my father."

"Pride. Ego. Embarrassment. Self-consciousness."

She scoffs softly. "And you went to the *one* man who took advantage of your weaknesses."

I shake my head. "I'm sorry, Nyla. I didn't want to do it. I really didn't want to do it—I shouldn't have done it." My hands leave her wrists and slide down to her waist. "I'm sorry. I'm sorry I agreed to return you back to him."

Her thumb grazes against my cheekbone. "Why are you crying?" She asks with a little waver in her voice.

"Because," I croak out, bringing her close to my chest. She straddles my lap and hugs me around my neck. "He knew Zineerah was in recovery." Her chest hitches against mine. "He knew every detail about my sisters and threatened me with it. He threatened me with Maira and Sky and all our friends. I'm sorry, sweetheart. I should've told you. I shouldn't have sold you out to him."

"You're right. It wasn't the right move. You should've discussed it with me first, and I would've helped you out by bargaining with Baba. Whether it was for Dua's education or Zineerah's medical bills, I would've taken on the show without hesitation."

"I was practically a stranger to you, Nyla. I couldn't have let you do that after I had asked you to pretend to be in a relationship with me."

"Shahzad, you don't have to know someone in order to be kind to them. I've been dealing with my father's bullshit for the past twenty-five years. Just because you were his bodyguard for a year and a half doesn't mean you had him figured out well enough to make such a detrimental deal with him." A nervous quiver in her chin. "The fact that you didn't *tell* me about the deal after our relationship had shifted hurt more than the actual act of making the deal. Do you understand what I'm saying?"

"I do," I reply with a heavy heart. "I wish I wasn't a fucking coward and just told you the mistake I'd made. I wish I'd been brave enough to come clean before our relationship took a different turn. It pains me to think about the hurt I could have spared you."

Nyla inhales deeply, carefully readjusting the heating pad on her stomach. "Where do you see our relationship heading? You've been putting in a lot of effort over the past eight months, and I believe you have a clear understanding of what you want."

I gently stroke her jaw, tracing a soothing pattern. "Remember our first date? You mentioned that once we've established ourselves in our careers, you'd want us to start considering our future together—marriage, kids, the whole deal."

She lets out a mock groan. "Oh, god, I really did sound like someone who's never been on a date before."

I tilt her chin up, peeling her hands away from her face. "I want to spend the rest of my life with you, Nyla. Picture us in a better place, wherever you want, raising a family together. It didn't take me eight months to realize this; it was clear long ago." My lips gently graze the underside of her wrist. "The day you walked out of my life, I saw our future unfold before my eyes, and I've been working every day since to make that vision a reality."

"That kind of a future needs a hell of a lot of trust, Shahzad. How can I trust you?"

"When's the last time you cooked for yourself?"

She blinks in surprise. "Uh, I don't know. I've just been eating what you make me."

"And why did you let me take you home on Valentine's Day, even with Mickey and Grayson outside the bar?"

"Because I trust—" She stops herself, biting her bottom lip and shaking her head, realizing my strategy. "Okay, fine. But how can you guarantee that you won't hurt me like this again?"

"To be honest with you, I can't promise our relationship will be perfect because life is unpredictable, but what I *can* promise is that I'll do my absolute best to understand you, support you, and be there for you." I gently lift my hand and trace the path to her chest, my index finger stopping just above where her heart resides. "That beating in there is the most precious thing in the world to me. And I swear, with every ounce of my being, to hold on to it for the rest of my life."

A sudden, unexpected swell of emotion tightens my throat, and I feel the telltale sting behind my eyes. Despite my best efforts to keep steady, my tear ducts betray me, and Nyla breaks, too.

"I've been doing my part," I continue, my gaze unwavering, "to help you heal. But, you know, you've done an incredible job giving yourself the love you deserve. I've witnessed your power and your strength. And it's time for a new chapter for us. From here on out, I want us to work on ourselves together. Starting with open communication like this. No secrets, no walls. Just you and me. Together."

Nyla sniffles and wipes her nose with the sleeve of her sweater before pulling me into a comforting embrace. "No more lying, Shahzad. If we need to talk about something, we go to each other. If we need something, we ask for it from one another." She draws back and waves her finger between us. "This? You and me? We're one body. If you're hurting, I'm hurting. If you're laughing, I'm laughing. I'm here because of you, for you, and with you. Got it?"

I blink away the oncoming tears, but she takes care of me by holding my face and wiping her thumbs over my lashes. My eyes shut from the complete relaxation of her warmth and gentle touches. "I'm a mess."

"You're *my* mess."

"Even better."

I tuck a stray strand from her ponytail behind her ear. "You know, I had a lot of time to spare these past eight months while begging for your forgiveness. So, I finally turned on the T.V. and watched all of your movies."

She tilts her head. "Your favorite?"

I huff, rubbing at my wet eyes. "I don't want to be a dickhead and say none simply because you kissed *every* co-actor in *every* movie, and that one sex scene nearly made me break my television."

She throws her head back laughing. "Is that why you never kept a T.V.?"

"I'd rather watch you in real life, next to me." I kiss her forehead. "Under me." Cheeks. "Over me." Nose. "And everywhere other than on a screen." I pause at her smiling lips. "But for the sake of the question, I really liked you in *The Remembrance*. Seeing you in those corsets changed the trajectory of my life."

She pulls her pretty lips in, cheeks flushed bright red as they stretch up high. Seeing her this happy because of me despite the hurt I put her through is . . . I don't think I'll be able to sleep tonight.

"Is there anything else you want to clear with me?" she asks.

I try to scrounge my brain when I'm suddenly whipped with a realization. "Wait, yes. I— Okay. Don't kill me for this."

She narrows her eyes. "*What?*"

"You know the day Maira and I came to pick you up?"

"Yes . . . ?"

"And she told you I'd drank a lot and punched a wall because of how much I missed you?"

Nyla starts glaring. She's already connected the dots. "Never happened, I'm guessing?"

I nod. "No more lying."

"Then tell me the truth," she says. "Did you threaten Connor about your pink-haired wife?"

I lift my chin. "Who's Connor?"

"Fourth of July."

Oh, shit. I completely forgot about that bastard. "I could've done much worse."

Nyla shoves my shoulder. "Don't do that again. You ruined Nova's chances with his best friend. Just be glad he didn't press any charges against you."

"Why?" I sit up in alert. "Did he hassle you with questions?"

"No," she mumbles. "I called it an early night and had Mick and Gray secretly take me home."

I rub my thumb over her chin. "I'm sorry I ruined your night."

"It's fine, I guess." Nyla flicks her gaze up, then rolls it to the side. "Listen, I have to go to Taipei for the next four weeks to work alongside the atelier for my debut."

"*Four* weeks?" I release a deep, guttural groan, letting my head fall back onto the plush cushions of the couch. "You're killing me, woman."

"It's nothing compared to the eight months I made you wait. I'll be back before you know it."

With a heavy sigh, I raise my hands in unwilling surrender. "I'll hold down the fort here, then."

She nods, seeming unsure of something within herself. "I need time to think about what we've discussed today. Is that okay?"

"If it's okay with you, then it's one hundred percent okay with me," I reply.

"All right, Chef," she whispers. "Lie down."

I help her off my lap and lie down, bringing the blanket over our bodies. My arm unfurls on instinct for her to rest in. She settles in and drops the heating pad on the coffee table, back pressed against my chest. Instead, she takes my hand and brings it under her shirt, resting it on her soft stomach.

At her whistle, Caramel hops onto our legs and snuggles under Nyla's arm. Sky's too big of a girl, so she curls up near our feet.

Nyla resumes her favorite movie, and I watch her.

38

Nylana and Shahzad

Nyla

April 16th

Mickey and Grayson drop me off at my house at around six in the evening. The flight back from Taipei has me tangled in some serious jet lag that'll take three to five business days to shake off.

I step out of the car and find my porch crowded with potted plants and colorful flowers suspended from the awning. There, on the welcome mat, rests the familiar woven basket containing my favorite pastries from Caffè di Matilda, accompanied by a neatly folded note.

"Miss Nyla, would you like us to take your bags inside?" Grayson asks, standing tall by the open trunk of the rover.

"Yes, please. Go ahead." I unlock the door for the boys to enter while I navigate the box of pastries, stuffing a cream roll into my mouth and unfolding the note.

I finish work at seven. Taking you out tonight.

I fold it and press it against my heart.

Being in Taepei and distracting myself with the textiles and watching from the sidelines as my designs were re-produced by professionals technically didn't allot any time for me to think anything through. That and also because sightseeing was a *must*.

No one disturbed me in Taipei for photos and autographs. To them, I was just another foreigner marveling at monuments and buying magnets for my fridge.

JFK Airport, on the other hand, bombarded me *big* time. Camera lenses inches from my face, fans overlapping one another like *World War Z* zombies for selfies and signatures, and the usual, bizarre questions the paps kept screaming. I needed ten airport security guards and my own to safely escort me to my car. Hell on Earth, I tell you.

Seriously, if I could spend the rest of my year living in the serenity of Rhode Island, I would. No more real estate ventures in cities like L.A. or New York; I had liquidated those properties earlier to fund my design projects and personal expenses.

After thoroughly inspecting my home, Mickey and Grayson bid farewell for the week. Jet lag has taken its toll on more than *just* me.

I decide on a warm bath to loosen the knots in my muscles. Afterward, I put on an oversized Yale University sweater and black tights.

As I blow-dry my hair, I braid it to the side and top it off with Shahzad's Yankees cap. My gaze shifts to his folded, pink notes on my bedroom wall, written with daily affirmations that uplift my spirits and remind me of my worth.

God, I can't wait to see his stupid face.

Jogging to Shahzad's house, I retrieve the key stashed in a ziplock bag beneath the cushion of his porch swing. He's such a grandpa for owning one.

The moment I swing the door open, the dogs are already on high alert, barking their joy. I drop to my knees, exclaiming, "Oh, hello, my babies!" Caramel is the first to reach me, showering my face with licks, like how I clean every plate of Shahzad's delicious meals. Sky sniffs around, circling me before finding a spot on my cheek to join in the affectionate licking. "Aw, I missed you very much, too."

After securing their leashes, I buckle them up and lock the door, tucking the key into my pocket. "How about we go visit your dad?" I suggest. Their response is an enthusiastic chorus of barks.

I've silenced my phone after responding to the Khan family and replying to Dua's birthday wishes. Maira sent a lengthy voice memo expressing how God reached the pinnacle of creation when making me. I make a mental note to visit her soon, especially with Shahzad.

Caramel stops right outside the lamp post of Caffè di Matilda to pee. I wave at the two boys skating down the sidewalk and smile at an elderly couple passing by.

Narrowing my eyes to see through the busy crowd of the café, I catch sight of a familiar bed of waves speaking with a young woman seated across from him.

My smile deflates as easily as it inflated.

He's laughing at whatever joke she's cracked. Naturally, my instinct is to measure myself against the elegance of the woman in a black bomber jacket and a frilly skirt. Unlike Dua or Zineerah, identifiable by their midnight-black hair, this woman's locks are a lighter, blow-out brown shade. Petite and finely sculpted, she stands on the shorter side.

The radiance in his eyes intensifies as he speaks with this mysterious woman. Extending both her hands, she receives an immediate and firm grip as he clasps them without hesitation.

I roll my eyes. *She could just be a family friend. It's you he's in love with, anyway, so.*

Shahzad stands all of a sudden and pulls her in for a hug that she half-heartedly returns. And then he stamps a kiss over her crown.

I gasp. "Are you kidding me?" Hand-holding is fine. Okay. Whatever. A hug is drawing the line, personally. But a kiss on the head? Now, that is just crossing every line in the universe.

I quickly turn to face the street, crouching down and pretending I'm petting my dogs.

Before I can even catch sight of what I'm assuming is a *gorgeous* face, she takes a right and starts strolling down the street in her casual attire.

Huffing, I stand and enter the café.

Shahzad's back behind the counter and taking an elderly man's order. When he sees the dogs and me, a pure shock of delight strikes his face. *Okay, well, that's a good sign.* Except I don't reciprocate back. And he easily catches on, quickly checking the customer out and handing the reins to Amelia.

I sit myself down in the corner, pulling Caramel onto my lap.

"You're back!" Shahzad exclaims, sliding into the booth seat across from me. Sky hops up and gives him wet kisses on the cheek. "At ease, honey." He reaches for my hand, but I jerk it back. A defeated sigh. "What did you see?"

"You know *exactly* what I saw."

Licking his lower lip, he relaxes back and quirks an amused brow. "You sure you want to play this game, Troublemaker?"

"It's my birthday."

"That's *today*?"

I kick him under the table. "Who was she?"

"Forgive me first, and I'll tell you exactly who that lovely girl was."

My molars grind together. He's so—*ugh*. I've planned out my forgiveness, so there's no freakin' way I'll take mercy on him in our favorite café.

So, I roll my shoulders back and shrug. "Fine. Don't. Get me my latté."

"As you wish, my lady." He gets up and, in a blink of an eye, squishes my cheek and presses a kiss on my left one. I shove him back and wipe my skin, watching him walk backward, pointing right at me and saying, "Sahara says hi, by the way."

"I hate you," I say with a smile.

"I love you," he says back, also smiling.

Throughout the remaining hour of Shahzad's shift, I sit and sip my drink, watching the fluid, professional movements of his muscled body. He serves drinks like he was a world-class barista in his previous life. He charms the fathers with his alarming collection of dad jokes, compliments the mothers' attire, and lets the jumping, sugar-high kids pet and rub Sky.

Gosh, it's like he's an animated princess.

I sigh into a smile and countdown the minutes to seven so we can get the hell back to our little private sanctuary.

"So, where's Nyx?"

Shahzad pulls a plate stacked with pancakes and settles it down on the dining table. "Viola, ma chérie."

I burst out laughing. "That was a *terrible* French accent, by the way."

He squeezes my nose. "Made you happy."

I snap pictures of my birthday pancakes with baby-pink frosting and edible black hearts. "Gosh, Shahzad. This is *so* cute. Thank you so much for this."

Smiling, he pokes candles shaped like the numbers two and six into the top and uses his lighter to ignite the wicks. He dims the lights a little and gathers the dogs—Caramel on my lap and Sky on a chair next to his. He watches me from across the table, the golden flames illuminating his rugged, sharper features. "Keep me in your dirtiest wishes, Troublemaker."

I scoff. "You're pathetic."

"For you."

FAKE IT TILL WE MAKE IT

Rolling my eyes, I clasp my hands together and conjure a wish inside my brain.

I wish...

I wish...

Gosh, when was the last time I made a birthday wish? Last year I celebrated with a tub of chocolate ice-cream and Cool Ranch Doritos in the bathtub at midnight. And the years before were all extravagant parties at my house that were business networking events in disguise. Pro-tip: never let your greedy, capitalizing father host your birthday parties.

"Nyla?" Shahzad's raspy voice slices through. "You don't want wax in your cake now, do you?"

"Sor—"

"No."

I sigh, grazing my teeth back and forth across my bottom lip. "I don't know what to wish for. My health is fine. My career's in motion. My mother and I are talking again. I have an adorable dog." *You should probably... do it now, Nyla.* My eyes flick up to his watchful ones. "What do you think I should wish for?"

A shrug. "Whatever's on your mind."

"You," I blurt out. My hands clap over my mouth in an attempt to un-attempt what I just attempted. "I mean—you—you should know that there's nothing—I don't have anything. On my mind. There's nothing currently being processed in my brain right now. As we speak. Right now."

Shahzad inhales.

Oh, boy.

His laughter bursts out like colorful confetti, erasing the tension and painting the room in vibrant shades. Painting *me*.

"It's not funny," I mutter.

"Yes, it is. It's *very* funny. You're very funny, baby." He wipes the ends of his eyes, faltering into light chuckles. "Oh, man. I needed that. Seriously."

I blow out the candles and cross my arms. "There. Eat."

Flat-faced, he rekindles his lighter and lights the candles again. But this time, he stands up and walks over to me, planting down on the chair beside me. "Hand."

I give him my hand.

Tugging me over, I collapse onto his lap, and Caramel hops onto the floor, joining Sky across the room. "Shahzad—"

"Be a good girl and make a wish." He ties his muscled arms around my waist and props his chin on my shoulder. "What's the one thing you *desperately* want, Troublemaker?"

You.

I lick my drying lips. "I don't know."

"You're not lying to me, are you?"

Shutting my eyes, I think of the first wish that pops into my brain, then quickly whisper, "Iwishtospendtherestofmylifewithyou," and *poof*!

Shahzad tenses, and that's my cue to stand. But he keeps me seated on his lap.

I relax back and toy with his rough-skinned fingers. I won't talk until he's ready. That wish was a direct translation of my forgiveness. It's about damn time I let this man in my door for the rest of our lives. God knows he might contact NASA and have them name an entire galaxy after me. He can save that tactic for our anniversary.

"You mean it?" Shahzad whispers.

"Mm-hmm."

"Words."

"Yes, I mean it. I forgive you."

His index finger turns my cheek to face him. Our noses brush in the action. "You forgive me?"

"I do."

Shahzad's lashes flutter close, and his forehead falls onto my shoulder. "You forgive me?"

I weave my fingers through the back of his head. "Yes, Chef. You're forgiven."

"You forgave me."

"Frankly, I almost said it when you brought Caramel into my life. After I left for Taipei, I had a lot of time to think over our conversation, but I only felt more and more alone. So, I looked at our pictures from last year, kept a couple of your handwritten notes to keep me moving forward, and . . . dreamt of you. Every night."

"You . . ." The vibration of his chuckle against my chest sends a rumble through my belly. He cocks his head back and grabs my face, catching me by surprise. "You—fuck. Okay. Wow. I didn't—I didn't think today would be the day, but—"

"Shahzad?"

"Yes, baby?"

"Shut up and kiss all my wishes out of me."

He wastes not even a millisecond before his lips are devouring mine in a desperate, messy, *needy* manner. "Upstairs," he whispers in between the kisses. "Can I take you upstairs?"

"First bedroom on your left."

He whisks me up in his arms, bridal-style, and practically races upstairs, telling the dogs to go play and to *not* eat the pancakes.

Shahzad opens my bedroom door and nearly drops me onto the floor. "My notes." His eyes, wide and, oh, *so* brown, take in the wall of affirmations. "Nyla, I love you. God, I love you so much."

I yelp as he throws me like a hacky sack onto my mattress and climbs on top, shedding his leather jacket and captivating my lips with his rough, adamant kisses. Tongue-tied, teeth against teeth, our hands itching to explore our skins after all these months apart. *Finally*.

"Let me touch you, please," he whispers, cracks in his hoarse voice. "*Please*. If I have to get on my knees and beg you, I will. You know I fucking will."

"God, Shahz. Hollywood could really use a dramatic man like you." I chuckle, removing my sweater and unclasping my bra. He tosses them over his shoulder and dives for my neck, massaging my breasts, the pent-up moans leaving my mouth.

Somewhere along the lines, I hear the clinking sound of him undoing his belt, the sharp sound of his zipper, and the curses as he rips his jeans off his legs.

Somewhere along my laughter at his desperation, he renders me speechless with his fingers slipping inside of me, thrusting at an uncontrollable pace for minutes, sweat beads breaking onto my chest, my face, and my back.

He suddenly sits back on his knees and memorizes different parts of my panting body. His cheeks are flushed red, and his lips are swollen like mine. "I'm giving in tonight, Nyla. I'm giving *all in* tonight. Tomorrow. For the rest of my fucking life, I'm giving in to you."

I can't find the words left in me to speak.

"Look what you do to me, baby?" He starts stroking himself. "Look at me. Look how desperate I am to finally touch you after a year of pure, torturous suffering. To taste you. Fuck you madly to make up for the two-hundred and eighty-seven days missed."

"Oh, wow. You were keeping count?"

"Like a prisoner tallying his days." He hovers over me, tracing my brow with his fingers. "You know what I need?"

I gulp at the wicked anticipation in his dark eyes. "W-What?"

"All of you," he replies, feather-light touch traveling down to my breasts and circling my nipples. "I need *all* of you underneath me, watching me with your jewel-green eyes, smiling at me with this pretty, pink mouth." He bites my bottom lip.

I squeeze my thighs together to find a bit of relief that he's stalling me from. Gently, he kisses my pulse and my faint collarbones, and then he's bridging his marks down to my stomach.

I stop him by covering my stretch marks around my gut, but Shahzad is quicker and more stubborn. He grabs my wrist and pins it on the top of my head, nearly knocking my breath out of me. "Don't even *think* about it."

"But—"

"Don't." He releases me and descends back down to kiss my stretch marks, trailing his lips over the white threads that mar my skin. "Your scars and marks? They belong with mine. I want to worship them. Cherish them with my mouth. Memorize their shape."

"God," I breathe out, curling my fingers in the sheets. "Shahzad, *please* just—"

"Suck in your stomach again, and I'll leave you on the edge, Nylana."

"It's a habit."

"I'll fuck it out of you." He caresses my belly, humming with satisfaction near my ear.

"Touch me," I whisper, feeling his muscles tense as I run my left hand over his back and wrap it around his nape, widening my legs for him. "Please, touch me."

His hand cups the area where I am *burning* for him, begging for him. His deep, delirious chuckle sets me aflame. I constrain a cry and arch off of his chest, but he keeps me glued to him, working his fingers inside me like there isn't a tomorrow.

"How should I make you mine, baby? Tell me again. Tell me what you need from me."

"You. I need you."

He pushes inside in one quick thrust, and the cry that leaves my mouth could be mistaken for a horror movie heroine's scream.

He moves painstakingly slowly for the first few seconds, pulling out to the hilt and *pushing*.

Harder.

Rougher.

Exactly how I need it. Vicious and mind-blowing.

I tear my nails through the sheets, tears gathering in my eyes. *God, yes, yes, yes.* His words and dirty speeches had tied knots in my stomach, and now, thrust by thrust, they are beginning to come undone in a symphony. "Shah . . . "

He pulls out abruptly and then drives back inside. His hand holds onto my jaw. "Eyes open and on me." Our eyes meet in a half-hooded embrace. "Doing okay?"

"Fantastic." I kiss him and completely wrap myself around him.

Shahzad pulls me onto his lap, and I use the remaining bits of my strength in this position of power. "In case I haven't been clear enough, I love you, Nylana." He buries his face in the crook of my neck. I shut my eyes and ride out the sensation that's lulling me into a dream. Unless I *am* dreaming of this again. *Please don't let this be a dream.* "I want all your mornings, afternoons, and nights." He lays me back and continues the pace of his ministrations. "What do you say, Troublemaker?"

I comb back his hair. "I take a lot of time in the shower."

"I'll join you to save our water bill."

"I get jealous easily. Seriously, you've seen it."

"So do I. It's one of our sexiest traits."

I peck his lips, whispering, "I'll make you pay for all our dates."

"An honor, truly."

The pad of my thumb runs across his bottom lip. "You won't leave me even when my life becomes overbearing and loud?"

He kisses my thumb. "I'll do everything in my power to protect you from the noise and never let go of your hand in the crowds. They'll have to cut it off my body, and even then, nothing, no one can keep you apart from me. I am yours, Troublemaker."

He kisses me to erase any doubts, pressing me down onto the bed.

"I'm yours," he whispers again. "I'm inescapably yours, Nylana."

"And I've always been yours, Shahzad."

And then we're both crashing down together, showered in sweat, lips strung together, and laughter.

His laughter.

The best sound I've ever heard.

39

See You In A Minute

Shahzad

May 31st

Watching Nyla sleep every morning is like sitting on a sandy beach, listening to the soft singing of the waves, and watching the sun lift and spread forth its golden-blue hues.

I delicately trace my index finger over her dark brows, down to her pink, lovely lips. She shifts closer with a wistful sigh at my touch.

I fix each rose-gold strand of hair away from her face and bridge light kisses on her bare shoulder up to her neck, jaw, and below her ear. "I love you so much, Nylana. So *fucking* much."

"Love you, too," she murmurs.

I raise a brow at her and back away. Green, shimmering like the sun's reflection over the ocean, greets me. "You're awake?"

"I can't sleep from how sore I am."

"I'm sorry, baby." I peck the tip of her nose. "I'll go even harder next time so you don't sleep at all, and we can fuck for a week straight."

She shoves my chest playfully. I take her small fist and kiss each finger.

FAKE IT TILL WE MAKE IT

The past month, since she's forgiven me, has been nothing but a blissful dream. I moved in with her, naturally, and gave Sahara back the keys to the house.

I've taught Nyla to cook. She's taught me how to use a needle and thread. Our dogs—*our: my new favorite word*—have bonded even closer with their shenanigans and howling at the most bizarre times of the day.

We go to the beach as a family, eat dinner together as a family, watch movies and T.V. shows together as a family, and, you know, it'd be nice to add another edition to the family that has hands instead of paws, but still crawls and wakes us up in the middle of the night. We decided on that tidbit of our future a little later.

Also, not that anyone's keeping count, but we've fucked 120 times now since her birthday, so.

"What are you thinking about?" Nyla whispers, grazing her knuckles across my beard.

"You."

She smiles into the pillow. "Not this again."

I wrap my arm around her waist, and with a strong tug, I pull all of her onto my chest. She places her chin over her hands, soft, long legs tangling with mine. "We don't *think* in this house, remember? Ask me again."

"We know," she says. "So, Mr. Arain, what are you *knowing* about?"

"Well, I know I want a family with you, Mrs. Ghilzai-Arain."

"Only Arain. Mrs. Nyla Arain. Ghilzai is my father."

Sparks burst within my chest. "You sure?"

"Absolutely, Mr. Arain." She pecks the tip of my nose. "What else is on the itinerary?"

"I want our first kid to be out of wedlock as a fuck you to the shitheads in our families."

"Agreed."

"We'll have another kid after you take my last name." She grins shyly. "Sky and Caramel will be there. And we'll adopt a cat, maybe. Or another dog."

She nods on a loop. "Where will we live?"

"In the outskirts of the city. A small house with a picket fence and a backyard with a century-old tree and a garden. Or Switzerland. Wherever you want, honestly."

"Can we add a tire swing to the tree for the kids? Oh, and a trampoline?"

"We'll build our house from scratch. Like Ryan Gosling in *The Notebook*."

"I do love that scene." I earn another sweet kiss.

"It'll have a big kitchen so I can cook my family whatever the hell they want. And a big office room where you can work your designer magic."

Nyla has her eyes closed the entire time, her enchanting smile growing with every word. "What else?"

"Then, as our children find a place in this world for themselves, I'll open a restaurant in the city, and you'll become a withstanding, prominent name in the fashion designing industry. But we'll still manage to make time for one another and for our children because no one made time for us." I swipe my thumb across her cheek, wiping away a single tear. "We'll have our fights and our arguments about how we're acting like our parents, about how we shouldn't be. You'll want your space, and I won't give it to you because I can't function without you near me."

She sniffles, chuckling. "Yes, you've proved that."

"So I'll call a truce and tell you that you're doing a great job, and I'm proud of you. And you'll say it back. And then we'll fuck for hours and lay like this, you tracing my tattoos and me admiring you as always, and we'll talk about what we'll do when our kids are married and how we should retire to Zürich and live on a farm. Then you'll open your eyes and realize that despite everything that's happened to us, everyone that held us back from one another, you and I stayed because we believe in one another."

Nyla slowly opens her glossy eyes and smiles brightly. "What if we took our kids to work with us? That way, we won't fight or argue."

"You think *we* won't argue, Troublemaker?"

"Over mundane things, sure. But I don't want to fight to the point I need space. You know I can't function without you near me, too. You're, like, *unofficially* my bodyguard again."

I thread my fingers through her hair, giving it a tug. "*Just* your bodyguard?"

"Sorry, I meant my *third* bodyguard. After Mick and Gray."

"Nylana."

She giggles. "You should know I considered you my boyfriend since the day we first kissed in that hotel room. I move too fast. I also fall too fast."

"As long as you're falling into me."

She bumps her forehead against mine and smiles so very brightly. "Ouch."

I flip her around and gaze down at my bride-to-be with golden-pink hair and knowing jade eyes. "Before I met you, all I saw was my past when I envisioned my future." Delicately, I place a kiss on her cheek. "Now all I see is you."

Nyla brings me down for an embrace, running her fingers through my hair. I lay my head on her chest, breathing in her fruity, vanilla scent. "I wish we could have all the time in the world to stay just like this," she whispers.

"We will, baby. We will."

"Not with our schedules. I have to be in New York next week for my debut show. You have Zineerah's wedding to prepare—"

"Let's just enjoy this, please?"

With a contented sigh, she kisses my forehead, and we both drift off into a peaceful sleep.

The Caffè di Matilda team gathers in the front alcove after hours for my farewell party.

"I'm going to miss you so much!" Matilda has been sobbing against my torso for the past five minutes. I pat her back as she cries about how I'm her muse for her fanart of Lord Voctoral De Ashburn, and without me, she'll lose all her patreons. Whatever any of that means flies right over my head.

I go around making rounds, giving Roger and Graham tickets to a Yankees game they've been wanting to go to since last month.

"Invite us to the launch of your restaurant, kid," Graham says.

"Opening night," Roger adds.

"Full-on VIP treatment." Graham.

"And keep in mind my seafood allergies. I don't wanna ruin everything by dying, you know?" Roger, again.

I clap the twins' shoulders. "Thanks for everything, boys. I'll practice my knife skills each day, especially that sandwich knife."

"Don't insult the sandwich knife," Roger tsks. "It's all about the precision of the cut, you see—"

"Have a safe flight to Toronto, kid." Graham pushes him aside before he can go off on a tangent about knives. It's disturbing how much the man adores his blades.

"Hey."

I turn around from Amelia's monotonous yet charming voice. She pushes a chocolate zucchini muffin into my hand—one of my favorite baked goods. "For me? Aw, mia Lia. You shouldn't have."

"God, I'm not going to miss you," she says as she hugs me. I contain my excitement and gently hug this little woman made of steel. "I'm proud of you, Shahz."

"Ditto, kiddo."

Nodding, Amelia backs up and smiles. It's an adorable smile, too. Dimpled and packed with sly amusement. Like she knows secrets I've only ever told my sisters, Nyla and Sky. "Make sure to RSVP for my wedding."

"I will."

"And don't forget the milk and ice ration for cold coffee."

"I won't."

"And it would be an honor if you could name a drink after me."

"Bitter or sweet?"

"Take a wild guess." She rolls her eyes, still smiling, and walks back to Kevin.

"Well, can't say that I won't miss you!" Devon grabs my shoulders from behind and turns me around so I can watch Nyla conversing with Rita. "It's disgusting how in love you are."

"Shut up." I shake him off. "As if you aren't that way with Rita."

Devon's playfulness simmers down. He stretches his hand and I clap it, pulled in for a hug. "Keep in touch, Shahz. I mean it. You leave me on read, and I'll take the first flight to Toronto to whoop your ass."

"Got it, Cake Boss."

"Good. Keep in mind the oven temperatures I taught you." He pats my cheek and heads off to the appetizer table.

Harry approaches me with a timid smile. "Hey, Shahz."

"Hey, buddy." I pull him in for a quick hug.

"I, uh . . ." I wanted to show you something that I got over the weekend." He rolls up the sleeves of his flannel. It's a small tattoo of a plate covered in dish soap bubbles. "Got this when I heard you were leaving."

"Jesus, Harry . . ." I take his arm, marveling at the ink. "You got this for me?"

"Yeah, you really inspired me as a dish boy, which sounds stupid now that I say it out loud, but . . . I don't care. I know it's not anything extraordinary like making soups or baking, but you made it feel that way. Gave me the confidence that it wasn't a low-level position."

"Dammit, kid. Come here." I yank his lanky ass in for a hug, rubbing his back. "Remember, every dirty dish has a story to tell. You just gotta look *really* closely between the chips and scratches, okay?" I pull him back and lower my head so we're talking eye-to-eye. "You're extraordinary, Harry. Don't think of yourself otherwise. And when you're a successful chemical engineer at Tesla or some shit, don't forget me. Your dishwashing sensei. Maybe gift me a Tesla as a thanks."

He snorts. "I will, Shahz."

The tinkling sound of a spoon against glass fills the room.

Donald finds a spot for his unwarranted speech. "Victor," he says, *still* not knowing my real name despite the large banner behind him that says, "*We hate you for leaving, Shahzad,*" made by his daughter. "Oh, Victor. I'm so proud, *so* proud of myself for hiring you."

Nyla joins my side, and I wrap my arm around her waist as support.

"Without Victor, we wouldn't be *victor*ious. We wouldn't have these sales and marketing *victor*ies that we've, mostly me because, again, I hired him."

"God help me," Amelia whispers, rubbing her temples.

"To Victor!" Donald raises his glass of whiskey, which he keeps on the top shelf of his office.

"To Shahzad," Matilda corrects, and the crowd follows her response. "It's Shahzad, Papa."

Donald furrows his brows. "I thought that was his middle name?"

"Let's get back to the party, everyone!" Devon announces, and the music fades out Donald's voice.

Nyla belly-drops onto her bed where I'm packing my suitcase. "That was *so* exhausting."

I chuckle, folding a pair of jeans for my carry-on. "Baby, you'll have to attend longer parties sooner or later."

"Don't tell me—"

"After parties, pre-celebrations parties, Oscar parties, A-lister parties—"

"Stop, stop, stop." She flips around and covers her ears. "I've set a strict rule with myself that I'll only attend parties for thirty minutes max." She crawls toward me, and I push my suitcase out of the way. Her arms snake around my neck, and mine around her waist. "That way, we can spend the entire evening together."

"I love it when you talk responsibility to me."

"Yeah?" She nods, smiling into our kiss. Just as I want to take it up a notch, she pushes me back. "Finish packing. You have an early flight to catch tomorrow."

"Five minutes."

"Nothing's five minutes with you."

"But the next time we'll see each other is at the end of June. What the hell am I supposed to do without you?"

Nyla huffs and goes to her closet. She returns with a handful of her colorful, lace underwear and throws it in my luggage. "Help yourself to those."

I don't complain any further.

In the morning, Nyla drives me to the airport in my Jeep—Sky and Caramel sitting in the backseat with their heads sticking out the windows.

I hold onto her hand, playing with her fingers, kissing them, confessing how *not* excited I am about planning my sister's arranged marriage. Definitely not looking forward to speaking with Raees either. But if Zineerah is on board with it, *completely* on board, then I have no right to meddle in her affairs or advise her any longer. I'll just have to hammer it into Raees' brain that I know several different ways of torture that I'd enjoy putting him through if he raises his voice at my sister.

A private limousine drives us to Azeer's private jet.

"Want me to look after Nyx while you're gone? I can have her delivered here to Rhode Island." Nyla hugs my torso at the first step of the jet. "I promise I won't accidentally crash her again."

My stomach tightens at my motorbike's mention. "Uh, no. It's fine. You won't have to anyway."

She furrows her brows. "What? Why?"

I smile and pull out a little gift box from my leather jacket. "I was planning on giving this to you on your birthday, but . . ."

Curiously, Nyla takes the pink box and undoes the golden ribbon. She lifts the lid. "What's this?"

"A key."

"A key to what, Shahzad?"

"Your studio."

Nyla pales. "S-Studio?"

"Yes, the design studio you wanted in SoHo." I pinch her chin and lift her sunken head. She's crying. "Happy tears, I hope?"

"How did—" Nyla presses the back of her hand to her mouth. She chokes on her next words and starts full-on sobbing. I'm unsure if I should join her or let out a little laugh. "Shahzad, how did you—?"

"Doesn't matter." I kiss her forehead, cheeks, and knuckles. "I've got to get going. Dua will kill me if I'm not at her apartment by twelve."

"But—"

I crush my lips against hers and inhale her scent. Knowing that I won't be able to touch her or hold her or listen to the sound of her laughter in real time is carving me open from the inside out.

"Shahzad," she whispers, hugging the gift box to her chest. "What did you do, love? I don't deserve this."

"And I didn't deserve your kindness when you paid for Nyx's damages."

"But you sold . . . " Her green irises flare. She bites down her bottom lip. As I continue to stare at her indecisiveness, she slowly starts to untie herself and gifts me with a long hug. "I love you."

"I love you, too, baby." I squeeze her until she's giggling and slapping my back to free her. "Make sure to eat on time and—"

"Slowly, I know."

I wipe away the last bit of her tears. She's been an emotional wreck these past few days, and as flattering as it is, it also shatters my heart to bits to leave her in Rhode Island while I'm in Toronto.

Caramel jumps up into my arms for extra kisses and cuddles. He then earns licks from Sky, too, running around our legs.

"Take care of him for me, honey," Nyla says to Sky, scratching her behind her pointy, white ears. She squints one eye as the sun hits her face and the air winds through her open hair. "See you in a minute, Chef."

I steal a kiss and let Sky take the lead up to the jet's entrance. Turning around, I exclaim, "Show the world what you're made of, Troublemaker!"

She bursts out laughing and blows me a hundred kisses I cage inside my heart.

I sit down with Sky next to me and watch through the window as Nyla walks back to the Jeep. She gives me one last air kiss and gets inside the car with Caramel, driving out of sight.

Four weeks and two days, 30 days in total, 720 hours, 43,200 minutes, and 2.5 million seconds to go, Shahzad.

40

EPILOGUE

Nyla

June 30th

Thunderous applause reverberates throughout the auditorium.

My closing model, Lily, and I hold hands and strut down the runway together. I bow my head in gratitude, soaking in the standing ovation of my *first-ever* fashion show as a designer.

Mama blows me a kiss, with Mark flashing me a thumbs up. Alina is woo-hooing at the top of her lungs, and Azeer joins in subtly. Maira and Layla wave with their arms stretched up, forcing Mustafa to take pictures of me from every possible angle. The seat next to him is empty, which is totally fine because Zineerah's wedding is *literally* tomorrow.

We all gather backstage, and I'm losing my shit alongside my models, huddling together as I coax them with compliments and kisses on their cheeks. Bouquets are being dropped in my arms, along with heartfelt congratulations from the workers, my agent Holly, and my sweet mama.

Inside one of the bouquets lies a folded note with the dreadful First Class Faces logo. I grit my teeth and squash it without bothering to read the contents of Baba's message.

"Would you like me to take these to your dressing room, Nyla?" Hye-jin asks, handing me a water bottle with a straw poked through the cap in exchange for the bouquets. I didn't want to trust another stranger as my assistant after what happened last time, so I proposed the job to the one girl who's volunteered and worked most of her life at Threads and Textiles and is studying communications in her first year of college.

"Yes, thank you. And let's have dinner this Friday when I'm back from Toronto, okay?" I start walking to my dressing room with her in step with me.

"Can't. Date with Tae."

"What? You're always with him. I'm not impressed by your lack of attention for me." She sighs. "Manipulator."

I pinch her cheek and open the dressing room door.

The water bottle drops from my hand and spills across the carpeted floor.

"Sh-Shahzad?" Here in New York? Instead of Toronto? Planning last-minute arrangements for his sister's wedding? And in a *black suit*?

Oh my god, I'm dreaming, aren't I?

"I'm going to go hold the crowd." Hye-jin shuts the door behind me.

"Pinch me," I whisper.

Shahzad mistakes that as "kiss me" and crashes his mouth against mine. I wrap my arms around his neck as he lifts me off my feet and spins us around.

Yes, yes, yes!

FaceTime has *nothing* over touching each other skin-to-skin. Tangible and tethered. *I can't believe he's here.*

"I can't believe you're here," I whisper.

Shahzad sets me back on my feet. "How could I miss my favorite girl's debut show? I'm so proud of you. Everything was incredible. Your clothes, the set, *you*." Another sweet kiss.

"You watched it all?"

"From the back. I know you saved me a spot, but Mustafa is still a little upset about me leaving Maira in Koreatown last year and being dishonest with him, so."

"Oh, love. I'm sorry."

"Don't be. He and I will figure it out."

I smile sheepishly, but then— "Zineerah!"

He winces through his teeth. "Yeah, no one knows I'm here, so let's keep it between ourselves."

I gasp. "Wait, Alina and Azeer are here!"

He smirks. "How do you think I got here to you?"

I attack him with kisses all over his rugged, handsome face. My red lipstick stamp, stamp, stamping his golden-brown skin. "Wait, I have a surprise for you."

I don't give him a chance to speak and grab my purse, rushing out my dressing room door with his hand in mine.

"Where are we going?"

"Someplace special." I take the back security doors, bypassing Mickey and Grayson. They take one glance at Shahzad and turn their heads, mentally clocking out.

My Mercedes is waiting in the private parking lot. Mama suggested I take a limousine to the event, but the comfort my car provides, plus driving on my own with my anxiety-reducing playlist Shahzad made for me, was a more suitable idea. And my air freshener smells like pine cones and cloves.

"After you, good sir," I say in a posh accent, opening the passenger door for him.

He shakes his head, chuckling, and gets comfortable. I take to the driver's seat and start up the car. During the five minutes it takes for me to warm it up, I kiss Shahzad everywhere on his face. His hair's long again, and whisking my fingers through the locks has dragons breathing flames in my stomach.

I drive us to Sun Tower Hotel.

Shahzad makes a comment about how we'll be attending Zineerah's wedding, which is at the Toronto Sun Tower location. He's also *not* excited to see Maya, having to avoid her the entire month of planning his sister's big night.

"Wear this," I say, handing him a silky sleeping mask I keep in my purse for long drives or traveling reasons.

Shahzad complies and slips it over his eyes.

I enter the private parking lot, shoulders shimmying from excitement. This surprise was for next week, but since *he* decided to bolt out of the blue, why not return the favor earlier than scheduled?

Parking my car, I hop out and open his side of the door. "Take my hand, love."

"You're not going to murder me for forgetting to FaceTime you last Friday, are you?"

"Saving that for the bedroom." I intertwine my fingers with his and lead him to a specific parking spot. Hugging his arm, I whisper, "Open sesame."

Shahzad tugs off the blindfold.

It drops onto the floor. Along with his sharp jaw. His dark eyes grow twice in size.

"No . . ."

"And, and, and"—I pace over to Nyx and point at her rear end—"upgraded to some turbo horsepower, something engine. I just told Paul to give her a powerful makeover, and ta-dah!"

"Baby." He rubs the beginning of a magical smile on his lips. "Nyla, you— I can't believe you." Heavy footsteps echo as he makes his way over and sweeps me up in his arms, tickling me with a hundred kisses. "I can't believe you're real."

I smack a loud kiss on his cheek. "I couldn't live with the fact that you sold your bike off to buy me a design studio, Shahzad. Thankfully, Paul hadn't sold her off because he said, and I quote, "Knew his sore ass wasn't going to let go of Nyx at all," end quote."

Shahzad melts into a lopsided grin and places me back on my feet, embracing me wholly instead of a kiss. "I missed you so much, Troublemaker."

"I missed you, too, Chef."

He cups my cheek, thumb caressing my cheekbone. No heartfelt monologue or a lengthy speech leaves his mouth. We stare longingly at one another for what feels like hours, ignoring the vibrations of our phones and the one or two cars that pass us.

Shahzad makes me feel unchained. Liberated. Stepped into a spotlight that he controls. Just seeing him from across the room, or up close and personal, makes breathing a hell of a lot easier. I don't even think I knew *what* freedom felt like until he touched me, body and soul.

"What are you thinking of?" I whisper, curling a stray lock of his hair around my forefinger.

"You."

"That was a trick question. I thought we didn't think?"

"My apologies. I am *knowing* of you. I know I want to take you onto this bike and to Cove Beach, in that little lagoon of ours, with no clothes in between." He skates the pads of his soft lips across mine. "Or I can take you upstairs now and give you a long, *long* congratulations you won't forget?"

"And who's walking your sister down the aisle tomorrow while you give me your long, *long* congratulations, Shahzad Arain?"

He sighs.

I nudge him back with a smile and pull the keys of his bike out of my purse pocket. Giving it a kiss, I toss it to him and wink.

Shahzad groans and wraps his hand around my throat, giving me a kiss. "You're such a tease, you know that?"

"Do you know Azeer's private jet has two bedrooms?"

"Yeah?"

I raise a brow, leaning my head forward.

Both his brows hit the roof of his hairline. "You're serious?"

"Mile high club for two?"

In the blink of an eye, he wraps me up in his arms, settles me down in the passenger seat of my car, takes the driver's side, and becomes every driving teacher's worst nightmare.

"Oh-em-gee, Nyla khala! You look like a princess."

Zoha flutters around me like the butterfly her mother calls her.

"And you, my love, look like the *most* beautiful princess in the kingdom of . . . uh, the kingdom of . . . Disneyland?"

"You don't have to talk to me like a baby," Zoha says with a deadpan expression. *There's her father's attitude.* "Also, I don't support Disney anymore. I'm a Studio Ghibli fan now, like Mama." *And her mother's influence.* She pinches the skirt of her mint-green lengha and rushes out of her bedroom.

Alina enters in a navy blue lengha adorned with golden glitter and sequins. "Hey, angel."

"Hey, Mama," I drawl, giggling as we both spin one another around. My lengha is—surprise, surprise—blush-pink with intricate, silver floral patterns starting from the hem like beanstalks and spreading throughout the mid-line of the skirt. My crop top is the same, with a netted dupatta practically choking me. "You look *so* hot!"

"Babe, *you* look so hot." She lowers her voice. "And wait till you see Raees Shaan." Alina begins fanning herself and awkwardly body-rolling.

"Shahzad refuses to show me pictures of him."

"Good. Because he's a man that's meant to be seen in real life. I'm talking The Metropolitan Museum of Art level hot—"

"Who are we discussing?" Azeer's sharp baritone cuts through. He leans against the entryway in a classic tuxedo, short but wavy black hair brushed back. "I do hope it isn't Shahzad's future brother-in-law."

"What?" Alina's high-pitched voice drags out, followed by a nervous chuckle. "Please, that guy? *Pfft.* We don't care about him. Or how he looks. Or the fact that he's six-five."

I gasp. "He's six-five?"

Alina squeals. "I know. I'm telling you, when you see him, you're going to *wish* your lengha didn't have this many buttons and strings."

Azeer marches up to Alina and, in one swoop, throws her over his shoulder as if she weighs no more than a feather. "Apologies, Nyla. I'm going to show my nuisance exactly how many buttons and strings are tying her lengha together."

Alina, who was once protesting like a banshee, perks up with a smile. "Really?"

"Before I toss her off the balcony," he adds and stomps out of the room. I hear Zoha complaining about creasing Alina's outfit, Azeer complying with his daughter's requests, and then the girls laughing at him.

"What the hell just happened?" Shahzad asks, entering the room. He freezes instantly like a deer in headlights. A ghost of a smile twists his lips upwards, and his fists clench together.

I do a little spin for him and pose with my hands on my hips. "If you start crying again—"

"Too late." He feigns wiping his imaginary tears, but when he's close to my face, he *actually* has tears in his eyes. "You're so pretty."

"*You're* so pretty."

"You're prettier."

"You're prettiest."

Shahzad huffs. "You're prettiest-est."

"Fine. You win." I pat his chest and rise up on my tippy-toes to give him a little kiss on his lips. "Can I ask you a question?"

"Shoot."

"Is Raees *actually* six-five?"

Raees *is* six-five.

And he's terrifyingly beautiful, too.

I use the term terrifying because he has zero display of emotions on his face as he sits on the couch positioned center stage, gaze narrowed like a hawk stalking its prey. I wouldn't lie if I said my heart did a gallop when our eyes locked and he gave me a silent nod as a greeting, or how Alina captured my hand and squeezed the shit out of it when he greeted her.

Beauty is in the eye of the beholder, as they say. And while our own partners are attractive in our eyes, Raees is universally handsome. Wavy, black hair with hints of salt-and-pepper texture close to his temples, the broadest shoulders, and a firm swimmer's physique. His diamond-shaped jaw is cut and gritted. The slope of his nose is perfect and pointed. And even from this distance, I am jealous of his dense, dark lashes.

Every woman and man in the room, from the youngest cousin to the eldest grandparent, fixates on him as though he were a rare exhibit showcased in the halls of The Metropolitan Museum of Art or The Louvre.

Move aside, Mona.

"Ah-hem!" Azeer clears his throat, snapping Alina and me out of our trance. "Are you two going to check up on Zineerah?"

"In a bit," Alina mumbles, zooming in on Raees's face and snapping pictures. "The interior design is so beautiful. Right, Ny?"

I study the archway of white and red roses and the shimmering curtain drop behind. "It's very beautiful."

She sends pictures of Raees in the group chat with the girls—Dua, Sahara, Zineerah, and me—and adds a text: *@zineerah*. With a heart-eye emoji.

"That's enough." Azeer plucks her phone out of her hands and points to the entrance. "Go to the dressing room. Now."

"Fuck you."

"The presidential suite is fifty floors above us, sweetheart. Don't tempt me."

Alina blushes hard and nudges him aside, giving me a sly smirk. She hurries off, and before I can follow, I glance at Shahzad, whose own eyes are settled on Raees, but not with admiration.

Zineerah will be fine with the girls tending to her right now. Even Maya, I suppose.

I take a seat next to Shahzad and rub circles over his back. He resembles a professional sniper ready to assassinate on command. "What's wrong, love?"

"Everything," he mutters.

"Talk to me," I whisper in his ear and plant my chin on his shoulder. "You never told me how your meeting with him went."

"It was fine. We had coffee in some café on Dua's campus. Murder wasn't on the menu, unfortunately."

I snort. "Then why are you glowering at him?"

"I'm not glowering. Only assessing."

I take another peek at Raees. As I mentioned, he's sitting blank-faced and with slitted eyes as if he's trying to make out the faces in the crowd. He doesn't look aggravated or filled with scowls like Azeer. Or exasperated and rolling his eyes like Shahzad.

He's neutral. Almost... anxious. The little shaking in his knee gives him away too easily, and how he's been irritating the band on his ring finger. He's even licked his lips ten times in ten seconds. Eleven. Thirteen.

God, he's walking on pins and needles.

If Alina was checking out his appearance, I'm observant of his behavior. He's marrying my future sister-in-law, of course I'd be quietly protective, too.

"I don't know," I mumble, looking back at Shahzad. "I think she's in good hands."

"I trust you." He kisses my forehead and stands when his phone buzzes. "She's ready to go." Taking my hand, he stands me up, but I stop him. "What?"

"I'll stay here with Azeer and Zoha. You go walk her down the aisle."

"But—"

"Go, Shahzad. I don't want to draw any more attention to myself than I already have. This is Zineerah's big night, okay?"

"You sure?"

"Yes."

"You *sure*-sure?"

"Shahzad Arain."

He doesn't give one flying fuck and kisses me on the lips in front of all his judgmental aunties and uncles. When he leaves, Azeer scoffs a chuckle from his seat.

"Shut up," I mutter, kicking his foot under the table.

"I think you two are *very* cute," Zoha says when I sit her on my lap. "Also, you're welcome, angel." *Sassy little bug.*

"For what, *angel*?"

"For telling Shahzad uncle where you were hiding last year."

Wait, what?

An unfamiliar Bollywood tune streams through the ballroom, and in between, I hear Azeer whisper, "Here we go."

Zineerah enters the venue with her smoky-black eyes searching the floor, her delicate frame stooped beneath the weight of her vibrant red shaadi lengha. The gown sparkles with a myriad of golden gemstones, each one adding to its extravagance.

I bite down on my lip, flushed with worry. Meanwhile, she shuffles along the aisle, each step heavy with hesitation. Her brows furrow, knitting together in a web of concern, and her eyelids press tightly closed as if shutting out the room's gossip. Shahzad gently grasps her arm, leaning in close to her ear, murmuring words too soft for anyone else to hear.

The girls are behind her, and *what the fuck is Sahara wearing?* A neutral-brown turtleneck with a high-waisted bohemian skirt? I will *never* understand her, but I can't wait to get to properly know Shahzad's favorite adopted cousin. Maybe offer her some style suggestions, too.

Sighing, I break focus from Zineerah and glimpse over at the stage.

Oh, my.

Raees stands rigid, his towering figure dominating the space. His broad shoulders stretch out, casting a strong silhouette against the light. A subtle gesture catches my attention—his thumb brushing the inner corners of his eyes. *Is he crying?* The doubt lingers momentarily until he confirms it himself. His hand moves to the outer corners of his eyes, wiping away any proof of tears. His nervous energy becomes noticeable as he fidgets, rubbing his sweaty hands against the fabric of his sherwani. Raees is a ticking bomb of anxiety.

"Is he supposed to be doing that?" I ask Azeer, pointing discreetly at Raees stepping off the stage and walking down the aisle.

Azeer chuckles deeply. "You mean taking my advice?"

I blink a few times, recalling how Azeer had caused a spectacle at his second wedding with Alina when he jumped off the stage and carried his bride all the way back.

Except Raees is smart enough to simply extend his hand.

Dramatic gasps and whispers flood the room, and a couple of people dart their eyes at our table, specifically at a smug Azeer.

And Shahzad is burning with agitation.

And Zineerah's long, thin fingers intertwine with Raees' longer, thicker ones.

And I'm holding my breath watching these two like they're my favorite Regency couple.

Raees offers his arm, and she holds onto it, the two making their walk back to the stage. He even shifts aside the cushions on the fancy, decorated couch and wipes the surface before she sits.

Silence.

Complete, utter, pin-drop silence.

Raees can't take his eyes off of Zineerah's stone-cold face and downcast eyes.

"It's like a rom-com," Zoha whispers.

FAKE IT TILL WE MAKE IT

Just then, Raees's mother, Rosie, and older sister, Ramishah, push the photographers to start snapping pictures. The crowd relaxes back and begins feeding coals to the gossip train. Maya marches up to our table and jabs a finger in Azeer's direction. Man, she's pissed at her nephew. "I'll have a talk with you later." Her eyes briefly glance over Zoha and me, but that grimace and head-shake are hard to miss.

Shahzad and Alina appear a minute later. He forces his chair out and drops down.

"*Fuck. You*," he grits out at Azeer.

I quickly cover Zoha's ears.

Alina is at her husband's defense in a second. "*Excuse* me? He just gave Raees the best goddamn idea, and you're going to berate him for it?"

"You know how Zineerah's anxiety gets, Azeer. Why the fuck would you tell Raees to pull that stupid, fucking stunt? Is it a sadistic habit of yours to ruin every single wedding?"

I pinch my lips to prevent myself from giggling. Alina lands a sharp jab against my shin with a ludicrous stare. "What? He's not wrong."

"First of all, I've ruined one wedding in total, which I paid the loveliest price for," Azeer says. Alina rewards his words with a kiss on his cheek. "Secondly, Raees is a thirty-five-year-old professor with a Ph.D. and a healthy, functioning brain. Peer pressure is the last fucking thing he'd give in to, Shahzad." He leans forward on his hands, all professional and cut-throat. It almost, *almost* reminds me of sitting in my father's office, preparing for a scolding. "And shouldn't you be happy that he truly cares about Zinnie to willingly let these leeches gossip about him?"

I take Shahzad's left fist and place it on my lap. "It's okay, love. I was watching him the entire time, and he didn't hesitate at all to meet her down the aisle. I think—no, I *know* that he cares for her."

"And if that isn't enough proof already." Alina scoffs, gathering our attention to where the newlyweds are sitting.

Raees . . . is using sign language to communicate with Zineerah. And she's communicating back with not-so-hollow eyes anymore.

"What did he say?" I ask.

"He's apologizing," Shahzad replies, looking calmer but still on edge from Azeer's stupidity. "Brokenly."

"It's the effort that counts," Alina states. "And you better apologize for raising your voice at Azeer. Don't forget that he's older than you." She proves his age by pinching his cheek.

I glare at Alina's sassiness and roll my eyes in secret—quick enough to catch Raees smile at Zineerah when his vibrant sister approaches them on the stage.

Shahzad's fist spreads out and grips my knee like an anchor because I know he saw it. I know he saw *her* smile, too. A faint smile. But still, *Zineerah smiled*.

"You trust me, don't you, Chef?" I whisper, sliding my arm around the back of his tensed shoulders.

Shahzad closes his eyes. Exhales deeply into his winning smile. Dark brown eyes pour their affection into my green ones. "With every breath I take, Troublemaker."

Acknowledgements

So, I wrote another book.

Surprise, surprise.

Nyla and Shahzad's story is one that I had to write multiple times before I could figure out the direction I wanted to take. I knew I wanted a space to talk about my struggles with BED after writing about my epilepsy for When Life Gives You Lemons. Many aspects of my battle with BED have been ingrained into this book. The insecurities, the over-thinking, the body dysmorphia, comparing myself to others' physical appearances on social media, eating less to lose weight, eating a lot at night and then not eating at all the next day to lose weight, only to binge-eat because of how hungry I got, and lastly, the fear of being unloved if I opened up about my torture—all of this was a neverending nightmare. It still is from time to time. Writing Nyla was a form of self-realization of how difficult everything was during that stressful period of mine—to have so much confidence as a child, as a teenager, only to come into your adulthood and lose it all because of standards. As for Shahzad, who is constantly trying and failing and trying and failing, while everyone around him is a natural on the first try, it stems from the burnt-out gifted student inside of me.

But, at least, I am still here.

I want to start by thanking my gorgeous beta-readers: Meghan, Simran, Ranah, and Kiera. You guys elevated this story's premise and character developments through the roof. I am so glad to have you by my side, as always. Thank you for your support and the warmth of girlhood you have surrounded me with. I love you all from the deepest dungeon of my heart. Also, Simran's "Just the tip!" comment about Raees being 6'5 will always be living in my head rent-free.

Thank you to the fantastic readers who supported When Life Gives You Lemons and have patiently waited for this book to come out. Your excitement and adoration for my stories motivate me to write and improve daily. I'm so lucky to have you all by my side, making your incredible edits or hilarious TikToks about my characters. I hope you enjoyed reading Fake It Till We Make It as much as I enjoyed writing it.

The third book in the Sun Tower Series will be out later in the year as I work on side projects. But let me say that Azeer and Shahzad have nothing, absolutely nothing against Raees Shaan, and I can't wait for you to witness Zineerah and Raees' love story.

Love,

Noor.

About the Author

Noor Sasha is a twenty-something-year-old who writes about wealthy (for the most part), pretentious Desi men who are explicitly over-the-top pathetic for their girlbossing, gaslighting, and gatekeeping women. If you're in the mood for arranged marriages, forced proximity, desperate pining, second chance romances, nemesis to lovers, and heated sports romance with a leading cast of diverse characters.

Instagram: @authornoorsasha
Twitter: @authornoorsasha
TikTok: @authornoorsasha
Goodreads: Noor Sasha